STOCKHOLM SERIES: III

REMEMBER THE CITY

STOCKHOLM SERIES: III

REMEMBER THE CITY

A novel
by
Per Anders Fogelström

*Translated from Swedish
by
Jennifer Brown Bäverstam*

The Stockholm Series:
City of My Dreams
Children of Their City
Remember the City
In a City Transformed
City in the World

Swedish copyright © 1964 Per Anders Fogelström
The third volume was originally published
in Swedish as "Minns du den stad."
English translation copyright © 2011 Jennifer Brown Bäverstam
and Penfield Books, Iowa City, Iowa, aka Penfield Press
Library of Congress number 2011941113
ISBN 978-1-932043-68-6

Cover design by M. A. Cook Design
Cover photographs by A. Jonsson, Stockholm, circa 1860,
and by Jennifer Brown Bäverstam

TABLE OF CONTENTS

v

THE AUTHOR

PER ANDERS FOGELSTRÖM is one of the most widely read authors in Sweden today. *City of My Dreams,* the first book in his five-volume Stockholm Series, broke the record for bestsellers. A compelling storyteller known for his narrative sweep, his acute characterization and the poetic qualities of his prose, Fogelström was highly acclaimed even before he wrote the *Stockholm Series.* Ingmar Bergman made one of Fogelström's earlier novels, *Summer with Monika,* into a film that is now a Bergman classic.

Born in 1917, Fogelström grew up in Stockholm and lived there his entire life. He was a vast resource on Stockholm's history with enormous archives on the subject, and published much non-fiction about the city. He spent his early career as a journalist, and in the 1940s, he co-founded a literary magazine. His own prolific writing resulted in over fifty books.

Fogelström's *Stockholm Series* has remained a favorite in Swedish literature among readers of all ages, and he continues to be greatly loved and respected as a chronicler of his people. Fogelström died on Midsummer Day, June 20, 1998, two days before the unveiling of a statue of him at the entrance to the hall where the Nobel prizes are awarded in Stockholm.

THE TRANSLATOR

Jennifer Brown Bäverstam has traveled and studied languages all her life. She has translated several books and articles from Swedish and French. She holds a degree in French and economics from Georgetown University and has studied translation at the University of Geneva. She lives in Boston, Massachusetts.

Translator's Note

Swedish place names are generally one compound word with the proper name at the beginning and the kind of place at the end.

Because most of the place names in the book have not been translated, the following terms explain endings for names of streets, hills, bridges, etc.:

backen: hill
berget, bergen: hill, hills
bro, bron: bridge
gatan: street

gränd: alley
holm, holmen: island
torg, torget: square
viken: estuary

I

REMEMBER
THE
CITY

The new century had dawned; the new era had arrived. But the city was still just an overgrown small town. Much of the idyllic country life still existed alongside rumbling factories and newly constructed office buildings. White sails of small cargo boats rimmed the waters, rattling carts rolled over endlessly empty squares, the echo of horses' hooves pounded between the buildings on bleak wide streets.

Beneath the calm surface the birth pangs of modernization were underway. On the desolate streets the processes of transformation were carried out so fast and so radically that many city dwellers felt turned into strangers in their own home.

In every part of the city there was construction going on: apartment houses, tall churches and stately schools. New streets were laid out, wide boulevards where recently planted young trees stuck up out of a sea of sand. A ring of residential suburbs grew up outside the old tollgates. The last horse-drawn streetcars disappeared; the first car showroom was opened. Electricity and the internal combustion engine were ready for use in continued dramatic changes to the city and to life.

So much of the known and the familiar were destroyed. Buildings were torn down, hills blasted away, gravestones and the bones of the dead were tossed aside. Nothing was considered sacred or worth preserving.

They were going toward brighter times; such was the law of development, the doctrine of progress. Behind lay only darkness and want, days to forget, memories to obliterate.

A new century, a new city. And a new human being?

On the way, marching toward the future and progress, the masses felt impatient. They wanted to be included now, to push their way forward to human dignity and justice. One demonstration gave way to another. Within a few years the labor movement had doubled its numbers many times over. The impression of mass and strength gave people a sense of self and self-confidence. Demands were formulated now from the People's Hall, the gathering place of the people, opened twenty years after Master Palm came to town and tried in vain to rent a locale for campaign meetings.

Attempts to quell the demonstrations only drew new groups of sympathizers to them. Workers, artists, and professors sang the citizens' song of the noble poet, von Heidenstam, who proclaimed it was a disgrace for civil rights to be equated with money. More threatening tones were heard in a newly translated song of struggle: Stand up, oh victims of oppression!

The demonstrations culminated in the first Major strike. A ring of reliable troops brought in from the countryside surrounded the House of Parliament, as within parliament discussed voting rights. Outside, the city lay silent and dark for three days: no streetcars or carriages rolled through the streets, no sloops glided across the inlets. Candles and water had to be rationed, fresh bread and fresh newspapers were not to be had.

Parliament set up a committee of investigation—in a kind of recognition of the principle of universal suffrage.

The lines began to be clearer. Increased opposition forced solutions to be found. The general strike gave the employers a reason to organize. Minor and disorderly confrontations and controversies would be settled by centralized negotiations and national agreements; disputes would no longer be valid between individuals, but between organizations.

The individual might feel doomed to be devoured by the new era and the new city. The movements, the organizations, dominated more and more. But along with them, as if riding on their wave, the person of the new era was propelled forward: the official, the negotiator, the representative.

A woman dressed in dark clothing came out of a doorway on Stora Badstugatan, a shadow out of the woods. Behind her lay the factory courtyard, silent and empty. The shiny cobblestones glimmered softly from the light of the windows in the upper story. The factory director had his home there. A window stood open to the winter evening, someone was playing Napoleon's March over the Alps.

The woman stepped out into the street and was lit by the streetlamp. Her pale face glimmered briefly in the light before she lowered her head and began to walk away toward Hötorget. She walked calmly, methodically, without being drawn into the beat of the march's melody.

Every single day for more than twenty years she had walked this route through the city. Morning and evening, in rain, in snow, in sunshine, in the dusk, or in the dark of night. She knew every house, every display window. But much had changed. A few years ago the large Hälsinge farmstead beside Hötorget had been torn down. Now Lutternsgatan's low houses were being smashed to bits. Soon the ridge beneath these ruins would be cut through for the new street, Kungsgatan. And where she had previously crossed Helgeandsholmen, behind the bazaars and the royal stable, the newly inaugurated House of Parliament stood.

When she thought of everything that had disappeared, people and houses, she felt old. She wasn't young anymore, soon thirty-five. And unmarried, belonging to the leftovers, the barren.

Still, she didn't feel like she had lived in vain. Maybe not so much happened to her directly—but she was always involved in what happened around her, with those who were close to her. She accepted and shared their experiences; in mirroring the lives of those around her she also got to participate in life.

In moments of joy and worry—and perhaps even pride—she could feel that she was something more than just a mirror, something more significant. Her home was their nest. A foundation, something to start out from, was perhaps what she was able to provide. As long as she had the strength, as long as she could manage to retain their trust and love.

As she walked, that March evening in 1905, through the familiar and yet so unfamiliar streets, she felt thankfulness toward a life that could give so much, berated herself for the many times she had felt only loneliness.

Longing to get home made her walk faster, she was a little breathless with the effort. But she didn't even glance at the streetcar that passed her on its way to Slussen.

EXPECTANT
HILLS

The lanes of the Old Town opened onto the water like narrow portals.
Through these openings, dark streams of workers poured through the Old
Town, on their way home from Kungsholmen's or Söder's big factories.
The whistles had blown seven o'clock, the workday was over. The shop
assistants stood in doorways and watched those who were now off work a
little enviously. They wouldn't get off before eight at the earliest.

The wind whistled around the open area beside the locks at Slussen. In
the harbor at Kornhamn, the cargo boats' forest of masts rocked softly in
the twilight. But on the side closer to the open Baltic, the wind took a
stronger hold. Fiskarhamn's dock with its stalls and customers was heav-
ing, water splashed, tugboats and small vessels pulled on their lines.

All was dark and heavy—the compact mass of houses in the Old Town,
the steep hills of Söder, the streams of work-clad, tired people, the thud
and shuffle of all the heavy boots. But the skies above the dark city had
some of springtime's soft light.

Streetcars ringing their bells rolled through the streams of people, carts
and carriages plowing their way forward. Steam launches drew small
sparkling light stripes on the waters and a train showering sparks thundered across the railroad bridge, Järnvägsbron, toward the central station.
Inside the black skeleton of the Katarina elevator, the faintly illuminated
elevator cars rose and sank.

Everything Emelie saw was very familiar, she saw it each evening on her
walk home. Still, it was different now. Maybe it was the gleam of the light,
the feeling of spring. It had been cloudy for a few days, now it was clear
and she could see that something was happening behind the blanket of
clouds: light and spring had crept closer. Normally it would all get easier
then; people wouldn't be cold and could arrive home before it grew dark.

Still, she was a little afraid of the light. With the light it was clearly visible how close the danger was, how her world was threatened.

They were blasting in the hills of Söder, and a new and broad road making the ascent was to replace the difficult hills on Stora Glasbruksgatan. They had already blasted down through the hill on Renstjärnsgatan a few years ago, and a wide ditch had divided Fjällgatan. The house in the back that Emelie had lived in for so many years had disappeared. Now there was only a steep precipice left, dropping down to the new road below. They had been able to move into the house closer the street, but that was also condemned, would have to be torn down in a few years. The new road, Katarinavägen, left many homeless. The Dihlström Institution was among those affected, but a new workhouse would soon be ready down by Hornstull.

There was a lot of building going on now, large apartment buildings in what had previously been a part of town with small, ramshackle houses. Open views, gardens and tobacco fields disappeared. The sun did not shine in anymore, the shadows broadened. The slum of hovels was exchanged for tenements, the draughts and discomfort of wooden houses for the chill and gloom of stone buildings.

Next time she moved it would probably be to an apartment building, with water and sewer connections and maybe even electricity. For her parents it would have been unimaginable luxury and comfort. And still she didn't want to move, instead wanted to stay where she was as long as possible.

Now she was beginning the climb, she had to walk more slowly up the steep hill. Darkness got the upper hand here again; the light strip of sky was no longer visible. The yellow balls of light from the gas lamps grew smaller and smaller and disappeared somewhere around the bend in the road. The house facades were dirty and crumbling, nothing was repaired here, everything was going to be torn down soon. The waste from empty slop pails floated past in the gutter.

A small group of people stood under one of the street lamps, some men and a woman with children. They were speaking a foreign language together; one of the men held a piece of paper in his hand and tried to read it. But he shook his head and the others gesticulated excitedly. Suddenly they took a few steps toward Emelie who grew nervous and tried to step out of the way—she couldn't help those people, couldn't even understand what they were saying.

But the man with the paper looked friendly, he smiled, pointed at the piece of paper. There was an address on Höbergsgatan, written with clearly printed letters. The man pointed at the address and at himself and his companions. She nodded in reply; she could understand what they meant. She pointed up the hill and they followed her. She had to walk slowly, otherwise the woman with the small children wouldn't be able to keep up.

The man tried to explain, repeated time after time his foreign words. Finally Emelie thought she understood what he was saying: apparently they were Russians. She had heard that a number of Russian refugees had come here after the unsuccessful Russian revolution attempt a few months earlier, fleeing the czar. Revolutionaries... She recalled her parents' friend, Thumbs. He talked about the revolution, at least he used to. Emelie had never been able to believe that revolutions were possible; the failed Russian attempt was surely new proof of that. These people had believed and tried—and had to flee. They were nice and friendly and she felt sorry for them. How would they manage here, in a country where no one understood what they said? But they certainly had some friends on Höbergsgatan; she had to help them get there. It was only a few houses away from Glasbruksgatan. She followed them to the door and they nodded and thanked her with words she didn't understand. And someone high up in the house opened a window and called down in that strange language—and the group on the street cried with joy and called back to him. They had found the right place; someone was waiting for them.

She turned and left them, felt the warmth of their joy. It was good when there was someone who waited, when the person who came was welcome.

She walked faster now that the hill was behind her, smiled to herself when she thought of those at home. Melancholy in her smile: scattered remnants were all that was left. Her youngest brother, Olof, had died in the sanatorium almost three years ago. He hadn't been more than twenty-two years old and had left a wife and daughter behind. Jenny and four-year-old Maj lived with Emelie. Together with Gunnar, the son of Emelie's older brother. Gunnar had turned sixteen a month ago.

She had the children of both her brothers living with her. It was strange that it had turned out that way...

Or maybe it was only natural. Did not women, seemingly weak, survive and endure? Emelie could remember her grandmother, little, wiry Washer-Malin. How the old woman almost disappeared behind the enormous cart of washing she pushed. And Mama, a widow with four children to support. Though of course August had been adopted by the wealthy Bodins, and had soon disappeared from the world of poverty of his siblings. And that fit in with the picture too: if the men didn't die they disappeared anyway, didn't have to bear up in the same way. When Mama died it wasn't August but Emelie who had to take care of her siblings, who had to have the strength.

The burdens and the duties sometimes felt heavy. There were moments when she wondered: why am I always the one who has to be on hand? Is there no one but me who can help out?

Such as the time Olof was in the hospital, when she had to go to August and almost beg for help. Yes, he had been kind and willing to help. But she was the one who had the responsibility, had to ask.

Yet it was true that the responsibility yielded mostly happiness. If those at home hadn't existed and needed her help—how would it have been then?

The thought scared her. She could survey them anxiously and wonder: how much longer? Now Jenny wanted a place of her own, maybe get remarried; she was still young. How long would Gunnar stay?

Still, they were there now. If they hadn't been remnants they wouldn't have needed her help. Their weakness and misfortune were maybe her good fortune. It sometimes felt that way when longing for them and worries over losing them were strongest.

Now they were waiting. She walked as fast as she could, thought she would tell them about those Russians—Jenny was so interested in everything that happened outside the walls of home. In the big world, as Jenny said. A child of the world was what she was called by a neighbor's wife who was a pietist.

The cobblestones of Fjällgatan gleamed white through the evening darkness. Bare, black tree branches grew tall over the fences on the north side, while the houses on the south side stood close together as if supporting each other. Widely spaced gas lanterns were held up by iron arms, which had been mounted on the rotting walls of the wooden houses. A little of the glow from the gaslights burnished the baker's golden pretzels on number 12. The windows of the upper story in the tall house reflected some of the light from the western sky.

Everything might appear untouched, just the same as always. But beyond the wooden house at number 12 lay the precipice, the newly blasted street. Inside the gate in the fence directly opposite were piles of torn down lumber and broken rock, and a hole gaped where the house that had been their home for so long once stood.

The old captain who had owned the two houses inside the fence and lived on the top floor of the house in back was gone now, dead. His heirs had sold it to the city. The owners of the neighboring houses on the south side had been forced to do this too, and the rows of houses in the back that had clung to the edge of the hill had now disappeared or were in the process of being torn down.

The house on the street where they now lived had an entrance from the yard. Emelie stopped for a moment at the gate. Demolition and blasting had expanded their view, but what was close by was mangled and broken. The scene she had just been looking at was only an optical illusion—nothing was the same; nothing could be what it had once been. The city and life were continually being transformed. Everything was transitory. This was true not only for the house where she lived, but for the people around her as well, those who were closest.

Yet they were still there.

When she opened the door the smell of burned food wafted toward her. Jenny had apparently gone out to pick up Maj. Emelie had to quickly take over at the stove. A minute later Gunnar, who was apprenticed to a carpenter, arrived. He worked on Kungsholmen and had a long walk home.

They ate the burned food and Emelie told them about the Russians she had seen. Jenny had also noticed some foreigners in the area; now they were probably Russians too. That was how things were with Jenny: without really knowing it she changed the actual facts. An Italian plasterer became a Russian revolutionary, a mouse became a big rat, and an everyday trifle became an exciting adventure.

Gunnar listened without asking anything or participating in the conversation. He had become involved in the Young Socialist Clubs through a workmate and there they talked a lot about what was happening in Russia. But Gunnar, who was new and unaccustomed, thought it was difficult to follow the debates: especially when some of the more superior youths in the club spoke a language only the initiated could follow. About the ideology of anarchy and the petty bourgeois Lasallianism under the aegis of half measures, about the capitalist coercive state and the struggle for emancipation of the working class. Sometimes he had wondered if all those foreign words might be Russian.

He kept quiet and listened, preferring not to reveal what he was thinking. First he wanted to be sure himself of what he believed. His caution was both inherited and dearly paid for by experience. He had been hit a lot for speaking up before he had moved in with Emelie.

He nodded good-bye and went out to meet his friends. Emelie didn't need to remind him to come home on time; he was seldom late. But she did it anyway. It was an old habit she had from when she used to have to remind Olof. She regretted it immediately—but Gunnar didn't get annoyed, he only answered calmly: no, he wouldn't be out late.

Maj fell asleep. Emelie sat next to the kerosene lamp to darn socks. Jenny reclined on the wooden kitchen sofa, sunk in twilight. She never sat like ordinary people, thought Emelie. Now that Gunnar wasn't home it didn't matter if she was improper, and Emelie had to smile: Jenny looked so funny, her arms slung over the back and sides of the sofa, her legs sprawling to the floor. As if Jenny was always playing someone, some role.

She was tired of embroidering, she said now. She had brought home jobs from a needlework shop where she used to work. It was more fun to stand in the shop, move around, meet the customers, see the people pass by on the street. It was for Maj's sake she had taken a job she could do at home. Actually she didn't want to go back to the shop either. Instead she would prefer to resume her artistic life, stand on stage, sing, dance...

Emelie had heard it all so many evenings, all of Jenny's plans and ideas. She felt some kind of reassurance: it never got any farther than plans. Still, she didn't really like Jenny entertaining these thoughts. Jenny was a widow and a mother. The memory of Olof and taking care of Maj should prevent her from thinking these foolish things. And Jenny was twenty-four years old in any case, not a child any longer. Her dancing days were over.

Emelie rolled up the finished socks, took out the next pair, looked at them a little crossly.

"Gunnar has gotten enormous holes in these," she said.

Jenny didn't answer, went over to the window instead and stared out over the debris from the demolition, the scaffolding and the water. She felt closed in, imprisoned. She had asked to live with Emelie, wanted to live here, liked Emelie. Still, she longed to get out and away, somewhere where more lights glittered and life pulsed faster. I'm still young, she thought. If only Olof had lived, if he had been healthy... It had happened so fast, they had been given so little time. He would have understood that she wanted to live, longed to get out.

Without anything to wait for or long for, life became dismal. Was that why she thought up one plan after another, tried to dream dreams?

She wept a little in the darkness before she fell asleep, wept silently so Emelie wouldn't hear.

SPRING ON THE OUTSKIRTS

The windows stood open, winter's smells of mold and mildew were being aired out. The grass was already growing high around the row of privies and sheds in the yard, fertilized by the kitchen slops. Clumps of burdock and patches of nettles shot up along the fence.

Gunnar ran down the steps, opened the door to the yard—and stopped a moment, blinded by the spring sun. Now the evenings had grown light and long, enticing people out from their cramped houses.

He greeted the neighbor woman politely. She had pulled a wooden bed out to the yard and was ridding it of vermin using a table knife and kerosene.

One of Gunnar's friends from the Young Socialists Club was waiting in the street. Acke had long been a member in the club, knew the people in the leadership circles. He would probably not have bothered to meet up with the quiet and insignificant Gunnar if they hadn't happened to walk home together a few times, and during those walks Acke had found something that both annoyed and attracted him: opposition. Gunnar didn't let himself become enthused like others. The kid was irritatingly doubtful and cautious. There was something to be won over in him—and Acke felt that it was his job to do it, convert the doubter into a believer.

They went down the stairs to the new Renstjärnsgatan, and followed the blasted-out excavation southward. Away toward Folkungagatan a red streetcar rolled in the direction of the tollgate. The bell clanged angrily and sparks sprayed when the pulley on the trolley pole ran along the overhead wire.

Acke told about his exploits at the Social Democratic Party's congress a few months earlier. He thought it was something that ought to impress Gunnar. Acke had been one of the many Young Socialists who had stormed the podium at the People's Hall and done his best to disrupt the proceedings. They had whistled and booed and put out the lights so that the congressional delegates had to sit in half darkness.

The objective of these actions had been to prolong the deliberations and thus harass the detested Youth League members. The newly formed Social Democratic Youth League was a direct competitor to the Young Socialists—and was expected to be recognized by the congress as the official youth league of the party, with whatever that implied in the way of moral and economic support. Now the question of the new Youth League's status did not get brought up before two o'clock in the morning during the last day of the congress. And then all the Young Socialists and their sympathizers had demanded the floor. In which case all their opponents had been forced to petition for it en masse as well, for the sake of fairness. After that the motion was easily made to remove the question from the agenda. In light of the general exhaustion, such a motion had to be approved. And there sat the Social Democratic Youth League members completely outdone, without the congress giving them the status they had hoped for.

It was a beautiful experiment in tactics, thought Acke. Something to learn from. You shouldn't let yourself be conquered by the reactionary elements of the working classes.

He waited for Gunnar's admiration, maybe some questions that would lead to a more detailed lesson. But his listener remained silent.

"So..." coaxed Acke. "Wasn't that cleverly done?" He was pleased to get to remain in the home of the Social Democrats even though there were certainly many who wanted to kick out the troublesome Young Socialists and instead get a more compliant youth movement.

They had turned onto Folkungagatan, the road down toward the tollgate and Acke's home. After one block the new buildings disappeared, followed by low rows of workshops. One side of the street had been laid out as a park where new, slender trees were protected by wooden railings. They sat down on one of the railings. Acke lit a cigar and spat. A freshly painted green pissoir gleamed beside the pump close to Erstagatan. It rose up like a magnificent fort over the enormous sea of sand.

"If I didn't feel welcome at home I would move," Gunnar said suddenly.

The answer had been so long in coming that Acke had begun to think about something else. It took a moment before he understood what the boy meant, that he was opposing him again.

"That's idiocy," he hissed. "You don't mean that we should leave the party willingly? No way. Membership still gives all too many benefits. You know yourself," he appealed. "You can think that your old man is a hopeless reactionary and argue with him—but you stay at home. It's probably the same for you…"

"No," answered Gunnar. "I don't live with my parents."

Acke began to be tired of trying to convince him. The kid was so young, couldn't yet appreciate finesse. He believed everything would be so uncomplicated. Gradually he would learn that it was better to hit below the belt than to lose.

"You probably mean well," he said, "But why don't you live at home?"

Gunnar tried to explain. Apparently the one he had called father wasn't his real father, at least it had sounded that way sometimes. He hadn't been able to stay living at home.

"Was he so hard on you?"

"Yes."

"Hit you a lot?"

"Yes."

"Then who are you living with now?"

That was almost harder to answer. He was living with Emelie—but who was Emelie actually? A friend of his mother's. But it didn't feel like that. Emelie and his mother had never really been such good friends. Emelie was much closer to him than if she had just been a friend of his mother's. She wasn't like a foster mother either, more like an older sister. He didn't know what he should call her.

"With someone I know," he said after he'd thought a little while.

"Someone who is so nice that you feel welcome?"

"Yes."

"Then you've been lucky," Acke said a little indifferently. He had caught sight of a girl he knew. She lived down near the tollgate; they could walk together a ways. It would be more fun to joke with her than to sit here and drag answers out of the taciturn boy.

"Well," he said. "I think I'll be getting home. I'll take this opportunity to flirt with that girl over there…"

He left. Gunnar stayed sitting where he was, saw Acke take the girl's arm and wander off. It was Saturday evening. Maybe they'd go out to the amusement park at Sickla. He didn't really know where he himself would go. With his quiet ways he didn't have an easy time making friends. For some people everything was so easy, like for Acke who just walked up and took a girl's arm without further ado.

He stood up, brushed off the seat of his pants. Looked up toward Erstagatan. He could swing by, just walk past… His conversation with Acke had made him think of his mother and siblings. He knew that he couldn't go in—his father or whatever he should call him—had said that the son of a whore wasn't to stick his nose inside their home, had threatened to kill him.

He could walk on their street at least—and he would be able to run away from his father who was sure to be drunk on a Saturday evening.

It might be foolish, but he went. Without being able to tell if he really felt any longing for his parental home. His mother had had so little time with him; younger siblings and home and work had taken the energy she had. From time to time she drank quite a lot, became quarrelsome and angry. She had hit him more often than she had caressed him. But of course he liked her. And understood that she had taken her part in saving him from his father and letting him live with Emelie.

Many of the dilapidated wooden houses on Erstagatan had been torn down; new buildings were being put up. The streets were becoming strangely bordered with what looked like uneven teeth, high and low indiscriminately. And groups of children had numerous opportunities for adventures and plundering now. They flocked to demolition and building sights and stole firewood. They were chased by the guards, climbed through broken fences, made their way into abandoned, tumbledown houses.

Barely a block from Folkungagatan—that was where his family lived—in one of the hovels next to a large house called Hagen. People claimed it had been Queen Kristina's hunting castle. Gunnar looked around cautiously before he slipped in through some broken slats in the fence and, after a couple of quick leaps, hid himself between the bushes.

He was in a forbidden area now, on enemy territory. He crept forward so that he could see the narrow yard between the small houses. He had never lived here, had moved in with Emelie before his family had moved here. So he didn't know the hiding places and escape routes that well.

A few small boys were arguing over a dead rat. They had found it in a trap and now the question was who would get the tail that the authorities would pay five öre for. The rat-tail meant two paper cones full of candy bits and the biggest of the boys already had his knife out when the door to one of the houses opened and a man came out. A black, unwashed chimneysweep—his father. Gunnar saw how he swatted at the boys who jumped aside, then he took the rat and went over to the stump for splitting wood. He chopped off the tail and stuffed it into his shirt pocket, throwing away the rat in the bushes. It fell at Gunnar's feet and he had to prevent himself from jumping back and being discovered.

His father went inside again. Gunnar stood there, hidden between the bushes, heard them bellowing there inside their little house. They were celebrating its being Saturday. Father must have some friends over; maybe they had invited the neighbors in. A man came out on the steps, stood there swaying a moment, dug inside his pants and let a out a stream that sprayed over the trampled grass of the yard. He had left the door open behind him. Now Gunnar's mother came out with a bucket of kitchen slops. She shoved her guest over to get past. But he wouldn't let himself be budged, grabbed her for support and managed to catch hold of her waist. The bucket swung out, some of its content splattering on her skirt. It seemed as if she hardly noticed. Gunnar realized she was pretty drunk too.

The man groped her and she started to laugh and smacked his fingers playfully. When he let go of her she took a few steps with the bucket and poured out its contents beside the neighboring shed. An old lady came rushing out, shook her fist and shrieked. His mother and the unknown man shrieked back.

While this tumult was going on, Gunnar sneaked off. He felt disgust and revulsion; wanted to get away, avoid seeing. He hid behind an outhouse while a gang of kids went past, wondered if any of his siblings were part of the ragged and dirty group. How old would they be now? Tyra would be about ten. That would mean Beda was eight and Erik six. The youngest, Bengt, couldn't be more than four. The children were surely out, even though it was almost nine o'clock. There was no room inside for them on an evening like this.

Now he felt how much Emelie had rescued him from. Without her help he would have also lived in the shed. He would have belonged to the "lumpen proletariat," as his friends at the club said, those who not even the advocates nor the champions of the poor dared believe in or hope for.

The children had disappeared. Gunnar sat for a little while behind the outhouse. He saw how the birds had built a nest between the broken tiles on the roof, how the dandelions were budding along the dark wall. He stood up and slipped off, turned off the path, walked in the dusk beneath some apple trees grown wild.

He heard a noise, froze with alarm. What if his father had noticed him after all.... But no one came. He heard the noise again. There must be someone behind the fence. He looked carefully through a hole.

The boy must have been about his own age, the girl a little older. She lay in the sparse grass, a thin girl with her dress tucked up. For an instant Gunnar wondered if he should help her, if she had been attacked—but then he saw how her arms and hands eagerly pressed the boy's body down and how she seemed to lift herself from the ground to come closer to him.

He wanted to go, couldn't see—yet he stood where he was. Then he heard footsteps approaching and was suddenly able to act. With a few steps he had disappeared among the trees, followed by curses and angry shouts from the interrupted couple.

He came out on the street on the outskirts, still dizzy and half stunned. He ran a little way before he calmed down: no one was after him.

He almost felt nausea. But at the same time attraction, longing. Of course he had fantasized and dreamed. He had certainly seen couples pressing against each other in doorways and passageways. But not like this, not so close.

He bent down, broke off some of the green strands of grass that were growing between the cobblestones of the street, placed them in his buttonhole. He plucked a few leaves from a branch. His buttonhole was filled with signs of spring; they spread out over his lapel. He thought how for the first time he could feel spring bubbling all around him, green life was pushing its way out everywhere: at house corners, between stones, over fences, on his coat. Smells had come alive, life was returning.

He looked across at the new church that was being built in the White Hills. The scaffolding shone white around the almost completed steeple. Under the gray colossus the hillside lay naked. The crowd of little houses closest to the construction site was gone. The church seemed so austere, so clean and dead. Not a tree or green leaf was visible in its vicinity.

He eventually made his way back to Fjällgatan and opened the gate. Home again, so safe despite the cleft below. He looked up at the house. There was a light on in the window: a square of welcoming yellow light. Emelie and Jenny were home. The light shone so calmly, soothingly.

Still he sat out on the steps of the outhouse, felt like he had to be really calm himself before he went in. He saw a shadow dance by up there, saw Jenny in the window. She was in her shift, must be going to bed. Just as well that he waited a while.

She caught sight of him through the window, waved. He waved back. Now it was best not to wait too long. Then they would begin to wonder. He didn't think Jenny understood that he wanted to leave her undisturbed. She didn't seem to get disturbed. It was more like he was the one who was unsettled by her—and then of course he could see that Emelie didn't like it.

They realized he was back at the house anyway. There was no reason for them to wonder about that.

When he came up they were already in bed. Emelie asked if he wanted more to eat but he wasn't hungry. He put out the light before he undressed, saw Jenny's eyes glimmering in the darkness. She asked if he had had fun.

"I only took a walk and looked around," he said and pulled the grass and leaves from his coat lapel.

"For girls of course," she laughed.

"Huh!" he said, and crawled under the blanket.

THE VISITOR

In spite of the fact that it was spring and light out, the office lay in shadow. Heavy, plush drapes blocked much of the daylight; whatever found its way in was filtered through tightly woven curtains.

August Bodin had lit the electric lamp over the desk, a little round ball of light made of frosted glass. He waited. And while he did he could not undertake anything else. The knowledge that he would soon be forced to interrupt his work irritated him. He shuffled through his notes. He had stockpiled far too many large bricks last fall; there were still many full pallets of them at the depot at Ragvaldsbro. They were hard to keep watch over; a number of them had surely disappeared. And expensive and difficult to ship; the brick carriers were a tough bunch. Building contractor Dahl, who was constructing the new workhouse institution at Hornstull, had managed to get the better of the carriers, had laid a rail from the dock to the construction site and loaded whole wagons with bricks for the joist structures. You had to be clever, find new methods. And at the same time stick with the tried and true, not rush into anything. There were so many innovations, there was a lot that was surely of doubtful worth. In one of the new buildings on Strandvägen an inventive building contractor had installed some sort of ventilation shafts that people would use to throw their garbage down. They had indulged in water closets in some places. And in the Cedarblom building on Östermalmsgatan they had attempted something appalling: central heating where heat was spread via warm water. People experimented too much; it was dangerous when there weren't enough knowledgeable people. Craftsmanship had been in decline since the journeyman and master examination had been abolished. Neither building contractors nor supervisors had enough skills.

August Bodin was a building contractor himself and these days seldom relied on others for the firm's construction projects. He took the certain over the uncertain, preferred to build a few good buildings to many bad ones. But he was of course dependent on knowledgeable supervisors, as well as able foremen and workers. Ever since they had begun to lay bricks in the winter as well as summer, it had been easier to keep together a steady core group.

Caution enjoined him to run the firm on a smaller scale, not let it expand too much. At the same time he needed more income, there were many who were dependent on his work. His own family had grown: four children now, wife, maid and nursery maid. And then his foster mother with a maid in her apartment. And his parents-in-law. Everyone was dependent on him. Sometimes it was difficult to manage it all. Especially when he had to make sure the firm had enough reserve capital to deal with the crises, which now and then shook up the construction industry.

With everyone he had to support it was hard for him to also extend himself for those he was not directly obligated to assist. While his younger brother had been sick and lain in a sanatorium he had had to help out there too; his sister Emelie had asked him to. Naturally he was glad that Emelie had come to him. He had wanted to help. After Olof's death it seemed that Emelie and his brother's widow had been able to care of themselves. He had spoken with Emelie a few times and it sounded as if they were managing. He had never met Olof's widow, he had been sick in bed during the funeral. The times he had met Emelie she had come up to the office after the workday was over.

They lived in their world, he in his. That was the way it was. His siblings had other requirements in life, not so great. They were used to living the way they did. He couldn't move them out of their world—it was too late now. But he could make sure they didn't suffer from need. And he wanted to do that. He had said to Emelie that he would do that. She knew she could come to him in a pinch.

Emelie was frugal, capable and kind. Maybe too kind. He knew that she had a boy living with her. One of Bärta's sons. Bärta was the

girl who had lived at his mother's during the time August used to
make a visit home every week. He had seen Emelie together with the
boy once, the year of the Stockholm Exhibition. But why had Emelie
taken on someone she didn't in any way need to take responsibility
for? Her incomprehensible goodness irritated him. What if there really was a reason that she took care of the boy?

Once upon a time... young and desperate, alone in his new family, longing for a girl. In utter secrecy he had had meetings with Bärta.
Which year was it? It must have been 88. But Bärta had soon disappeared, met the chimneysweep whom she had then married. Naturally
the boy was the son of the chimneysweep. Hadn't Emelie said that too
once a long time ago? Though of course he could also be the father of
the boy, so careless he and Bärta had been in their ignorance.

If that was the case, then he had a responsibility, couldn't leave
everything in Emelie's hands. It was difficult. He had never said anything about Bärta to Ida. If only he had mentioned it earlier, while it
was still easy enough to talk about. Now he couldn't go to Ida and tell
her. It was too late.

The boy was surely the son of the chimneysweep, he thought. Bärta
would have certainly said something otherwise. Even if she had clearly understood that August would not marry her. She would have
demanded support, of course. She wouldn't have let the chimneysweep believe he was the father of the child in order to get married.
Emelie's taking care of the boy wasn't so strange either, unmarried with
her conscientiousness for looking after and helping others. Maybe she
thought the boy had been neglected and therefore had intervened; she
had always been a little meddlesome.

He didn't want to think about it anymore. But just today it was difficult to stop since he had left the message that he was going to visit
Emelie. He wanted to see how they were living, that his brother's
widow and little daughter weren't in any kind of distress. He had said
to Olof at the hospital that he would help if needed. He had felt obligated to promise, in spite of everything.

He stood up, turned off the lamp. I'll take a coach from Gustav

Adolfs torg, he thought. I'll walk a little ways, there's plenty of time. It felt good to get out, get away from those foolish thoughts.

The statue of the king stood surrounded by wooden planks. A new and magnificent pedestal had been promised by a rich brewer and wholesaler but not been put in place yet. Horse manure lay in piles where the carriages stood waiting; the pigeons and sparrows were having a feast. The city looked dirty and smelled bad despite the spring evening being lovely and cool. The street cleaners' strike had gone on for almost two weeks, and the students who filled in with brooms weren't enough. It was wrong for people to strike like that, whenever they felt like it; the innocent suffered. In the construction industry they had managed very well during recent years. It's true there had been a short-lived struggle a year ago, but the Bodin firm had been one of those who had agreed to a separate settlement. Of course he had had to hear some jeers because of it from his fellow employers—but he had felt satisfied with himself, felt he had shown solidarity with his roots in the working class. Besides, it had been an economic necessity. He had been in need of money and didn't receive it until construction was finished. But now he had applied for membership in the building contractors' association. At the same time he was proud over that separate settlement, it had been his little manifestation. He hoped that it was forgotten now. There were actually quite a few who had negotiated in a similar manner, yet it was never good to push anything too far.

Next to the horse-drawn hired cabs was an automobile taxi, a so-called "cockroach." He wondered if he should take it, it might be fun. He had only ridden in an automobile one time before, one Sunday with his family on Djurgården. But its motor might not be able to handle the hills of Söder. The old horses were still safest. Besides he would call attention to himself. People would come pouring out of every rickety house on Söder to see the automobile. He wanted to arrive unseen, as unseen as was possible for an upper class gentleman on a poor street. He nodded to one of the horse coachmen who climbed down and opened the door.

August arranged himself comfortably. The vehicle rolled across Norrbro and along the water of Skeppsbron. At Slussen rows of street-cars stood on both sides of the bridges; the northern company had blue on one side and the southern company had red on the other. The coachman took the route toward Hornsgatan, and turned up onto Ragvaldsgatan. Then it went eastward on Högbergsgatan turning in on Fjällgatan. August stepped out, paid, tried to read the numbers on the rusty sign on the fence. To think that this had never happened before, even though he had planned it so many times.

He stood there a moment while the carriage turned and disappeared. That's right—the street had been blasted away over there. Wasn't the handle on the gate the same as the one on their old home on Åsöberget? He had lived just about like this once upon a time, in a tumbledown old house on a street in the outskirts. A long time ago. And now he was coming back. It was like meeting the past. He felt like he barely dared open the gate. He could recall those who no longer existed: Mama, Papa. As if they were inside, asking: "August... have you been gone so long?"

I've been to the cemetery a few times at least, he thought in defense. I laid a wreath... when was the last time? He couldn't remember.

But he couldn't stand here any longer, people would begin to wonder. He opened the gate and saw the crater from the blasting, the excavation where the new street would go. The row of outhouses, not so far from the precipice. The house had crumbling plaster. Well, it was natural that they weren't repairing anything here; everything was going to be torn down soon.

The steps were freshly scrubbed and he wondered if Emelie had done that—just because he was coming. But she probably scrubbed them even if nobody was coming. She was probably like Mama, always busy with the brush.

Then he knocked and Emelie opened the door. He stepped inside, looked a little surprised at a young girl in a red blouse. She had her hair combed down around her face, just like the beautiful dancer,

Cléo, who had danced at the Circus Variety last year. It had become so popular. Who was this girl who was visiting Emelie? She couldn't possibly be the widow?

But she took his hand and said—as if they were relatives—of course they were: "Good afternoon August, I'm Jenny."

"So nice to met you, Jenny," he said. But he thought: Good God, a kid, a little minx... and Emelie who had all the responsibility. The room was small, closing in on them. Everything was hopeless.

But the child who was sleeping seemed well cared for and healthy. There wasn't any sign of the boy. Maybe he had moved back home with his parents. August didn't want to ask.

When Emelie had lit the kerosene lamp and they had drunk coffee and sat and talked a while everything felt easier. The room was no longer so small, he thought, it felt more sheltering than suffocating now. He had to get up and look out several times, he didn't have such a fine view himself.

Jenny didn't seem so impossible either now that he had gotten used to her speech and mannerisms. She was certainly a little silly, with her hair draped loosely around her face and her large red mouth. Quite thin. Never sat still, got up and down and wasn't embarrassed to show her ankles. But he had heard that she was some sort of artist, would have gone well with Olof who had also been a restless type.

She was friendly and nice, not shy, not impudent either. It was easy to talk to her. Emelie was much quieter, she actually seemed shy. She had a hard time telling him how things really were with them. Emelie said either yes or no—and Jenny added the rest. He didn't know if Emelie was grateful for this or not.

"As you understand, Jenny, I promised Olof to help if it was necessary," he said.

"Thank you," she replied. "We are grateful for that. Things are alright now—but you never know..."

Yes, they were getting by, he could see that. They weren't suffering from a direct lack of anything. The room was neat and tidy; everything was mended and clean even if it was worn out and simple. The promise felt easier to make and he was glad that he had come, he reassured himself. He didn't have to worry too much, he could give them some help from time to time, but he wouldn't have any great responsibility. Their aspirations weren't so great either.

Jenny brushed a lock of hair back from her eyes, smiled with her wide mouth. When she leaned forward he was aware that she wasn't as thin as she had seemed, at least her bust was round. A rather merry widow, it wasn't in her nature to mourn too much. Maybe she would remarry someday, have another child with another father. Things would be less of a burden for Emelie then. But Emelie would really be lonely then. If that boy wasn't still living here, that is.

While they were still sitting at the table Gunnar arrived. He bowed, sat down on one side, accepted a cup of coffee. He looked at Emelie as if asking her to excuse him; he hadn't thought their visitor would stay so long. Emelie had asked him to go out a little while, her brother was coming over and they had a little business to discuss. Was he disturbing them now? But Emelie didn't seem displeased, she urged him to take another bun and he ate contentedly.

Their distinguished visitor was Emelie's brother, the building contractor, Bodin. A capitalist and purchaser of labor, a man from the upper class. Close up he seemed rather human—an ordinary person, though in fine clothes. But then of course, he was Emelie's brother as well.

The visitor asked him his name and age.

Gunnar Karlsson. Sixteen years old.

And what was his line of work?

He was a carpenter's apprentice.

That was good. One should learn a trade from the ground up. Good carpenters were needed, a building contractor knew that much.

"What if Gunnar were to get work on one of your construction sites?" Jenny said suddenly.

Emelie looked anxiously and almost admonishingly at her, but Jenny didn't notice.

When Gunnar was done with his training he should come to the

Bodin office, August said. Then he would get a good job.

"That's super!" cried Jenny.

But August already regretted what he had said, hoped that Gunnar wouldn't come.

But still he continued, "Yes, come over, you must do that."

"Thanks," said Gunnar. Emelie kept quiet.

It had grown much later than August realized; he had planned on staying only a little while. Now he jumped up and excused himself, knew that they had to get up early the next morning.

He promised to come back, waved good-bye and left. When he got out onto the hushed nighttime street he regretted not ordering a carriage ahead of time. But he could probably get down to Slussen on foot. These were streets he had walked on as a child. Still, he looked around a little anxiously. You never knew, there were a lot of hooligans and rowdies in this area. But no one accosted him. For safety's sake he did not take Glasbruksbacken, took Götgatan instead. It was a bit of a detour but he avoided passing the dens of fornication and the darkest passages.

There were coaches on Södermalmstorg. Now he could tell that he was tired and wanted to get home quickly.

The coach rolled down Brunnsbacken; music wafted out from the lit-up iron veranda on the Pelikan restaurant. The bazaar building stood black and burned out with broken windows after the fire a few weeks earlier. Despite it's being late the night was still unbelievably light, so blue. Some windows still glimmered on the hill behind him; the street lights glittered.

Everything had gone better than he had dared hope. And the boy was assuredly not his. At least, they didn't look like each other. A funny girl, that little widow. He recalled the lock of hair over her mouth, the curve of her breasts, how she had swung her ankles. She was really a funny one.

He felt like he had been relieved of a burden. What he had seen was in spite of everything not worrying, more picturesque and light than heavy and troublesome. He didn't have to add any more worries to those he already had, could stay quite calm.

But those piles of bricks that were still lying down by Ragvaldsbro—he would have to take care of those tomorrow, send a foreman to hire some brick carriers. It wouldn't do to avoid those troublesome carriers, there would only be conflict. And he had always tried to avoid conflict.

OUT
IN THE
WIDE WORLD

The city dozed in the summer heat; the lanes on the hillside lay still and silent in the haze of the sun. Clouds of black flies swarmed over the garbage heaps in the yards and the heat pulsated between the walls of the houses. Some mechanics lay in a cleft in the rocks and played cards. They were unemployed because of the lockout. In the baker's garden on Fjällgatan a sweaty ice deliveryman sat and drank beer. Outside on the street his horse stood in front of his cart. The melting water created a puddle between the cartwheels. The heat was oppressive; if the sky hadn't been so blue it would have seemed like a storm was on the way. And beneath all the seeming calm there was an inescapable anxiety: how would things work out in Norway? The Norwegians had declared King Oscar deposed and the Union dissolved. In Sweden an extra session of parliament had convened and the consumption of arak punch had risen to an alarming degree from all the toasting to king and country.

During these critical days the new Social Democratic Youth League had held a congress. One of the delegates, Fabian Månsson, had encouraged the representatives to go down to Bern's Café and demonstrate for peace—and slug those "patriots" in the jaw if they gave any trouble. A sensational flyer spread across the city, the exhortations of the socialists' congress: Down with weapons! Peace with Norway!

The ice deliveryman had received one of these flyers and read the dangerous words in a low voice to an attentive baker's apprentice: Sweden's working youth should refuse to mobilize if they were called up—"knowing full well that weapons, if they were to be aimed at anybody, should not be aimed at the Norwegians."

"Whoever wrote that should be placed on bread and water for a lifetime," said the baker's boy.

"You can be sure," grunted the deliveryman, and hid the dangerous paper. He dried the beer foam from his mouth with his shirtsleeve: it was best to drive on while there was any ice left. He picked up the large pair of shears and walked through the archway to the street.

A young woman was standing, leaning forward a little carefully, and feeding the horse with a crust of bread. She was wearing a light summer dress, looking so airy and light in the heat, her hair glistening in the sunlight. The deliveryman felt young and glad to be alive when he saw her, wanted to express his joy somehow but couldn't find the right means. He only ended up giving a whoop and slapping her backside; it stuck out when she stood that way. She jumped aside and shrieked with anger. Didn't he have the nerve though!

"I couldn't help it," he laughed as he bent over to unwind the reins from around the horse's front legs. But he hadn't had time to more than take hold of the reins before he got such a kick from her pointy boot so that he almost fell over.

He got up, angry and red in the face.

"That didn't hurt, did it?" she asked. "I just couldn't help it either."

He had to laugh as he climbed onto the driver's seat. As the wagon rolled away he turned around. She had a child beside her now, a little girl who had apparently gotten a cone full of candies at the baker's.

He waved to them. And they waved back.

"That was a real woman," he said to the horse. "A hell of a temper—but she doesn't hold grudges."

Jenny had to laugh. So typical of guys. She couldn't stay mad at the ice deliveryman for long, it was just like he said: he couldn't help it. It was his way of showing his appreciation, to say that summer was lovely and a girl was nice.

"Let's go," she said to Maj. "You have to change your dress before we leave."

They walked up the dark stairway, opened the door to the room that was comfortably cool since it faced north. The dress was laid out on a chair. Jenny washed the girl's face and hands and got her dressed. The dress was perhaps too fancy for everyday, but she wanted Maj to look pretty when they went to the needlework shop. She brushed her hair, tied her bow. She took out the tablecloths she had embroidered and rolled them carefully in paper. She tried to see her own image in the little mirror, combed back the annoying waves of hair.

Now they could go.

When they reached Nytorget the ice wagon and horse stood in front of the butcher shop. But the deliveryman was nowhere to be seen—and it was probably best that way.

She remembered how she had walked down this street once long ago, with Olof. That day when things had been decided between them. They had been on their way to Hammarby Lake to rent a rowboat. That was the day she had learned that Olof was sick. And they had realized that they belonged together, even if their time together would be short.

It was right here where they had walked and the butcher had stood in the door and lifted his cap and smiled in such a friendly manner. Now the butcher, Amilon, was also dead. His horrible death had been the subject of conversation for many years: murdered, stabbed, his corpse stuffed in a barrel that had been thrown in Hammarby Lake. The same lake they had swum in at that time. And where Olof's mother had drowned when she was rinsing laundry in a hole in the ice.

She shivered in the summer heat. So narrow and confined the world was, so close everything terrible lay. She never went to Hammarby Lake to swim anymore. And it wasn't only because the water had gotten so foul.

A little farther from home it was easier to feel free. They walked down Götgatan and there were many shop windows to look in. Wagons rattled over the stone paving, the drivers spinning their brake handles so their speed down the steep hill wouldn't be too perilous. The windows stood open in the Vega Restaurant on the corner of Sankt Paulsgatan. But they were so high up that she couldn't look in, otherwise she would have wanted to see if any artists were sitting in there. It had been their old haunt before. She didn't know what it was like now. She thought of Olof's friend, Arthur. She had heard that he had been committed to a mental institution. So much had happened in a few years—despite the fact that she usually felt like nothing happened.

On Hornsgatan it was ugly and rundown, as it had been for a long time. Part of the cemetery had been dug up and half of the street blasted away while the houses scaled the hump on the other half. The dark excavation pit in the street had never been finished and cleaned up; there were mostly old wheels from the equipment and piles of trash down there.

Jenny urged her daughter on, began to be anxious now, wanted to reach the shop and have her work checked and approved. She knew that she wasn't particularly good at embroidery. She had such a hard time sitting still and fiddling with small stitches. It was easier if she could choose the patterns and colors herself. But usually everything was all set and decided. She could only follow the designs traced on. There was no chance of improvising, inventing.

The shop lay on the other side of the hump and the owner was waiting for them. She barely had time to look at what Jenny had produced, so Jenny got off easily—at least for the time being. They had promised to send some embroidered pillowcases that were a rush order—a wedding present. And they didn't want an ordinary courier to take them—a clumsy boy could drop the pillowcases in the dirt. Such lovely and finely worked items should be delivered by a woman, someone who understood the value of the workmanship and felt responsible. Could Jenny do it? Maybe her little girl could stay in the store while she went?

Jenny preferred to take her with her. Where was the package going?

All the way to Kungsholmen, close to the church. It was probably easiest to take the steam launch across.

This was going to be a real summer outing. Jenny grew excited, she hadn't gotten away from Söder for close to a year now. It never happened, it was hard to get away. The package wasn't heavy, the assignment was a pleasure.

She received money—for her work, for the assignment and for the trip. Somehow it came out to a little more than she had calculated, so she bought two sour candy sticks at the shop next door. Contentedly sucking on them, mother and daughter climbed down the countless outdoor stairs of Maria trappgränd, down toward the water at Söder Mälarstrand where the steam launches had a mooring.

The sun shone on the glittering water. The launch glided across as if on a mirror, as if breaking up small pieces of glass that splintered and were tossed into the air, sparkling once and disappearing. At the wooden dock by Munkbron and alongside the quays of Riddarholmen, lay rows of white Mälar boats; cloth canopies shone brightly from the stalls around Kornhamn. The launch glided in among some shoals of black coal barges. Soon Strömbadet's yellow towers and spires were gleaming before them. The numerous smoke-stacks of the gasworks protruded like black sticks beside Central Station, and from out of the greenery on the hillside above Kungsholm's church, small red cottages glistened. The windmill, Gamla Eldkvarn, was a somber gray beside the water. Between the windmill and the yellow houses of the Karolinska Institute lay an opening at Eiraplanen. That was where the boat was going to tie up.

At first Maj had been a little timid faced with so many new things. Now she was standing in the bow and laughing out loud when the foam splashed up. Jenny held tight onto the child's dress, leaned against the back of the wooden bench, closed her eyes, and felt the wind ruffle her hair.

This was how she would like to travel around for days, gliding over the waves, out into the wide world. Once she had actually traveled far away, all the way down to southern Sweden. On tour. If she got another chance—then she would probably want to go out again. As soon as her daughter got a little older.

A bell rang, then the clanging ceased and the launch glided in toward the quay. The windmill stood silent; business had ceased a few years earlier. The city had bought the property and something new would be built here, maybe a courthouse with a prison on the ground floor. A prison on Kungsholmen would be appropriate, thought Jenny. There was so much else that was dark and gloomy in the area: the morgue, the sanatorium, all the hospitals.

But the picture she saw wasn't gloomy. Despite their functions, the buildings seemed light, pleasant. And the narrow street that climbed up toward the interior of this part of the city was truly pretty. Holding her daughter by the hand, Jenny passed by Kungsholm's church and poorhouse. On the other side of the street the sanatorium and the lying-in hospital stood side by side. Women were taken there, the infected and the pregnant.

She hurried Maj along, wanted to get away from the neighborhood of the sanatorium. They arrived at Scheelegatan. That was where she was to leave the package. The street was like a country road, bordered by gardens and fields. Just beyond a field of rapeseed a fairly large building was visible. The new police station was being built there. And next to the old Piperska gardens rows of apartment houses began, and a fireproof gable stuck up covered with advertising.

Everything was correct; the address she had received was the right one. A friendly woman opened her door, thanked her and took the package. The errand was accomplished.

She felt lighter—and empty. She recognized the situation so well. There she was without knowing what she should do next. Relieved but also a little at loose ends. Now there was no excuse for her to be out and dressed up in the middle of the day. Home to her embroidery again!

But as long as they were out... Nothing was forcing them to take the same route home again. They weren't so far from Kungsbron right now, they could take that way back.

The smokestacks around Klara Lake, beside the Separator and the gasworks and over by Rörstrand and Atlas, were belching out smoke. The long and narrow lake was surrounded by greenery and small houses. Wooden docks jutted out from the beaches, and rowboats lay tied to them. The streetcar rolled past from Fleminggatan; a train chugged off northward. Beyond the docks across the lake and the railroad, just a few steps from these outskirts, were suddenly the city's liveliest streets and most urban areas.

They walked along Vasagatan, past Majestic, high buildings with shining verdigris green towers, alongside tempting shop windows, past the impressive, heavy red sandstone walls of the new post office. At Centralplan the street opened up and the sun shone in everywhere. Glistening, light-colored awnings were unfolded over almost every window, and gave one the impression of walking along a quayside where hundreds of boats were letting out their sails to dry in the sunshine.

Rows of carriages waited outside the Continental Hotel, all of them open with their tops down. Maj grew tired and began to whine, didn't want to walk any farther. Riding in a carriage was unthinkable, but they could splurge on a streetcar to Slussen.

They stood and waited for the streetcar. Fine gentlemen in top hats walked in and out of the hotel entrance. And suddenly one of them tipped his hat politely at them. Jenny was so taken aback that she curtsied. But then she recognized him. It was Herr Törnberg whom she had gone on tour with. He had grown older, of course. A little stouter, with some gray hair. But his face was as pink and smooth as before, almost a little too child-like. He looked like a bon vivant—and that was just what he was.

He had to talk to her a little, had to hear how things were with Jenny. He knew that she had gotten married. Her husband was an artist, a painter, wasn't he?

Indeed... what a tragedy, he begged her pardon for asking, would never have believed she was a widow, she was so young. But they shouldn't stand there on the street talking. Could he invite her for a cup of tea? It would surely be quiet inside the Continental this time of day.

What an adventure, Jenny thought. To sit in a fine restaurant. She wasn't nervous about going in; during the tour they had eaten in restaurants every day. And her dress was certainly good enough.

Besides, it was probably a little dark in the dining room.

They were given a table in an alcove, with a velvet-covered sofa. She ordered tea and Maj got a pastry. Jenny felt like she was being treated like a fine lady. Herr Törnberg hadn't been this polite on tour certainly. At that time he had made it clear that he was an artist and she was just an uneducated kid who had been allowed to tag along. She remembered how she had cried sometimes when he had been especially difficult.

Now he wanted her to call him Julius and asked if she had really thrown over the artistic life. She who had been so promising.

The words felt good to hear; she had of course dreamed and planned. But she couldn't believe his words. She remembered things all too well.

She would have to see, she said. Her daughter was still so little, needed to be taken care of.

He remembered Jenny so well as the girl dancing in The Hooligan's Waltz... that was really a worthwhile number. He could at least get her address, you never knew. Something might come along that would be perfect for her. Of course he understood that she couldn't go out on tour now while her daughter was so small—but, maybe it was possible that she could tear herself loose a few evenings?

After she left he sat there looking at the name and address he had entered so carefully in his notebook. Jenny Nilsson, that was her name now. Maybe. She wasn't exactly beautiful, her mouth was too wide and her hips were too narrow. She didn't fit into anything in the romantic style; people would laugh if she sang any languishing love song. Yes, they would laugh and that wouldn't be the worst thing. She was funny, that girl, fit into comic roles. She wasn't so shy, either. He remembered how she had swung around in that waltz, her skirts fluttering, her neckline cut low.

Well, well, he'd have to see. There was nothing for her now. But he had a presentiment, a foreboding. "The famous singing duo" might split up any day now. There had been friction for a long time. He was going to be abandoned; Rosa was going to leave him. They had been a handsome and pleasing couple that people had liked to both see and hear. Alone, he would only be an aging, slightly overweight torch singer. Collaboration with a woman of Jenny's kind would mean something new. Although then he must not be afraid of being a comic, making himself act silly. The romantic singer would become a comedian. Could he handle that?

As long as it was possible he would try to avoid the change that was threatening. Nothing had been decided yet. Rosa might regret her decision and then he would try to forgive her misstep. But his meeting with Jenny offered him another possibility, a kind of insurance. If Rosa left, maybe he could begin to play the monkey with this zany girl.

He drank and made a face. It was hard for a charmer to grow old, for a duet singer to be alone. If he worked hard with Jenny she could be something. Of course she was ignorant, but she wasn't stupid and she looked like a heck of a lot of fun. It might actually be quite stimulating to work together with a young woman who was full of life.

He ordered more to drink. Recently he had felt so unhappy and alone; now he had found new possibilities.

They were back on the hill again. Maj had to put on her everyday dress and go out in the yard. Jenny opened the window, the old room felt stuffy. She took off the light-colored summer dress, combed her wavy hair into place in front of the mirror. She took a few experimental steps, began to hum—then she danced before the cramped spaces, turn after turn around the table until she sank down, panting, on the wooden sofa. She wasn't so accustomed; it had been a long time. She had to get in shape in case anything came of all those plans, if Herr Törnberg, Julius, meant anything by what he said.

That tour had really been a disaster it seemed. But it hadn't been only her fault; everything had been so hard at just that time.

I will never be a real artist. That's what she had said to Olof when she came home that time, distraught. And was she prepared now to try again?

Whatever the case, it suited her better to perform than to embroider. Today had been an adventure that made it more difficult for her to return to everyday life.

Maybe she would hear from Julius. Maybe the door would open, maybe she would get to dance, whirl around on a stage again. Olof would have understood. But Emelie? Emelie might think that she was betraying Olof.

Well, she'd have to wait and see. Now those tablecloths with tracings on them seemed duller than ever.

She hid them in the sewing basket. They wouldn't ruin this day, at least. She laughed when she thought of the ice deliveryman. That must have been a real good luck kick she gave him.

CHOOSING
WITHOUT
CHOICE

Fall and the pre-Christmas season arrived. The days grew shorter but workdays longer. Emelie walked morning and evening through a dark city, didn't see much daylight. The room where the packers sat was facing the narrow factory yard.

She heard horses' hooves on the cobblestones and looked quickly through one of the small windows. Some horses were being led across the yard to the stable. The fine horses, the ones that were only harnessed to the factory owner's private carriage. That meant he had returned from his meeting, would call for her at any moment. There was something he wanted to talk to her about.

Once she would have been worried, wondered what he wanted and tried to figure out if there was anything he might complain about. Now she had grown used to being called into his office. The factory owner seldom complained, but often wanted some of her views regarding the work in the packaging room. He was surprisingly simple and reasonable; things would never have been this way during the old factory owner's time.

Emelie had been with the company much longer than the present owner. She had begun as a twelve-year-old the same year she had finished school. He had arrived as his uncle's chosen successor a few years before the summer of the exhibition. When old Melinder no longer had the strength, it was his brother's son, Konrad, who became the factory director. A few years later he married and turned the upper story of the factory building facing the street into his residence. To Emelie he was still the "young director," despite the fact that he would soon be thirty-five.

It was as if he heeded her judgment. She didn't understand why, could hardly believe that this was the case. Though it had even happened that he called her in when he had visitors, salesmen for sheet metal and glass manufacturers who were recommending their packaging materials. She had forced herself to say what she thought, even though the salesmen had sometimes grown angry and tried to prove that she was wrong in criticizing their products. Sometimes the factory director thanked her afterward, declaring that her opinions were invaluable.

Presumably he wanted to show her some new packaging now. A lot of new things had come along during recent years. At one time all containers had to be useful in an additional way to their original use. Soaps were to be made small and round so they could be placed in a container that could then become an eggcup, perfume bottles could become cream pitchers, jars of salve used as glasses, and velvet-lined bottle cases used for jewelry boxes. The workers had had a lot of trouble with all these irregularly shaped containers which were difficult to pack. They had to be handled so carefully and wrapped in wood shavings and cardboard. During the past few years she thought it had gotten a little better, with not so many strange shapes. But one never knew what the factory director might dream up; he was so keen on anything new.

The message arrived. She straightened her hair with a comb, hung up her apron and brushed off her skirt. She took the shortcut past the cellar stairway where the small beer keg stood with a scoop for those who got thirsty while they worked, and then she emerged in the soap boiling room. She nodded to the man who was standing up in the midst of the steam at the edge of the deep cauldron and stirring the soap. He was tethered from the ceiling by a strap that fastened to his belt. In this way he didn't risk falling down into the bubbling paste if he slipped.

The world inside the office was a different one from the factory's. It was quieter, tidier. She always as out of place when she entered, felt like the smells and dust of the factory clung to her hair and her clothes. The discreet black-clad office clerks sat on high stools and bent their backs over the bills and account books on their desks. She could hear the scratching of the steel nibs of their pens. On a lower table in a corner stood a strange apparatus: a typewriter that was seldom used because none of the gentlemen knew how to write on it with more than one finger at a time.

She knocked on the factory director's door, waited for an answer, then stepped inside. He was talking on the telephone, waved her to a chair with his hand. She sat down and waited, looked at the portrait of old Melinder and remembered the old man tottering around the factory. She wondered what he would have thought if he had lived to see all the changes, and if he had seen her sitting here. In his day no employee could sit down in this room. One stood in a corner and waited, one stood in front of the table and received orders. A lot of things would have made him upset and angry if he had seen the factory today, she realized. He would surely have liked to have everything stay the way it was.

The factory director finished his phone call, laid down the receiver. He sat silently and looked at Emelie. Then she began to feel worried, knew that he didn't have a pleasant message for her. When he wanted to show her something new and had plans, he grew excited, began to talk as soon as she came in the door. But when it was something unpleasant or troublesome he had a hard time getting started.

"What should we do with her, that Strömgren?" he said at last.

Emelie knew what this was all about. But she was unsure how she herself should approach the problem. She had to have solidarity with the firm, but also with her colleagues. The packaging department, her department, had to produce satisfactory work. And Hanna Strömgren was a sloppy worker and impertinent and slovenly as well. But with two kids and no father, if she lost her job both she and the children would not survive.

Melinder leafed through the letters on the table, the complaints. Things that had been missing in shipments, goods that had been poorly packaged.

"I should have checked up on her more," said Emelie. But she knew at the same time that it was impossible. One person can't control everything ten people do. And Hanna Strömgren tried to avoid being checked on. She became insulted every time Emelie wanted to see what she was doing more closely. It was tempting to get rid of the cause of the trouble.

Still, she couldn't pronounce judgment.

But Melinder said, "We will have to fire her."

Wasn't there any other solution, she asked? Although she could see that he didn't like it, that he wanted to quickly go on to something more interesting.

"Suggest something," he said.

"Ink bottling maybe... if she can be switched with one of the girls in there."

It was said and done, and she had the responsibility. The supervisor in ink bottling and the girls there would not be happy—except for the one who got to change departments. Hanna Strömgren would certainly consider it Emelie's fault that she got an inferior job. Everything would have been simpler if Hanna had been fired, then it would have only been a question of a short moment's discomfort. But Emelie felt like she couldn't take that as her responsibility. Everyone wanted to force her to decide. When there wasn't a chance of making a good choice—then they asked her to choose. Then it was Emelie who decided, then it was her fault that things turned out the way they did.

Naturally it went as she had expected. The women in ink bottling thought that if Emelie couldn't keep that slut Strömgren then she should be fired. Emelie tried to explain: in the ink bottling department they didn't run the same risk of making mistakes that could damage the factory's reputation. And surely they knew that the Strömgren woman had children to support? Couldn't they let her try?

Hanna Strömgren swore and screamed that Emelie had kicked her out to work with the hussies in the ink bottling department. Emelie ran gossiping to the factory director, everyone knew that. She kissed his ass, pandered to him so that it was repulsive to watch. They should go on strike, demand that Emelie be fired.

Hanna had to be fended off, but came back several times, stood in the door and screamed: "Arse licker!"

The choice was a bad one, almost meaningless; everyone complained. The Strömgren woman quarreled with her new colleagues, the supervisor of the ink bottling department complained about all the sluts Emelie sent to her.

Where did one draw the line for solidarity?

Emelie felt like she could see Gunnar's serious face. He had asked what she thought. His friend Acke in the Young Socialists Club had said that the workers had to show solidarity in their struggle with the exploiters, the buyers of labor. Acke thought that if possible they should sabotage their work. The skillful and capable workers were traitors who, through their competence, increased the exploiters' power. The workers were slaves—and slaves only carried out the work they were forced to do unwillingly, under protest. The Young Socialists' task was not to increase, but to diminish the wealth and power of the exploiters.

No, she had answered. That's not the way it should be. To work could never be anything bad and ugly. It was the meaning of life. If companies made good products that were sold and profits rose, then the employees' conditions improved as well. Of course there were many injustices and disparities, but one couldn't do anything about those by undermining one's work. Quite the contrary. Hadn't he noticed how the capable and skilled were respected; even the employers respected their wishes. The others were only viewed as unreliable troublemakers. No one listened to them. He didn't believe that the workers' elected representatives in the labor unions and the party were unreliable and unskilled workers, did he? Surely, the opposite was true. Those who had shown they were capable in the workplace were chosen for important positions within the unions and there they could work for a better future.

She thought he could find better company than that Acke and the Young Socialists who talked so much nonsense and speechified about bombings and acts of sabotage. How about in the Socialist Democrat Youth Clubs? The person who had been responsible for that peace demonstration last spring had of course been convicted of raising a mutiny. But to encourage people to stop shooting each other couldn't be a real crime.

In spite of Acke she was not worried about Gunnar. He didn't allow himself to be misled so easily. He was like August, stubborn and cautious at the same time.

Gradually things calmed down, at least outwardly. Hanna Strömgren and her new workmates began to get used to each other; there were no longer as many reasons to complain. If Hanna was sloppy and a few half-full bottles of ink arrived in packaging, nothing happened other than that they were sent back to ink bottling again. Factory director Melinder must have thought that Emelie's choice was a good one. No customers complained. The problem had been solved without the culprit being fired.

But for Emelie it was not so easy to be content. Being forced to make choices had given her an enemy, actually several. Hanna Strömgren intended neither to forget nor forgive. She hated. And her hate was contagious. It was easy and felt good for those who considered themselves overlooked and scorned to have someone to lay the blame on. The girls in ink bottling acted hostile when Emelie walked by. Their supervisor, Fat Tilda, who had been Emelie's friend before, felt passed over: it was Emelie who the factory director called for and talked with, despite the fact that Tilda was older and had been at the factory just as long. Previously, Tilda had been able to acknowledge that Emelie was quicker with her hands and ideas; Tilda had admired her colleague. Now she heard what the girls were saying, began to wonder if there wasn't something to what they said: wasn't it true that Emelie curried favor? Emelie did have a brother who was a fine gentleman. There was something strange about that. It might actually be a conspiracy, the rich were spreading their nets, they had their spies. She told the girls about Emelie's wealthy brother. Could someone who had a capitalist for a brother feel solidarity with the workers and poor? Should someone like that even work, take bread out of the mouths of those who needed it more?

Emelie sensed their distrust and their hate.

When she arrived home one Friday evening an even more difficult decision awaited her.

Bärta was sitting on her kitchen sofa crying. As soon as Emelie entered the yard she guessed that she had a visitor. Bärta's two younger sons were standing in the darkness and throwing stones at the lamp out on the street, trying to break it. She took them inside with her. They roughhoused and fought with their two sisters and Jenny's daughter. To get the children to be quiet, Emelie asked Jenny to open a pot of jam. It was made from the currants that had grown in the now demolished garden.

Bärta was only two years older than Emelie, thirty-seven. But she had led a harder life, given birth to five children, labored as a mortar girl on construction sites, drank. Bärta was old, toothless and bloated. Her breasts and belly hung like half-empty sacks. Hair yellow like straw straggled in wisps around her face, which was swollen from crying and from liquor. She smelled of filth and sweat, didn't have the energy to keep herself up.

It was Johan, she complained. He had been her life's misfortune. She had stood it for seventeen years, now she wanted to leave.

Emelie tried to calm her. Things had been all right between Johan and Bärta for long periods. How would Bärta manage with four children who were not provided for?

Things could hardly be any worse than they were now. Johan no longer had any work. No master chimney sweep could have a drunkard like him staggering around on the rooftops. He refused even to look for work; he just lay at home in their hovel and badgered Bärta and the children to get him aquavit. The kids could beg and Bärta could walk the streets, he had said. Bastards, he had called them. But he was father to three of them in any case, he could never deny that.

Emelie shushed her. Bärta shouldn't say that. The children could hear her.

So what? They had heard most of it—and Jenny's kid was too little to understand anything.

"And don't imagine that he leaves me alone," she cried. "Hardly one night goes by, though he's not good for much. But if I stay there I will have even more kids to support."

Emelie looked at the children who were sitting around the table and scraping up the last bit of jam. Ten-year-old Tyra who already had an insolent look in her eye, eight-year-old Beda who looked skinny and sickly. And the boys: the six year old was really boisterous, wild and bold. The youngest was surprisingly plump, as if still undeveloped. All four were ragged and dirty; Jenny's little girl stood out as a bright and shining clean contrast. Jenny was actually quite conscientious after all, though Emelie sometimes felt she was a little sloppy. But now she was really able to appreciate her sister-in-law.

Those four children would be damaged if they were living this way, be ruined, all of them. Could she do anything for them? Did she really have the strength? And could she really ignore them? They were Gunnar's half siblings after all.

"But what can you do?" she asked. "Can you support yourself and the children if you leave Johan?"

Bärta had hopeful prospects for a job, as a bottle washer in a brewery. It didn't pay much but it was still something. They would probably get by as long as they didn't have Johan harassing them.

He absolutely destroyed the children. Of course children needed to be spanked. But there had to be some moderation. Emelie could see how bad Beda looked, couldn't she? Tyra and Erik were able to stay out of his way. But he would get a hold of Beda and the littlest one, whip them with his belt until blood ran.

Emelie remembered the difficult years when Johan and Bärta were her neighbors. How she couldn't bear to see Gunnar abused and had to bring him to stay with her. Gunnar was August's son; the excuse for her action had felt particularly compelling. But the four around the table were also small people, just as worthy, just as poorly treated. Beda was surely sick, should see a doctor. If Emelie persuaded Bärta to return to Johan it could mean a death sentence for Beda.

But what could Emelie do for them? Gunnar was working, of course, wasn't earning much since he was still an apprentice—but it was still a few kronor. And Gunnar was Bärta's son. Even if Emelie and he barely got by themselves, Bärta should get the kronor Gunnar was able to earn.

And lodging?

Bärta should ask around. Somehow that could be arranged. Now she didn't dare return to Johan even for one night. Could they crowd into Emelie's place for a few nights?

They were already four living in the little room. It couldn't take so many more. But Emelie knew of a room that was standing empty in the house next door. The people who were living there had moved since the house was going to be torn down. Emelie would go over there right away and find out if Bärta and the children could live there for a short time.

She returned a half hour later, tired and humiliated. The man who was in charge of the house had been difficult. She had had to plead with him and beg until he gave in. Emelie understood that the money he demanded from her would never reach the owner of the house. Bärta and the children could live there in secret, apparently against the orders he had received. And they had to be prepared to leave with very short notice.

Emelie put together what she could spare in terms of bedding and followed along with Bärta and the children when they went over. They lit a candle and looked around the filthy hovel. It would soon be demolished; no one had cleaned up when the previous occupants had moved out. But Bärta claimed it was no worse than what she was used to. Though she would have liked a swig of something to wash down all her misery. Didn't Emelie have anything at home?

No, she didn't.

Well, she would have to get along without. Bärta arranged things for the children on the floor. The man Emelie had made arrangements with came by and Bärta struck up an acquaintance with him. After a while she returned with a bottle.

Emelie returned to her home. Gunnar had returned and was already in bed. Jenny was still sitting at the table. She probably wanted to talk about the evening's occurrences. But Emelie didn't really feel like it, wanted to first think over what had actually happened, how much her responsibility had increased. She gave brief answers. And Jenny grew tired of it, yawned and got up to get ready for bed.

There was a violent pounding on the door. Jenny, who had had time to take off her dress, sat on her bed while Emelie went to open it. Johan was standing outside, drunk and furious.

"Bärta and the kids are to come home," he shrieked. "I know that they're here."

"No," Emelie answered calmly. "They're gone."

"Gone—where?"

"Bärta has probably left you forever," Emelie said. "She couldn't take it any longer."

At first it seemed as if he was going to burst into tears. But then he let his rage well up instead.

"It's your fault!" he screamed. "You're a devil putting on airs. You have always despised ordinary workers. You're going to pay for this!"

Emelie couldn't feel afraid of Johan. He wasn't strong, he was mostly frightened. And then she remembered him from the time he was a poor hounded apprentice boy. She had helped him back then from time to time. She knew he didn't dare do anything to her.

His tone turned whining, beseeching.

"I want Bärta to come home."

"She was afraid you would beat the children to death," answered Emelie.

"Those children of that whore and the devil deserve what they get."
Now he was sounding cocky again.

"Beda is sick," said Emelie. "You should be put in jail, the way
you've beaten them."

"A man has the legal right to whip sense into shrews and brats."

"You get going now." Emelie spoke low. "And you're never to come
back here again. Do you understand?"

She raised her hand, as if she meant to box his ear. He stumbled
backwards, almost lost his balance but regained his footing, and lum-
bered silently down the stairs.

Jenny sat there on the bed, frightened. Gunnar had also sat up. He
was pale, held his belt in his hand. He'd apparently planned on inter-
vening to help Emelie.

Suddenly she smiled a tired smile.

"There," she said. "Now we can sleep peacefully. He's not coming
around here anymore. Don't worry, I know him well."

She stroked Gunnar on the cheek quickly and almost shyly. She
would have liked to hug him, calm him. But it felt as if she couldn't;
life in some way had been too hard, too cold. None of the tenderness
was left on the surface—only hidden deep down, like an ache, ready
to burst. There had been so little use for expressions of affection, as if
she had never had the time or the opportunity to try them out. Now
when she would have liked to show what she felt she wasn't capable.

But in the darkness, once she heard that Jenny was asleep and that
Gunnar was still lying awake… Then it got a little easier to be gentle.
Hidden in the darkness she could stretch out her arm and take his
hand. She felt how tightly his fingers closed around hers, how even in
his sleep he held onto her hand. She lay awake, couldn't fall asleep.
Her arm was growing numb but still she didn't want to pull her hand
away. She felt like he needed something to hold onto, feel that someone was there. Even if it was only Emelie.

On Sunday evening Bärta came crying and told her that Johan was
dead. He had hanged himself from the large oak behind the shack

where they lived; a neighbor had come by and told her. His drinking buddies hadn't heard anything despite the fact that they were sitting inside there and drinking. They were living there now, by the way.

"I never should have left him," Bärta cried. "It was my fault."

And Emelie wondered how long it would be before Bärta said: "It was your fault. You drove Johan away."

A LITTLE
CIRCLE OF
FRIENDS

The first morning in November was gray and cloudy; the city lay in fog. It wasn't too thick, however, for the outlines of buildings and towers and the shorelines to be visible like light pencil sketches.

Just before nine Jenny put away the pillowcase she was embroidering, threw a shawl over her shoulders and walked out into the yard. She called to the children who were playing by the outhouse. Bärta and her children were still living in the neighboring house. The planned demolition had been delayed. The two little boys and Jenny's daughter played well together. They had built a little circle of friends in which the six-year-old Erik was the self-appointed leader.

They rushed over, full of high jinks. A little bit behind came Beda, who had been sick and was still home from school. She was sniveling, looked as if she had been crying. It was hard to figure that girl out. Jenny tried to ask Beda sometimes if she was in pain or was sad. But she never got any comprehensible answer. Beda had such a bad stutter, was so bashful and confused. Jenny thought that Bärta probably shouldn't drag her feet any longer about taking Beda to a doctor.

Now the children had to be really quiet and listen, Jenny told them. Something was going to happen soon. Wait and see! Around Norrbro and in the center of town the streets and shorelines were probably black with swarms of people who were waiting.

Far off from Kungsholmen could be heard a steam whistle, a rumbling from on of the factory smokestacks on Söder joined in. And then a collective shout from the whole city, from all the factories on Söder and Kungsholmen, from the boats along the quaysides, from the galley wharf and Djurgården—from every direction the factory whistles and steam whistles joined the chorus. Then they grew quiet; one single tone went on a little too long. The bells in the church steeples began to chime nine. At that moment "the purely Swedish flag," without the old symbol of the union with Norway, was to be raised over the whole city. There it was. It was fluttering from the tower of Kastellet on the other side of the water. They could make it out—but if it was "pure" or not was hard to determine.

Suddenly a cloud of smoke rose from the cannons on Skeppsholm and Kastellholm. The shots thundered so that the windowpanes shook. Erik shrieked with delight. Maj and Bengt yelled too. But Beda was frightened by the shots. She began to cry and hid behind the outhouse.

The new national flag had been consecrated with pomp and ceremony. A little less ceremonious was the consecration that took place later that day, only a few blocks away from them. It was at an asylum for homeless bachelors that opened on Tjärhovsgatan—three large rooms with beds for one hundred fifty men.

Jenny calmed Beda down and then went up to finish her work. She thought about the girl while she filled in the initials on the pillowcase. She thought how she usually could understand children easily, gain their trust. But she couldn't laugh and joke with Beda. The girl withdrew, wouldn't join in the games.

Well, there was nothing to be done. Jenny had only promised to look after the younger children a little and give them sandwiches. Actually Bärta's children were used to taking care of themselves. And Maj played so well with the boys; Jenny could work with less interruption than previously. That was good—even if she didn't mind having her boring work interrupted.

The little children played store out in the yard. Erik had gathered together a supply of pieces of bark, stones and withered strands of grass and set up a counter with a board. Maj and Bengt shopped and had to pay with pieces of glass. Beda came over and wanted to play too, but she was so clumsy that she knocked over the board and all the store supplies fell down on the ground.

The three younger children hadn't wanted to include her in the game; she didn't belong to their circle. They had difficulty understanding her stammer; she irritated them with her clumsiness. Now they chased her away; she ran away with them following her. Erik punched with his fists and yanked her braided hair. Even though she was bigger, she had a hard time fighting back and screamed when they pulled her hair. Instead of defending herself she held her hands in front of her face, stood and took the blows until they grew tired and left her alone. Then she crept away, sniveling, and hid herself in the woodshed.

They tyrannized her with childish cruelty. To them she seemed like a "big kid"—and an oddity in being an unthreatening "big kid." They could give back for the persecution they themselves had received at the hands of the bigger kids, for the beatings the adults gave. When ten-year-old Tyra came home from school it might be their turn to be bullied, if they didn't get Tyra to go along in their persecution of Beda.

The limited world that enclosed them could be cruel. Erik and Bengt were used to slaps and beatings; as long as their father had been alive they had constantly felt threatened. People beat the weaker ones and received beatings from the stronger; that much they had learned. But they had also gained strength through being a group that stuck together, which created a defense or carried out attacks in common.

Jenny's daughter, Maj, had grown up differently, alone and sheltered. Still, she moved easily into the little circle of friends, found company and there were continually new adventures. Something that for the boys might be the result of bitter experience, for her might be something new and gay, an adventure. She liked being with them when they tormented the stupid and annoying Beda who came and interfered with their games.

The thrill of the hunt had been awakened. Beda had hidden herself in the woodshed, like an animal in its burrow. They would capture her, tie her up, torture her. Erik had the string in his pocket. As silently as possible they opened the door to the woodshed, pulled it closed behind them so that no grown-up would notice, looked around in the dim light of the shed.

Beda was sitting against the woodpile, trying to hide behind some empty sacks that were hanging there. They could see the terror in her eyes; it stirred them up even more. Now she couldn't get away. They could have gone right for her, simply taken hold of her. But those were not the rules of the game. They had to creep closer, slowly surround her, prolong the suffering and the enjoyment.

They crept in the darkness. But Bengt was too little; he spoiled some of the fun by rushing straight at her. He pushed his sister lightly, laughed and ran away as if he thought she would chase him. Erik followed around the front of the woodpile. Maj crept behind it. And at the same moment that Maj fell down on top of Beda, Erik grabbed his sister's feet and pulled the string out of his pocket.

Beda tried to protest. But the words never left her; they got stuck. And the hunters cried out with the thrill of the hunt. They fell on the defenseless one and got her down onto the sawdust.

If Beda had had strength and willpower she could have kicked her legs free rather easily from the poorly tied string, shaken off the smaller children and fled. But she just gave up, lay like a bundle and let them carry on. Erik sat down on her, trying to force sawdust into her mouth. But he didn't really succeed; she pressed her lips together at least.

Then the door opened. Anxiously they looked up. Maybe they were trapped now?

It was Tyra who had come home from school. They were unsure of her, didn't know what she would do. She might decide to free Beda and box their ears. She might even feel like tying up one of them— and if Tyra did the tying it wasn't easy to get loose.

She closed to door behind her, smiling a little superiorly.

"What are you doing?"

"Beda broke my store," Erik defended himself.

"We've tied her up!" Maj was proud, filled with the adventure.

Tyra bent over, looked at her sister.

"Whiny baby," she said.

Tyra was on their side. They didn't have to be afraid. But they were still a little cautious anyway; now it was the "big one" who took the initiative.

"Badly tied," she said and felt the string around her sister's legs. She pulled on the string. Beda whimpered, curled up even tighter and tried to hide her face against the floor.

"Why can't you let the little children play in peace?" Tyra asked angrily. "You should leave them alone. Do you hear me, you dimwit?"

"Get the strap that's hanging in the corner," she said to Erik.

He obeyed silently, afraid now.

"You can each have a turn hitting her," she said. "Then you'll see that she doesn't do it again."

She stood over her sister, twisted her and turned her over, panting with the effort. She pulled up Beda's double skirts, exposing the skinny gray white body. The small children stood silently and trembled.

"Bengt can begin," ordered the executioner.

The little boy received the leather strap in his hand, not really knowing what he should do, let it dangle and bump against his sister's leg. Quickly and anxiously he wanted to be rid of it. He looked at the others.

"Now it's Maj's turn."

No, she didn't want to.

"Then you'll have a taste of it yourself."

Maj hit carefully, sniffling. Gave the strap to Erik.

"She broke my store!" he repeated. He hit, harder than the others, but still without strength. It seemed as if Beda barely noticed what was happening.

"Give it to me—you can't even do it!"

Tyra arranged herself, took hold of Beda's skirts with one hand and hit with the other. Beda cried out now. The blows were hard; red stripes were visible from the strap.

"Untie the string," said Tyra. Erik was in a hurry to obey.

"Hang up the strap," she told Maj. Then she let go of Beda. Her sister fell on her side but made no effort to shield herself or get away.

"Remember that you were all a part of this," said Tyra. "No one can tattle because everyone participated."

"But if Beda tells…"

"She can't even talk, the dimwit."

Quiet and afraid, they slinked away. They knew that it wasn't actually Beda but Tyra who wouldn't let them play in peace, who was dangerous.

A moment later they were upstairs with Jenny asking for sandwiches. Since it was a holiday they got jam on their bread. Maj asked if she could get one for Beda too.

Maj opened the door to the shed, ready to flee. What if Beda were to take revenge now that the boys weren't here? It was so quiet. Had she left?

Maj looked around. A boot was sticking out from behind the woodpile. Beda had tried to hide, but as usual had failed.

Maj held out the piece of bread. At first Beda just looked afraid, as if she thought that the outstretched hand was going to hit her.

"It's for you," said Maj. "Take it!"

"Sh-sh-should I-I-I…?"

Maj nodded.

Beda took the bread, ate it, wiped her mouth. Then smiled suddenly, a hasty and sorrowful smile.

A moment later she came out of the shed, looked around as if she expected to be accosted once again, hurried across the yard, out onto the street, and home to the bare, cold room in the demolition site.

The winter and the snow arrived. Tyra and Beda went to school, the little children played in the yard during the hours of daylight, then they had to be inside with Jenny. She lit the kerosene lamp, listened to their chatter and games while she worked. She felt how needed she was at home. Of course it would be hard to leave the children alone all day long. So it was just as well that she had never heard from Julius Törnberg. Still, she was disappointed, would have at least liked to say no. It had only been polite talk, what he had said when they had last met. But she felt how she must get out sometime again. She was at home on the stage. Her embroidery could never be more than compulsory duty.

The children needed her, they kept her at home. In fact it was only Maj she had responsibility for. Bärta's children had had to manage alone before and would have done it now as well if Jenny hadn't volunteered to take care of them. Of course sometimes she might complain of the trouble. But she wouldn't have wanted to let them go. She saw how her care yielded results. They had grown healthier and plumper, more pleasant to deal with. When the boys had come they were small savages, ate with their fingers, peed in their pants. As if it was a game, she had gotten them to go along with her, given them new and better habits.

That was true of the boys and to some extent true of Beda also. Tyra had avoided Jenny's influence. That girl went her own way, stayed out with her friends, seldom went to Jenny's, instead went straight home in the evening. In some ways it was of course calmest like that. When Tyra was there the other children became unsettled. She both bullied them and drove them to revolt.

Beda was not so easy to approach either. The girl's backwardness and sluggishness, her difficulty with speech—all this created a sort of wall around her. But Jenny thought she could see how the girl sat shut inside the wall silently appealing for help, asking someone to have the strength to persevere and break down her isolation. Her mother wasn't able to do it; in school Beda had been placed in a class for misfits. What could Jenny do?

It was only by coincidence that she came up with the idea to teach Beda to knit. At first the girl's fingers were stiff and clumsy. She dropped stitches, pulled too hard, made a mess. Jenny helped her unravel it, explained again, held onto Beda's hands to give them a better position, encouraged her to try again. This was hardly necessary; the girl was so eager herself, wanted to do it so much. Every day she came and sat beside Jenny and tried again, listened patiently to her criticism, unraveled and started over. And when Jenny was able to praise her work Beda blushed red with embarrassment and joy.

Jenny got some old tangled skeins of yarn from the sewing goods store, and straightened them out together with Beda. Now the girl could do her first complete project: a pair of stockings. When Bärta came to get the children Jenny called Beda over, lifted the girl's skirts and showed off the new stockings. Bärta couldn't believe that Beda had been able to knit them all by herself. She praised the girl. And Beda, who was unused to receiving praise from her mother, began to cry.

Bärta scolded her; she could never figure that child out.

But Beda went on knitting; she preferred not to stray from Jenny's side. There she sat safe; the smaller children didn't dare attack her. Tyra stayed away. And Jenny smiled at her little workmate. Even if the girl did not say very many words she was there. Jenny could talk to her even if she seldom could get an answer out. It wasn't quite as boring and dull when there was someone else working in the same room.

SECRET MEETINGS

The Young Socialist movement found itself in a period of seething activity. Skillful agitators, inflammatory slogans, suggestive meetings and the rhythmic invocations of the poets of the struggle whipped up a wave of enthusiasm. And felt like this wave might become large enough to wash over and crush and eradicate existing society.

The Young Socialists gathered like conspirators behind closed doors. Security at the meeting was increased; new members were carefully vetted. Hinke Bergegren urged the meeting's participants to join the riflery club; society would be overthrown with weapons paid for by the state. In the discussion for which minutes were not kept, it was also declared that "shorter weapons" might be needed.

"The dagger in the flesh!"

The slogan was formulated in the pamphlet "The Yellow Peril," whose front page was embellished with King Oscar's portrait signed "King of the Thieves." The newspaper was confiscated and the one responsible for its publication quickly emigrated to America.

A time of struggle, of want and hate. But also of playing in the dark, exciting pranks, sensations. Church doorways were covered with posters calling for atheism. In one night a flyer was distributed to military personnel across the whole land inciting them to mutiny.

Perhaps much of this was a game—but the game was dangerous. In other countries similar endeavors had taken on another character, turned into bloody earnestness. In Finland a general strike and riot had followed in the steps of the Russian revolution; it had gone as far there as bank robbery and murder. And in Stockholm a group of hundreds of Russian refugees had held a secret congress, among them the Bolshevik leader, Lenin. Not until the congress was over could the

Young Socialists triumphantly report what had happened while the bourgeoisie slept.

Society responded to the agitation of the Young Socialists with new, tough requirements, anarchy laws, the muzzle laws. Thousands of people crowded together in the People's Hall when Bergegren and Axel Holmström spoke out against attempts to silence the opposition. But forty policemen and stenographers were among the audience and the speakers were sentenced to prison.

Revenge for all the injustices: The dagger in the flesh! And at the same time an inflammatory international pathos: War is fratricide, throw down your weapons!

These phrases were heard from a chaos of contradictory voices. People both worshipped and despised violence, dreamed of light and wrote verse to the darkness of the depths. Spoke of universal solidarity but found traitors everywhere.

Leon Larsson with his enormously thick and wavy dark hair, wrote his poetry, sang the songs of hate. They were read at the meetings and the listeners imagined they could see the masses storming forward, the blood spurting, the blazing conflagrations:

Our solution is only one: Ignite, ignite,
Knock down and annihilate, crush,
Let the sea of fire burn high into the outer regions,
Let the world be reborn through flames!

In every single issue of the Socialist newspaper, "Fire," new poems by the poet were published. They were read at meetings all over the country, were copied out in black oilcloth booklets, were learned by heart.

Ignite! The laws of a society of thieves could not apply to these subversive elements. The uprising had to create its own laws. They were still not written, had not yet been given any coherent formulation. What was said at secret meetings was one thing, what was said publicly was another. Which orders should people follow? Where was the line drawn between permissible and forbidden for those overthrowing a society? Who could condemn their Finnish comrades?

The roar of the enormous wave drowned the whispers of the cautious.

Yet the wave was still actually not much more than a ripple on the surface. The Young Socialists were few, politically rather meaningless, a few thousand rabble-rousers whose voluble propaganda had begun to concern the leaders within the large labor camp, the party. More and more of the calm and thoughtful ones now spoke up to say they should "come to terms" with those who were hurting the image of the labor movement. They should pass a resolution to drive the anarchists outside the walls, out into the desert.

Many of those who felt the pull of the wave were torn between the wish to float along with it and an instinctive need to cling fast to the firm ground of the shore. Gunnar belonged to them, a young and unremarkable member or the movement's periphery, one of those who were never summoned to the secret meetings.

There was a lot that attracted him, a lot that repelled him. Of course he wanted to participate in the adventures, the nightly flyer-posting raids and the clandestine meetings. But at the same time he longed for friends with less violent and more reality-based plans. How could these zealots build an inhabitable and organized society?

He had just recently turned seventeen and was right in the middle of his years of rebellion and dreams. But still there was much of calm and gravity within him, so much so that it prevented him from lifting off from grounded reality and flying away. He agreed with the revolutionaries that society had to be changed. But they dreamed so much. The dreams might frighten the bourgeoisie with their bad consciences—though he probably wondered if the zealots weren't mostly dangerous to themselves. There were those among them who would take any sort of risk to carry out a prank successfully.

He attended the meetings he was asked to attend, never participated in the discussions but followed closely what was being said, though it was often difficult. They thought so fast, they referred to so much he didn't know about. Those who set the tone were not the workers, but the professional revolutionaries, he felt. It was hard for those who worked all day long to have the time to get involved in the problems. And Gunnar had never been one of the quick ones.

Gunnar went down the stairs in the People's Hall one evening after a meeting. Acke was with him. They came out into the great hall with its glass roof looking up toward the spring evening's sky. The debaters stood in small groups in the hall and up on the long balconies that went up four stories, one above the other. Sellers of all kinds of socially subversive literature cried out their wares.

Once out on the street, the boys stopped a moment and breathed in the fresh cool evening air. They began to walk toward Norra Bantorget. But they hadn't taken gotten very far before someone called to them. It was the poet.

He had something to discuss with them. Couldn't they go to a café?

The boys felt honored. The poet was known by all in the movement. A gangly twenty-three-year-old with dark, shadowed, sunken eyes, and long hair that stuck out over the collar of his coat.

He leaned across the table with the steaming cups of coffee. Gunnar felt like his gaze burned through him.

It was about the revolution. Everyone had to be ready to sacrifice himself. Now it was the Finns who first and foremost needed weapons.

Acke nodded. Both he and Gunnar knew that the poet had Finnish friends living with him. Someone had guessed that the Finns were bank robbers; they had a suspicious abundance of money.

Dangerous things, Acke thought…

What of it? In the worst case then… couldn't the revolution and liberation demand something when capitalist oppression daily devoured millions of people's lives and health?

They didn't have to decide right away; he only wanted to know where they stood. The plans were still uncertain. The poet said that they should begin to create a secret revolutionary league that worked side by side with the Young Socialist movement. A small chosen group of reliable people could get more accomplished than a large group where traitors could sneak in. He would let them know.

The boys walked home through the city. Acke grew excited by the plans; now they could really do business, something would happen. But Gunnar remained thoughtful, didn't want to promise he'd go along. He had to think about it first. Did Acke really believe that Berggren knew about this?

Assuredly. He had said that they should join the riflery club to get hold of the weapons. Hadn't Gunnar heard that? Well... it was a secret of course. But in any case this was to get them weapons without having to take the trouble to apply for membership in some reactionary organization.

What if they asked Bergegren for help?

That would not work at all. And Gunnar could certainly see that if someone came along and asked a responsible politician like Bergegren if he would help plan a robbery or smuggle dynamite, that politician would only have one answer to give. And then the politician would make sure that the person who asked him got kicked out of the movement. You can't have those kinds of idiots involved. For Acke it was enough that the famous poet was a member; that was a guarantee that everything was above board.

The next few weeks were troubling for Gunnar. He didn't want to be a traitor, not show cowardice. If it was truly right to steal dynamite and smuggle it out of the country—then he would participate, despite the risks. It would have felt good to be able to talk to somebody, not only with Acke. But he couldn't disturb Bergegren, and besides, Acke had said that famous politicians would not be able to answer honestly.

Jenny wouldn't be able to understand this. But Emelie?

Emelie was an authority to him, he could rely on her. She never laughed at his questions and always tried to give real answers. But he knew almost exactly what she would say. Even if he didn't use the word theft when he asked, she would understand that it might be involved. Acke and the others probably thought she was a malleable and dumb Branting follower, one of those who stood in the way of radical measures.

During the days that passed he tried out his questions, tried to gauge her possible answers himself. Of course society needed changing, she would reply, but you couldn't gain justice through stealing and breaking laws.

She would point out the changes that had occurred, talk about how it had been in her parents' day, show what the workers had won through perseverance and peaceful work. She would say that only those who had the stamina to endure and wait could accomplish anything. All those who hollered and kicked up a fuss hadn't achieved a fraction of what those who worked calmly had succeeded in doing.

He knew what she would say. The restlessness and youth inside him might object—but the calmness and gravity that were also there made her right.

Smuggled dynamite could mean people's deaths. One could hope the oppressors'. But it might only result in increased oppression, more casualties. They had robbed banks in Finland, shot down a few innocent guards and bank workers. If the revolution was a great and sacred thing—could it be well served by such events?

Emelie would say no. She was perhaps a little reactionary, always so cautious.

Of course: he was cautious himself. That was his character. And it wasn't just caution, but something else as well. "War is fratricide."

The longer he thought about this, the more clearly he thought he could hear Emelie's voice, the more convincing her argument seemed. However reactionary that might be, he agreed with her.

It was even wrong to murder a capitalist. He returned to that. And the thought flew through his head once again when he stood in the doorway of Drottninggatan and saw the sign:

Aug. Bodin. Building Contractor.

Almost one year ago Emelie's brother had said: Come when you are done with your apprenticeship. You must do that.

Now Gunnar was standing here, holding his certification as a carpenter from his master on Kungsholmen. For safety's sake he had asked Emelie first. She seemed a little unsure and pensive before he reminded her of what her brother had said. "You can always try," she had replied then. "But don't hope for too much."

But since building master Bodin had said it that way, so insistently—then he must have meant it too. Gunnar held onto things that were said, remembered them, made his decisions based on them. If Emelie said anything you could count on it, that much he knew. That was why he dared believe that her brother was also reliable.

He knocked on the door, stepped inside. A large office, a gentleman who looked up and wondered what the visitor wanted. A fine gentleman who grew pensive when he heard that the youth wanted to speak with the builder himself. Bodin was in but his clerk didn't know if he could receive anyone. Did Gunnar have an appointment?

Yes, from a long time back. He had been invited to come.

And what was the name?

Gunnar Karlsson.

The clerk went in. It took a while for him to return. Gunnar stood with his cap in his hand, looking around cautiously.

The builder couldn't recall that he had arranged any appointment, said the clerk. But he would receive him anyway.

August Bodin was standing by the window. He turned and looked at his visitor. Then he remembered, extended his hand and greeted him.

"Of course, now I recall," he said. "I had forgotten that your last name was Karlsson."

He was a trained carpenter now, Gunnar told him. That was why he had come.

August remembered. Those hastily made promises had irritated him many times. He wanted dependable and skilled people, they were the kind he knew. Certainly the boy appeared to be good, but August did not actually know him. And then there was that history with the boy's mother in the far distant past, something that had to be absolutely buried and gone, not pop up again in any way. If the mother, Bärta, thought that his employing her son was any kind of rapprochement or even admission of... But his word was his word. He was bound to give the boy a try, at least. Punishment for his being so dumb and giving a promise needlessly. If it helped Emelie then she was worth it, of course.

He took a look at Gunnar's certificate. It was fine, nothing wrong with it.

"We have a construction project going on where the carpenters doing the interior will start in a week," he said. "We can always fit in one more man. I'll talk to the foreman."

His visit was short. August asked how Emelie and Jenny and her daughter were, and Gunnar answered that everyone was fine. Then it was over.

Since it was his day off he took the road past the People's Hall. He took a look inside. Some of his acquaintances sat in a corner, Acke was one of them. Already from that distance Gunnar recognized the gangly figure, the large red necktie and the rounded hat that bobbed around over his sticking-out ears.

Acke took him immediately aside and asked in a low, conspiratorial voice: so, had Gunnar made up his mind? Was he going to go along with them?

Gunnar shook his head. No, he didn't believe that such plans were useful for the movement.

Acke grew angry. Did Gunnar really think that he understood this better than the others? Now he only hoped that Gunnar would be so honorable as to keep silent, that he wouldn't go and give anything away.

And Gunnar answered, rather loudly now, that he did not know anything and did not want to know anything either.

Of course he did want to know. In the time that followed he often

wondered what Acke and the others were up to, if anything was becoming of their plans. One evening he had walked with Acke to a meeting
and had counted on keeping him company on the way home afterward.
But Acke disappeared together with the poet and a few others.

Gunnar walked home in the light evening. Summer had arrived. In
the better areas of town they had begun to chalk the windows so the
sun wouldn't shine through and bleach things while the apartments
stood empty for the summer. The builder of course had a summer
house out on the island of Stora Essingen. A couple of the guys on the
carpenter team had been out there for a few days and repaired a glass
veranda.

Gunnar felt alone, shut out. Damn that caution that held him outside of their camaraderie. Adventure was so close—and he had said no,
thank you to it. He had chosen to work and obey. He knew that Acke
had slacked off work for a whole week to participate in something. A
transport of some kind, maybe that dynamite they had spoken of. It
sounded as if the Finns had explosives. But hadn't the poet advocated
using dynamite in Sweden? He no doubt wanted to blow the national
bank to bits. They talked so much but no one really knew who had said
what. If it was actually the poet who had said that, then they couldn't
take it seriously—the poet didn't talk like ordinary people.

Now Acke sat there and planned, was part of the secret meetings.
But Gunnar remained outside.

It was as if he had given up youth and the revolution for the orderly and the secure, for everyday toil and the few coins in his wage envelope. His workmates on the carpenter team were all older, calm and
stable. Anything but revolutionaries. Professionally capable men who
had been employed by Bodin for a long time, so long that they had
begun to feel a certain security in their environment. Sometimes they
might emanate some kind of self-satisfaction, knew their worth and
thought that men roaming around and looking for jobs had themselves to blame to some extent. Bodin had a nose for good people, they
said. Incompetents didn't grow old in his firm. He seldom hired anyone who was still green; it was important for Gunnar to hang in there

so that the team's contract wouldn't be at risk.

They reprimanded him. Even about things that didn't directly connect with work. One morning when he arrived they had thrown a pile of wood in the corner where he usually put his lunch bag.

He understood what they were waiting for: the initiation. Whoever was new at a workplace had to provide his initiation with a bottle of aquavit. Gunnar had waited with the purchase. He had hardly believed that his comrades who were so much older and more skillful wanted to be paid for by a young boy. And it also went against his grain; he did not want to drink himself and did not want to invite the others to either. He wasn't part of any temperance association, but he had seen too much of drunkenness close up.

But the tradition had to be observed, they had made clear what they wanted. He bought a bottle and it went around the team, was consumed "orally," as they said. When it came to Gunnar he passed it on without tasting it. He didn't want to—and what he didn't want to do he didn't intend to be forced to do. And the old guys were not especially bothersome; they joked about it a little and that was that. He had paid for his initiation and thus been approved. Like one on a team, one of the secure and the settled ones. A reactionary?

Part of the team and still a little outside of it. The only young member. The old men lived in their world, were fathers of families, had adult problems. Gunnar felt both solidarity with them and a separate status, just like among the Young Socialists.

Wasn't it always that way—in his family, at work, among his friends—that he was a little outside, close camaraderie but still not really a part? Caution, shyness and stubbornness hindered and bound him. He himself could see how it was, note what it cost him. And still he didn't have the least intention of changing himself, just the opposite. He felt like this slightly sulky stubbornness was the most precious thing he owned. It was who he was.

As he walked home through the silent evening city, he looked around a little irritatedly, as if he was looking for someone to quarrel with. Stubborn and foolish, go ahead and say it. Go ahead and hit me and try to subdue me! I don't intend to give up. As long as I live and breathe I will fight to remain who I am.

There was no opposition. The streets lay so empty that his steps echoed between the walls of the buildings. Only a few girls passed by; they looked at the bumptious guy and giggled.

He looked at himself in the reflections of the dark shop windows and couldn't find anything to laugh at.

THE
DOOR
OPENS

"Stand by for the blast!!"

A blue-clad worker waved his frayed red flag and the elegant man in the straw hat and light-colored suit stopped obediently. The man looked down the endlessly long stairs he had just climbed, surprised that people wanted to live in such an inaccessible part of town. Well, there were easier routes to take, of course. But research required effort. He had just walked along Stadsgården to observe the harbor's stevedores; he had come across a funny song that should be sung by a really comical longshoreman. Yet the guys working there had not really corresponded to his expectations. The figures on the stage would probably have to have more characteristics taken from the humor magazine "Strix" than from reality.

The shot went off, the rumble came rolling toward the man, clouds of smoke and dust rose from the crevice between the walls of the hills. The worker in blue rolled up his flag and returned to his workplace; the road was free.

Carefully the man with the straw hat crossed the broken rocks of the street, found that he still had one set of stairs to hurry up before he arrived at Fjällgatan, which now had been split in two by the deep excavation. Grunting he continued climbing, thought he'd had enough exercise now—even if he had grown a little rounder with the years and needed to get in shape before the adventures that waited.

From the stairs it was only a few steps to the house where he was headed. For safety's sake he checked the address in his notebook. Now if only the inhabitants were home and not out doing errands. Maybe he should have written and said he was coming; he hadn't gotten around to it. The man in the straw hat seldom took action before he was obliged to, but now he was in a hurry. She knew nothing of what awaited her. What if she dug in her heels... or if she had moved, disappeared? No, she was certainly still there. No one else would have noticed that there was something about her to take notice of. Or was he only imagining that?

She lived almost like she was in the country. A row of small stone and wooden cottages, dandelions that bloomed between the cobblestones, and against the dark fence were green trees. Some children in large pinafores sat at the edge of the gutter and dug, each with a broken off spoon. Though across the street was an ordinary apartment building.

He pushed open the gate in the fence, grimaced when it squealed on its unoiled hinges. He looked into the yard. A woman was sitting on a bench sewing. She stood up when she saw him, came toward him.

"Why, it is Mr.... Julius."

"Look at that. I found the right place. And here is Jenny, sitting and relaxing in the summer heat."

"Not exactly relaxing," she answered. "Working, embroidering. But how did it happen that you...?"

Actually, he had something to talk to her about, plans.

It was probably best that they went upstairs. There were so many curious people, she said in a low voice and looked quickly at the open windows on the bottom floor of the house. If he waited a moment she would just check on the children playing in the street. Her daughter was there.

He lifted his hat and dried the drops of sweat from his forehead, watching as she dashed off. Just her way of walking was worth the price of admission, would put people in a good mood. He had calculated right; she was useful. Though a little vulgar. Sentimental love songs were not what one sang with her. Norlander's songs suited her better, such as, *That One with a Little Motor in Back,* from the revue last year. It had become so popular.

Though one had to be careful. It was easy to get too coarse. And that type, that girl, would tend to emphasize the coarse. If you put a propeller on her backside it would be too strong. It was probably wisest to refrain.

She came back, walked undaunted up the stairs ahead of him: Julius had to take things as they were. And certainly the room was small and simple, but clean, light and neat. He sat down on the wooden sofa and longed for a whiskey and soda, politely declining the coffee she wanted to offer him. He had so much to do, couldn't stay very long. But now she had to listen to him really carefully.

What he had to tell her made her shiver with excitement and nervousness. Of course she had waited for him, almost a whole year. Had hoped that he would get in touch, at times suspected he wouldn't. But now when he arrived and said that everything was ready, that he had an engagement for both of them—then she grew frightened. She wondered how she would get away, how she would dare stand on the stage again, what Emelie would say. A whole seven years had passed since that summer when she had gone on tour. And then Julius had been so dissatisfied with her.

Was his wife also going along?

He shook his head. No, they were divorced. She was going to leave the stage, remarry. That was why he needed a new partner.

But she couldn't sing those songs... people would laugh if she tried.

He would choose songs with her that were appropriate for them, more comical things. He had had the opportunity to study Jenny, knew what her strengths were. That she could make people happy, get them to laugh—this was no small task. And Jenny had the temperament and humor, was not afraid to put on a show.

She didn't reply. Just sat there and wrapped her feet around the chair legs, like a young girl.

Now everything had developed faster than he expected. He hadn't had time to ask her—but the conversation he had with her the previous summer had convinced him that she was willing to join him. He had already made arrangements with a good friend, a showman who he had traveled together with before. At first there wouldn't be any long continuous tour, instead there would be appearances mostly on Saturdays and Sundays. Later on in the summer it might be a question of longer tours. Jenny could get a few small roles in the comedies, simple one-act plays that the troupe would put on. In the immediate future it would only be musical numbers. Their first performance would be in a little less than two weeks.

Less than two weeks? How would they have time? She had to learn the lyrics, rehearse, get clothes.

They would surely manage. He had arranged a space for rehearsals, a private party room in a tavern that was empty during the day. He would get costumes for the performance with the help of the touring company; a pianist was already engaged. She would receive the lyrics without delay.

It was as if he had led her into a gilded trap; she could only say yes now. And of course she wanted to, she had longed to get out the whole time.

And money? What would her terms be? She asked lightly in passing, as if she wanted to pretend that she didn't depend on it.

How low did he dare go? The money would be paid to him, every krona he could draw off her fee would increase his own. But the girl wasn't stupid and he couldn't afford to lose her; it was too late to find a replacement if she said no.

"Ten kronor per evening," he answered against his will. "The showmen pay transportation, food and lodging. Not so bad—eh?"

No, not in comparison to her embroidering, nor even if she thought of what Emelie earned. But an artist had to dress well, buy make-up and powder. She waited with her answer, wondered if he might raise his offer.

"There will be extra for the small roles later," he said.

She nodded, accepted it. He got up, promised to send a messenger with the lyrics to the first song early the next day, told her to take note of the time and place for the first rehearsal. She gave him her hand to say good-bye and he took it, kissing it. The hand kiss felt like a tickling greeting from the adventure that awaited. From a world with other manners, where the heavy tread of everyday living was exchanged for merry pirouettes.

She made a deep curtsy when she opened the door, a playful farewell gesture. And he laughed to himself as he walked down the stairs. The girl was too funny, would surely work out well. That one with a little motor in back...

Emelie had expected it for a long time. Jenny had told her about her meeting with the singer, had never really relinquished the dreams she had had. But it had gone so long without anything happening. Emelie had been able to convince herself that it never would become anything more than a plan.

She thought, naturally, that Jenny should not perform again. But now that the decision was made, Emelie felt like she had known the whole time it would turn out this way. Jenny couldn't be stopped. Jenny hated embroidering, Maj may not have been able to keep her job much longer. Her employer wasn't completely satisfied with the results. And apparently the kind of work that Emelie didn't find exactly suitable was just what suited Jenny.

Emelie couldn't understand Jenny, couldn't comprehend that anyone would want to stand on a stage and make a spectacle of oneself. She remembered how upset she herself had been that summer when she had sat in front of a public audience and wrapped soaps. But Jenny could hop around and show her legs, wear those low-cut dresses. If Jenny herself wasn't ashamed, didn't think she was hurting her daughter or the memory of Olof—well, then there was nothing to say. And they certainly needed the money.

It was only worth discussing the practical problems. How would they arrange for the children when Jenny was out traveling? Bärta's children had fended for themselves earlier, but it would be best if someone could look after both Maj and the little boys. There was the wife of a bricklayer in the neighboring building who had her own small children. The woman seemed reliable. Jenny would ask her.

Of course Jenny was funny. There were certainly many others

besides Emelie who would find cheer in seeing and listening to her. There was no harm in that, it couldn't hurt anyone. Still Emelie felt uneasy, wanted in some way to protect Jenny. It was as if Jenny was giving herself away.

But she was happy now. And Emelie had to recollect Olof, how his happiness had also frightened her. He wanted to paint, didn't take care of himself, wore himself out. His happiness was also his destruction. Would it be the same with Jenny?

All the next day Jenny waited anxiously. It wasn't until evening drew near that a boy arrived with an envelope—it was thick with music and lyrics. There wasn't a chance that she would learn everything before the rehearsal next day. She sat beside the kerosene lamp for a long time that evening, trying to figure out the melodies she had not been familiar with before, humming as she learned the lyrics. Emelie and Gunnar had fallen asleep. The summer night was warm; she was sitting in her camisole. She looked out the window that was partly open: the dawn had begun to creep over Östermalm's compact rooftops, but the surface of the water was still a glistening black.

The lyrics didn't seem especially remarkable when you saw them like this on paper, strings of simple amusing remarks, coarse jokes from time to time. But she let her thoughts play with the possibilities, made up gestures and facial expressions, saw characters and scenes appear. There was more to it than just showed on paper.

Mostly Emil Norlander songs, nothing really new. The song about Anders de Wahl that was to be sung by a young girl, who would stand with the great actor's portrait clasped to her breast:

Oh, oh, oh my Anders de Wa-a-wa-wa-wa-wa-Wahl,
So far you are the ladies' choice swain.
Oh, du lieber A-anders,
You, you must needs heed our call,
Yet you cause us such pain.

What if she wailed it as if she were in real pain… and hugged the portrait… and turned her back to the audience so they saw her arms wrapped around her own back… and burst out with a shriek?

And that part with Oh—you—my kissy kiss—my little one—there they could sit on their heels and jut their heads forward and pucker their lips, she could gape with her large mouth so it looked like she intended to eat Julius up.

She began to laugh to herself as she sat there: if she could only get to play things up, let it all hang out. It wouldn't be pretty—but it would be funny.

But the first rehearsals didn't turn out especially funny. Julius sweated and grew crankier and crankier; the room was close and stank of smoke from the previous night's partying. The cleaning ladies peeked in the doorways; the pianist was bad-tempered and fell out with Julius time after time. And none of them wanted to really listen to her; Julius's opinion was that he himself knew better. It didn't really work when they followed his ideas; he was stiff and boring, didn't see the opportunities for getting laughs.

But once the rehearsal was over and he had caught his breath over a grog, he calmed down. It would go more smoothly when they got used to each other. He would think about Jenny's suggestions; something could probably be used.

The following days they rehearsed number after number, tried to figure out new possibilities. But the days were few; they were in a hurry. Julius grew impatient if Jenny didn't immediately understand his instructions. He was whiny like a spoiled child, she thought.

At the same time she felt she had to acknowledge he was right. There was so much she didn't know. She really should have had a lot more rehearsing, but now they had to scramble through the program. She was nervous before the first performance, almost regretted what she had set herself up for. Public sacrifice, she thought, go to the block. How would she get people to laugh with her and not at her?

At home she kept quiet about her anxiety, afraid that Emelie would try to persuade her to give up. It was too late now. Even if it were wisest to flee, she was obligated to appear on stage. And as long as she was obligated—then she needed all her self-confidence, didn't dare listen to any warnings.

They sang their songs, in park after park. Their first performance was a little tentative, but soon she felt how things loosened up. She knew how to do this, liked getting people to laugh. In Julius's case it was more difficult. She tried to pull him along with her, overacted—but people were amused.

Usually they performed outdoors, in new and rather primitively furnished public parks. The dressing room might be a tent that was used as a kitchen for a café. During the first evenings she tried to hide in a corner, but there was neither time nor space for such prudishness. She had done this before, soon got used to it all over again. She routinely kicked off her Fia Jonsson costume-plaid skirt and striped pants-without shyness, and swore at some peeping toms staring through holes in the tent.

Sometimes they had to perform indoors, in assembly halls where there was neither curtain nor stage, or in theater barns that smelled of greasepaint and sweaty hair, and where the stage lights flickered dangerously close to her whirling wide skirts.

It had worked, she had succeeded! She wasn't any great artist, only one of the many small and impoverished ones who moved from park to park, from barn to barn. But she entertained people, they laughed and applauded, sometimes she even received a flower. Her name appeared on the posters: The Famous Comedy Duo Julius Törnberg and Jenny Fält. She used her maiden name. Julius thought that Jenny Fält sounded much better. To be named both Jenny and Nilsson was probably not such a good idea for a little music-hall singer.

Maybe she was happy, she didn't really know herself. This was her life, what she was good at. But it was hard to be away so much from Maj. And from Emelie.

THE BOMB

The economy had been good for a long time. It showed up in an increase in construction. On all the islands of the city new apartment buildings were being built. The streets were being widened; sheds and small cottages were being demolished. Stora Badstugatan, which sometime in the future was to be turned into a boulevard, was widened adjacent to Adolf Fredrik's Church. Graves were dug up in the churchyard and were moved closer to the church or to a green park in the middle of the street. Birger Jarlsgatan was extended to what had previously been called Träsktorget. Trebackarlånggatan, which had become Tegnérgatan, was blasted out through Gråbergstadens hill toward Dalagatan and the old fishing shanties along Återvändsgränd were torn down.

On field and hill where once there had been just been a few solitary shacks, new apartment buildings were erected close together, side by side. Land began to grow expensive in the city, there were suggestions to dynamite Skeppsholmen and Kastellhomen till they were level and then fill them with apartment buildings. Rows of houses on the street and houses facing backyards were shoved aside in crowded neighbor-hoods. Rows of new windows looked down over cement paved narrow courtyards where there was barely room for more than garbage cans.

But the outskirts were still green. Over the summer whole tracts of small housing settlements had sprung up. It was a new idea that had quickly caught on.

Gunnar worked on a construction site on Norrtullsgatan, quite close to Odenplan and the new church that had been consecrated that summer. One of the guys on the carpenter team was from the area. He could tell about the carnival that had been there during his child-hood—with swings, carousels and bird shooting. Now a house was being put up in contemporary style, with many bay window-like projections and something almost like the tower of a castle on the street corner itself.

He looked out the window while he plastered an archway. The widened cross street was being paved with stones but the workers were on break and dozed in the sand on the yet unfinished sidewalk. A horse with the reins wrapped around his front legs stood in front of his gravel wagon and munched from his feedbag; the driver lay beside the horse and ate from his lunch bag.

The summer had been warm and fine; Gunnar had gotten a good job. He should certainly be content. But then there was his loneliness. It had become so abnormally quiet at home since Jenny was away so much. And Emelie was a little downcast, though she tried to hide it. He knew she was having a hard time at work. Fat Tilda and Hanna Strömgren were doing what they could to get to her.

Gunnar was too restless to sit inside during the evenings, he was looking for something without really knowing what. It got so that he wandered through the streets on his own, in the silly hope that he would meet someone he knew, that something would happen. He went to the Young Socialists' Club when there was a meeting, but didn't find any real friend there either, not since Acke had deserted him. Acke was a part of that secret gang, the conspirators. There was a lot of talk about them and their plans; it leaked out despite their carefulness. One person had heard that they planned to blow up Trondheim's Cathedral when the Norwegian king was being crowned there. Another said that the poet had been down in Hälsingborg and laid plans for robbing all of Aller magazine's cash. But no one took all the talk of coups and attacks seriously. A lot of things were part of the jargon they had gotten used to as well: storming the barricades, setting fires, overthrowing society.

Mostly likely something was about to happen. But Gunnar didn't get to hear anything more than rumors and hints. From what he heard he created a picture of what he believed to be the truth: it was the poet who drove things, who laid the plans.

The club was taking a Sunday outing to Haga Park, an autumn get-together. He would go with them. But he didn't dare hope that his isolation would be broken, not even if he showed himself prepared to pay the high price to get to be with Acke.

They gathered on one of the hillsides that were slightly yellow from the drought. Someone unrolled a banner with the words: Death to Militarism. Acke and the other co-conspirators had not come. But Emerik Larson, the brother of the bard, sat calm as usual, with his friendly smile, listening to Birger Svahn cutting down the military, clergy and capitalists. Emerik worked at a bookbinder's; he was marked by consumption.

The photographer who had been asked to be there arrived and ordered the club members to crowd together for a group picture. They squeezed closer, jostling each other. Flowers, bows and feathers bobbed on the large straw hats of the girls; the boys straightened their rounded derbies and floppy newsboy caps. Some lifted up bundles of their newspaper, "Fire," to show that the campaign hadn't been forgotten in the midst of all the partying. Others crossed their arms and stared sternly at the camera: here is where we stand, subversives and outcasts, the sworn enemies of society.

All were dressed in their Sunday best, a well-groomed proletariat. No tatterdemalions or alcoholics came to their meetings.

Those who had been standing and sitting in groups gathered round, ordered to the center by the photographer. Gunnar suddenly found himself next to a girl in a white hat with a red ribbon and a gray jacket over a white blouse. He glanced at her a little sideways. His glance met hers and he turned hastily away. He felt how he blushed and cursed his bashfulness. She smiled he still had time to see.

She was sitting together with another girl and a boy with whom Gunnar had exchanged words sometimes. Before he knew it, Gunnar was caught up in a conversation concerning events, which had nothing to do with the Young Socialism movement, such as the number of fires that summer and the poor selections available at the cinemas.

They all walked together from the meeting through the park, arriving at the south entrance where the streetcar with the red signs stood waiting. But they walked past it; no need to ride on such a beautiful evening. Otherwise, Gunnar usually took that car to his job on Norrtullsgatan. It ran every morning carrying the workers, and then the fare from Slussen didn't cost more than five öre.

The gas lamps on Norrtullsgatan had been lit now, a long glittering row of lights in the dusk. When they strolled past a house that was under construction he thought of telling them that he worked there— but didn't get around to it. And it wasn't so very much to tell either. His everyday life could hardly be of interest to them.

If he had been alone with the girl he might have said it anyway. But when there were four of them together it felt different.

Since the streetcar now came along and passed them he asked instead what they thought of the new system—that you purchased your tickets onboard.

It had been easier with the boxes for collecting the fares, the girl said. And now the conductors would have change machines too. They would never be able to manage those in the winter when it was cold and their fingers grew stiff.

They had arrived at Odenplan and the other couple was continuing eastward; she was a maid in a building on Karlavägen. And Gunnar found himself suddenly alone with the girl in the white hat. He walked by her side and wondered what he would find to talk about. He didn't need to worry, she chattered on.

She lived out in the vicinity of Hornskroken. Did he also live on Söder?

Yes, though in the Katarina area.

Did he usually go to the club meetings?

He did, although he hadn't seen her there before.

No, she had just come by chance. Her parents weren't especially fond of the Young Socialists and their activities.

From what she told him about herself and her work, (she worked at a candy factory), he thought he understood that she had gone to the Young Socialists' meeting to protest conditions at work. She told about the inspection when workers passed through the iron gate to the factory area, about the woman guard who found pleasure in humiliating them. If it was still deemed necessary to inspect them, it could at least be done in a decent way. There were even workplaces where employees could receive a little of the goods they had made. Her father worked at Reimerholm's Distillery and there the worker's received a schnapps with their meal every day, until recently, when they had gone over to giving the workers a liter of aquavit every Monday. At the candy factory the workers didn't get one single piece of candy.

The way seemed shorter because of their conversation. They had walked up Vasagatan, heard an evening train rolling out from Central Station and beneath white clouds of smoke thunder out onto the railroad bridge. The water lay dark and shiny, reflecting lights from the windows of the compartments gliding by, the gas lamps along the quay, and the multiple rows of windows of Norstedts printing works. A ferry was waiting; a church bell struck ten. The girl was in a hurry now, it had grown later than she realized. What would her parents say?

They hurried toward the ferry. She extended her hand and said good-bye. No, he didn't need to accompany her; he lived in a completely different direction. They would surely see each other again, when the club held a meeting.

The deckhand lowered the boom, the ferry chugged out while the water foamed from the churning of the propellers, smoke rose in the air, there was the glimpse of a white hat, a hand waved farewell. She was gone.

He took the footpath across the railroad bridge, watching the ferry as it became an ever smaller speck of light against the dark surface of the water, and at last disappeared. He wondered if he would meet her again, she had said he would. Why hadn't he even asked her name?

It felt as if finally his isolation was about to break, as if he was going to get there, be included. When the club held a meeting, she had said. He would be there, waiting for her.

But he never met her again. And he guessed that it was the bomb's fault. After that thing with the bomb her parents would never allow her to go to the Young Socialists' Club.

The bomb didn't actually exist, had never been assembled. But they wrote about it in the papers—and the ingredients had been there.

A few days after the club outing the newspapers claimed that bomb making had been going on in the home of the revolutionary poet on Västmannagatan. The Finnish Red Guards chief and four other Finns had been captured. Five Swedes had also been caught—they were known as Young Socialists and had laid plans to rob several banks.

A large contingent of police and detectives had swarmed into the apartment on Västmannagatan and seized a wooden crate with cartridges and dynamite. An informant had given the names of those implicated. Among those who were taken was the poet's brother, the worker at the bookbinder's. Emerik had been picked up at his workplace and transported to the police station at Mynttorget dressed in his gluing apron and wooden clogs.

Both the poet and Hinke Berggren denied any knowledge of the plans for making a bomb or committing armed robbery. And all the Swedes involved had to be let go, there was no real evidence, only a lot of rumors and uncertain information. The Finns who were living in the apartment took responsibility for the dynamite found there.

But the newspapers raged and demanded an inquisition of the subversive Young Socialist movement. They blamed the Social Democratic Party who hadn't taken a distant enough position from Bergegren's propaganda. The party was now reaping what it sowed. Branting and several others from the Social Democratic leadership were driven more and more to a sharp condemnation of the young agitators, and after a vote within the party, Bergegren and Schröder, the editor who had participated in writing the pamphlet "The Yellow Peril," were suspended.

A few months later a new scandal occurred which gave renewed force to the accusations: Young Socialists from Skåne had shot dead a mail coach driver on a train and stolen registered mail. The robbers

were found on the membership roll of the Malmö club, even if they
hadn't paid their dues for several years—and a worried member of the
board had torn out the compromising pages from the members' direc-
tory and burned them. Now the Young Socialists were both mail robbers and membership roll falsifiers, and the Social Democratic party
members thundered: the boil had to be surgically removed, the lice
picked out from the red banner's folds.

Gunnar continued to go to the club for a while, in the vain hope
of meeting the girl from the Haga outing. Neither Acke nor the poet
was to be seen. There was a lot of talk that those who had dishonored
the club should be expelled—but no steps were taken at all. And
Gunnar began to feel like a stranger in the association, more ashamed
than proud of his membership. The mail robbers had kept the money
for themselves, one of them was to be married and had bought furniture before he was caught. And Acke and the others who had talked
so much did not stand up for what had been done. Now they snuck
off and blamed it all on the Finns.

The guys on his work team knew that Gunnar was a Young
Socialist and they teased him sometimes. And even though he might
think they were a little too tranquil and self-righteous, he listened to
them in another way now. Perhaps they were privileged, would benefit more from reforms than revolutions. He recognized that—but also
that he himself was better suited for calm yet hard work than for violent plans and café politics.

He began to pull away, didn't go to meetings any longer. And one
day he enrolled in the Social Democratic Youth Club, the formerly
hated archrival.

One evening he ran into Acke on the street.

Gunnar nodded and stopped. But Acke pretended not to see him.

IN THE
MORNING
DARKNESS

A light rain was falling; the drops glistened in the glow of the street lamps' gaslight. The morning was dark and cold. Two small girls pressed themselves against the walls of the building that vibrated from the rumble of the large newspaper presses inside. They were waiting for their mother who had gone inside the distribution hall to fill her sacks with the fragrant newly printed newspapers.

The church bell struck five. At the same moment their mother came out of the doorway lugging the heavy sacks. A little irritated, she called for help and the girls scurried over. They took hold of one of the sacks; their mother slung the other over her shoulder and began to walk.

The larger of the girls lifted their sack up onto the smaller one's back, the little one bowing under the weight. Then the bigger girl lifted the sack from the bottom, and they tried to follow their mother as fast as they could. While the little girl toiled on she felt how the sack grew heavier and heavier. It wasn't just increasing tiredness—the bigger girl eventually gave up and in the end satisfied herself with just holding the corner of the sack.

That was how every morning began. The girls were roused from their sleep, got a piece of bread in their hand, and stumbled half awake down to Slussen and the worker's train. Then they had to wait at the distribution center while their mother stood in the newspaper delivery line and then haul the sacks to their district in the Town between the Bridges, the Old Town.

Their mother had set down her sack outside the entrance to the first building on Västerlånggatan. The girls put theirs down beside

hers. The little girl straightened herself; her back felt like it was broken now, she was puffing with the exertion. But the bigger girl had
already opened the sack and started counting out newspapers. Each
one of them had their own building to make deliveries in.

Up the stairs, stop at the right mailboxes, fit the newspapers inside,
then down again. Out onto the street and deliver to the next building,
moving the sacks with them. They had to hurry, get done in time to
run home to Söder and to school. The teacher would threaten them
with the cane if they arrived too late.

Tyra and Beda had begun to get used to the work. Their mother
had been a newspaper deliverer for a couple of months now, ever since
she had been let go from her job as a bottle washer at the brewery.
With her daughters' help, Bärta could take more papers and increase
her earnings. It was typical that newspaper deliverers had their own
and others' children to help them. The girls were not more than ten
and twelve years old, but there were younger children who worked at
it. The income was still quite meager. If the girls had not been among
the many who received food every other day in the school's dining
hall, they would have nearly starved.

When the sisters were done, each one hurried off to her school.
Tyra ran easily and lightly during her deliveries, she could rest or walk
slowly from time to time. She had selected the easier buildings and
was done sooner. She could take care of herself—and she could also
take care of the teacher if necessary. It wasn't hard for Tyra to find the
right words.

It was harder for Beda. If she arrived late it was hopeless. She could-
n't come up with any defense. All she could do was, obediently and
hiccupping with fear, lay her fingers on the teacher's desk for a rap
with the pointer.

Her nose ran and she panted when she ran. Fumbling, she tried to
wipe away the snot hanging from her nose. She almost always had a
runny nose, had holes in her boots and walked around with wet feet.
When she ran her legs felt numb from all the rushing up and down
stairs. In the evenings the pains were so bad she could hardly fall asleep.

She ran—even though she knew that she would be late today also. Deliver the newspapers, get there on time—her duties couldn't be synchronized. Whatever she did she was doomed and would be punished.

The girls had only just vanished when Bärta was done and came out onto the street. She picked up the empty sacks, took them under her arm and began to walk home.

Bärta was able to work more calmly than the girls; she didn't run on the stairs, there was no cane driving her. If she had been able to think more carefully how to plan their work, and if Beda had been able to clearly explain her situation—then Bärta could certainly have taken a few more newspapers so her daughter could get to school on time. But she had divided up the papers equally between the three of them and felt in that way it was fair. People received their newspapers as early as possible and didn't complain.

Maybe she did actually increase her pace at the end. She would grow thirsty, long for a beer. She usually stopped at a beer bar on the way home where she met the other newspaper deliverers and sat a little and talked. Then she would continue home, drink a shot and sleep for a bit. It had gotten like that; she couldn't do without aquavit. Though time after time she had promised Emilie to try to give it up, for the children's sake.

The boys went to Emelie's every day after school. They played together with Jennie's daughter and were given supper there before returning home for the evening. Before, Emelie had given Bärta some money now and then, the larger share of Gunnar's salary. Later she had found it was better instead to keep the boys fed. Because of this the boys grew well-behaved and well-nourished and Bärta was naturally grateful. If she had received the money herself she might have drunk it away. No matter how badly she wanted to see the children healthy and fed, it just turned out like that. First she took just a coin for a sip… and then she didn't know how it happened, she couldn't quench her thirst.

The man who supervised the house slated for demolition was standing on the street and yelling, "Time's up! You and your kids have to be out of here, they're going to begin tearing it down early tomorrow."

Bärta grew pale, felt like she had to sit down. She knew that the news was going to arrive any day, that the demolition really should have happened over a year ago. Each day they had been living on charity. Still, the blow felt severe when it came.

"Couldn't they delay it a few days at least?"

But she knew that no prayers would help. No one could be allowed to live here; everything had to be ready for it to be torn down.

"Take out the stuff you have in there and put it in the shed," the man said. "It can stay there a couple of days but not any longer. And I can't be responsible for your things."

"Can we sleep in the shed for a few nights?" she asked.

"In the shed? You'll freeze your butts off. It rains in and is full of drafts."

The man went inside with her, took a shot, tried to make out with her. But Bärta didn't have the energy, pushed him away.

"What should we do?" she asked helplessly.

"Go to the councilor who's in charge of your ward," he answered. "Maybe there's a place for some shelter at least. I'll help you carry these out," he said, and got up. "Someone might want to come and look at this dump before the demolition begins. Then there'll be real trouble if they find out anyone has been living here."

He shoved Bärta aside and began to drag the broken mattresses and tattered patchwork quilts with stuffing sticking outside—their few meager belongings.

Bärta washed at the pump on the yard, making herself as tidy as she could. She fortified herself with the last drops in the bottle and rinsed them down with beer. Pulling herself up as straight as she could, she tried to walk as steadily as possible down Nytorgsgatan and out toward Katarinabangata where the councilor had his reception. She knew that the old man would grow furious, she had gone for charity housing before.

Tired, ragged and frightened people sat in the anteroom and waited. Some came out, snuffling from weeping and hurried away.

"Next!" he bellowed from inside.

Bärta gave a hiccup, sat down on the wooden bench, tried to come up with something that could move the immovable.

The councilor worked quickly, he knew his visitors and they knew him. Bärta, however, did not belong to his most frequent customers. Therefore he dealt with her a little longer than usual once she was inside.

"Anyone who wants charity should not come here stinking of beer!" he shouted.

She had only been offered one little bottle, she assured him.

Then she should have asked to keep the money instead.

Look, she didn't want to beg...

Then what was she doing here? Wasn't she begging for money from the municipality instead?

She supposed it was necessary, she was a widow with five children after all, four of them were young... they needed shoes.

She should talk to the school about that.

It was housing she had come about primarily. They had nowhere to go, their house was due to be torn down tomorrow.

Is that so... so they had been squatters more or less?

Not exactly, she had received permission.

The only thing he could arrange was a few weeks in a shelter. How old were the children? So, the girls and the little boys could live there with her. Her eldest son was too old; the shelter was only intended for women and small children.

She made sleeping arrangements for the boy.

The councilor filled out a form; she would have to go to the shelter and hear when they could be admitted. He couldn't do more than that, he wasn't a magician and thought for the most part that people should have the good sense to take care of themselves. Those who asked for assistance were wretches and should be treated accordingly.

Now she could leave, he said, and tossed her the paper.

Oh, and she was so cold... had such poor clothing. Couldn't she have a little money too?

Both she and her eldest son had gainful employ? And she had received space in a shelter. She shouldn't believe she could come and beg for as much help as she wanted from the public. Out, drunken woman! He certainly knew what she wanted money for! Next!

Bärta cursed the old man as she walked to the shelter on Bondegatan. A gruff female supervisor received her, complaining that the councilor had sent her even more homeless people. But there would be a spot available for them in a few days, there were several who should be evicted now. No one was supposed to stay for more than two weeks. During that period Bärta had to make sure that she found something else. The shelter was considered transitional housing only.

Bärta and the girls spent a few nights sleeping in the shed; the little boys got to stay at Emelie's. The shed had been a summer pavilion at one time before the area had deteriorated into a slum with the threat of demolition. Now several of the colored windows were broken and behind them no summer idyll was visible, only torn sacks hung up to screen from the rain and public view. Cracks let in drafts and it dripped from the ceiling when it rained. Even though Bärta and the girls tried to create a protected corner on the floor and lay with all their clothes on, they were cold from the draft and didn't get much sleep. There was no fireplace and they couldn't light candles; it shouldn't be seen that someone was living there.

Something positive came of the nights in the shed in any case—it felt almost good to be able to move to the once so dreaded shelter.

The shelter was a large hall, which had been partitioned with chalk lines and clotheslines to make room for as many households as possible.

Each little household tried to create an environment of privacy in this public space. Dirty cloths and rags enclosed the stall-like small compartments. They didn't go all the way up to the ceiling since the lights in the middle of the room had to provide light for everyone.

Outside the large room was a small room where people fought for a turn to cook meals on the kerosene stove.

The attempts at creating seclusion were doomed to failure. When the room was aired out the cloths fluttered; some fell from their lines and revealed miserable tatters, half-clothed people, private matters. And even if someone managed to block the view, there was no chance of living undisturbed—people participated in everything, every noise carried. The pops when the three old ladies in the corner pulled the corks out of the bottles of beer, the cries when the children were hit or hungry, the panting when a girl was paid a visit behind the rags from her "fiancé," the welfare workers' lecturing words to the beer-drinking old ladies and their ingratiating wheedling for a coin in response. Everything was heard, everything was exposed.

Jenny had been home for a few days from her tour and decided to take the opportunity to do some baking. Emelie filled a bag with bread and went to take it to Bärta.

The superintendent stood in the doorway and blocked her path, wanted to know who she was looking for—this wasn't an ordinary house where you just dropped in and had a cup of coffee. Emelie showed her the bag and explained her mission. Unwillingly the superintendent let her pass.

The hall had not been aired out; the stench of sweat and filth hit the visitor full force. Inside the doorway a little open area had been created. A woman and some children had sat down there to bind wreaths, they had poured out heaps of pine branches and moss from some sacks. Emelie was gripped with despair, felt like she wanted to flee without completing her errand. But then she caught sight of one of Bärta's sons who was standing and peeping through a crack. She called to him.

He showed Emelie where they lived, pulled a cloth aside and let her in. Their space was quite far from the lights in the ceiling, and at first it seemed completely dark within. But then Emelie could make out Bärta who was sitting on a chair and Beda on a pile of clothing on the floor. The girl appeared to be knitting despite the darkness.

Bärta looked up, confused.

"It's me, Emelie."

"Oh, it's you."

Bärta hardly seemed interested, slurred as she spoke.

"Jenny has been baking," Emelie said and handed her the bag.

Around them were cries, coughing, the clearing of throats. The noise of people eating and drinking. Dresser drawers were shoved in, chairs were scraped, beds creaked. Noises and smells made it obvious that a child was sitting on a potty within the enclosure behind Bärta's back.

"But you can't live like this..." Emelie said, appalled.

Bärta got up, tried to pull herself together. She didn't want Emelie to realize what bad shape she was in, that she could barely stand up straight. Emelie was a little bit snooty, didn't understand that those who lived in misery had to fortify themselves. Everything would be all right for her with her fine brother—those who had to manage alone had to cling to whatever they could get a hold of.

"Shall I tell Beda to boil some coffee?" Bärta asked.

No, of course not. Emelie had drunk some at home, was only going to leave the bag with her.

"We can only live here one more week," Bärta said. "Then they're throwing us out on the street. Or taking the children away from me."

"Something has to be arranged for you. Have you tried every possibility?"

"Never mind... there aren't any," Bärta answered, a little evasively. She herself knew that she hadn't put her mind to it enough, had sat in her compartment with a bottle instead of going from house to house looking for somewhere to live.

There was no point in trying to reason with Bärta, she could hardly answer. Emelie left shortly after and knew that she was fleeing. Outside the building she found twelve-year-old Tyra standing and hanging out with some of the young hooligans.

The children would be damaged by living this way. And soon they might be kicked out completely, end up in an orphanage. They were

Gunnar's half siblings, they were small people she had watched growing up and were in close contact with her, people she felt she couldn't
abandon. Someone had to do something—and there was no one to
transfer the burden to.

Did she blame herself for telling the truth to Johan? Was it her fault
the children had no father and their mother drank? No, of course it
wasn't. And still it was as if she felt some guilt, had to do something
for them.

She had only gone to August one time earlier and asked for help,
for Olof's sake, when he lay sick with consumption and had to get
medical care.

Could she ask August to help Bärta? Wouldn't she then have to tell
him what she couldn't tell him, the secret: that August was Gunnar's
father? Sometime she would like to be released from her promise to
Bärta and tell the truth, for Gunnar's sake. But now the situation
didn't concern Gunnar. It concerned Bärta and her other children.

Maybe there was a solution, a way around. If she asked on her own
account. If she told him the house was going to be torn down and ask
if August could help her find another cheap apartment, preferably
a room with a kitchen so Bärta could live in the kitchen with
her children.

She would be tying herself down, be too close to Bärta. Much of
her freedom and comfort at home would disappear. But was there
any alternative?

THE TENEMENT

Södermalm was being transformed; the area of the city with the small cottages was being turned into an area of tenement houses. The development had been going on for a while, but now it was happening faster than before. The tall apartment buildings dominated; all the low stone cottages and wooden sheds seemed suddenly to have become dilapidated and ready to be pulled down. They clung fast to the rocky knolls in the shadow of the new buildings—but blasting reports and demolition crews drew ever closer.

At Stadsgården they had taken down the large haunted Dubbeska house; a "skyscraper" was going to be erected there. Emelie looked over the fence as she scrambled across the wooden walkways that had been laid alongside the blasted out Glasbruksgatan. Everything was chaos as yet; nothing of what was planned could be detected.

She took the route past Fjällgatan and their old home. The house was still standing there, someone still lived there. It felt as if she had betrayed it and fled. Of course the house was going to be demolished any day and she had been obliged to find someplace new, as well as help Bärta and her children. But each time she passed by the old house she felt a stab: we could have still been living here, avoided the tenement houses.

Their new home lay not far away. She walked down the stairs and along the blasted away Renstjärnsgatan. It soon grew narrower and more pitted, ran along between the tenement buildings and the collapsing houses until somewhere out in the evening darkness it disappeared up into the White Hills and became a footpath.

On Kocksgatan a row of small houses climbed the hillside, as if they were trying to sneak away from the rock blasters who had their shed on a cut away part of the street. A group of harbor workers stood in the middle of the street; they were surely on their way to the tavern, Masis Knosis. It was still there in the large wooden house right across from them. One of the men waved and Emelie saw who it was and waved back. Thumbs, her parents' friend. He was beginning to look old and tired. Things were difficult for him; his wife Matilda was sick and their youngest son had given them a lot of trouble. Now Mikael had gone to sea; maybe it was best that way.

Thumbs came over to her, took her hand and greeted her, wanted to know if Emelie had heard anything from her sister. Gertrud was married to Thumbs' oldest son, the streetcar conductor, Rudolf. But Rudolf and Gertrud and their children lived so far away, in Siberia, as the city's northernmost region was called. They didn't get together very often; time didn't allow it.

Knut, their second son, had another daughter, Thumbs told her. The two married sons had ever growing families, ever shrinking prospects of helping their parents. And Mikael was not one to be counted on. Thumbs would be obliged to go down to the harbor as long as he could carry himself there. And then after a day's labor he had to go home and take care of his wife.

Emelie saw how tired he was. She felt as she did so often: she ought to have time, ought to help out in some way. But she already had too much, couldn't do any more. She could only press his hand, hope that things would be better.

She watched him leave. Thumbs who had been so raucous and happy, who had looked as if nothing could crush him. Thumbs who had been going to overthrow society.

Once Emelie had been bitter over him, thought that it had been him with his fanaticism and his activism that had divided her siblings and forced August out. Thumbs had never been able to accept that August had been adopted by the wealthy Bodins and become an employer himself. Traitor? But what should August have done, what should Mama have done when the Bodins offered, when the childless wanted to take a poor child as their own? Thanks to the Bodins, August had been spared much—and thanks to August the siblings had been able to make things a little more tolerable. He had helped Olof before, now he had managed to get them this apartment. The building didn't belong to the Bodin firm, it belonged to a businessman August had connections with.

Emelie wasn't sore at Thumbs any longer. She understood that independently of what he thought and said, the siblings would have still grown apart, become strangers to each other. They would have separated, like August and Gunnar.

Gunnar was probably already home. She walked faster.

She turned onto Åsögatan. This same street ran all the way to the hill where she had lived as a child, where Thumbs and his Matilda still lived. But it looked different here; there was nothing of the hill's expanse and freedom. Only a dark trench between the high walls of the buildings. In the middle of the neighborhood, a hill still stuck up between the new buildings, forcing the same street to become a narrow lane. On the rocky ledge eroded by blasting stood a little group of condemned stone houses in disrepair. Maybe they would be gone in a month, maybe they would be standing there for ten years or more. Everything depended on whether or not some building contractor thought it would pay to blast and build.

She walked into the doorway opposite the rocky knoll, the four long and dark flights of stairs up to the little apartment under the attic. Through the stairway windows she could look out across the courtyard with its rows of outhouses, the overflowing garbage cans, the children playing. She opened a window, leaned out and called to Jenny's daughter and Bärta's little boys. They should come up now, she didn't want them staying out now that it had gotten dark.

The door from the entryway led directly into the kitchen where Bärta and her children lived. It was cramped and messy in there. The stove, countertop, pantry and firewood box took up much of the floor space. Besides, Bärta had a hard time keeping things in order; clothes and cooking pots often lay in a pile. Bärta took out so much but put so little back.

Emelie hoped that their arrangement to live together wouldn't last too long. It was an emergency solution. At the very latest it would have to get better in a few years when Tyra could begin working and the boys might earn a little money on the side while they were still in school. Then she would try to help Bärta find a room. And Gunnar would be able to move into the kitchen here. He was almost an adult and it wasn't really proper for him to be sleeping in the same room as Jenny and Emelie. Jenny didn't really think about the boy being grown now, and she was so unabashed in her ways. Kind and cheerful but unthinking.

The plans for everyone moving out were still only future dreams. Now when housing was so scarce and Bärta had money troubles they had to be happy that they at least had a roof over their heads.

Bärta sat and dozed on the kitchen sofa. She had been drinking as usual; there was no point in scolding her. Emelie had given up hope on Bärta; it was the children who mattered, those who she could not neglect helping. If it had only been Bärta she might not have been up to the effort. But she saw how the children felt better from eating well every day and from receiving a little care. She couldn't let them be destroyed.

Bärta stood at the stove, her face sooty. She had been unsuccessful in lighting it. The fire in the stove was smoldering and it felt cold in the kitchen. Despite all her bitter experience, Emelie had left a krona for Bärta to buy wood; she hadn't had time to take care of it herself. But when she opened the firewood box there was no wood there, no bought firewood. Only a pile of wet board stumps. Bärta had sent the children out to steal fuel at the building sites. Emelie had said so many times that she didn't want them to do that, they could be arrested, accused and punished in school. But Bärta persisted, was of the opinion that children had always taken wood from building sites. This should neither surprise nor upset any sane person. It was only Emelie with a brother who was a building contractor that could come up with forbidding such a thing.

"You didn't buy any wood?" Emelie asked.

"Didn't have time," Bärta said. "I'll buy it tomorrow. The boys got a few pieces from a construction site."

She ought to have asked where the krona was but felt like she didn't have the energy, wanted to believe that what Bärta said maybe was true, that she hadn't had time, that the money was there and would be turned into a sack of firewood tomorrow. Still, she knew that it was gone, that it was wrong to trust Bärta with money.

She hurried into the room to get ready to take care of her duties. In here it was neat and tidy, everything in its place. Gunnar had hung up his work smock. Emelie took a cardigan and an old apron out of the wardrobe. She looked around, turned down the kerosene lantern when she went to leave the room. Felt a sense and a thrill of happiness: they had made it nice in here, simple but clean. It was a home—although so close to the agitation and disorder of the kitchen.

The fire was crackling in the stove when she went back into the kitchen. Gunnar had a fine touch with a fire; he split the boards into thin splinters and got the acrid fuel to light. Emelie took out the bowl with the leftovers from the previous day. She saw finger marks: it was surely the boys who had been into it. Of course she wanted them to eat—but not with their fingers and directly out of the bowl. She brought out the boiled potatoes, together with the piece of sausage that Gunnar had bought. The children came storming in from the yard. Gunnar had to take them in hand and make sure they wiped their feet and hung up their jackets. At last Tyra arrived too. She stayed out as long as possible. But she wanted to eat, so she came home for the evening meal.

The girls had to set the table, Bärta moved her chair a bit to one side and sat there, finished, and looked at them. She thought she couldn't manage without at least one beer, a little something to pull herself together with. Emelie surely had money. But then there was that krona, to both admit that it was gone and ask for more—that was too strong, wouldn't do. Maybe Gunnar had some money. But he was impossible, she knew that much. That silly boy imagined he knew what was best for his mother. If Johan had lived Johan would have told him straight: out with the money, your mother needs it.

Johan would have understood. Johan who was dead, who Emelie

had driven away when he came. Certainly Johan had been difficult—but aquavit was something he could always get a hold of.

"I don't want any food," she said. "I'm going out for a while."

She pulled on her shawl, hurried out before they could ask or protest. She tripped off toward the old shack by Hagen where she had lived with Johan. Maybe some of his cronies had a drop to spare.

They ate, perhaps a little quieter than usual, unsettled by Bärta's sudden flight. But the young children soon got going, especially Erik and Maj. Those two were the liveliest. Now they were teasing seven-year-old Bengt who had gotten caught on a fence when they were stealing wood; he was walking around with half his backside exposed. Emelie had to have a look, Bengt got up unwillingly. No, it didn't look too good. The only pair of pants he had.

"Take them off so I can try to help you," Emelie said. "But we have to do the dishes first."

The girls helped her. Then it was as if Tyra simply glided off, disappeared.

Beda placed the china in the cupboard, the younger children jumped around on the floor. Bengt had his rump bare, then Erik lifted Bengt's shirt and he and Maj laughed till their faces turned red.

Emelie shushed them. They had to calm down, not carry on that way. Beda made their beds; after they washed they had to go to bed. Beda helped them, trying to clean their necks and ears. But they squirmed and splashed her and she got almost wetter than they did.

At last they were lying down, the boys in their bed in by the kitchen counter, Maj in Jenny's bed in the main room. Jenny was away for a few days again. Gunnar had gone out, was going to meet somebody. Emelie didn't ask very much, Gunnar didn't cause her any worry. Maybe sometimes she might ponder over his being so serious and well-behaved. He had so little of the restlessness and pranks of youth. But August had also been calm like that. It was strange that at one time August had fallen for Bärta, that they had had a child together. No one had any idea that they had been together until long afterward when Bärta had told Emelie who Gunnar's father was.

August who seemed so cautious and well-behaved. What if Gunnar too met some girl, if he too… No, Gunnar was so shy, blushed thoroughly when Jenny joked with him.

Her thoughts went round like they usually did when she sat alone and worked, in careful tracks around those who were closest, as if they were spinning a net of hopes and apprehensions, of dreams and worries. Sometimes they drifted away from home to the factory and her work colleagues. It had gotten somewhat better there; Hanna Strömgren had left, the girls in ink bottling had calmed down. But Fat Tilda would never be Emelie's friend as before. Tilda couldn't handle that the factory owner sought Emelie's advice at times.

Bärta out, Jenny away, Gunnar at his haunts. Maj and the little boys asleep, Tyra hadn't come back yet. Emelie felt alone, abandoned. Here she sat and patched the trousers that Bärta should have taken care of.

But Beda? Had the girl gone to bed? Emelie put down her work, quietly opened the door to the kitchen. Beda sat there alone in the dark, staring through the door of the stove into the last glowing embers.

"Are you sitting alone here in the dark?"

She asked without waiting for an answer, it took so long for Beda to answer.

"Come in and sit by the lamp a while. Do you have anything you're knitting?"

The girl shook her head. She didn't have any yarn left. Her mother had told her she would buy some; she had sold a few pairs of stockings that Beda had knitted.

Emelie searched through her drawers, found a little embroidery yarn and a piece of cloth too. And somewhere Emelie should have an old pattern left. Gullpippi who had lived with them while Mama was alive had left it behind.

She looked among her belongings, heard some tissue paper rustle: the handkerchief she had once received from her father, on her eighth birthday. In childish handwriting which she could barely recognize were some words printed in pencil:

Gift from My Father on My Birthday 1878

And she imagined she could still see her father's pale face beside her in the darkness, his friendly eyes. So long ago, so young when he had died. Two years younger than she was now.

The letter E and forget-me-nots decorated the old handkerchief.

So long ago, so different. If Papa and Mama could have seen her now, if they had lived like Thumbs and Matilda... She had almost forgotten, so far back in time; there had been her home, there she had never been alone.

But now she had almost forgotten Beda. The girl was also alone, perhaps even more alone than Emelie had ever been. A child needed someone to be close to, to feel someone's warmth. To have the strength to become an adult, to have some closeness to remember.

"Come see this," she said and she placed her arm around the girl.

Emelie showed her the handkerchief, told her about it. If Beda could try to sew a handkerchief like that... Emelie would help her.

They sat by the light of the kerosene lamp, bowed over their work. Didn't say many words. But felt cozy and together. Emelie even made coffee and Beda got half a cup.

After the girl had gone to bed Emelie sat and looked at the little crumpled piece of cloth where the letter B had been filled in with verdigris green stitches. Gradually Beda would surely learn to embroider, just as she had learned to knit.

Tyra ought to come back sometime; the girl shouldn't be out running about late at night. And Gunnar was certainly taking longer than usual. He was going to meet an acquaintance, he had said. And Bärta—how would she manage to get up and deliver newspapers if she drank half the night?

Bengt's trousers were ready in any case, as good as they could get.

Now she would just make sure Maj's clothes were in order for school in the morning.

When Emelie was done for the evening she went to the window, stood in the darkness and looked out over the rows of apartment houses.

So many windows. So much life, so much loneliness, so much poverty and weeping. And some joy also, someone who was laughing aloud on the other side of the wall.

She had never lived like this before, room to room, window to window, house to house. So close and so alone. In the small cottages people fell to chatting more, met in the yards, were friends.

Now there was someone at the door. It was Tyra coming in. A moment later Bärta came in too, boisterous and in a good mood. Emelie had to quiet her down a little, otherwise the neighbors would complain.

But Gunnar took his time. Though she didn't have to worry about Gunnar, he was so sensible.

GATHERING FORCE

They waited, anxious, but also impatient. Like an oppressive, warm summer day when the sky is still blue but the first thunder clouds are creeping across the horizon.

There had been a few good years, with work for both entrepreneurs and employees. But during those years the opposition had also grown stronger. The liberal government had been replaced by a conservative one at the same time as the number of labor representatives in parliament had doubled. The labor unions had grown in strength and even the employers' associations had been consolidated. Unity within the organizations was stronger on both sides than previously. And funding for the struggle had grown, as well as the opportunities for wounding each other.

The apparent calm had time after time been disrupted by difficult conflicts. Names such as Mackmyra, Sandö and Amalthea told of evictions, riots, sabotage and life sentences. A new law that curtailed freedom of speech sent many agitators to prison; another law that granted all Swedish men over twenty-four the right to vote would perhaps send some of the condemned further on to parliament.

In the city they had not had any serious workers' struggles since the big workshop dispute had been brought to an end. When the strong economy began to give way, the first serious threat arrived: building contractors wanted to lower the hourly wages of their employees by five öre and their piecework by fifteen. When the proposal was rejected they answered with a lockout. The conflict lasted for fifteen weeks and ended with the construction workers keeping the wages they had. But the funds to support their struggle were depleted.

A victory for the workers? It was certainly that. But the conflict had only been about lowering an existing wage that was being endlessly devalued by rising prices.

To speak in favor of increased wages and reforms no longer seemed realistic. Now what mattered was to salvage what could be saved. The good years had yielded a certain amount of overproduction. The labor unions dreaded that the employers might literally welcome a conflict; diminished production would send prices in a strong upward direction.

And the prices continued to rise at the same time as the number and magnitude of the disputes grew. The increased price of food, which was partly a result of higher food tariffs, became especially sensitive for the poorer population.

Increasingly, people felt that these developments would necessarily lead to a more or less decisive encounter. The employers had gotten a new and energetic leader, the circuit judge von Sydow, who had made clear that his goal was to break down the opposition. "Without unnecessary excesses" – but which ones would be seen as necessary? Wages and working conditions must be laid down, workers' self-will and presumption stifled, and the employers' supremacy over factories and workshops be restored. What would make this possible was the employers' paragraph 23 that established that employers in all contracts would retain the rights to hire and dismiss workers according to what they thought best and regardless of whether said workers were organized or not.

This meant that those active in the unions would be driven away from the workplaces and strikebreakers would be rewarded, claimed the workers. Workers' unions would be rendered completely meaningless. Such demands could not be accepted, there would have to be a fight. And people felt the threat pushing closer, this threat that was mixed with hope: It is the final struggle...

The brief general strike of 1902 left behind a memory of how impressive the collective strength of many small people could be. The general strike was a weapon which could also be accepted by the meek and cautious. They had found a formulation that appeased many: The crossed arms revolution.

The dream of the revolution was there. But also a promise that a bloody conflict would be avoided. They would neither need to build nor to storm barricades. They had only to sit down and cross their arms. And all the wheels would stop; the whole city—even the whole country—would be crippled.

The best-informed leaders within the union movement were dubious of the outcome of such an action. They knew how the funds had dried up during the preliminary conflicts, how difficult it would be to draw lines when it came to granting permission for work that, in spite of everything, had to be carried out, how much hunger and how many tears a strike would cost.

But they were also jeered at. They tried to compromise, gave way during contract negotiations accompanied by catcalls and whistles of the agitators. Though the retreat didn't give any hope, there would apparently have to be a fight—or capitulation. Unemployment had been great during the winter. Spring arrived with a string of lockouts that led to decreases in wages. Prices continued to rise.

WARNING SHOT

The evening sun shone over the summer city. But it had sunk far down in the west and no longer reached the street excavations; the awnings had been rolled up over the store windows.

Gunnar was on his way home. He still worked for August Bodin, now at a construction site on Tegnérgatan. It was natural for him to walk along Drottninggatan on his way home to Söder—and still it felt as if he was sneaking along there in order to spy. Asta worked on Drottninggatan, in a tobacco shop. She lived in the same building as him on Åsögatan. She was a beauty he had admired for several years from a distance, but never dared to approach. She smiled in such a friendly way at him sometimes, but she was always in the company of different young gentlemen who escorted her home when the cigar shop closed at eleven o'clock in the evening.

If she saw him through the windowpane she would think he was walking past there to look in at her. That wasn't completely wrong, he probably wanted to see her at the same time as he was afraid she would catch sight of him.

He peeked carefully through the window when he passed by, could only see some backs in there: gentlemen, customers. He knew that she would be found in their midst, joking and laughing. A smile for everybody, probably even for him if he stopped by and bought a cigar. Maybe a twelve-öre "Pour la noblesse," that the boss usually bought on paydays.

But Gunnar didn't smoke, had no reason to make a purchase. As he walked on his gaze followed a row of shop windows. A bookstore. He stopped there for a while, maybe mostly to be able to glance sideways and see if any of those gentlemen were exiting the tobacco shop. Whatever that would be worth for him to see.

Several copies of the same book stood lined up in the window: a new arrival. He couldn't afford to buy books, but read the title that was written in flaming red letters: "Enemy of the State." Strange that a good bookstore would display that. He had to look a little closer, noticed the name of the author in smaller and black letters: Leon Larson.

Now he grew deeply interested, he would really like to read that book. The price was there on the cover too: 1.50. It was expensive, almost three hours' work. Still he was well-paid, he was proudly aware of that. People also said that it was the construction workers' high salaries that drove up the rents. He didn't want to subscribe to that, of course. Besides, he had heard Bodin himself say that it was mainly land speculators that made life tough for building contractors.

Leon Larson: "Enemy of the State." It was remarkable that a respectable store had it in its window, that a book with that title didn't get covered up. But perhaps the police didn't care about books that were sold in better stores. They only confiscated the kinds of pamphlets that coal porters went and sold to the workers.

Should he buy it? Then maybe he would know something about all those things that were such a secret.

He had two kronor of his own. That meant of course that he wouldn't drink coffee or buy himself anything for a while.

He would probably have stepped inside and bought the book if the shop hadn't been such a fine one. It wasn't a place where an ordinary worker could go, maybe he would be outright laughed at or driven out. He saw the fine gentlemen behind the counter, the even more refined customers. Possibly if he had been wearing his best suit. But his lack of assurance would give him away.

He stood there, couldn't tear himself away. There, in front of him, for sale, lay the answer to many questions. And he couldn't buy it, even though he had the money.

Someone had come and stood beside Gunnar, to also look in the window. Gunnar had barely noticed it, was too preoccupied. But when he finally went to leave he saw that it was the building contractor. That's right, his office was in the same building. Gunnar hurriedly raised his cap.

"So," said August Bodin. "Karlsson is interested in that book?"

"Well..." He didn't really want to acknowledge it, what would the building contractor think then?

Bodin smiled, as if he had come across something funny.

"Wait a minute," he said. "I'll get it for you. It might be useful reading for a young man."

Bodin walked into the bookstore and Gunnar stayed where he was, even more astonished than before. The whole thing was unbelievable. That the building contractor was going to give him a book—and a book like that!

Bodin came out swinging a little package by the string, handed it over to Gunnar.

"Read and ponder," he said. "It seems to be a very revelatory story. Greetings to everyone at home, by the way!"

Gunnar went off in a daze, trying to find make sense of what had just occurred. But when he walked out onto the narrow truss bridge or the Mousetrap, as the bridge was known, toward the Riks Bank, it was as if he was woken up by the cool evening breeze along the water. He looked around, shook his head—and suddenly began to run. He was in a hurry, had to get home and read the book.

It was short, only around a hundred pages. Gunnar was not a frequent reader, he read and had to reread and still he had a hard time comprehending everything. The book was about a young boy named Magnus who didn't like working, preferring instead to write poetry. Magnus went to the People's Hall and met with Young Socialists. Their leader was the editor Stockman who published the newspaper, "The Torch." Stockman and his cronies came up with lots of criminal plans. Through these people Magnus soon came into contact with Finnish revolutionaries, traveled with them to Copenhagen, smuggled dynamite and planned break-ins and burglary. Finally Magnus understood that the Young Socialists were the enemy of the state and the people and left the group.

For someone who had participated, if only on the fringe, it wasn't difficult to figure it out—once the pattern was made clear. Stockman was Bergegren and "The Torch" was "Fire." And Magnus, he was the poet, naturally.

Everything was clear—and still so unclear. As Gunnar had experienced it and understood the events, things hadn't happened this way. It was the poet who had been the soul of it all and who had said that Bergegren shouldn't know anything.

Gunnar, who had left the Young Socialists a few years ago, had no reason to defend them. His resignation had been a form of criticism. But the poet's book made him so indignant that he trembled where he sat in the twilight by the window. What kind of a world was he living in? Here the poet was blaming others for what he himself said and did—and the book was sold for a lot of money in fine bookstores. And the building contractor who had said that he should read and learn from it. Learn what—to lie?

In defense of the building contractor it could be said that he probably only had read something the newspapers had written and that he probably couldn't be aware of the actual circumstances. And the newspapers? Did they know anything—or did they just write anyway?

He continued reading despite the fact that the printed letters almost floated away, disappearing in the summer evening's dusk. He couldn't stop and didn't want to light a candle, then Emelie would wake up again. She had woken up several times and asked if he wasn't going to bed soon. Soon, he had said every time. Now it was too late, there was no point. It was light outside when he read the last pages. He stretched out on the bed for half an hour, couldn't fall asleep, didn't try to either.

Before he went to work he stuffed the book in the bottom of the drawer where he had his possessions. He hid it so no one would get a hold of it and read what was not true.

But he showed it to Emelie a few days later. Had thought of talking about its content with her—but Emelie seemed most interested in the fact that Gunnar had received the book from her brother, the building contractor. She came back to that time after time, wanted to hear every word her brother had said, how things had gone when they met, how he had looked.

When Gunnar said that he was thinking of burning the book she insisted on taking care of it. Save it as a souvenir, she said.

Just something to remember. He figured it had to be as she wished. Was she thinking of reading it too?

If she had time.

But she never did.

The book gave rise to long-winded and passionate newspaper debates. Bergegren and other Young Socialists protested. That was no young innocent youngster who had joined the movement as a poet. Now they found out that he was a criminal, an incendiary. Moreover, the poet had embezzled the dynamite that the Finnish revolutionaries should have had. All the criminal plans had been his: he had planned to attack and murder bank messengers, he had thought of shooting the king and blowing parliament up into the air, plundering the cash reserves of the social democrats and the cooperative. The poet replied by telling in countless interviews of the persecution he had endured and the intense attempts he had made to prevent Bergegren and the others from committing all the evil deeds they now accused him of having planned.

Outsiders could hardly discern what was the truth in this cascade of accusals and counter accusals. Under the circumstances, what people saw as revealed was that a vast number of criminal plans had been talked over in the Young Socialist movement. The Social Democrats could, with a light sigh of relief, remind people that already one year earlier they had expelled the Young Socialists leaders who had then created their own party.

The poet's book and the debates surrounding it shook up the Young Socialist movement, which, a short time earlier had undergone sharp criticism for the mail burglary in Skåne and the Amalthea exploit. Much could have been viewed as rather innocent revolutionary frenzy with theatrical daggers, harmless bombs and loose warning shots. But the mail robbery and the Amalthea affair had cost blood and lives. It was no longer a question of playing games.

At the end of June the Tsar paid a visit to the city and was received by King Gustaf, the old King Oscar having died two years earlier. His visit aroused criticism. The Tsar was called a blood-stained tyrant and many feared assassination attempts on the part of exiled Russian revolutionaries. When the Tsar and his retinue stepped ashore at Logårdstrappan, the police had cordoned off all of the Old Town. Those curious onlookers who had gotten there before the barricades were set up were not numerous, despite the magnificent weather.

The following day the shot that had been dreaded was fired. But it was a random shot. It was not fired by some coldly determined exile against a tyrant. Instead, it was fired by a desperate Young Socialist at a completely innocent Swedish officer. The attacker had time to take his own life before he was arrested; he had several issues of "Fire" in his pockets and a letter in which he blasted society.

The deed gave rise to new frictions within the revolutionary circles. The most zealous members blamed Bergegren for cowardice when he did not want to publicly defend the attack. The Young Socialist Club members from Kungsholmen made a procession to the attacker's grave, laid a wreath with red and black ribbons on it, and gave three cheers for the dead man's derided and defamed memory. The speaker was taken away by the police, as well as a bakery worker who had pulled out a revolver at the graveside.

It was said that Bergegren was tired and overwrought and wanted to withdraw. He disappeared from the scene, no one knew where. A succession of Young Socialists sat in prison, others stayed out of sight, waiting for the storm to blow over.

While the unavoidable large workers' conflict drew ever closer, the Young Socialists had lost all opportunities to have any influence. Their shots had frightened themselves as well as their opponents.

What was going to happen now? How many more days until they stood there without work and therefore no money for rent or food?

It didn't help just to work as usual. Thinking about things made people anxious.

The building contractor came down and looked around worriedly. A strike right now wouldn't suit him at all. But he had a lot to do, had recently fought his way through the long struggle over the five-öre cut in pay. Building contractors did not belong to the employers' association, which had just warned of a lockout. But if there was a big lockout among other professions the contractors could fear that their workers would respond with a general strike. And then they would be back where they were again, in a long period of inactivity and losses. If only it would drag on at least several months so they would have time to get this building finished.

He felt how he himself became a little ingratiating in his manner, he spoke with some of the older more secure workers: they surely didn't believe that there would be a conflict again? As for himself, he had not enjoyed that lockout they had held, they certainly knew that. He had been forced to go along with it.

They smiled when he left: Bodin sure seemed nervous. But they weren't the ones he should be talking to now. He should deal with his colleagues.

At the end of July the employers initiated their expected lockout. On the first day eighty thousand workers were shut out of their workplaces. It was expected that eventually the number would double.

The national trade union confederation answered that a general strike would begin on the fourth of August if the lockout was not revoked before then.

Many people were gripped by panic. Over the course of a few days every revolver available for sale was bought. People stood in line in the large weapons and sporting goods stores. Bank tellers were among the first to arm themselves; there had been so much talk of the Young Socialists' plans for bank robbery.

A period of lawlessness was anticipated, of riots and assaults. A volunteer citizens' defense corps was formed. Protests were heard from the workers' side; the unions intended to maintain order themselves within their ranks. The temperance organizations demanded prohibition. Firms advertised canned meats and powdered milk, good for storing if food transport was stopped. On the streets more and more carts for hauling were seen; those who had the opportunity stocked up on provisions. Many stores enacted large price increases; everything could be sold for a price.

ONE FOR ALL—AND ONE

The first and most important command was solidarity; that was the prerequisite for the strike to succeed. The command was impressed on people via speeches and articles. If everyone leaves work, then everyone will be running the same risks, it was claimed. People should strike in collective troops and no one return to work if all were not allowed to return.

One for all and all for one.

Many might feel they were fully part of a collective; they would do as the group decided, did not need to be faced with any choices. For others it was more difficult, worst of all perhaps for those who worked in small workplaces or who had reached such a high position that they could hardly figure out if they were among those who should heed a call to strike.

Emelie was one of the undecided. Relatively few of the employees at the cosmetics factory were organized, but it was obvious that all the workers there would strike. How should foremen and supervisors behave? She had cautiously asked a number of them; some intended to strike, others didn't.

Any day now she could be called in to the factory director and questioned. And she didn't know what she would answer. In certain respects the strike didn't concern her. Melinder ought to be considered a good employer, he hadn't lowered any wages. And Emelie herself as superintendent had been better paid than the workers. She had nothing to complain about.

But of course she was a worker, a working woman. And as such the expected strike did concern her as well. All of her closest relatives and friends were going to strike. With the exception of Jenny, of course. Artists were neither workers nor bourgeoisie; they couldn't be categorized, lived instead in their own world.

She had to speak with someone who understood what this strike was all about. She considered Thumbs for a moment, but what he would have to say was obvious. She wanted to talk to somebody who had thought the matter over and didn't have any preformed opinions.

There was one person who was informed about the situation and who ought to be able to give a well thought out answer: Rudolf, her sister's husband and Thumbs' son. Rudolf had once been active in forming the streetcar labor union. Recently there had been a lot of talk as to whether the streetcar workers would participate in the strike or not. Rudolf must have had reason to think things over.

Emelie didn't get time to visit her sister's family very often. They lived far away on the northern outskirts of town, in Siberia as it was called. But a few times a year she would go and pay a visit, usually in connection with someone's birthday. And now Gertrud's second oldest daughter was turning seventeen. That was an excuse to come and Emelie could even count on being expected.

Gunnar had promised to make sure the children got their supper so Emelie wouldn't have to go home after work. But she didn't want to arrive at Gertrud's too early either, in which case they might think they had to invite her for dinner. They had plenty to feed as it was.

If it had been a normal day Emelie would have stayed at work, there was always something to prepare. Now she didn't dare, the factory director might look in and, if he saw someone was there, start to ask questions about the strike.

She stopped for a moment outside the entrance and looked around, not quite sure which way she should go. She took the road heading north after all, although it was way too early.

Stora Badstugatan was dark and gloomy, even in the summer evening's mercifully mild light. It was closed in by shacks and dilapidated stone buildings, most of them rather low, housing small industries, breweries and farmers' quarters. Inside the gaping archways hundreds of horses stamped their feet between carts and lumber scraps, hay sacks and piles of dung. On the high hill behind Lilla Badstugatan the observatory was visible with its tower, and an old farm stuck up from behind the bushes on the gravel slope.

City and country merged on the ragged outskirts, a settlers' camp and a dumping ground. Odengatan crossed over Stora Badstugatan on a concrete bridge; streetcars rumbled along across the bridge. The viaduct had a stately name that told of plans to come: Sveabron. One day both Stora and Lilla Badstugatan would be made into one, and grand Sveavägen was the intended outcome. But that was something that would happen in a future swathed in mist; for the time being it was it was just a short stretch of deserted street on the edge of town that had been honored with the new name.

Emelie looked around a little irresolutely. In fact she didn't like going outside her routine; back and forth to work she walked through a city that was safe and well-known, almost friendly. Here she didn't feel at home, here dangers could lurk and here were all kinds of opportunities to get lost. She had to keep moving, otherwise she might be accosted. She tried to walk as if she had a goal, climbed up to Odengatan, followed it all the way to the new church at Odenplan.

There was a lot being built beside the church; the whole block seemed framed in construction scaffolding. Everywhere were buildings and people she didn't recognize, a foreign world. It was as if she was being driven out into it, out of her usual, safe environment. That strike... She did not want to take part in it at all, wished that everything could stay the way it had been, that she could walk her familiar route between home and the factory, keep her quiet corner of existence. She felt like she didn't have the strength for more worries than she had. Bärta just dumped her responsibilities on Emelie, counted on Emelie to manage her children. It was a shame on them all if the children went around dirty and ragged. And she herself couldn't eat if the children in the kitchen didn't get something too.

As long as they had work she could keep them from extreme want. Gunnar made a very good living, Jenny paid her own and Maj's way. But Bärta seldom contributed any money. She hardly ate at home either, of course—but her children did. The boys were hard to fill up.

Worries followed Emelie through the unfamiliar streets. The old, usual worries and the new troubles. One for all—and all for one. When she grew tired and dispirited she thought how only the first part of that expression—one for all—fit her case.

She got as far as Sankt Eriksbron, a new bridge that she had not seen before. She walked out a bit between the iron structures, looked at the new skyscraper on the Kungsholmen side and the billowing smokestacks at the Atlas and Rörstand factories next to her.

Still a couple of days left, then no smoke would be rising any longer; everything would be still. A long period of famine. She would not be able to go to August this time, not now that there was talk of strike and conflict. It didn't help that they were siblings; they had landed on either side of the dividing line in any case.

Had she already made up her mind? No, but if. If.

What would Rudolf say?

She felt in her pocket for the soap she had been able to buy cheaply at the factory, the birthday present. Then she began to walk back to the road.

Emelie was the only guest; there wasn't much of a party and celebration. Rudolf had come home late and sat and ate. He was going to a meeting again that evening. There were strong forces in motion pushing the streetcar workers to strike. But a strike meant a breach of contract; as the contract was worded neither the streetcar company nor its employees could start a such conflict. It was mostly for appearance's sake that the other strikers wanted the steetcar employees to participate. They remembered how impressively quiet it had become on the streets during the short general strike a number of years ago. If the streetcars were running the public would not feel the situation's gravity, would not feel the paralysis.

The pressure continued to mount; people wanted something called "street peace." That was why they were holding another meeting tonight. Rudolf couldn't predict how it would go. But he was going to speak up and say the contract had to be kept, he had helped push it through and he didn't intend to break it. There would surely be those who called him a coward and a traitor. Whichever way the vote went he would naturally abide by the decision that was reached. Solidarity was the most important thing; what he himself thought was secondary. But the contract... How upset would they have been if it had been the company who had broken it?

There were some who had a suggestion. They should ask the company to cease operation during the strike so there wouldn't be any conflict. Though he himself would speak in favor of the suggestion he did not believe in it; the company would not agree to it. They would not be able to if they were to keep their own contractual rights; they of course had an agreement with the city that transportation had to be kept running.

If the company could... if they were so decent that they did not force their employees into an impossible situation where they had to choose between breach of contract and breach of solidarity.

The company had been decent many times. They had arranged a pension; working conditions were better than in most professions. And in the last two years they had even gotten a vacation.

Vacation? Emelie had to ask. What was that?

Well, they had one week off every year with full pay.

Had one ever heard of such a thing? It's true, Emelie had heard that Rudolf had taken time off, but had taken for granted that it was unpaid leave. She had assumed that the streetcar company could not keep all the cars in use during the summer when it was fine weather and people would just as soon walk as ride.

Rudolf seemed tired, as if he had failed. When Emelie saw him this way she liked him better than when he appeared as the somewhat overly self-important family patriarch. Once she had loved Rudolf, or at least believed that she did. It had been a difficult time when it turned out that Rudolf preferred Gertrud. Now what had happened felt like it no longer had any importance. Many times she had even thought it was a good that things had turned out the way they did. Rudolf could be quite unbearable with his self-righteousness and he treated Gertrud condescendingly. Emelie knew that she never would have been able to resign herself to it as Gertrud had.

But now for a moment she could see the boy again, the one who had not hardened into self-satisfaction, who wasn't so completely sure and instead dared to show a softer, more human side.

She would have liked to console him, encourage him. But it wasn't her place. He had Gertrud. Instead she had to voice her own concerns.

"What should I do?" she asked. "What do you think?"

He inquired about the stipulations and the work, asked how others in her position were going to act. He sat silent a minute, looking as if he did not like giving the answer he had come up with.

"It really depends on who you want to stand in solidarity with, what you feel yourself to be. If you are a worker…"

"What else would I be?"

"It's a matter of unity now. If we did not have our contract it would be obvious that we should strike, no one would hesitate for a minute. In your case it is only a question of where you belong. If you are a worker then you should strike if you are not counted among the few that are exceptions to this. Electric lighting and water will not be shut off, refuse collection will continue, animals shall be attended to and sick people be cared for. But otherwise—nothing.

She was quiet, waited.

"I think about our parents sometimes," he said. "Your father—did he get to turn thirty-five before he was worn out by our society? My father, who still works at the harbor though he doesn't have the strength, my old mother lying there crippled with rheumatism. One day there has to be a change. Sure we have it a little better. But I can't imagine that our kids will have lives like ours. What would be the meaning of a life like that? Now they want to break up our organizations and lower wages. If they succeed, they will roll back all our progress. Young people will stand in the same old spot we once stood in."

It was seldom Rudolf said so much. He saved his speeches for union meetings.

Gertrud and the children listened, hanging on his words. It was as if he was addressing Emelie in a different way from his family. As if she was capable of understanding in a way his closest kin never could.

"I don't want to give you advice," he concluded. "You are the one who is going to have to pay, whatever you do."

Now she didn't have to ask any further. She knew what she had to do. The words about their parents and the children were the determining factor. Every time she thought of her parents' toil and misery she wanted to weep. And if something like that awaited the children—then it was better to die. And under all circumstances important to strike.

She did not stay very long; the way home was long. Rudolf, who was going down to the People's Hall, kept her company for part of it. Then she continued on alone, up the hills, through the familiar streets that she knew so well. But this evening they were strange, nothing was familiar, nothing was safe and secure any longer.

The next morning she went herself and asked to speak with Melinder. He looked at her a little questioningly; she normally never asked to see him.

"Excuse me, director," she said and sat down though he hadn't offered her a seat. "Excuse me—I would only like to say that I am going to strike."

"What is this? What is there that we don't agree on?"

She saw that he was trying to joke but that didn't make it any easier. The tears welled up in her eyes. She shook her head.

"Nothing. Everything is fine."

"Have the others tried to coerce Emelie?"

"No."

"So Emelie wants to do this herself?"

"Yes," she answered in a low voice.

There was so much she thought of afterward that she should have said: about solidarity, about the masses that the lockout had forced to go without work and without bread. Maybe also some of what Rudolf had said. But it was impossible for her to answer, the sobs caught in her throat. And the words wouldn't come. She could not explain what she felt.

"I won't stand in the way," he said. "Some have expressed their willingness to work so we will try to keep on operating. And Emelie understands that this makes it impossible for me to take you back as superintendent once the strike is over."

She nodded.

"But there will always be a place for you here in any case," he said. "I simply don't understand the meaning of this. Emelie wasn't even in the union, correct? To be superintendent means to have been entrusted with confidence—in which case one must not betray this confidence when the company undergoes difficult times as well. But perhaps it isn't worth talking about it. Go and do what you can now before the nuisance begins. Emelie isn't thinking of starting to strike before the others at least?"

He sat and watched her leave, close the door. Well... what was there to say? She was crying, poor thing. He should have taken her on, bawled her out, rid her of these foolish notions. But she had always thought of what was best for the company before, he couldn't really be sore at her. It must really be the others pressuring her, maybe her relatives too, friends. His old uncle who once upon a time had hired Emelie had told him about her circumstances at home. She certainly had not had an easy time of it.

Sometimes he understood that the workers reacted, understood it better than he ought to in his position. And in the bourgeois newspapers as well, there were lines of thinking that supported this understanding. Now with the crisis and all the prices going up—it was clear that many would become desperate. That lockout had been a bad business actually, starting trouble just as the season was at the door.

The season, yes. She would have been needed now, belonged in any case to the few one could depend on. It hadn't been the very best workers who had notified him that they intended work despite the strike.

Well, well, after a week they would get hungry and come back. And then maybe they would all make it through the season...

DREAM AND REALITY

Gunnar examined his work tools before he placed them back in the tool shed. He wondered how long it would be before he got to take them out again. He had sharpened and polished them, as if he were saying good-bye. It would be good to have perfect things the day work started again. He did not doubt that he would get to return to the building site, Bodin would surely keep his "steady fellows" and then Gunnar too would get to come back. All or none, that's what the fellows had said.

One of the carpenters stood up and cut off pieces of wood long enough for a lunch box. He had apparently decided to build up a miniature supply of wood over the last few days. Gunnar nodded good-bye and walked through the opening in the fence that they had set up around their workplace. The boss stood waiting with the padlock in his hand.

It felt strange to know there was no work waiting tomorrow, a weekday. He had not had time to get used to the idea of time off yet. What would he do all day long? During a general strike you couldn't get any odd jobs, all work was to cease. Some of the guys were going fishing. Others had relatives in the country and were going to travel there. They might even be able to find work there because it was not the intention for cows and pigs to suffer because of a strike. A bricklayer who was a Young Socialist had invited some friends and their girlfriends to go along in his rowboat and set up camp on an uninhabited island in Lake Mälar. He had invited Gunnar too, but since Gunnar didn't have any girl to bring along he declined. If was safest that way, the bricklayer had said that those who went along would become "nature worshippers" and live as if in paradise. It might have sounded tempting—but Gunnar actually preferred life on earth.

The giant dark stream of work-clad people wended its way through town. One would not have guessed that anything remarkable was happening. Most of those who hurried by looked as they usually did: tired, perhaps a trifle impassive but also eager to get home. Nothing of a revolutionary tone could be overheard.

The summer evening was light and warm. The open area around the locks lay bathed in the western sun. Drottsgården, the first skyscraper on Söder, was nearing completion. The brownish red walls glowed in the sunlight. The enormous building towered ten stories high over Stadsgården and faced the as yet unfinished Katarinavägen.

When Gunnar approached the building where he lived he saw that someone was standing in the entryway to the street. A light dress shone against the gray background. It was Asta's sister, Hjördis. A few years ago she was just a kid who turned around and stared big-eyed when he walked past. Now a young girl with her hair put up and long skirts. She might well be around seventeen he guessed. Still a kid, of course. He himself had turned twenty.

She asked if he was going to strike now too.

Yes indeed—and she?

Of course. The factory where she worked counted on having to shut down completely.

"Beautiful weather," he said, and looked up at the roofs that were still glistening.

Suddenly he was gripped by the desire to act. Out of courage—presumption? This was not a day like any other, there was no real reason to just get up and eat and go to bed. No work awaited him in the morning; he could sleep half the day if he wanted. And it could be fun to go out with a girl, just go for a short while. Even if the girl was a kid and didn't stand up to any comparison with her big sister, Asta.

"Shall we go out and walk a little?" he asked. He regretted it almost as soon as he asked.

"Oh yes!" The answer came quickly, too quickly. She closed her mouth and blushed.

"I'll just go wash and change," he said. "How about in a quarter of an hour?"

Supper would have to wait even though Emelie would fret that he wouldn't have time to eat. But she didn't say anything, seemed dejected. She was probably thinking about what the director had said, that she would not be allowed to continue as superintendent after the strike.

Hjördis was already standing in the doorway waiting when he arrived. She had on a wide-brimmed picture hat over her light, pinned-up hair. From under her tight-fitting dark jacket billowed a full gray skirt.

He walked a cautious little distance from her, tried to think of something to say. It wasn't as easy now as it had just been; now he felt that he had gotten himself into something new and maybe dangerous and it paralyzed him. She was also quiet, glancing sideways at him from time to time, but said nothing. They had gotten as far as Glasbruksgatan before he came up with an idea.

"There is a Frenchman who is going to fly up in the air over at Gärdet I heard. Shall we go have a look?"

"Fly? In a balloon of course?" She had seen that once at a workers festival at the athletic grounds.

No, in some sort of machine. That's right, it was called an aeroplane. But if they were going to have time to see anything they would have to take the streetcar.

He grumbled to himself a little over this luxury now when it was so important to save every cent. Two transfer tickets at ten öre each. But at the same time he absolutely refused to accept the ten-öre piece she offered him. They traveled on the ring line along Skeppsbron and across Norrbro, round Kungsträdgården and past Norrmalmstorg all the way to the square at Stureplan. They were lucky; a streetcar on line 2 came from Birger Jarlsgatan's north side and drove up to the square. With that car they could go all the way to Karlaplan.

She gripped his hand when they stepped off, as if she was afraid to be separated from him and get lost. Gunnar, who had been on construction sites in many parts of town, knew where they should go. He held tightly onto her hand; it gave a new and pleasant feeling. As if she were seeking protection and he could protect her.

"We have to hurry," he said. "Otherwise everything will be over when we get there."

Throngs of people had assembled around the field at Gärdet. The Frenchman, Legagnieux was his name, had already made some attempts to get into the air the previous evening, but the plane had risen so imperceptibly that many spectators wondered if it had even left the ground.

Gunnar asked: had anything happened? Yes, the Frenchman had been up once, surely five or six meters off the ground, and flown as far as Borgen, where he had disappeared behind the hill. Now the plane had been wheeled back to the starting position. You couldn't see very much of it. You had to pay an entrance fee to get very close. In any case, it was rumored that the Frenchman was going to go up again.

Just at that moment they heard a murmur; a gasp went up through the tightly-packed onlookers. He was coming! The rickety, open plane rose above the people over there. It was sailing away—they saw it go up even higher. Now there was no doubt that the strange machine really was up in the air. Ten meters up, fifteen. The audience rewarded the flyer's bravery and death defiance with cries of bravo and thunderous applause. The plane went out in an arc, dipped down for a moment, enough so that they were afraid it would crash, righted itself, soared back toward the crowd, landed and continued for a ways on the ground with functionaries running after it.

Jubilation broke loose, people screamed and shouted hurrah. The spectators rushed forward to congratulate the brave aviator who, with a champion's pride, climbed out of his plane. But the non-paying spectators couldn't see much of that; they could only see the seething masses, hear the cries.

Apparently the show was over. People began to disperse, eagerly discussing the miracle they had just witnessed.

Gunnar and Hjördis walked back toward home. He still held onto

her hand. They followed along with the flow of people in the direction of Strandvägen where there were also many people in motion, on
their way to and from exhibitions out on Djurgården.

The exhibition, "The White City," was out at Friesen's Park.
Neither of them had been there to see it. They had heard of the water
slide that went out in the water. And the exhibit that showed the
destruction of the city of Johnstown during a flood. The flower clock
and the haunted castle...

And the open-air dance floor, said Hjördis. That Pinet's dance floor
was supposed to be especially sensational. That's where the well-
behaved girls went to dance, not just those who didn't care about their
reputations and frequented Gröna Lund amusement park and the
dance halls. Everyone was dancing the Boston now. Just think if they
could go to the exhibition sometime!

It was expensive he had heard. He had to stop her. That bit about
the dance floor worried him; he didn't know how to dance.

Yes, it was sure to be expensive. She resigned herself to the fact.

He told her about his big childhood memory, the exhibition of
1897. Emelie had worked at the exhibition, in the cosmetics factory's
pavilion. He had been able to go with her every day that summer, had
been able to ride through the Fairy Grotto where the women from
Dalarna rowed the boats. That exhibition had been larger, even better.
Had Hjördis been there?

No, she was so little then.

He felt big, grown up.

When they got to Slussen she pulled her hand out of his. He wanted to try and take it again but she pushed him lightly aside.

"No, not here," she said. "Someone might see us."

She was right, of course. Someone could see them here and
think something.

He shoved his hands in his pockets, but in the dark passage and on
Glasbruksgatan's narrow wooden walkways he got to hold her hand
again, help her so she didn't stumble. She held onto her wide skirts
with the other hand.

They said a brief good-bye in the dark entrance to her building. One last moment her hand grazed his, then she opened the door and was gone.

Pensively he continued upward. Of course it had been fun to go out with Hjördis. But that part about going to a dance floor wasn't for him. And anyway she was just a kid. He had better pull back in time.

But the feeling of her hand remained in his, something of its scent too. When he lay down he put his hand under his cheek, sniffed silently. Then he angrily shoved his hand under his pillow. Now he would sleep. Tomorrow they were striking.

While Gunnar was falling asleep the streetcar personnel were gathering in the People's Hall. Now they were deciding how the strike would go for the streetcars.

As expected, the request that the company cancel streetcar operations had been rejected.

The mechanics from the north and south lines had voted to strike by 82 to 3. The traffic personnel on Söder had come to the same decision with 102 votes against 14. The votes already taken placed a certain amount of pressure on the largest department, the traffic personnel from Norr, when they went to discuss their position.

According to the bylaws, the question had to be decided by secret ballot and in order for a strike to be effected, three quarters Majority was required. Each department had to decide for itself how to act.

It wasn't until four in the morning that the votes were counted. 415 had voted for the strike and 176 against. The requisite Majority was lacking.

A tremendous row ensued. Many of the mechanics had attended the meeting and now took part in the wild debate. Hardly anyone could make himself heard; the chairman banged with his gavel in vain. The most agitated rushed onto tables and chairs and held speeches without having been given the floor. Those who had voted against the strike were traitors of the working class, the board of Department 1 was made up of a bunch of cowardly wretches who placed the contract with the company above solidarity with the working class.

At last the department chair managed to calm the uproar with the promise that the union board would meet immediately and discuss what could be done. After a short while the board communicated its decision to revoke the provision that every department maintained the right to act on its own. Instead, the votes would be counted together, giving 599 for the strike and 193 against. Thus, by five votes, the required Majority had been secured.

At five o'clock in the morning the director of the Norra company on the north side was informed by telephone of the decision. The employees of the Södra company on the south side made their appearance an hour later and informed their employer that they had gone on strike.

Tired and upset by the violent debates, Rudolf was finally able to go home. As long as possible he had held out for their contract: by breaking with the contract they renounced any right to return. He had been answered that solidarity meant more than pieces of paper. And he should not worry about his job; everyone was going and they would all set the same demands in order to return. If the streetcar company wanted the cars up and running again they would be forced to accept the workers' demands.

Naturally he yielded to the Majority decision. It wasn't the strike that he was against, only the route taken to get there: breach of contract and annulling the bylaws.

Some of the most aggressive wanted to follow Rudolf out of the meeting to continue discussing things. But they were advised by others: don't occupy yourselves with him. He is decent although he is impossibly literal minded. The day the workers take power he will hammer out the bylaws first before he goes along with it. But he will take part in things then too.

They squabbled a little, rather lamely and without any real desire.

When they came out onto the street they stopped for a minute and breathed in the fresh morning air.

"Tomorrow the bourgeoisie has to leave," one said and

smiled contentedly.

"And we will have to pull in our belts," another one answered tiredly.

That morning no bellowing demonstrators marched through the streets, no revolver shots were heard. Those who had feared rioting and violence and cautiously peered through the cracks in the curtains found a city in a peaceful Sunday mood. Holiday clad workers came gradually out of their houses, wandered slowly through town, glanced perhaps in passing at the People's Hall to see if any acquaintances had placed themselves by the entrance at the feet of the giant harbor worker statue.

No streetcars clanged, no workers' carts squealed, no horses' hooves clopped along the cobblestones. Here and there a wheelbarrow went by, loaded with food and pushed by someone who hadn't had time to go shopping until the last minute. No automobiles were running; cab-drivers and hired coachmen had gone along with the strike. The sought-after "peaceful streets" were as good as total. On Vasagatan however, a hearse rolled out toward the north cemetery. The coach-man wore the Trade Union confederation's exemption warrant in his cap, and behind this one wagon the funeral guests proceeded on foot. On the outskirts of town, haulers could be seen leading their horses to pasture. Steamboats and ferries lay still at quaysides since the stokers were also striking.

The changing of the guard received an unusual number of specta-tors. Other idlers placed themselves where they could watch the luck of the many people fishing from quays and bridges. Neither the work-ers' prefects nor their safety corps was visible; however, the number of police on patrol was unusually large.

The summer day was warm and peaceful. No one who saw the calm, sober and quiet city would guess that a massive strike was under-way. The nightmare seemed to have been turned into an idyll.

EVERYDAY ON STRIKE

Gradually the feeling of festivity and of the "final battle" cooled, even if it was supported by enormous meetings at Lilljans wood and Hornsbergs meadow outside Karlberg. As soon as the masses of people were on their way home from these, some of their everyday worries and concerns crept in their path. Coin purses and food supplies began to shrink and there were no signs indicating the opposition intended to give up.

The first four days of the strike were the big, quiet, peaceful ones. No real opposition was offered. Streetcars stood locked in their garages, only a few coach owners were out driving, with the exemption warrant in their pockets or the Red Cross flag on their wagon. Typographers also went on strike. The large daily newspapers came out on small duplicated or hectographed scraps of paper, while the strikers, in contrast, had their own newspaper, "The Answer," which was printed in large editions. The workers were charged with trying to stifle freedom of speech and the understanding that some of the newspapers and employers had felt earlier for the striking workers was diminished.

At around ten o'clock on the strike's seventh day, a Monday morning, the doors to the streetcar garage were opened and a streetcar rolled out. Policemen stood posted on both platforms, the company's driving supervisor was the conductor and at his side stood the executive director and the chairman of the board. A number of striking streetcar employees ducked aside, some worried at being recognized; others hurried over to see what was going to happen. A messenger was sent to the People's Hall.

The streets lay silent, without any vehicles other than the lone streetcar that rolled along down deserted Birger Jarlsgatan, between seedy-looking houses and fireproof gables plastered with advertising flyers. Once it was past Stureplan the picture changed. The sound of the streetcar caused the people in the fancy apartments along the boulevard to rush to their windows. Women leaned out and waved with white handkerchiefs and the director lifted his hat in reply. Strolling gentlemen stopped, raised their walking sticks and shouted bravo. A few passengers climbed on board at the stops, either out of a taste for adventure or to demonstrate.

The streetcar followed the length of the ring line, over Norrbro, Skeppsbron and the locks at Slussen. At Kornhamnstorg it met another streetcar driving on the line in the opposite direction. The company traffic inspector, who had taken his place on the oncoming car's front platform, asked politely how the journey was going. Reports were exchanged: everything fine.

Meanwhile, outside the People's Hall on Barnhusgatan, large groups of strikers had gathered. When the car with the director on the platform slowly rolled through the packed route, people moved aside unwillingly. The director looked around grimly, but also felt something of the victorious commander's satisfaction: the critical part had been managed without incident. But on crowded Badstugatan they were held up. The tracks there had been filled with sand and mud again. The director stepped off and pulled down the lever while the chairman of the board cleaned the tracks with his walking stick. People flocked around them; a few protests and derisive remarks were heard. The police climbed down but did not have to intervene. The tracks were ready, the journey could continue.

Twelve streetcars were put into circulation the first day, each one under police supervision. A couple of days later the cab owners informed their drivers that driving rights would be rescinded for those who did not have at least one cab in circulation. That meant that one hundred cars and horse-drawn carriages began to circulate. The volunteer citizens' defense corps took it as its main task to supply the streetcars with those willing to work, and several lines were able to be opened. The popular actor, Axel Hultman, worked as a conductor and was interviewed by the newspapers, which were being printed again since office workers and others ready to work had taken over the presses.

The actor and the other defense corps members lived in the Continental Hotel where the corps had its headquarters. The narrow Vattugränd was closed off and signs with "access forbidden" were set up. Outside the barriers bitter strikers stood in clusters. In the hotel vestibule, visitors were greeted by guards. At night there were also guards on the roof. There had been fears expressed of bloodthirsty Young Socialists sneaking across the roof and throwing bombs down the chimneys.

But still, calm and perseverance were predominant. After two weeks the number of strikers in the whole land had not diminished by more than a thousand, and no greater disturbances had occurred.

During the strike Emelie had time to think over her situation. Normally she was too harried to really have the energy to think and plan. Then it was perhaps easier to say yes and take on more burdens than to resist entreaties and pleas. Now, when she had the time to see and reflect, she found she had taken on way too much.

"You are too kind," Jenny had said many times.

Emelie didn't see it as a question of kindness. Sometimes it was more a feeling of responsibility, most often fatigue, the inability to push things away. Sometimes she had also fallen for dreams and hopes, believed that everything would take care of itself and change into something better.

Such as the question of living arrangements. Of course it had been necessary for Bärta and her children to have some place to be; the authorities had threatened to place the children in an asylum. But Emelie had not expected that their living together would be long-term. Just the opposite, she had said to Bärta that it was only a makeshift solution. The big dream had been in the background the whole time: one day Emelie and Jenny, together with Gunnar and Maj, would be able to afford to rent both a room and kitchen. There were three of them working and earning money, so she had thought the possibility ought to exist.

Now more than two years had passed, the temporary inconvenience had remained.

Emelie had had what she now saw as some silly ideas that Bärta would change if she came into a more settled situation. It had not turned out that way at all, quite the opposite. Bärta had given up completely. She felt responsibility for her children but didn't show it, couldn't cope. It had become easier for Emelie to take on Bärta's burdens than to constantly plead and argue.

She had gotten herself into a mess! Not only for herself. Maybe Jenny wouldn't have been out on the road touring so much if she had been able to make it a little nicer here at home. Wasn't Gunnar also beginning to stay out more than before? And Maj—were Bärta's sons such good company for her? The girl was always together with the two boys, seldom or never played with other girls.

The person who takes on one load after another finally ends up not being able to carry anything. When one takes on new burdens one's strength and resources are not enough for those who were there first, one's nearest and dearest. The lifeboat will sink if everyone is to be saved. The one sitting at the oars is forced to be tough, has to shove some people away, be deaf to prayers, blind to suffering.

That was how it felt now, now that she maybe had too much time to think and brood.

There are tasks you can never accomplish, people you can't help, who perhaps don't even want to be helped.

Bärta did not want to be helped. She only wanted to have someone take care of her children and give her a place to sleep. If Emelie ever tried to talk some sense into her she grew angry and snapped, "Sure I've promised. I know I've promised." It seldom was more than promises.

Tyra was also a part of the impossible tasks. She received meals and had her clothes cared for, accepted it all sullenly. And went her way, hardly answering when spoken to.

With Beda it was different. She truly needed help and there was no doubt that she was attached to Emelie. Yet it was still so difficult. It would require an enormous effort if Beda were to get any real help, much more than Emelie had any possibility of giving. Beda should get to live in a place where they could take care of her.

And the boys? Things were fine for now, as long as they didn't get any bigger. But Erik was ten years old now and had begun to be evasive. He sold "The Answer" and surely was making a few coins though he was careful not to show them to anyone. As things were now during the strike Emelie certainly ought to have demanded money from him. But she didn't really feel that she had the right; his mother was closest to him.

Something would have to be done before Jenny and Gunnar grew tired of living this way. But as long as the strike continued it couldn't even be considered. They would just have to try and stick it out.

Emelie cleaned while she ruminated. She cleaned in the kitchen too though Bärta clearly showed that she didn't like it. Some mornings when it was especially fine weather Emelie took the children with her and went to the woods beyond the tollgates to pick berries. Their harvest was not particularly big; all too many others had already been out on the same errand. But they were fun outings for the children and Emelie found that she too felt better leaving their dark apartment and getting out into the woods. And even if they didn't get so many berries they could take home a few sacks of sticks and pine cones for burning.

One day she baked bread. The children gathered round. When the first loaf was done she cut a fragrant slice for each of them. Even Tyra had come in to take part.

Emelie wrapped one of the loaves in a piece of paper and took it with her when she went out to visit Thumbs and Matilda who were still living out on Åsöberget. It wasn't very far, but still she didn't get a chance to visit them so often. They had grown so old, marked by hardship and age. Matilda had been bedridden for several years. Thumbs walked around and tried to tidy up when Emily arrived, but it didn't amount to much.

She gave them the bread and saw how they lit up with happiness, though naturally they said she should take it back home with her. In times like these she couldn't afford to be so generous with them. Yes she could, she had baked it and would no doubt get by since Jenny had not been affected by the strike.

Had she heard anything from Rudolf?

She told them what she knew. That Rudolf had been of the opinion that the streetcar workers shouldn't strike angered Thumbs. Some of his old self peeked through, the agitator who couldn't be struck down. But it was only for a moment, he didn't have the energy to be enthusiastic any longer.

"After the strike they won't take me back at the harbor," he said. "They have been wanting to get rid of me for a long time. I'm too old. There are younger men who can work harder than me."

"As soon as the strike comes to an end Knut will come and help us a little again," his wife said soothingly. Knut, their middle son, was a bricklayer and the one who supported his parents the most even if he first had to think of his own large family. Rudolf was not as considerate; his thoughts seldom went beyond the walls of his own home.

And Mikael? Had they heard anything from him?

No, not for a year now. He was presumably still at sea.

Emelie didn't stay very long; Matilda was much too tired. But when she left she thought it felt good and had been the right thing to do despite the remembrance of sickness and poverty. As if an old broken bond had been tied together again. Thumbs and Matilda had during all those years been her parents' close friends. After Mama's death the siblings, except for August of course, had lived with them for several years. She should look in on them from time to time, repay something of all they had given.

She who had been going around for days and wondering how she would reduce her tasks! But this was different, no responsibility, only a little kindness.

The days passed and no end to the strike could be discerned. Long lines wound outside the People's Hall; people tramped patiently for hours to receive, in the best case, one of the bills that were called emergency currency and were good for purchases in the cooperative stores. The Trade Union Confederation received economic support from its fellow organizations in other countries, but those in need were so many that no resources seemed to be enough. The city's bricklayers found that the amount they had to divide up was five hundred kronor; that didn't even come to fifty öre per organized member.

The lines grew outside the Milk Drop's distribution centers as well. Mothers with young children waited to get a splash of milk. In many families people had to be satisfied more and more often with watery gruel for supper. School began and in many places meals were arranged for the children who suffered most from hunger. But the ones who asked to eat far outnumbered those who could be fed.

People began to talk of the enormous army of the starving.

For the organized workers it was camaraderie and its demands that strengthened their powers of resistance. Among the unorganized a number of people began to waver and regret that they had gotten involved in the struggle. Some of them carefully made inquiries with their old employers. Those willing to work arrived at more and more workplaces looking for work. On the streetcar line by the end of August there were more than three hundred newly hired; in addition ten of the old personnel had returned.

Those striking guessed what this might come to mean. The day they requested to be allowed to come back in an assembled contingent, their employers would answer that they couldn't fire the ones who had helped the companies during the difficult time of the strike.

Each person willing to work meant that victory grew ever more distant and the risks after a defeat ever greater. Hate for the traitors, the strikebreakers increased. There were no serious clashes, but people gathered outside a number of factories in protest.

Unrest grew especially among the streetcar employees. Rudolf came to Emelie's apartment and told how people had turned to the strike committee to have them bring an end to the strike. The response had been no. Instead the decision had been taken for all the labor unions to boycott the streetcars.

It looked like the conflict would never end.

On the first of September the strikers once again held a giant meeting out by Hornsberg. There were estimates that forty thousand workers showed up. But the mood was not the same as at earlier meetings. Many of the listeners asked themselves if it wasn't really defeat that was being announced, even if it was in veiled wording. The strike general, Herman Lindqvist, said that a change in tactics would be undertaken, a "rational split."

The split meant that people on the whole should go back to work. Only the companies who belonged to the employers' association, which had declared a lockout, would be exempted. The return would happen on the following Monday, the seventh of September.

A few days later a number of employers announced that they, under penalty of five hundred kronor, pledged by all available legal means to protect those who had worked for them during the strike. All who by word or action molested those who had been willing to work would be punished or fired. Among the undersigned was Melinder's cosmetics factory.

The general strike had lasted something over a month. On Sunday, the day before many were to resume work, street life was more animated than usual. People wanted to get out, had no peace sitting at home and imagining how things would go the next morning. Maybe the door was shut, the places taken by strikebreakers. Or maybe everything would work out, maybe they would receive work and money again, would be able to eat a real meal, take home what had landed in the pawnshop.

Everything would work out. Or be lost.

THE RETREAT

Once again the sounds of a workday morning were heard: the rumbling of heavy, tramping work boots. The stream of workers welled through the streets of Söder, filled Glasbruksgatan's narrow and dirty passageway, squeezed in between long fences and buildings slated for demolition. Then the street widened, formed an outlet. In the open space in front of the elevator the stream dispersed in whirls toward various destinations. The workers from Söder were on their way to factories, construction sites and workshops again. The day of retreat had come.

The factory owner had said she could come back, though not as supervisor.

While Emelie walked she wondered if he would remember and stick to his word. Or if he had regretted it as the strike dragged on. Maybe he had hired so many strikebreakers that that there wasn't room for the old workers anymore.

Of course she was glad that the strike was over. She missed the security that work gave, felt anxiety about receiving the confirmation that she would be allowed to resume. But the time of the strike had also been the first real time off she had had since finishing school as a twelve-year-old. If scarcity of money and worry about the future had not ruined so much of it, it would have been a time to remember with a certain amount of joy. For once she had had time. Worry had been there—but also calm. And thanks to Jenny they had not had to starve even if food had been scant. The last week they had lived mostly on gruel and potatoes.

On Stora Badstugatan, close to the factory, a little group of people had gathered. Emelie meant to pass by at first, but then she saw it was her workmates gathered there. She felt a stab of fear: had they not been allowed in?

She went up to them and joined the group. She found out that they had decided to congregate and designate a few of them to go and talk to the factory owner, hear if all of them would get to return.

Some figures hurried quickly by, in through the doorway.

"Scabs! Traitors!"

Hold off, they weren't allowed to shout. Hadn't they seen the advertisements? Melinder belonged to the employers who had pledged to fire those who threatened the strikebreakers.

It was one of the men from soap boiling who warned them, one of the few who were union members. He had a certain authority and the others obeyed.

Then Fat Tilda arrived. She did not sneak past as those who had been willing to work just did. Maybe she didn't feel like a strikebreaker since she was supervisor. She greeted them—but not many answered.

They were gathered. It was time.

"We should choose a delegation," the soap boiler said, who knew words and procedures. Two or three who will go in and negotiate.

The soap boiler was the obvious candidate; he was named right away.

"Emelie," the women from packaging suggested.

"But she's the supervisor!"

"She has gone on strike like the rest of us. That should be enough."

It was one of the women from the perfume department who was speaking on Emelie's behalf, one of the ones who had often been critical of her before.

"Will these nominees do?"

"Yes."

"Then we two will go," said the soap boiler.

Emelie had wanted to decline the task. But the woman's words gave her courage; it felt as if she had their confidence and couldn't let them down. Nevertheless, she stepped a little hesitantly away from the group and looked around. There was warmth in their glances, support in their bearing. Old grudges and talk seemed forgotten. It was clear that they depended on her and wanted her to be their spokesman. Her steps became more assured.

Well inside the entryway, where the gaze of the others couldn't reach them, her insecurity returned. But the soap boiler seemed so confident. He grabbed her hand, gave it a hasty squeeze, and said, "We'll manage this fine. Melinder is someone you can talk to."

The factory owner had come down from his apartment to the office. Usually he didn't come down until a few hours later. He had seen the group on the street from his windows on the second floor, had guessed that they would send some people to inquire. For a moment he had feared there would be trouble and thought of calling in the engineer and the head foreman. But then he saw which ones were coming. The soap boiler was perhaps opinionated and obstinate, but absolutely not any troublemaker. And Emelie, she didn't scare him. She had had his trust. Now apparently she had that of her colleagues.

It might feel like she was betraying him. But it was also a sign that she was trustworthy.

"The strikers have chosen us to negotiate about resuming work," the soap boiler said in his most businesslike voice.

Melinder stood at the counter that normally divided visitors from clerks. The office workers had not yet arrived. He did not ask the two to come into his room. The soap boiler's words irritated him a little. Negotiate! It wasn't a question of negotiating now, but of asking politely. They had lost their strike.

He waited with his reply, playing with a pen.

"So," he only said.

It could be the right moment to get rid of a few difficult and less skilled workers. But he had only hired two new employees while the strike was underway. The season was waiting; everyone would probably have plenty of work. There would be a lot to do and a whole lot of overtime. To a certain degree he was dependent on the experienced and knowledgeable workers' desire to take care of what was behind schedule. Of course their strike had annoyed him, their solidarity had felt like disloyalty and an unjustified blow at someone who considered himself to be a decent employer. But, he had not been able to avoid a certain admiration. They must have sacrificed quite a lot, perhaps starved themselves through it.

"We hope that everyone will get their job back," said Emelie.

He heard how she made an effort to make her voice sound steady. He had the urge to smile but controlled himself.

"So, that is what you want," he said.

They waited. He had to give them an answer now, not keep them on tenterhooks too long.

"Let's agree to that. But supervisors and foremen who have gone on strike cannot count on getting back their old positions of responsibility. They will have the same requirements as the others in their work. For Emelie it will be the same as the other women in packaging."

The soap boiler glanced at her swiftly. That was for her to answer, he was not one of the supervisors.

"Yes, I know," she said. "The factory owner said that before the strike."

"Then we are in agreement. And remind all the others that those who have worked during the strike are under no circumstances to be made uncomfortable. Anyone who is guilty of harassment toward them will be fired immediately."

He turned and walked into his room. The two of them stood there a minute, as if they were waiting for one last word before the factory owner closed the door.

Outside on the street their workmates were waiting. They had drawn closer to the entryway now, looking in time after time. They felt like the negotiations were taking a long time, dreaded reduced wages and being given notice. When Emelie and the soap boiler came out they were immediately surrounded; the whole group squeezed into the archway at the entrance.

How did it go? What did he say?

The soap boiler gave an account. The previously worried and tense faces relaxed. One of the women suddenly burst into tears. The soap boiler ended by reminding them that anyone who said anything to the strikebreakers would be fired.

They streamed in.

"The boss can rest easy," grumbled a liquid soap maker. "We won't say a word to them. Do you hear? Not one word!"

Some of the women gathered at Emelie's side asked, "Who's going to be our boss now?"

"Tilda, I imagine."

"That cow! She can't manage it!"

Inside the workrooms some of the "scabs" were waiting, keeping in close range of each other. Now they might regret that they hadn't been part of the Majority, ask themselves if they had been as smart as they once believed. The reasons for their behavior were strong enough. They understood from their colleagues' contempt that things would never be the same again: they were outcasts, were considered traitors. They felt the hatred and they hated. Their comrades, themselves, maybe even anxious wives and hungry children who had driven them where they now stood.

The only one who didn't seem to feel despised and expelled was Fat Tilda. She came over, self-important and satisfied, to the packers' big table, placed herself at Emelie's old spot, and began to get the work materials in order.

"I'm in charge of packaging now, girls," Tilda announced. "The factory director wants it that way. Now you must really try to do your best since there is so much to catch up on."

No one answered. They knew their job, knew what they had to do. Tilda, who had never worked in packaging before, but had instead been in ink bottling, shouldn't try to teach them anything.

Emelie looked around, didn't know exactly where she should sit and which job would be hers. One spot was free, one of the younger girls had apparently not returned after the strike. The girl's job was one of the simpler ones, but it had to be done as well. Emelie sat down quietly, began to lay out bundles of stickers.

At Melinder's Cosmetics Factory work had been able to resume without trouble. In other places many of those who had gone on strike had been fired; their positions were taken and employers didn't want to let go those who has shown themselves willing to work during difficult times. The motto "All for one and one for all" could not be adhered to. People had neither the means nor the money to show solidarity any longer. Many went without; there were plenty of workers to be had. At the companies who were members of the Swedish Employers' Association the strike was still on.

For many, membership in a union felt more like a burden, an extra risk of bring drawn into conflicts and be among the first to be laid off if any cutbacks were made. More than one third of the Swedish Trade Union Confederation disappeared from the rosters.

It was especially worrisome for those strikers who had worked on the streetcar lines.

When Emelie came over to see Thumbs and Matilda one evening, Rudolf was there; he had plenty of time on his hands. While they were at his parents' he didn't say much about his difficulties. The old people had worries enough of their own. Thumbs had been allowed to return to the harbor, it was true, but he was viewed as so old and frail that he had been given the role of "signal man," giving signals with his stick, watching over the loading and unloading. It was good to not have to carry anything, but it didn't pay as well.

Emelie and Rudolf left at the same time, keeping each other company through the darkening evening streets on the edge of town. Many years ago they had walked together like this. At that time she had been so proud to get to walk with the handsome Rudolf. She remembered his uniform with the shiny buttons. Now he was walking in ordinary everyday clothes; the streetcar company had demanded back its uniforms from the strikers. He was a little bent now, had aches in his joints. Not many conductors were able to avoid this. For over twenty years he had stood on the open platforms of the streetcars, first as a coachman, and then as a driver. In snow and rain, in chilling wind and burning sunshine.

He was bitter. Everything looked like it was going as badly as he had feared. They couldn't make progress toward any negotiations. The union had put together a committee, but the company refused to receive them. The company didn't want anything to do with the organization any longer, not after the breach of contract. Those who wished to return to work had to apply. Those accepted by the company had to sign personal contracts. The union was apparently going to be completely eliminated, not recognized as a party in the negotiations.

Under such circumstances there was nothing to do but to go on striking. And as time went by, the chances of the strikers making themselves heard diminished even further. They grew ever more destitute, while the company continued to hire more and more strikebreakers. Soon the old workers were not needed; the newly hired ones managed things just as well. Attempts had been made to initiate an effective boycott of the streetcars, but it didn't appear to succeed. People complained about the discomfort walking in the raw fall weather. It was no longer a question of solidarity. People wanted to ride, even if the cars were driven by strikebreakers.

Enticed and then forced into breaking his contract, forgotten when the "rational split" had been carried out on regarding who was to return to work after the strike, now betrayed and deserted. Rudolf was sick and tired of everything. Nobody had wanted to listen to him when he had warned them; they had screamed that he was a cowardly traitor. Now some of the screamers were ready to crawl to the cross, now they were willing to sign a contract that made their union superfluous. He had once participated in building the union, been one of the active members. He didn't think the company would hire him if he applied. He didn't feel tempted to try either. Those who came back after the strike would be considered new employees, he had heard. If he was rehired those more than twenty years of employment would be wiped out and he would receive a salary as a beginner.

They had lived carefully, he and Gertrud. Pinched and scraped to save a small sum. Never indulged themselves, not even to go without having a boarder living among them. He had not been ashamed of accepting relief during the strike—he was worth the money at least as much as those who had squandered their pay during the good years.

They had some money saved. He didn't intend to sit with his hands folded while it dwindled away. Now the money would afford them a new life.

Something clicked inside Emelie. What did he mean?

He had made his decision. They were going to emigrate. Already a few weeks ago twenty streetcar workers had left. Mostly youths.

The two of them had gone down Åsögatan's Stairs to Borgmästaregatan. The light from a projecting gas lamp shone on the wet autumn mud. On the other side of the street the compact blocks of apartment buildings began.

The tears welled up in Emelie's eyes, everything looked mistier, the sheds beside them almost disappeared in the darkness.

Travel away forever?

Yes, of course. Such long journeys were not journeys for pleasure. They were made only once in a lifetime.

Wasn't there any other possibility? Couldn't he become a truck driver?

No, he was tired of currying favor. Hauling contractors would certainly not be happy to admit an active union man. It was just as well to clinch the matter. There would be streetcars in America too.

And what did Gertrud say?

She was going with him.

He reached out his hand, said good-bye. Walked down the hill toward Folkungagatan. Didn't turn around, didn't wave. She hadn't expected it either. Rudolf wasn't like that.

In fact, this was just like Rudolf, she thought. When he and Gertrud had gotten married they had not stayed close to relatives and friends. They had moved as far away as they could, all the way to Siberia. And now they were going even farther away, putting enormous seas between themselves and everything old and familiar. She could not understand them. Did Rudolf know anything about America? How would they manage when they didn't even understand the language? She remembered those poor Russians she met, their bewilderment. They had moved to save their lives—and Rudolf who didn't even want to try to be a truck driver...

And Gertrud. To think that Gertrud could go along with it. Once more Emelie had to think how fortunate it was that she and Rudolf had never become a couple. He would certainly never have gotten her to go to America. Hardly even to Siberia.

A few weeks later Rudolf and Gertrud and four of their children left. The oldest daughter, who was nineteen and had a fiancé, stayed behind. Possibly she and her fiancé would follow later on, if everything in America turned out to be as good as people said.

Emelie walked down to the train bound for Göteborg together with Thumbs. He had quite a difficult time walking. Streetcars rolled past them, but they didn't even consider riding. You didn't arrive in a streetcar to take leave of a son who the streetcar company forced to go to America.

Gertrud and Emelie and the girls cried, Thumbs sniffled carefully, didn't want to show what he was feeling. But Rudolf stood calm and almost cold, setting his watch against the station clock. He told Knut, who had also come down, that they had completely different times in America. It was day there when it was night here. As soon as they got there they would write and tell about it. The city the boat would arrive at was called New York.

It was time to climb aboard. Thumbs slapped his son on the back, couldn't say anything.

They waved as long as they could see anything of the train. Then the long way home awaited them, the steep hills. And Matilda who lay in her bed and cried.

Of the more than one thousand streetcar workers who had gone on strike at the two companies, not even one third were given back their jobs. As many as one hundred of the streetcar strikers emigrated to America.

AS USUAL—AND YET…

Jenny had come home again. During the summer and the fall that had just ended, her engagements had been more numerous than before, her tours long and her days off few. Naturally it was good that she had had plenty of work during the period Emelie and Gunnar weren't earning anything. As long as the strike had gone on she hadn't had to worry about Maj either. Emelie had been home all day long.

She had had sufficient work, earned a good amount too. But it was strange how little there was left over, the money just disappeared. It was expensive to be out roving, to always have to be well dressed. She couldn't economize like she should either. Emelie would be beside herself if she learned how often Jenny took a cab. But what could she do? For those who lived in a hotel room it was so difficult to do laundry and iron, and especially like it was now in the fall, the streets sometimes looked like mudflats, particularly in the small towns. However she tried, her skirts dragged in the dirt.

Sometimes she wondered if it was worth it to wander around in this manner, if the earnings balanced out what it cost in other respects. It was hard to be away so much from Maj. Emelie did what she could, but she worked in the daytime, and during the season she often got home late in the evening. Maj was always together with Bärta's boys. There was certainly nothing wrong with the boys—but when Jenny had been away for a period, as she had this time, she thought she noticed how Maj was changing. A tomboy who fought and ran wild, who never played with dolls and never kept company with other girls.

Maj became more and more her own master. Rather tall and gangly for her age, soon turning ten.

Jenny stood alone in the room; outside the street lay in darkness. The light from the kerosene lamp on the table did not illuminate the entire room, but made the veneer on the dresser in front of the window shine. The dresser hadn't been standing there when Jenny left.

She looked at it, a rather clumsy piece of furniture with three drawers and thick round blocks for legs. She recognized it, had seen it at Rudolf and Gertrud's before. Maj's grandmother, Lotten, had received it as a wedding gift from her mother who had saved the money over the years so her daughter would have a white wedding dress when the day came. Lotten, who was of a practical nature, bought a dresser instead.

But after a while nothing remains. People only live and then disappear without a trace.

Out in the kitchen stood yet another piece of furniture from the broken up home of the émigrés. It was the bed which Emelie and her sister had slept on when they were small. Bärta's boys were using it now. It stood folded up in a corner and was undeniably a practical thing in the crowded kitchen. The accordion bed they called it—and she smiled at the name.

While the potatoes were boiling, Gunnar came in. He washed up at the kitchen sink and she thought to herself how he seemed broader in the shoulders, was more a man and less a boy than she usually pictured him. Then he went into the room and changed.

"So you're going out and about?"

She had to tease him a little. Ask him who the girl was he was meeting. Before he had usually just muttered, but now she thought he seemed confused. Well, well. This time she must have hit the bull's eye.

Gradually they were all gathered, everyone but Bärta. They ate, sat together a little while after the food was done and talked. Jenny had to tell about her new adventures; the last tour had gone as far as Finland. But then Gunnar had to hurry off and the girls began to clear the table and wash the dishes.

As so often before, Emelie and Jenny sat alone in the twilit room.

Jenny asked about Gunnar and Emelie answered, yes it was probably as she thought. He was going out with a girl in the building, Hjördis. She seemed to be a good girl, though her sister had a bit of a bad reputation—she was followed to the door by all kinds of gentle-men and was dressed so provocatively. But Hjördis was different, a completely normal girl. She was probably fine. And Gunnar was so careful.

Jenny smiled quickly. So typical of Emelie… anyone normal was good, everything normal was good.

The new, she thought, the deviating and unusual, everything she herself thought was fun and exciting—this frightened Emelie.

She must have frightened Emelie herself many times, would come to do it again. The first period they were living together she had some-times felt disapproval and distance. It wasn't so any longer; they knew each other. And could appreciate each other, despite their differences.

Everything was the way it always was, Emelie said. Nothing unusu-al had happened since Gertrud and Rudolf had emigrated.

Still, Jenny thought that Emelie had changed in some way, as if she was missing some of her normal calm.

Emelie talked about her work, about Fat Tilda's troubles as super-intendent, about how she herself had been pasting on labels until the factory director had happened to come out to the stock room and become upset at finding her sitting at such a simple task. Tilda had defended herself by saying Emelie herself had chosen this seat and Emelie had explained that it was the task that had been available since one of the youngest girls had not returned.

Tilda had been called into the office later, had returned very upset and reassigned the tasks. The packaging department was not being run effectively, did not get as much done as before. In the department they thought that Tilda was always running to the director's office tat-tling and complaining.

A letter had come from Gertrud; Emelie showed it to Jenny. They had arrived at New York and found a place to live. Rudolf had tempo-rary work, once he got a little used to the language he would try inquire about the streetcars. In this strange city the streetcars looked almost like trains and ran on bridges high over the streets or in tunnels under-ground. But Rudolf said it probably wasn't any harder to drive them than ordinary streetcars, even though they went much faster.

Gertrud asked Emelie to write and tell how Rudolf's mother, Matilda, was. And it wasn't a cheerful answer Emelie had to give: Matilda did not have long to live.

There was that frightening thing again: change, disappearance. Gertrud and Rudolf who had traveled so far away and never would return. Matilda who was fading away and soon would die. And Gunnar who had met a girl and one day would get married and move out.

Her existence had been shaken. Suddenly it appeared that everything could change. People who had been so close disappeared. Relationships at the workplace had been altered; old trust between employees and company executives was gone. And she could sense that this was only the beginning, that so much new waited, so much old would disappear. Perhaps a moment of uneasiness was what one felt before a departure. Perhaps the road would lead to something better. Emelie had won a lot, principally her colleagues' new and strong faith in her. But she had also lost something, part of which was the belief that everything would remain the way it had been.

Now Emelie took up the plans she had: the possibility of finding another place for Bärta and her children to live.

Jenny supported her idea, had more reasons to than she revealed just yet. It would be pleasant for them all if Bärta wasn't so close; Emelie could not manage it any longer as things stood now. If they didn't move too far away, the children could still come and eat, get a little help with their clothes sometimes. In any case, it would be a great relief if they could place a little distance there. Not to speak of how convenient it would be to gain a little more space. Jenny would do everything she could to share the costs.

She ignited Emelie's enthusiasm, had suggestions as to furniture they ought to buy and how they would arrange everything. Emelie did not really believe all those purchases were necessary—but of course it was fun to plan and try to imagine how nice they could make it there.

Then Jenny grew silent, looked pensive. Maybe she was tired, Emelie thought, she had been traveling so much. It must be time to go to bed. It had been so enjoyable to have someone to talk to, so pleasant to sit a while. Being together with Jenny had made her feel calmer. Some of the familiar and comfortable feeling was still there. It was good that Jenny was there, that she had come back again. Even if she was away a lot and would soon travel again, Jenny had become such an important part of her existence.

Jenny said something. Emelie did not hear it at first, was lost in her thoughts. She had to ask: "What did you say?"

"I have to get married," Jenny said. "I'm expecting a child."

Emelie sat as if paralyzed. She how everything else that had happened to her recently was meaningless compared with this: Jenny and Maj would also leave her.

What she had left of her siblings was disappearing. August's son. And Olof's family.

She would be completely alone.

But the apartment—a moment ago had Jenny not spoken of how they would arrange it for themselves?

"For several years I have resisted," Jenny continued bitterly. "Said: 'no, no, no.' Finally I didn't have the strength. Maybe you don't understand... But one feels so alone sometimes. You go from place to place and you stand on the stage and clown around. I like it of course—but sometimes you long for home, you even long for just another person. And then there is one there, all too close...

"Julius is nice, perhaps. And of course one feels sorry for him, dumped by his wife, alone and unhappy. But still I didn't want to; I wasn't in love with him. I said no and I locked the door. But no matter how I behaved he still showed up. He was just there. And, you understand, when one is out the way we are... close quarters and sometimes no dressing rooms at all. You can't go around and be prudish then. And so it happened the way it happened. Do you think I have betrayed Olof?"

"I don't know. Olof is dead."

"Despite that it feels like I have betrayed him. I have not loved anyone else. I have only gone to bed with someone else, because I was so alone and tired and didn't have the strength to resist."

Silence returned. Emelie hardly dared move; the decisive moment felt so near, as if the slightest movement would trigger it.

"Emelie... can I still live with you? May I? Even if you think I have betrayed Olof?"

"But... aren't you going to get married?"

"I have to have a father for the child, that's why I am getting married. But I will never move in with him. Never! Not even if I have to leave here."

"You don't have to move. You can live here as long as you want. I am so glad that I have you all."

Emelie could not hold back her tears.

Jenny seemed relieved, her face lit up, looking almost as if she had forgotten her troubles. Her liveliness returned, she got up, pushed in her chair.

"Oh, it's so nice to be home again," she said.

The dreaded loneliness was no longer so near. Jenny would stay.

Everything would stay the way it was for a time, as usual.

And yet, and yet.

WINTER DARKNESS

Scabby Tilda, they now said. Cow. Blabbermouth.

Yet she had been well-liked before the strike. Tilda was plump and cheerful, pleased to chatter and gossip with those who worked under her. The girls at ink bottling had gotten along with her and she had gotten along with them.

Things had started to change when Hanna Strömgren arrived. Hanna was quarrelsome and always discontented—and she passed this on to others. It was hard to look happy in Hanna's presence, one felt almost shamefully childish.

Didn't Tilda see how ignored she was? That Emelie was always running in to the director's office. Of course Tilda knew that Emelie had a brother who was a capitalist? Emelie was in charge of the exclusive packaging department, while Tilda, who was older and more experienced, had to muck around in ink bottling. It was unfair—and everyone thought Tilda was crazy to let herself be pushed to the side without uttering a protest. Tilda who was so skilled, who had been there for so long...

Hanna had wormed her way into Tilda, filled her with discontent. Gradually Tilda began to realize how she had been misunderstood and passed over. She accepted Hanna's compliments gratefully; they were soothing. The capable and dedicated employee had become consumed by the intrigue. At the same time Tilda could not resist stating that the flatterer was an incompetent slut who wanted to talk but not work. Emelie had made sure to get rid of the Strömgren woman. Why should Tilda be thankful and accept someone who wasn't good enough for Emelie?

Hanna's flattery had made Tilda feel unusually skillful and overlooked. But at the same time as Hanna sowed envy toward Emelie, she also brought about her own dismissal. When Tilda really saw how clever and dutiful she herself was, she went to the factory director and

made him fire Hanna. She could not be held responsible for having
such an incompetent coworker. And Hanna had to leave, believing
that her dismissal was Emelie's doing.

When the strike broke out, Tilda stayed on the job, wanting to show
that she felt solidarity with the company, that she was an under-appre-
ciated faithful servant. It was a calm period; there wasn't much to do
when no goods were being produced. The director was around the
workplace quite a bit, and Tilda had opportunities to speak with him.
Melinder said a few friendly words and Tilda lapped them up. Yes, it
was just. She was worth the praise. She had not run off and gone on
strike needlessly, like others who wanted to be liked by everybody.

She did not believe she had taken any risk by working. Good God,
those who were striking must have understood that a supervisor was
not an ordinary worker.

Now it seemed that they apparently had not understood. The fault
must be Emelie's, the one who had been a supervisor and set an example that bosses could strike too.

Fat Tilda felt like a martyr. In her faithfulness she had brought
upon herself her coworkers' displeasure. But they looked up to the one
who had evaded her duties; it was Emelie here and Emelie there.
When they needed advice and instructions they went to Emelie. And
if Tilda wondered why she who was supervisor didn't get asked they
answered: we ask someone who knows how.

If they had not been afraid of being fired, they would surely have
been even more insolent, calling expletives after her. That much they
did not dare do—and if they had she would certainly have gone to the
director. But they whispered and giggled, talked about her behind her
back. They were careful not to talk to her, gave barely a word in reply
when she spoke to them in a friendly manner.

The most difficult and dangerous part was that Tilda was not as
established in her job as those she had to lead. A few times she had
managed to give the wrong instructions and a couple of the most
spiteful shrews had sat there and destroyed a whole parcel of paper and

stickers instead of pointing out her mistake. It wasn't any better when Emelie sometimes asked if they were really supposed to do what Tilda had said. That impertinence was hidden behind a mask of harmlessness! She would become enraged, scream: "I'm the one who decides here! Remember that! Keep quiet and do as I say!"

Right after that, when she had calmed down, she might be obliged to change her instructions anyway, tell them to do as they had done before.

Tilda, who had earlier exploded in roars of happy laughter, now exploded in roars of anger. Insecurity and the feeling of hostility scared her, fear brought out anger. Rage was something external, a barking watchdog who sat outside the house where fear hid itself and cried over its inadequacy. The sought-after appointment as supervisor for the exclusive packaging department gave none of the joy she had anticipated. At times she thought of going to see the director and asking him to move her back to ink bottling. But she understood that it would never be the same as before there either. If she was going to have peace she had to totally conquer her opponents—or flee. She kept watch over Emelie, hoped to catch her at something that would give the director a reason to fire her most dangerous opponent, the one who had to be defeated first.

Emelie kept still, tried to mind her own business. Of course she liked the signs of friendship and loyalty she received, thought it was nice to hear that her colleagues wanted her back as supervisor. Yet she tried to calm them. It was impossible; the director had made up his mind. Now they had to do the best they could, otherwise they only risked being fired.

Though it was hard. Tilda did not tolerate any interference, wanted to be the one who decided things entirely. Sometimes though, Emelie had to speak up: things couldn't be done that way. But it was so unpleasant each time that more and more often she kept silent and worked following Tilda's orders, even when it meant that the work would get muddled up and take longer than necessary.

When the season was in full swing, it became even clearer that packaging couldn't keep up like it used to. The orders that were not filled began to pile up, customers complained about late deliveries and threatened to switch to the competitors. Tilda was called in to the factory director's office and came out red-eyed and scolded them for being lazy. Overtime work began earlier and became more intensive than before, but nothing seemed to help.

Emelie knew: more than routine work was necessary if the packaging department was going to keep up. Some amount of joy and good will was needed, of solidarity and common work spirit— everything that was no longer there. Now many were of the opinion that good work results would only place Scabby Tilda, the traitor, in a good light. More or less consciously they sabotaged her, laughing maliciously when she was called into the factory director's office to clear things up.

They didn't grudge her that.

People talked more than usual that winter. Emelie heard the whispers. She did not say very much herself, a habit left over from when she was supervisor. She listened to what they said sometimes, drifting off into her own thoughts in between. She worked mechanically; it was good to think during this time, talk too if it were called for.

One of the girls knew someone who in their turn knew the coalman who had discovered the poor murdered cashier at Gerell's exchange agency on Malmtorgsgatan. The deliveryman had entered the office and found the woman on the floor in front of the counter, bathed in blood. The door to the safe was standing open. And the murderer had been living at the Temperance Hotel on Bryggargatan, but hurried to take the Number One boat to Vaxholm to his father's cottage in the archipelago.

A steelyard had been the murder weapon. And the murderer's name was Ander.

Ander... Emelie had heard the name before. From her memory appeared the picture of a dream city, towers and minarets. It was so long ago, the big exhibition. When the director had been new in his post and scared the old Melinder by hiring a space at the exhibition. Emelie had sat there and wrapped soaps. At that time she had had the director's trust. Her position of honor at the exhibition had later led to her becoming supervisor.

There, at the exhibition, a scandal had occurred. A waiter named Ander, who worked for restaurant keeper Svanfeldt at his main restaurant, had served batch mixtures of drinks as unmixed and had poured low-grade cognac into fancy bottles.

Now the cheat had become a murderer, killing an unfortunate girl.

He had stood there cold and unfeeling before the murder victim's body when he was taken to the morgue, whispered one of the girls.

And Emelie's thoughts ran onward, to death. She had also stood before a dead person, only a few days ago. Matilda had departed. She had been in such pain, lain in bed for so long. It was merciful that it had happened. But it was hard on poor Thumbs; he would be all alone now. Two of his sons were gone too. Rudolf who had emigrated, Mikael who never got in touch. And Knut had his large family.

Matilda had been something of a mother for them all, the years after Mama died, when they had to live in the house on Åsöberget. She had never made much of a stir, was just there as someone quiet and secure in the background, behind the lively Thumbs who drew all the attention to himself.

Now Thumbs was not so lively anymore. Old and tired, he had moved in with a workmate in one of the wooden shanties on Kocksgatan.

The girls beside her were still telling gruesome stories. Now they had gone on to all those horror films, *In the Pirate's Lair* and *Buried Alive* and whatever else they were called. Names like Oriental and Gothic and Tip-Top were mentioned, the cinemagraphic theaters.

But Emelie was thinking of Bärta, in hopes that they would find a place to live for her and her children, and gain a little more space at home. Now it was necessary for something to happen, before Jenny had the child she was expecting. Jenny was still able to travel and perform. When she came home she would take the time to go from house to house and inquire she had said. Jenny would certainly not give up before she had found something.

Emelie smiled at the thought of Jenny, the enthusiastic and lively Jenny.

Wasn't it a little lighter than usual outside the windows, in the narrow courtyard?

Spring was surely on its way.

In the spring Beda would be done with school. If it had been like before, during the good times, then Emelie might have dared talk to the factory director. Told him how things were, what kind of girl she was. Beda could probably manage some of the simpler tasks. And Emelie could have watched over her a little, talked to her workmates, explained things to them. If... But now this was impossible of course.

But it was surely a little lighter out, a little closer to spring.

When the workday was finished she hung up her large apron, made herself ready for the long walk home. She was seldom among the first to leave; it was her habit to look over her work and make sure she had everything ready for the next day.

She came out into the courtyard, saw a lonely little figure with a large shovel, a boy who stood in the light of the courtyard lamp and cleared snow. Only in play, it was the director's son after all.

"Look!" he said, "Look how it's running."

He had dug a canal in the snow and snowmelt was flowing across the sloping courtyard.

"It's enormous," she said. "And isn't that a boat coming?"

A wooden chip lay in the snow and she placed it on the water. It moved with the stream.

"A big boat," said the boy.

The chip managed to bypass the shallows and jutting out points, gliding onward toward the cesspool.

The boy shouted for joy.

She had to laugh at his excitement.

She waved to the boy. A dark shadow hastily pulled back from the window in the floor above. The director? Maybe he didn't want her talking to the boy, not now after the strike.

She came out on Badstugatan, disappearing into the streams of people, a gray shadow among shadows. The smile and the presentiment of spring had disappeared as well. The evening felt cold, indeed life did. It had been so different before the strike, so much easier.

Melinder stayed standing by the side of the window. He had seen Emelie talking and laughing with the boy.

There was something a little different about that woman. He had believed in her, relied on her. She was so well informed about everything that concerned the department. He had been able to confer with her, take her advice at times. A real difference from that fat one now. She seemed muddleheaded and when she came to talk to him it was only tattling and complaining he got from her. He heard from her a number of complaints against Emelie as well.

He could not really forgive Emelie for striking. When she had chosen sides she had not chosen his side. She had to be made to feel that she had behaved wrongly, that she had disappointed him. It wasn't the principle, it was something else: perhaps wounded self-esteem, bitterness. He had believed in her—but she had apparently not believed in him.

It was too bad things had gone the way they had gone. That Tilda was truthfully not much to have in the way of supervisor. But to change the arrangements would be like giving in, as if to say he was sorry. And he could not do that in any case.

He opened the window, called to the boy to come up.

But things could not go on this way. Packaging had to run smoothly. It was impossible to cram more people in the already crowded workrooms. They had managed before, when Emelie was in charge. The work had not expanded since then, unfortunately.

He shut the window, felt irritated.

She could laugh! But he had to worry over the difficulties, left in the lurch. Apparently she did not care a bit.

SPRING BRIGHTENS

The winter after the long strike had grown dark and dreary. Many still were unemployed; it took a while before the lockout was settled. But even those who had work had worries; old debts had to be paid, pawn tickets redeemed, as much as possible restored.

When spring finally arrived it felt lighter than other springs, more longed for. People could begin to hope for normal times again. Gradually at least some of the wounds after the big battle would surely heal. And some of it could be forgotten, forgiven.

The big subject of conversation that spring was Hinke Bergegren's lecture, Love without Children, which time after time was repeated to a packed Auditorium A in the People's Hall. Bergegren had once again caused violent debate and flaming protests. Parliamentary representatives spoke in favor of a new law that would forbid all propaganda for birth control. And Hinke answered that a law that would defend people's rabbit-like procreation should be called by its proper name: the rabbit law. He himself invited them to membership in the Society for Humanitarian Procreation.

Emelie could not help hearing a lot of this talk even if she thought that people should not speak about these things. She had mistrusted that man Bergegren ever since Gunnar had been part of the Young Socialists movement. Wasn't he out to get attention again?

Still she could feel some understanding for what she heard. She had often thought that it was a bad situation with all these kids milling around the houses of the poor. No one had time and energy to watch them. Those who were born unwanted died when they were small. Neglected, hungry, sick. Without love.

Bärta's children... they did not receive the care they should. If they had continued to live with her she would have been troubled at the thought that Gunnar and Jenny and her children did not have a home to flourish in. Now she would have to feel like she had pushed Bärta's children away.

Of course it had become neat and pleasant at home since Bärta had moved. So calm, so tidy. And the children came and ate; they only lived a few blocks away, in a little room with an iron stove, which Jenny had managed to find. Jenny was good and took care of the boys' clothes, the girls took care of their own things quite well themselves. But when evening came Beda and the little boys had to go to their own home. They disappeared, without anyone able to keep track of them. Beda and Bengt probably went home properly, but Erik was harder to keep in line, he preferred to hang out in the streets.

And in the room with the iron stove Bärta sat and tippled with Johan's old buddies. Sometimes one of them slept over as well. It could be dangerous for the girls. That was no place for children to live. Now Emelie had no way at all to influence Bärta any longer; now Bärta had her own place and did what she wanted.

It was all so difficult. However Emelie handled it she felt the blame. Should not have let them go, had to do it.

Maybe he wasn't so wrong, that Bergegren. It was probably better to have love without children than to have children without love.

As in Jenny's case. She felt no love for her Julius. But she was expecting a child with him. And they were married, without living together. It was a strange wedding they had. They had gone to see a minister together with some witnesses from their actors' troupe. Then they had eaten supper at the Hasselbacken Restaurant and Jenny had stayed at her husband's apartment overnight.

From time to time she still went to spend the night with him. He had to have some small pleasure from having a wife to provide for, she would say.

No, it was something incomprehensible. Jenny took it all so lightly, as if she were playacting then as well.

Rustling of paper, whispering and giggles, Tilda giving out a bellow, thumping from the machine in the room next door. Everything blended together to form the sounds of everyday. But outside the small windows facing the narrow courtyard it grew ever lighter.

Spring had arrived. Everything would take care of itself.

Often when Emelie came home in the evening Thumbs would be sitting in the kitchen and talking to the children. He always looked a little surprised when she came in: Was it already so late? He did not want to sit in their way. And it was ridiculous that he ate at Emelie's so often. But it was not difficult to talk him into it, he was glad to stay.

Of course he liked it on Kocksgatan, in the room he shared with an old comrade from the harbor. But Thumbs belonged to those who liked to talk and get a reply to what he said. His friend was the quiet type, worked days in the harbor and in the evening he wanted to sleep.

Thumbs liked to joke with Jenny, she gave quick and caustic answers and he enjoyed it. But if she didn't have time he satisfied himself with the children's company. And they listened delightedly; Thumbs knew how to tell stories. About what it used to be like in the world, about Maj's grandfather who had been his good friend.

Jenny listened to Thumbs' stories too sometimes. She didn't think she really recognized Henning in Thumbs' stories. Olof and Emelie had never described their father this way. As a real freedom fighter...

Emelie shook her head when she heard the stories. Thumbs shouldn't put so many ideas in the children's heads.

But Thumbs went on recounting. And in the spring's light there was the image of a young newcomer to town, an idealistic portrait, a Henning who had never existed but took shape in the mixture of reality and dream in the stories.

Fat Tilda was sick for a few weeks. A message came from the factory director that Emelie should step in and take responsibility for packaging during this period. She let the work continue as Tilda wanted, to introduce changes for a short time would only lead to conflict and quarrels when Tilda got back.

A change was noticeable, nonetheless. When Tilda was away along with the irritation with her, it was as if the work spirit returned. After all the chatter and intermittent idleness, they suddenly felt a longing to really dig in, push their limits. The bickering quieted down, they didn't have time for that. It was as if a fresh spring breeze had been let into the previously stale room. They urged each other on, sometimes laughing without cause. Tilda's absence gave a feeling of freedom and pleasure in work.

They cleaned the place up. Old orders that had sat there and waited a long time were able to be sent off. The office clerks who took care of billing had to really get to work again.

One day the director sent for Emelie.

She had not been in his office since the day they resumed work after the strike.

There had been talk that Tilda would return the following week. It wasn't far-fetched that Tilda had said something about not wanting Emelie in her department. Tilda had threatened many times that there had to be a change. She had gotten it into her head that Emelie set the other women against her, got them to sabotage the work. If Tilda had said something to that effect to the director...

She knocked on the door, a timid little knock.

"Come in," he shouted, and the raised voice was like a confirmation. He was mad now, intended to fight.

But he pointed to the chair. She hesitated.

"Sit down," he said. And she sank down on the outer edge of the chair.

He seemed tired.

"It can't go on like this," he said. "There has to be a change."

She remained silent.

"If I could only understand why Emelie went on strike..."

I have to answer, she thought, must make him understand. He mustn't believe that it was aimed at him.

He saw her lips move but he waved, fending her off.

"It doesn't matter now," he said. "Done is done. You can't just think about the past. The important thing is that it's all wrong as we have it today and we have to make accommodations so it will go better in the future."

"Tilda Nyman has complained," he said. "She is of the opinion that Emelie is setting the other women against her. Is this true?"

Now she felt the tears but also wrath.

She stood up, looked at him when she spoke.

"No," she said. "It's not true. I have gone so far as to say that they should do just as Tilda says even when it's crazy. But still, when it's too completely crazy, I have had to ask if we couldn't do things like we usually do since it's faster that way."

"Sit down," he said again. And she sat down, a little more confident now, as if nothing could have an effect on her in the same way any longer.

"I have received reports." He leafed through papers, read a few figures, looked up: "A remarkable change has occurred these last days. Why do you all have time to do so much more when Nyman is away?"

He did not wait for her reply.

"Tilda Nyman has resigned from her job," he said. "Of her own accord."

They sat quietly. And Emelie had to feel sorry for Tilda. At one time they had been such good friends, had kept each other company walking home to Söder at the end of work. Whose fault was it that everything had changed? Did she herself bear any guilt that it had gone the way it had gone?

"It's probably best that it happened," he said. "Otherwise I would have been obliged to move her. I might as well admit that I made a mistake, took a person who was not experienced enough in the work she had to lead."

Emelie looked at him, saw how much he disliked saying this. But precisely for this reason she had to like him, he was honest even if it cost him something.

"So Emelie understands..." he said. "It will have to be as it was before. We will forget that whole terrible story. Take care of the department and make sure it becomes as efficient as it was before. And we will take a look at your salary as well."

She almost ran back. The women around the table ceased their work for a moment, looked at her.

"I'm treating everyone to coffee during break today," she said.

The pressure had been released. Of course it felt good to be rid of Scabby Tilda. But the most important thing was to get to end the battle itself, the constant opposition, everything that had poisoned their everyday life.

Someone opened the window onto the courtyard. The air felt mild, it was really true that spring had arrived.

MEETING WITH
THE PAST

The workday was over. On the street the clamor and noise was laid to rest, the light had taken on evening's softer, milder aspect. But it would still be several hours before the lamps were lit in the many small cigarette shops along Drottninggatan.

August Bodin stood at his window, saw how the streams of people dried up. They tried to get out and away. He had his family out at their summer house on Stora Essingen Island, but did not travel out there every evening himself. Ida had company anyway; her mother was with them in the country. His mother-in-law had become a widow last spring when old Henrik Wide had died, almost eighty-five years old. Ida's mother was considerably younger, not yet seventy.

August had a number of projects underway, work associates he was to meet. Someone who ran his own business could never take a break. It was important to always be on hand, snap up anything new. But he was not one of the ones who were too hasty; others had to try it out. When they had figured it out he would follow.

More and more, natural stone was being used in facades now. And tile, handmade. He was going to meet with a representative from the tileworks in Hälsingborg this evening. He had also begun to think about the possibility of working with whole framework constructions of reinforced concrete. They had done that at Myrsted and Stern's construction sights on the not yet completed Kungsgatan. The method undeniably gave a lot of advantages—once you had gotten the beams on the girders you had room to move around when it was time to build the walls.

He saw and listened, learned.

Others looked for what was called modern, chased after the trends and wanted to create sensations with their buildings. Everyday when he walked home he had the chance to see the large building being put up on Strandvägen 7. Oriel window after oriel window, surely a record on that street. And the roof—an enormous waste. They would have had room for more stories instead of that gigantic roof that was only made for show.

No, such was not his style. His strength was moderation and good sense. A certain dignity. Whatever he built would be well built, a solid building for a solid client. Honest work, genuine handicraft. Perhaps a little unexciting, preferably so. Those who were in search of whatever was in vogue would find nothing of interest in what August Bodin was doing. Respectability did not interest them.

Respectable. It was a word he gladly used, that he also would be glad to have people use regarding himself.

He had grown up in a poor home. There had been a lot of things that were hardly spoken of among "better people:" tuberculosis, unemployment, poverty. But to his impoverished parents' honor, it was still a question of respectable poverty, without lice, drunkenness or adultery.

Still, he had hidden his past from the people he had met later in life. Not because he was ashamed of what once had been his. On the contrary. At home among his family he willingly spoke of his impoverished childhood. It was good for his children to hear how their father had lived, that everything they were surrounded by was not just a matter of course. But it was nobody's business outside of the family. To them he was one of the Bodins, one in a chain of men who had created and carried on today's reputable company.

It might be time to go now, take the opportunity for a walk through the city. It was so calm and peaceful out now. Hardly a person to be seen from the window, only a decrepit drunken woman standing and loitering in a doorway across the street.

He fetched his hat and coat, took his walking stick. He stopped a minute in front of the large map in the front room. Had the right time come? Maybe it would be wise to buy land in the outlying areas now, if it wasn't already too late. A proposal had been made that the local railroad lines should connect the suburbs with the city. A streetcar line had been extended as far as Sundbyberg. A new residential suburb was to be built north of Karlbergsvägen. There were still those who had not noticed what was happening, how the city was growing. It was imaginable that something could be bought cheap, built up when the right time came. One evening he would travel around and look. But one should not invest too much either, not tie up too great sums.

Bodin's had to maintain its reputation: a safe company, good customers.

He closed the door, tested the lock. Walked slowly down the stairs, secure, smiling calmly.

The smile was still on his face when he stepped out of the doorway to the street. The sun shone in from the cross street, running west. He stood blinded a moment, waiting for his eyes to adjust.

"Building contractor! Building contractor!"

Someone was calling. He saw who it was: the drunken woman he had noticed from the window. He hurried on, wanting to pretend that he hadn't heard anything. Sometimes it happened that he was accosted by one of the old mortar girls who had been on his construction sites early on. It must be one of them. Of course he could give her a coin—but he didn't like to have to stand and talk. Somebody might see him, wonder what building contractor Bodin could have to do with a person like that. Those who had nothing to do with this environment could have no idea of how many strange figures one encountered in such a company over the course of the years.

She seemed not to give up, came staggering after him.

"Doesn't the building contractor recognize me?"

She was slurring, rocking from side to side where she stood. Her hair hung straggling from under her hat, which had probably fallen in the street many times. Her dark skirt was stained and her blouse was missing some buttons. Her whole being was an image of ruin and misery.

And despite everything there was something that he recognized, a shadow or perhaps a ghost from the past. He felt a shudder of fear mixed with worry.

"No," he said and only knew that he wanted to leave again.

"It's Bärta," she slurred. "Bärta who lived at your mama's once."

The window. Suddenly he remembered a winter night over twenty years ago, how they had stood here on the street and carefully made sure that the light was out inside the windows, that no one was left inside the office. Like thieves they had sneaked in, he and Bärta. To the velvet sofa that had been new then but long since discarded. He had not wanted to keep that sofa, felt it reminded him all too much of a disaster, of something that must be forgotten forever.

And now she was standing here.

"I only meant to ask for a coin. Work has been scarce for me for a while," she whined, and came so close that he shrank back because of all the fumes that enveloped her.

He did not know how quickly he could find his wallet; his hands were shaking as he searched. He wanted to get hold of a five but didn't have less than a ten. He handed it to her.

She grew almost speechless with joy. For a moment he was afraid she would throw her arms around his neck.

"Thank you, kind, sweet building contractor," she said. "I will never forget this."

He half ran away from there, against all his principles.

Never forget. Yes, forget, forget, let everything be forgotten. Don't remember me, never come back.

He kept quiet and ran.

She was still calling: "Thank you, thank you, kind building master!"

Gradually the shock began to wear off. He slowed his steps, panting. He didn't dare look at his image in the shop windows, he probably did not look like the respectable building contractor Bodin anymore.

What if someone had seen them, if someone had guessed the connection? What a great story to gossip about.

Bärta. The girl he thought about from time to time, happy and rather plump, not exactly beautiful—but still really nice. And now this horrible woman, bloated and babbling. It was unbelievable.

The thing that scared him the most was the thought that he could have had a child with her. She had not said anything about her son. The boy was the chimneysweep's, must be. Hadn't Emelie said that this was so?

He had worried needlessly. But now he regretted that he had not set a condition on his gift just now: that she was never to come back. Why hadn't he said anything instead of just running away?

Now he would be continually threatened by the past. It was harsh—a punishment that did not stand in proportion to the crime. He had lain with her, of course. But that was more than twenty years ago and he had been so lonely and miserable... Besides, he had actually been seduced. She had offered herself to him; she had been unemployed then and needed money.

Others had a lot of complications with women even though they were married; he had never been unfaithful to Ida. He had tried to live a clean and upright life. And then this had happened.

But if it was really true that he was father to the boy that person would have naturally said it now, to get more money. So that subject he did not have to worry about at least. He began to think of what to say if she started to come up to the office. An old mortar girl who had fastened onto him, an alcoholic wreck they should not let into his office. They would have to say he was on a long business trip.

Now he felt the danger, now he had to look sharp, stay out of the way.

It wasn't going to be easy to sit and discuss tiles this evening. But it was too late to cancel. He would walk slowly through the streets, calm down, comfort himself.

Far away lay the past, the people he had been close to but lost sight of. He could almost romanticize the past sometimes when he told the children about it. Now it showed an ugly and terrible face. He had to push it back again, not let himself be caught. Maybe she would never come again.

But like a nightmare she remained, haunting his thoughts, troubling and unsettling.

Across all the years there had been a barrier, something that had prevented Bärta from looking up August. He should not suffer because of her. It was she who had come to him and not he to her. That there could ever be anything lasting between her and August had never been her belief; they belonged in all too different worlds. That was why she had decided when she met Johan: I will have him—that way she found a father for the child she had conceived with August.

It had been practical, everything had been resolved. And she had liked Johan as well, in another way from August, of course. Maybe the way poor people like each other. They had hit each other and quarreled. She had never been afraid of him; she had been the stronger one. They had drunk together and when Johan was young he had been a real guy, despite everything. He had not been more difficult than most guys. Though tough on the kids, so tough that she had finally left him.

That thing with August had been her pride. No one had found out the story, she had kept her secret. Well, she had told the truth to Emelie during the difficult period when Johan had been out traveling as an apprentice and not been able to send any money home.

Emelie had taken care of August's son. She had helped in other ways also. It had been for August's sake. Emelie had paid for what August was responsible for.

But August had been spared. Bärta had not asked him for a penny. She had borne the burden alone. Well, there had been Emelie, of course… But still: she had kept it to herself, not bothered him.

Now she had been without work for a while. She had gone through whatever the children had been able to pool together. Nothing was enough, her thirst was too great.

Finally she had not been able to resist any longer. The barrier that had held during all these years was suddenly so easy to lift. Only a few words.

And the earnings had been beyond all expectations. He had given her ten kronor, without further ado.

When she sat bent over her beer bottle and glass she felt a satisfaction mixed with nausea. She had revealed her miserable condition to August. Done was done. And this meant that it could be done again. He would give her more money, to be rid of her. And she had not used the most effective means of exerting pressure yet: Gunnar.

A FUGITIVE TRAPPED

People's capacity and strength seemed boundless, the wheel of progress rolled steadily forward. During the strike some gravel had gotten into the machinery, but now the voyage continued toward a new and better world that awaited.

The city began to look more and more like a Major city; over the last sixty years its population had more than quadrupled. More and more shining sheet metal automobiles rolled proudly chugging through the streets where previously horse-drawn wagons had rattled past. Baron Cederström made a series of jubilant ascents with his aeroplane over the crowds of people on Ladugårdslandet. Large palaces and schools were built. The modern steel and concrete department store, Sidenhuset, was completed, as were the new police headquarters and Östra Secondary School. Regeringsgatan and Malmskillnadsgatan were laid out on imposing viaducts across the not yet finished Kungsgatan. Meadows and fields on the outskirts of town were transformed into new suburbs; trucks with rows of wooden benches on their platforms transported the suburban pioneers to and from their workplaces in the inner city. A Swedish film production company was begun. A series of films were shot with the era when Sweden was a great power as the theme. And when Ander the murderer lost his head, it was not with the primitive broadaxe, but with a new and ingenious guillotine.

So many new things came along, replacing the old. On Söder, the Lindgrenska Ragged School for Delinquent Boys was closed. On Skeppsholmen the old bathhouse for women closed its doors. On Nybergsgränd on Östermalm the last shabby, dilapidated houses were torn down for new construction that was going to be carried out by the Bodin firm.

Everywhere work was once again underway. The year after the difficult strike had to be seen as a good year.

But August Bodin felt no joy or pride. Of course he was a part of the new development; business went on as usual, opportunities grew. But for him everything happened in the shadow of his fear, the happiness of the present disappeared in the face of his worry over the past.

She came again.

In vain he tried to flee. She kept watch for him patiently. To not be discovered he was forced to remain at the office until all the employees had left. He sat there like an idle prisoner while the precious time passed, all too wrought up to be able to work.

When he had given her money the last few times it had happened with the promise that she would not come back. Now he knew that it wasn't worth extracting any promises from her. He would never be free of her anymore.

He looked cautiously out the window. She had not moved. Today he would have to force himself to attain some result, he could not give up. He would have to threaten her with the police if nothing else helped. Only luck had saved him from being found out. At any time an acquaintance could catch sight of them together, the gossip would begin.

This time he would not try to escape. It did not pay off either. Even if she was drunk and looked like she was half asleep where she stood. She would still notice him when he came, begin to shout if he did not stop. That dreadful person. He could not think of her as Bärta, more like a monster who had swallowed up the Bärta he had once known. And who now threatened to swallow him up.

He got his hat and coat, stood a moment in front of the mirror— as if he had to rehearse the dismissive face he would affect when she approached him. He went to the window again. Now she was gone. Had she given up, guessed his resolve?

She was standing in the entryway.

"I had thought of going up to see if the building contractor was still there."

She gave him a friendly smile. Her expression and tone of voice indicated that she felt herself a welcome visitor.

"But I have made it clear, I don't want to have you running in and out of here! We had agreed on that, you made a promise."

But now it was the rent... She was obliged, for the childrens' sake. She couldn't let them end up in the street. The landlord would not wait and she had been sick and couldn't work.

She smiled, undeterred and used to this, conscious that her words actually lacked meaning. What did he care if the money was needed for rent or drink, he didn't pay in order to help, he paid to get out of it. Old lies worked as well as new.

He knew also that it wasn't worth pointing out that he had already paid that rent. But still he said, "But I gave it to you last time."

No, that was for the milk store. If she had said rent that time then she had been wrong. But he had probably misunderstood or remembered wrong.

In any case, this had to end now, he said, and tried to be decisive. There is no point in coming back. If I am not left alone I will report you to the police.

She looked up. The smile that had just been on her face returned. It frightened him more than words. What did she think was so funny? What did she really want?

"The building contractor shouldn't get carried away," she said as a kindly reprimand. "The police will probably also understand that I need a little help. I who have had responsibility for the boy all these years."

"The boy?"

"Yes, of course it was the building contractor... he certainly remembers. Up there in the office many years ago. It didn't happen only once. And so things happened the way they happened. Emelie has surely told you?"

"It's not true," he exclaimed violently without daring to look at her. "The boy was born long after Bärta got married."

"So... the building contractor has worked things out in any case. But Johan was not the father of the child. And he knew, you can depend on that. He couldn't bear the boy. He would have beat him to death if Emelie had not taken in the child."

"Before this I had him of course for many years," she added. "August shouldn't believe that Emelie bore all the expenses and care-giving." Bärta was clear about this, even if her thoughts and words ran adrift in a fog of alcohol.

"Johan was out traveling as an apprentice at the time. It was not easy, I can tell you. Poor and alone as I was, without an öre of support."

She became very affected by her tale and began to sob. But he remained hard. Did not want to believe her.

Though his tone was no longer so assured. He knew all too well: it might be so.

"Ask Emelie!" she urged him.

Now he couldn't take any more, wanted to hurry away despite all his resolutions. But she grabbed his coat.

"A little money, all the same…"

He produced a few kronor.

"If this is true as Bärta says… Then I will see to it that some com-pensation is paid. But it will happen through Emelie. I will not lay down one öre in this manner. And remember that I cannot be forced, that nothing can be proven. If Bärta comes here again I will go to the police—and blackmail is severely punished."

She intended to reply with something, did not want the money to be paid through Emelie. But he managed to tear himself loose and ran away.

Fortunately they were not expecting him at home; he had a meet-ing. He would be spared being at home with his troubles, be spared looking in their eyes.

He walked through the cold streets, was chilled by the cold wind. Shut out, expelled. Had he not always been? As a boy he had walked like this through the streets, felt like his childhood world of poverty viewed him as a traitor, while his adoptive parents' world viewed him as an upstart and interloper. When he had felt unhappy and alone he had had his trysts with Bärta. Later on everything changed; he grew into his new environment, much of it thanks to Ida. Now he would feel like he had been false to Ida. As he had been false to the son Emelie had to take all the responsibility for.

Behind the curtains in the windows the evening lamps shone from warm and cozy homes. There were happy people there, people with a sense of community. As for himself, he wondered if he would dare go home again. The secret must certainly show on his face. As soon as Ida saw him she would know.

Of course he intended to tell her everything. One thing was still lucky for him: he could hope that she would understand. But first he had to talk to Emelie. Whatever he told Ida would have to be true. And there was still a small possibility that Bärta had lied. He remembered her smile. Did she smile because she was fooling him and was so sure she would succeed?

He had to talk to Emelie as quickly as possible.

It did not happen very often that Emelie received a letter. Now one was standing there, leaning on the vase on the bureau, waiting for her. She read the address several times. Even if she did not really recognize the handwriting, she knew it was from August. The envelope had the Bodin company imprint on it.

He wanted to talk with her. What had happened?

She got more dressed up than usual when she went to work the next morning, worrying all day that she would get glue stains and dust on her skirt, despite the apron that protected it.

Beda had gotten a job in ink bottling. Factory director Melinder had been so kind: of course the girl could give it a try. And it went really well for her; the work was simple and her workmates had been nice and taken care of her. Beda was proud of having a job but she didn't get to keep anything of what she earned. She went around in outgrown and tattered clothing. So that it wouldn't look too bad, Emelie helped her sometimes with something new.

They kept each other company to and from work. But today Emelie had to part ways with her at Drottninggatan. She reminded the girl: she should go straight home, hurry there. And Beda nodded in assent, almost breaking into a run as she went.

Emelie opened the door. Here was where August had his office, in a fine house with a wide stairway. He came and let her in himself and she followed him into his workroom. Emelie felt unsure and out of place. August had a much finer office than factory director Melinder. And once again she had to doubt that they really were siblings, that August was the same August who had once lived together with them in the crowded room on Åsöberget.

He was troubled; she could see it.

She pulled up with a start when she heard his question. She didn't know what she should answer, what she could answer. At one time she had promised Bärta to keep silent. So instead she replied with a counter question:

"Who has told you that?"

"It was Bärta."

"Bärta?" She almost shouted it. Bärta who had kept quiet all these years, who had insisted almost savagely on keeping the secret.

"She has pursued me all summer," he said wearily. "When I didn't want to give her any more money she said that I ought to pay for her having had sole responsibility for the boy."

Emelie flared up.

"She hasn't taken care of Gunnar, not since he was little! I'm the one who has taken care of him."

"Is it for my sake?"

The question confused her. Was it really for August's sake?

"Maybe mostly for Gunnar's own sake," she answered. "Johan beat him so badly that he could not remain at home."

"But he is my son?"

"Bärta says so. And it would have been strange if Johan had been his father. If so, then Gunnar was born far too early."

He sat there defeated.

"Sometimes he can be just like August," Emelie said slowly. "Not in appearance. But in his manner. So quiet and pensive—the way August used to be, at home."

"Gunnar is a good boy," she added, more persuasively, assuringly.

"August can surely be proud of him. Now that things stand the way they do, now that Bärta has said it at last."

Proud? That's not how he felt now.

And why had he not been told anything all these years? Why?

Bärta had not wanted to. Not even Johan knew of it. He believed at first that Gunnar was his, that was why he married Bärta.

"Didn't that chimney sweep ever find out that I...?"

"No. He only found out that Gunnar was not his. I forced Bärta to tell him so Johan would let the boy go. Bärta would never have said anything to August either if she had been the way she used to be. It was a kind of pride of hers that she never said anything."

"What am I going to do?" he asked. "Good God—what am I to do?"

He leaned over the table, sank his head onto his arms. Horrified, Emelie saw that he was crying.

She would have liked to console him, calm him. But she didn't dare. She only sat there quietly and waited. Finally he lifted his head, looked at her.

"Forgive me," he said. "This has been a difficult period. But nothing gets any better by giving up."

"Does August intend to say anything to Gunnar?"

He felt ashamed. He hadn't even thought of that.

He quickly made a decision, wanted to promise before he changed his mind: he would tell him himself.

Gunnar would soon turn twenty-two. It wasn't any child he was getting as a son. And he had grown up in another environment, with other habits, other ideals. If this had happened ten years earlier he could have done something about it. At that age Gunnar would have been the same age August himself had been when the Bodins adopted him. Now it was too late.

"I want him to know who his father is," he said. "And he will be entitled to his rights when the day comes, if there is anything to inherit at that time. Ida will naturally be told of the situation. But here at the firm perhaps it is just as well that things remain the way they have been. There will just be a lot of talk otherwise. If Gunnar wants to continue his education or has any special wishes, it can be arranged. And I will see to it that he receives every possibility of advancement here."

They sat there a long time and talked. Emelie felt how some of the old closeness returned. She felt like she recognized the old August she remembered from their childhood, the boy who had been one of them. And now as then he needed her help at times.

He didn't need to worry; she would take care of Bärta. How much had he meant to give her?

If he offered Bärta a thousand kronor—did Emelie think she would keep quiet after that?

No, he shouldn't do that. Such an enormous amount of money! She would drink herself to death. And if she survived she would certainly go looking for August again as soon as the money was gone.

If August was feeling so generous... then she would like to suggest that he give Bärta one krona per week. Bärta ought to be able to get by now. Both her daughters were working and the boys were running errands and delivering papers on the side while they went to school. Emelie would make sure that Bärta received her allowance every week and she would make it clear that it would cease if Bärta bothered August anymore. Bärta knew that Emelie kept her word. Bärta would take care not to go seeking out August.

He raised it to three kronor a week and Emelie unwillingly agreed to it.

Finally he called for a hired car and insisted on driving Emelie home. She protested, it was completely unnecessary. But he got her to go with him anyway, and they drove through the town, up Götgatan, over to the pot-holed and bumpy road where she lived. It was the first time Emelie had ever ridden in an automobile and she held onto her armrest anxiously, waiting for the journey to end any moment in an accident. But everything went well.

Ida was awake when August came home, waiting for him. Wasn't it his story, his confession she was waiting for? She had noticed that something was troubling him, that something was going to come out.

And Ida understood. Understood how things had been for him and how he had felt. And of course it had been so long ago.

"There is nothing to forgive," she said. "I wasn't there, not for you."

As they lay beside each other in the darkness of their bedroom she said, "Imagine, I wondered if he was your son... Do you remember that time during the summer exhibition of ninety-seven? We met Emelie and the boy at the exhibition. When Emelie came to our house later you asked about the boy and heard who his mother was. You looked surprised, became so unsettled."

"Too bad I didn't say anything to you then! I should have told you. But I thought it was so foolish, something old and forgotten that didn't have to be brought up anew."

"And now this happened... My poor, poor August."

Everything had been easier than he had dared hope. Ida understood and forgave. Emelie would take care of Bärta. Now all that remained was to meet the boy.

I will have to ask them at the office to call in Karlsson tomorrow, he thought.

A HAPPY TIME

In the middle of February the ice began to pack together at Strömmen. The whole area between Skeppsbron and Skeppsholmen froze. For a few days the ice cover stretched as far in as Strömparterren under Norrbro where the water usually rushed freely during the coldest winters. Steamboats and ferries lay frozen fast at the quaysides. People began to go out on the ice; the most daring made their way between Karl XII Square and Strömparterren.

Jenny leaned out against the sturdy railing of Norrbro and watched those intrepid ones. They were performing, she thought, providing a show for many spectators. Another day she might have been more keenly engaged in their performance. Today she didn't really have the right spirit.

After several months of discussion back and forth they had drawn up their divorce settlement. Julius had really hoped that they would finally move in together, that he would be able to convince her to. She had tried sometimes to forget who he was, pretend that he was someone else. But it was difficult: his fat body, the smell of pomade and sweat, everything was just all too clearly Julius.

At last he had given in. He would pay for Elisabet, who was not yet one year old. Jenny did not want more. Now she wanted to begin work again, manage on her own. She had figured out how she would find somebody to mind the girl while she was out. Jenny could of course not consider any touring, but she would probably be able to take on smaller jobs in town.

She wound her boa tighter around her neck. It was time to move on; soon they would be waiting for her up at Horse-Nisse's office.

The old sign with the dancing stallion still hung outside the premises on Beridarbansgatan. Once large numbers of horses had been sold here to the streetcars and breweries; now the seventy-one-year-old former horse dealer Nilsson had gone over to a completely new line of business. He had become the owner of a chain of cinematographic theaters with the Majestic Oriental Theater at the top.

During the course of a few years, before and after the strike, the cinematographs had had trouble attracting people and therefore had expanded their programs with artists of various types. Jenny had sung in several of Horse-Nisse's theaters. Now and then she had overlapped with the little, round Anna Hofman who had been a star of the variety shows in her youth, and later director of Svea Theater and the Crystal Salon. Anna Hofman still performed, had played the role of Fia Jonsson in "The Gilded Ocarina" and sung her songs at the cinematographs during the bad years. She had married an acquaintance of Olof's, the journalist Uddgren.

And now Anna Hofman was going to make films that would be shown in Horse-Nisse's theaters. Her husband had written "Stockholm Temptations or the Adventure of a Gentleman and Lady from Norrland in the City of the Beautiful Sinner."

There were some comic minor roles that Jenny would fill perfectly. And she would be close by and well-situated during the filming also, since she would mostly take part in the indoor scenes that would be shot up on the terrace of the Moseback Theater. The story was about a farmer from Norrland who had won the lottery and come to the city to have some fun and shop. This last was not the least important part—he was to make purchases in a number of well-known stores who would pay to be in the film.

Jenny agreed to the terms gladly. For three days of work she would receive fifty kronor and that was more than she could normally make in several weeks' work. And the work was easy; in the films there were no lines to learn.

When she came up to the terrace on the first day she suspected that it was not going to be as easy as she had believed. On top of the snow-drifts they had built something that looked like an outdoor theater and set up the borrowed theater decorations on the stage floor. On this the actors were to act and give the impression that they were indoors. Jenny was to wear a rather low-cut dress.

She shivered even though she had her coat on, stood and waited for the filming to begin. The photographer and the camera had been placed on boards in the snow. A few laths had been laid across the stage floor—the actors were not to go farther than these.

The scene under the open winter sky was to represent a ballroom. Luckily the sky was clear, no snowfall would ruin the scenes. But it was cold; the winter sun could not make it up past the buildings behind the terrace.

Anna Hofman directed; they got to rehearse for a brief while with their outer clothing on. They would dance, then the door in the background would open and the farmer and his wife enter. After being doubtful and then persuaded, the old woman would allow herself to be drawn along into the whirl of her pleasure-seeking husband. And then it would end with a huge commotion. The eager old man would tumble down while dancing and pull others with him in his fall.

Someone asked for music, they would have to have music if they were to dance.

"You can't hear anything in the film anyway," the photographer said.

But a piano was already being brought out. Some musicians would be in the scene.

Then it was time. They had to throw off their coats and jackets and stand up on the dance floor. They danced frenetically to stay warm, flying around so energetically that Anna Hofman and the photographer time and again had to remind them to stay inside the laid out laths.

Would they have to do it again?

"Yeah, right," said the photographer. "Film costs a lot of money."

The farmer couple tumbled in. Now the others were to back off and give the actors in the main roles center stage, since the camera could not be turned.

And then the end of the scene: Jenny gets a shove on the backside and flies out of her partner's arms, up into the air, and bang, down onto the floor. The fall was almost too great; she stood up sore and stiff.

"That didn't work," the photographer said. "You jumped too high, I didn't get your face."

They had to reshoot the last part, the collision had to take place a little more inside the stage and Jenny had to fall forward, toward the camera. And there she sat again, with an aching backside, and in a completely natural way was able to make a face expressing just what she thought and felt about the clumsy farmer.

Finally they got to put their coats back on.

Despite everything it had been fun to be a part of it. Without hesitating she accepted a new offer. A young woman journalist had written a short film that she hoped would contribute money toward a stipendium for her sisters in the profession. The film would be called "Ex-King Manuel in Stockholm or She Got the Job!" and tell the story of job-seeking young woman journalists. A chief editor was putting the ladies to the test—the objective was to see who could capture and interview the ex-king who was visiting the city incognito. The actors were a few newspaper women, among them the author. For Jenny it was a question of putting a colorful touch on some of the small roles.

This time they did not dare use an open-air stage; the weather was too unreliable. They had rented a dance floor out in Sickla Park. They had to ride in cars as far as they could and then plow through the snow to the dance floor where the snow that had come in had to be swept off, and scenery representing the Grand Hotel's vestibule was set up.

Jenny knew what to expect this time and had put on as much clothing as possible. Luckily she also got to keep her outer clothing on. Still it got pretty cold. As long as it stayed light they continued filming and there was no possibility of lighting a fire.

But she liked it. There were happy moments when they took breaks and drank coffee from their thermoses. It was stimulating to meet the young women journalists and Jenny almost felt like she was one of them.

During the last day of filming it grew dark before they had time to pack up the camera and equipment and the last car could head toward town. When they approached the customs house they saw the glow of the flames. Up on the mount at Klippans Berg the old barn was burning where the tradesman Amilon had been murdered.

The films were a real success. The one about the farmer from Norrland was shown at the exclusive Oriental Theater and attracted an audience for a couple of weeks. The journalist film ran for a week at the Apollo Theater on Hamngatsbacken. The most important thing for Jenny was the fact the she had new and good connections and been promised more work. Horse-Nisse and Anna Hofman had plans for more films and there was always a need for small comic effects, the humorous figures in the background. That was where Jenny belonged, not in the center of the film where they wanted to feature famous actors or newly discovered beautiful heroes and heroines.

Jenny might feel young and unsure, inexperienced as an actress. Still, she had begun to be something of a veteran, had been performing for a good number of years now.

She turned thirty. Such a milestone gave a reason for celebration even if she thought it was probably best for people to forget that she had grown so old. Her closest friends and relatives gathered for a coffee party.

They sat around the table in the room on Åsögatan. Not so many any longer since Gertrud had emigrated and Bärta moved. Thumbs came. And Hjördis stopped by; it was no longer any secret that she and Gunnar were together. Beda and the boys had stayed on after dinner; they still came and ate every day. Bärta didn't have the energy to even pretend that she belonged in their home any longer, and Tyra would often disappear for weeks at a time, returning torn, dirty and hungry—like a half-wild stray cat.

Emelie served the coffee. She had grown calmer and more assured recently, thought Jenny. It apparently meant a lot that the struggles at her workplace were over. She had Melinder's trust once again; it was as if it gave her a certain position of dignity. And then Emelie did not have the secret about Gunnar to carry around any longer. Gunnar knew who his father was now. Though they would never feel like father and son. August lived in his world and Gunnar in his. But Gunnar could feel more secure, he could always count on work and if he wanted to start his own company sometime August would help him. He had gained security, would certainly be able to marry his Hjördis soon.

Beda too had it better. Before they had often wondered how the girl would manage in life, if she would ever be able to handle a job. Things had worked out, thanks to factory director Melinder's kindness. Beda attended to her tasks in ink bottling, the work was simple and poorly paid—but still it was a giant achievement. Now she sat with the grown-ups around the table, quiet and as if alone in the din. It was as if it was kindest not to address her; the girl only grew disconcerted and anxious if anyone said anything to her.

Jenny sat and looked at the little group that had gathered together to honor her, was able to rejoice. Everything had turned out better than they had dared hope. Perhaps sometime they would remember this evening and this time as a happy time.

THE LINE

People had perceived the course of humanity, the advance of progress as a giant stairway: from the darkness of the depths up toward the light and the sun. Of course they had experienced periods of stagnation and even decline. But that the journey was still going upward and onward was something very few ever doubted.

So much could be interpreted as confirmation, evidence that the belief in advancement really was well founded.

The new voting law had meant a breakthrough for democracy; along with the number of votes grew the influence of the people on progressive reform. A first attempt at public retirement security pensions had been passed by parliament. It was true that the expenses and payments were far too small for the reform to have any real meaning, but the measures indicated a new view of society and its obligations.

And the capital city in this new society grew, acquired even more magnificent buildings and even broader streets. They were able to inaugurate the vast canyon of Kungsgatan, which cut through Brunkeberg's ridge, as well as to inaugurate Katarinavägen with its gradual climb up the steep precipice over Stadsgården wharf. The youth of the world congregated at the Olympic Games in the new romantically heraldic stadium-fortress that had been built where previously a simple recreational park had been. The number of automobiles increased without cease. Horse-drawn cabs disappeared after having their last renaissance during the summer of the Olympics when every resource had to be used.

But also opposing forces grew. Increased voting rights meant increased resources to the voters, increasingly greater demands put forward. Liberals and socialists stood opposed to the monarchy and the conservatives. The controversy surrounding the question of defense became especially heated. The demand for lowered arms costs launched Staaff's government—and blew it apart. The debate also created schisms within the Social Democratic Party. Branting had to fight many skirmishes with the youth on the extreme left who placed demands for total disarmament and called for a republic when the monarchy went too far in its eagerness to arm.

Sven Hedin issued his pamphlet, "A Word of Warning:" through their absurdity the Swedish people had lost the security that the union had given; now they were in the same situation as one hundred years earlier—with the Russians before them and the Norwegians at their back. Both were neighbors one should be on one's guard against. He evoked an image of an occupied city where the Russian main guard requisitioned Rydberg's Bar and Operakällaren Restaurant was turned into a military hospital, while the barbarians' horses were watered in Molin's Fountain behind the back of the statue of Karl XII.

One million copies of the pamphlet were distributed. The Social Democrats answered with a manifesto for disarmament and making all people brothers, and the most radical members printed an antimilitary handbook, "The Fortified Poorhouse."

Those in favor of defense started an enormous subscription for the procurement of a new armored vessel. Farmers and landowners organized a demonstration: thirty thousand rural inhabitants traveled to the capital to demonstrate for stronger defense. The king received them in the castle courtyard and gave a speech, the content of which made clear he was taking a distance from the views of the government and the Majority of the people. Fifty thousand people gathered for a counter action, a workers' demonstration which, with its red banners, marched right past the castle. They stopped instead in front of the government offices to honor Staaff's government with its demands: the will of the people alone would make decisions in their country. A split between the king and the government ensued; the liberal Staaff tendered his resignation and a right-wing government was formed.

Military defense was the big subject for debate. But many thought that stronger weapons were not enough, a strengthened morality was also needed. The licentiousness of the times worried people. It took expression in propaganda for "free love," in new dance halls and in dances such as tango and ragtime, in communal baths, in art and literature's degeneracy.

Then a line was drawn.

On June 28, 1918 in Sarajevo, the heir to the throne of the Austro-Hungarian Empire and his consort were murdered. One month later the great powers were mobilized. On the first of August world war broke out.

The agitation that had begun before the fall elections was as good as paralyzed. And despite the fact that the election then gave the opposition an increased Majority in parliament, the right-wing government remained in place. Now people were avoiding conflict and change. The opposition declared that the government could depend on the full support of a united people only if they would maintain an unbroken neutrality.

A line had been drawn across all the old issues, across party conflicts and moral bickering—and also across a suddenly antiquated and almost ridiculous faith in progress.

But it was also a dividing line: between an abruptly vanished time that now appeared almost idyllic, and the new chaotic one that had been brought in by the roaring of the cannon.

Whatever was going to happen, it was clear that the past had collapsed in a heap. Nothing would ever be as before. One might think that the old century had extended up to the time of the war, that now people were seeing the new one, which had been born too late, stepping forth.

In an instant, once self-evident authorities: moral, religious and political, disappeared in the whirl. Everything and everyone had deserted and therefore could be deserted. The socialist leaders who had so recently preached internationalism and brotherhood made themselves ready to commit fratricide in the name of the fatherland. The priests blessed the weapons.

Who was there now who would not find everything cast into doubt?

However things might go—the world that would step forth from the chaos of war would be a completely different one.

Freed of its illusions, robbed of its faith.

THE LAST SUNDAY BEFORE CHRISTMAS

Even what seems to be impossible and untenable can become routine. The war had gone on for more than two years, frozen in parallel formations.

Now the third Christmas of the war was coming. The countries that had not been directly affected by the war were also feeling an increasing war weariness. The telegrams and victories and defeats did not manage to engage them as before.

Stockholmers got a vague idea of how a large part of Europe's youth was living by seeing the trenches that had been dug at the entrance of Rosendal Castle on Djurgården. The lack of food was felt increasingly in the city. Ration cards were distributed among the poorer population, but when the women had stood in line for hours to buy up what was on their cards, they might be met with the message that the provisions they had waited for were sold out. People cursed the wholesalers—now they were earning fortunes by exporting meat and fish and butter. There began to be a shortage of wheat for bread as well. And the lack of sugar meant that housewives could not preserve jams and fruit syrups as usual. Those goods that remained rose to unheard of price levels.

The supplies diminished, the lines grew. But now they would still try to celebrate Christmas as best they could.

On the Sunday before Christmas, the last day for Christmas displays in the store windows, large streams of people thronged the streets. Alongside the most popular windows the police organized lines that advanced slowly. Children and adults crowded around to look at the tin soldiers making war in the Carpathians, or the elves sledding and sewing on Singer sewing machines. The Husqvarna shop on Norrmalmstorg had a display of "the devastation of war" in one of its small windows and "the blessings of freedom" in another. The devastation had been vented on copper pots and other household utensils, while the blessings were made up of Christmas breads and ginger snaps ready to be taken out of the oven. Long lines stood in front of the butcher's window; the onlookers had a hard time tearing themselves away from the sight of all the hams and preserves.

People were milling and pushing everywhere. A little of the irritation of everyday made itself felt now and then; they had become all too used to using their elbows during recent years. They had stood in so many lines.

A young boy made his way forward, his eyes shining under the shadow of a wide-brimmed hat. The girl hanging onto his arm laughed and whooped. The policeman in the spiked helmet looked around quickly, but saw no reason to step in. Only a guy from Söder with his flame. And in a line in front of a display window the risk of disturbance was not so great.

The girl stopped, tugged at her guy's arm. "Wait a little! Now we've lost Bengt again!"

"He's coming there."

The missing boy slowly made his way forward to them. He was big and strong and could have easily moved aside anyone who stood in his way. But he was good-humored and of a quiet disposition, would rather wait than disturb. The broad face under the cap lit up when he saw the people he was looking for.

"Is there anything to see?" he asked eagerly

"Tons of Christmas hams," answered Erik. "It just makes you hungry."

"It's getting to be time to go home," said Bengt. He was always hungry and now he barely dared glance at the goodies in the window. Emelie would not have a chance of offering them anything like that; meat and bacon were expensive and hard to get hold of.

He had said home and that's how it felt and what he meant. Home—it was home at Emelie's. It had been many years since he had lived there but the feeling was still there. Every Sunday they went there and ate dinner, the moments he looked forward to with anticipation. Not only because of the food, it was just as much the atmosphere and security he longed for. Everything that was at Emelie's. Their own room where they lived always felt cold and dismal.

Erik was not as interested in Sunday dinner. He had a completely different means of taking care of himself. He would have a suspicion where a good deal was to be made, and lightening-quick seize the opportunity. And he thought that most of what they talked about at Emelie's was uninteresting and insignificant. He found both Emelie and Gunnar tediously cautious and petty reactionaries.

But Maj's mom, Jenny, was funny, he had to admit that. If he came along and ate it was mostly for Maj and her mom's sake. Otherwise he wasn't one to bow and scrape, he could find a meal elsewhere.

Erik held onto Maj's hand, pulled her after him through the crowds of people. She in her turn held onto Bengt, did not want to lose him in the crush. She noted well enough that Erik tried to shake his brother off, wanted to be alone with her. But she was a little afraid of Erik, and also afraid of herself. It was safest to be three; if you were three then you were buddies. If you were two it could turn into something else— and she did not want to go there, at least not now. She was only sixteen, after all.

They made their way out of the crowd in front of the window, hand in hand through the throng, as if in a ring dance.

"Is there anything good showing at the Kino?" Maj asked.

But they knew that this evening there would be no movies. Maj would not be allowed to go on a Sunday evening when there was school the next day.

Maj often heard how privileged she was to get to go to school. She had to look out for herself, take advantage of her opportunities.

But Maj was not at all grateful, envied the boys who worked and earned money. And it was these boys she still hung out with, not her schoolmates.

Erik was the oldest of the boys. He was also the most unafraid, could be aggressive at times. He was always in a hurry, wanted to explore, try things out, go farther. But at the same time he was soft, not afraid to appear kind, almost sentimental. This could be a dangerous combination when he made advances.

With Bengt it was never like this. He was probably also interested in her in a new way, she realized. But he was shy; it never got to be more than that he sat a little closer to her than was necessary. And that he looked happy when she took his hand and they walked hand in hand, all three.

Söder seemed dark and silent when they came from the streets glittering with the lights of the stores. Katarina elevator's powerful iron scaffolding stood black against the black hillside. The elevator cars were small lights that were raised and lowered in the darkness. But there was no longer any black smokestack emitting sparks up high on the tower. For a while now the elevator had been run by electricity.

Behind the elevator and the big, tall buildings on Stadsgården, Katarinavägen ran in a broad stroke eastward up over the rise. And here, as if on a shelf lifted above the city and the water, the young people stopped a moment at the sturdy stone railing, and looked down. During the afternoon a gray mist had sunk over the city. There was no snow on the streets and the rooftops, but there was a white, snow-like tone in the gray fog. Now the darkness had arrived, it was cleaner, clearer—the milky mist was gone and the lights from the streets and the harbor shone as clear as sparks.

Maj stood, shielded by both boys. Like this, when they were a threesome, she felt her safety most strongly, she liked it best. It would have been scary to walk alone here in the darkness; there were so many boys from the big gangs, so many old drunks. She placed her arms around her friends.

"It is still beautiful," she said.

"Um," grunted Bengt.

But actually she had spoken to Erik, almost appealed to him. Sometimes he could at least agree with her, acknowledge what was there.

But he only spat over the railing.

When they walked farther on he took hold of her arm roughly, spoke vehemently. One day this city and this country would be conquered from within, by its own people. That day was not so far off any longer. The capitalists had thrown the world into war and were in the process of destroying themselves and each other. Their downfall would be the proletariat's victory.

Emelie had made mashed turnips. Mashed turnips with Icelandic herring—a rather strange combination, but the wartime menu was not decided by taste but by availability. They had just received herring with their ration cards. But the potatoes that they would have liked to have with herring were impossible to procure. The local dealers had incorporated their own system: those who wanted a liter of potatoes had to simultaneously buy at least three turnips. In this way Emelie had obtained a supply of turnips that were good to have now that the potatoes were completely finished.

Those who had money could get most anything. But ordinary people had to try and stand in as many lines as possible and take advantage of whatever was at a reasonable price.

In spite of its being difficult, Emelie really wanted to maintain the tradition of Sunday meals for Bärta's children. They took their places around the kitchen table. It was rather tight; there were eight of them who had to fit. Beda and the two boys, Jenny with her two daughters, Gunnar and Emelie. Tyra usually never came.

Jenny had to eat hurriedly. She had a steady engagement. A cabaret theater had opened—"The Happy Salmon"—in a building on Nytorget, and she appeared in two shows there every evening.

She dashed out at the last minute; luckily it was only a few minutes away.

There was probably nowhere in town to compare to The Happy Salmon, at least not anymore. It was a kind of reminder of the old workers' variety shows on Bännkyrkagatan where Jenny had met Olof the first time. A humble locale with low ticket prices, fifty öre. People could come to The Salmon in their work clothes. Harbor workers and factory workers went there in their blue clothing, butchers in their bloody aprons, bakers with flour-covered pants, spinning girls from the factories and bottle washers in knitted cardigans with scarves around their hair.

Jenny was something of a prima donna at the little theater. Most of the performers there were completely unknown talents and she at least had been on the scene for a number of years. A group of Danes made up part of the ensemble, among them a skinny little boy who sang and made jokes. His name was Max Hansen but he was called Little Caruso in the advertisements.

Jenny was billed as "The Real Stockholmer" and what she had to sing or say had to be done in Söder dialect. Sometimes she wondered if she would ever learn to talk properly again; it became such a habit to talk slang that she did it at home too.

At a place like The Salmon her inhibition and delight in creating odd caricatures were assets. Taking a strong lead using somewhat coarse techniques was what was called for here. And she laid it on. Saturdays and Sundays when the audience was especially easy to please, the cheering and volleys of laughter could carry her away so that she almost lost control of herself. Afterward she had to wonder: what did I actually do?

But they had laughed; she had made them forget their everyday worries for a while. And then she had fulfilled her mission. She did not have any dreams of becoming a great actress. She supported herself; she entertained those who most needed to be entertained. That had to be enough. But she would probably try to give her daughters somewhat greater opportunities. If they would only take advantage of them. Maj wasn't attending to her schoolwork, as she really ought to.

Now it was Jenny's turn.

She stretched her large mouth as close to her ears as she could and hopped on stage with flapping movements, curtsied deeply to the audience, lifted her skirts and showed her big white underpants.

"Go ahead and spank now, fellows! Today is the last Christmas display Sunday! And any more ham than this you won't see this Christmas."

TROUBLED SPRING

There was a lot that troubled people. Chicken pox had arrived; case after case was reported from every part of the country. Food shortages were felt even more acutely, supplies diminished at the same rate as prices rose. A bread card was instituted, oatmeal was obtained only with a doctor's certificate, lack of coal meant that street lighting had to be restricted.

Out in the world the war intensified. The German submarine terror increased, America stepped in. In March the revolution that had been expected in Russia for decades broke out; the czar was overthrown and imprisoned. People sensed that this was only beginning. Powerful forces had suddenly been unleashed.

Russian émigrés passed through Stockholm, revolutionaries on their way home to the revolution. One of those who came was Lenin; the Left Socialists were down at Central Station and received him.

Some of the revolutionary fervor gripped the workers in the city, in the whole land as well. The Russian uprising was welcomed in their Auditorium, which was completely filled. And on the walls of buildings and fences flyers were posted: Revolution on May 1!

In the middle of April the workers in Västervik put down their work and demonstrated outside the city's grocery stores. It was the signal. A few days later hunger demonstrations had spread like fire across the country.

Times were new—and revolted against the old. The Left Socialists had risen out of the Social Democratic Youth League. The youth formed the large party's outermost layer. Earlier the Young Socialists— as if by a centrifugal force—had been thrown out of the party. Now the Youth League had landed in the same situation, and given rise to a new and more radical party, the Left Socialists. One could guess that a third youth league, more loyal to the Social Democratic Party, would soon be built.

Now it was up to the new party to lead the streams of people. There was so much pent-up irritation, hunger and fatigue, suspicion and bitterness. And there was the knowledge of what had happened in Russia, what could happen. People blew on the embers—and they caught fire.

During previous years of unrest the military had been called in at times to put down the demonstrations. The Russians had shown that such a weapon could be twisted out of the hands of those wielding power, and even turned against them. Worker and soldier counsels had been formed in St. Petersburg and other Russian cities. Now such alliances were being formed in Sweden also.

Erik and Bengt had joined the youth club, Reveille. In the beginning they were not especially active, were among the youngest members. And Erik had other interests that took up his time. He had tried different lines of work, had difficulty being a subordinate, was not happy in boring, everyday routines. What he occupied himself with outside of work was more interesting. He had always had a certain ability for finding extra sources of income. As a boy he had sold "The Answer" during the general strike, later the Young Socialists' newspaper, "Fire." Now he had gone over to the Youth League's "Alarm Bell" and he also picked up subscribers for the Left Socialists' daily newspaper, "Politics." The Young Socialists and the Syndicalists were a little too crazy, he thought. They would never be able to have any real influence on politics, and therefore neither would they ever be able to transform society. The Left Socialists focused on a completely different way of taking power, they had plenty of practical people. Erik could very easily imagine being with them one day and taking care of some of society's many practical tasks, the kinds of things that those crazies surely despised.

Until then he made himself useful selling newspapers and small pamphlets. On the side of this more idealistic trade, he also dealt in Christmas cards, soap and coffee substitutes, razorblades and birth control. Selling was not only a means of income; he also saw it as his duty. And he felt like those who bought from him showed solidarity, not only with him, but with the movement as well. They supported a worker, avoided fattening private capital.

During this troubled spring he had a hard time taking care of his business like he usually did. There was a lot pressing on him, tempting him—demanding his participation. Now the movement needed everyone who could do something useful. Without a doubt he was one of them, had an easy time striking up conversation, was unafraid and had a persuasive way with others. People like him had a lot to do.

Maj felt the pull of the outside world from where she was forced to sit idly on the side during all the developments.

It was school that got in her way. School and home. Her mother could be convinced of this; it would have been easier if Jenny had been home evenings. So Emelie felt she had the responsibility for Maj, and it was impossible to persuade her otherwise. Emelie considered school extremely important, could not understand how Maj did not want to sit with her books every evening. The din of the streets was nothing to long for, thought Emelie. Was there anything bigger or better than being able to learn?

But everything exciting and important was happening out there, almost outside her window. And she had to sit and plod on with something that had nothing to do with life whatsoever.

She was lucky she got to see the boys on Sunday anyway. Erik had a lot to tell her now. Reveille had had a meeting on Thursday and two hundred sailors had come marching from their base on Skeppsholmen to take part. There hadn't been room enough in the club headquarters at Adolf Fredrik's Square, so they had had to stand out on the stairs. When the sailors were going to go back they had met a commander that had been sent out to get them. Then there was some excitement for a while; people were expecting an encounter. But the commander satisfied himself with setting them to a march and following them back to the garrison.

There was talk moreover of the military command placing machine guns at strategic locations around the city and that the upper class was in the process of organizing a private citizens' defense corps, as they had done during the general strike.

On Saturday morning there had been a large demonstration outside the House of Parliament. Workers from Pumpseparator and Bolinder's had marched; there must have been ten thousand people assembled outside on the open square. But... this time the extreme left had not gotten to the forefront in time. It was Branting who spoke—he had stood out on the stairs of the House of Parliament—and Hansson, the editor for the Social Democrats' paper, "Sossen," formulated their resolution. It would surely have been a more raucous go of it if the left had taken charge of the initiative.

This evening yet one more competitor for the favor of the people would be in action—the Young Socialists were holding a meeting at the People's Hall on Söder.

The boys and Maj swung by there after dinner to see if anything was happening, out by Södra Bantorget and Fatbursgatan. And look at that! The Young Socialists had also managed to mobilize the military. There were easily more than one hundred men from the Svea Engineer Corps who had come marching from Kungsholmen.

But nothing very exciting came of it. The three of them stood and waited a little while, then continued along Götgatan toward town. Down at the Royal movie theater on Stora Vattugatan the *Birth of Venus* was playing, at the Oriental the *Panther of Death* was playing and at the Imperial they were playing the *Suffragette's Bridegroom*. As usual they had to satisfy themselves with just looking at what was showing. Erik might have been able to take them, but he wasn't big on that.

The made their way up toward Söder again, a little disappointed. They stood a moment in the darkness of the doorway. Everything out there seemed so sleepily quiet and still, the street lay empty. But up toward Götgatan maybe something was happening... They thought they could feel the pull and the buzz.

No, Maj had to go up now. Emelie would be beginning to wonder.

She shouldn't give a damn about what Emelie was wondering, was Erik's opinion.

Now he was tired of all the well-meaning, mildly reactionary Social Democrats. Revolution was at the door, the day of liberation longed for by the proletariat for centuries—and Maj was going upstairs to sleep.

His mother drank, hardly knew what day or month it was. But Emelie and her like knew just as little, had no idea of what times they were living in. They probably went around being afraid that they were going to be freed from capitalism. They loved their shackles.

Well, Emelie was actually kind and well intentioned. But that was exactly what one could not be now.

Suddenly it seemed like Erik lost interest in Maj. The hand that had stubbornly stayed put at her waist was suddenly pulled away. It seemed like he was in a hurry, wanted to get rid of her quickly.

There was no point in his standing here like this. If Bengt had not been there he would have shown Maj a thing or two.

Now he wanted to get over to Götgatan one more time in any case. Just to be sure.

Of course Maj could get mad at Erik. But her life would have been boring without him; he opened the doors to everything exciting.

Next he came by already on Tuesday evening and wanted her to come out with him. The Katarina Club was going to have a meeting at a place on Kocksgatan. Texas Ljungberg and Kilbom were going to speak.

Jenny was just leaving for the show when he arrived, didn't have time for any discussions. Jenny gave in, had said yes before Emelie had time to oppose her.

Groups of people had gathered in the street outside the locale, some in expectation that something was about to happen.

A few hundred horse guards had squeezed in through the doorway. They had come marching through the whole town to the meeting. Erik and Maj pressed themselves against the wall, there were no longer any places to sit. But in the first row, all the way under the speaker's platform, sat old Thumbs. He had apparently gotten there in very good time. Some of his old animation was still there. He twisted and turned to catch everything; it was clear that he was enjoying himself. And Maj thought she could hear his well known: "Henning should have been here for this!"

Texas and Kilbom spoke—about deprivation and profiteers, about the revolution that was the hope of the poor. Now was the time to come with demands, now was when something must happen, now soldiers and workers were standing side by side while the bourgeoisie cried out in powerless rage.

The soldiers who were going back to the barracks farthest out on Östermalm had to break up the assembly quite early. The meeting participants followed them out to the street. Huge swarms of people had gathered there and ten policemen on horseback plowed through the people.

The guardsmen placed themselves in the lead. Thousands of people followed them in a dark stream that flowed down the new Katarinavägen. Streetcars were stopped and stood angrily clanging their bells in the middle of the multitudes of people. The police gesticulated wildly and tried to direct the stream, but were swept into it.

Maj walked as if in a trance, held on tightly to Erik's arm, shouted and cheered. They walked across Slussen, down Stora Nygatan, onward across Norrbro. More and more people were swept in. They continued along Birger Jarlsgatan, across Stureplan and up Sturegatan.

Were they going to storm the barracks? It was as if they walked without knowing where or why, as if only in the desire to walk as conquerors, shock the bourgeoisie.

At the gates of the horse guards the civilians stopped, waved and cheered as the military men filed in. Someone shouted, "About face, march!" and the crowd turned back toward Söder again. This time they took Götgatan up and dispersed, finally, at Södra Bantorget.

It had been a real hike. But they had walked, borne along by the atmosphere. And Maj had forgotten her promise about coming home early. Not even when the march was over could she induce herself to go home. She hung onto Erik's arm, as if still drunk with the mood. And the feeling of recklessness and adventure was still there when they stood in the doorway.

This evening she was not afraid of being alone with Erik. She only laughed when he kissed her hard and eagerly.

"I'm crazy," she said suddenly. "I should have been home ages ago."

He said a rather hasty good-bye, as if he had grown a little afraid, and fled.

Naturally they were sitting and waiting, anxious and wondering. Maj tried to tell them about the march, about the mood. But Emelie only thought it was terrible that Maj had been out running around far into the night.

Maj understood that it would be in vain to attempt to get permission to go out again any evening soon. But she wanted out.

The next evening she sneaked out without asking.

She went in the direction of Götgatan. There had been a rumor that something would happen there this evening. Erik would surely be there.

The whole street was like a seething cauldron when she got there. Hundreds of boys were trying to stop the traffic, bawling and bellowing. When the police arrived with sabers drawn they scattered, but a new crowd gathered on Bangårdsgatan. Stones flew through the air, streetcars and automobiles were surrounded, masses of people were packed together and screaming at each other.

But there was no sign of Erik.

Now she regretted going out. Without Erik it wasn't an event. Now the difficult part remained. She pulled herself out of the crowd. Ran through the dark back streets toward home. It would soon be eleven-thirty.

Her mother had not arrived yet. But Emelie was sitting up and waiting. And that was enough; she was upset. Didn't Maj understand how dangerous it was for a girl to go out in the streets alone when everybody was in such an uproar? And how was her schoolwork going?

Emelie both pleaded with her and admonished her. She sat for a long time on the edge of her bed. Maj cried, begging her forgiveness. But she could not sincerely and whole-heartedly promise to improve, that would be like promising to stop living. And school... she was so unhappy, could not stand to stay there any longer.

No matter what happened, she had to finish the term, said Emelie. And if she really ended up quitting she should try to make her final grades as good as possible. That was important for someone looking for her first job.

Maj would try, she promised at last.

Emelie put out the lamp. Maj cried a little to herself in the darkness. She heard her mother come in; they talked for a long time out there in the kitchen. She could not make out the words. But it sounded calm, as if resigned. And she felt safer, for Mama would certainly understand.

And suddenly everything felt easier. She fell asleep calm, consoled.

THE POTATO LAW

There were no potatoes to be had, or turnips either. People were boiling fodder beets but the beets stubbornly refused to become soft, even if they were left simmering all week.

Though of course people knew there was food; those who had enough money could buy it. If the shopkeepers got in a few sacks of potatoes these would surely go to the "steady" customers, those who bought a lot and gladly paid what it cost.

Some women were standing outside O.P. Jonsson's food store on Nytorget. Thin, tormented by the complaints of their husbands and children, tired of being jostled in lines. When there were no more potatoes… then it didn't matter any more, they didn't have the strength.

One of them was almost positive that the woman who had just come out of the shop had a bag of potatoes in her string bag.

Why should some get to eat as much as they wanted and not others? What were they to do to feed their husbands and kids? No potatoes, no grain, no milk. There wasn't enough bread. All the working people on Söder were starving; that was the truth.

They grew louder, people began to gather around. The woman who thought she had seen a bag of potatoes was now completely convinced. There were potatoes; the shopkeepers were hiding them.

The sun glittered on the corrugated metal roof, made the unfurled white awnings shine. Out on Nytorget enormous piles of the fuel commission's firewood supply lay rotting behind barbed wire. Behind the display window the shopkeeper stood and wondered what those agitated women were up to next.

The most impatient women suddenly swarmed into the store. Behind them were many others pushing forward; there was a bottleneck at the counter.

Potatoes! They wanted to buy potatoes, demanded to do so.

He was sorry, the owner replied. There was not a potato in the store. He didn't even have any to cook for himself.

Hah, he should not try to fool them. Someone had just seen one of his better customers leave with a bag of them.

Only beets, nothing else. If they didn't believe him they were welcome to choose a representative to come in and look at his supplies and assure herself that he had not hidden anything.

The offer made them hesitant. Naturally he would try to deceive them. No one wanted to commit to the risk of being the one who would be deceived—or in any case be regarded as the one who had been deceived.

A woman in a moth-eaten fur cap and stained coat finally pushed forward. The shopkeeper smiled, showed the way into the supply room.

Perhaps the rest would be so kind as to wait outside.

The representative came back after a moment, a little subdued. The shopkeeper had opened every door, pulled out drawers, opened up boxes. She had not found a single potato.

Well, even if Jonsson had a clear conscience there were certainly others...

They were going to go on.

They continued across the street to Wahlqvisten's. Now they knew how they would operate. They demanded immediately that two representatives be allowed to inspect the supplies. The shopkeeper did not want to offend the women here either; he went along with their wishes. The result was equally negative, and angry voices insinuated that those who had made an inventory of the shop had allowed themselves to be bribed.

Someone came up with the idea the Jonsson had storerooms in a neighboring house—that was naturally where the potatoes were kept. Despite everything, they had been deceived. The growing group of women returned to Jonsson. To their disappointment he had nothing against showing them that storeroom as well.

Tired and angry, the women stood in clusters out on the square. They had just felt some hope, for a moment they had dared believe that their action would be crowned with success. Somewhere there had to be hidden sacks, somewhere there were supplies that were intended only for the good customers.

They were still standing there when Bärta woke up that afternoon. She emerged just as someone called out that Carlsson on Södermannagatan according to completely sound rumors had several sacks hidden in a garden shed.

Those who had been standing where they could hear this began to move. Others noticed that something was happening and followed after them. Small streams of people were drawn out of every passageway and back street, unitied to one army that marched away to besiege Carlsson's grocery store on the corner of Södermannagatan and Katarina bangata.

Bärta followed along without actually knowing why; she was not out looking for potatoes.

The entire crossroads outside the elementary school was filled with people. The shopkeepers had hurried to lock their doors and people crowded around, screamed and threatened. Not until the police came did the store open. The police organized the line. Bärta, who had pushed her way forward, was being shoved away and she thrashed about wildly.

Everyone except the very closest could disperse, screamed a policeman. There wasn't much to go around.

So there was something there! The rumor had been true. Instead of dispersing even more people tried to press forward. The rumor grew in even greater circles about even more sacks.

There were only four liters of potatoes. The first eight people in line each received one half liter. Bärta had elbowed her way forward to be the second to last of the fortunate ones.

She came out onto the street, waving her bag as if she had won a prize. And was stampeded by all those who, incited by the sight, did their utmost to push forward to the same reward.

"There are no more!" yelled the policeman. "Disperse!"

But they did not hear, did not want to hear. And if there was anyone who wanted to give up and turn back, it was no longer possible. Too many people were pushing from the rear.

The police had to call in reinforcements. While the masses of people grew denser, the riot squad arrived and a group of mounted police. Södermannagatan was closed off; the masses began to be forced back toward Nytorget.

At Skånegatan the paving stones had been broken up for the current repair of the streetcar tracks. Some of the people stopped, picked up stones. Here were weapons; here was the opportunity to get revenge.

"Move on!" screamed the police. "Damned bitches!" shouted one and swung his whip.

Protesting futilely, the women had to yield to the horses. They herded together at the sides of the square while raucous boys whistled.

Bärta was not so mobile. She was getting caught between the piles of wood and the mounted police. She tried to grab hold of the bridle of one of the horses to ward it off, but got a stinging lash of the whip across her fingers and saw a couple of the potatoes, ruined by such travail, roll away to be plucked up by greedy hands.

"Give them back! Give back my potatoes you thieving hags!"

She thought she saw horses hooves above her and began to scream in violent terror. But the policeman had managed to bring the shying horse under control. A kind person pulled Bärta out of the way but could not bring her to her feet again.

Now they were throwing stones on Skånegatan; many people went in that direction. Drawn sabers flashed, police cars' doors opened and arrested people were thrown in. Now undoubtedly one hundred police were deployed, formed new chains, divided the masses of people into smaller groups, struck with sabers and whips to break up the trouble spots.

Daylight had begun to fade, shifting from yellow to blue. Some women who were bleeding from saber wounds shrieked hysterically. Bärta, who found herself left alone, set free and abandoned, began to crawl along the wood piles, only wanting to get away, escape. But she collapsed against one of the piles, no longer had the strength. All of a sudden she began to kick and scream aloud, as if in mortal anguish.

Bärta had ended up in the hospital together with the rioters, and Emelie went there to find out what had happened. She was called in to see the doctor, who gave a few explanatory words. Bärta had suffered from delirium tremens, or drunken lunacy as people called it. Probably the condition had been caused by her falling and injuring herself during the riots. The patient was in very poor condition; her heart had been taxed.

The next time Emelie came to the hospital, she was frightened by how weak and miserable Bärta had become. Much of the swollen corpulence had disappeared and her skin lay in empty pouches.

Bärta was unusually lucid that day. For the first time in a long while she could see the situation as it was.

The picture worried her and she cried.

Now she knew what she had suspected before but not consciously wanted to know: she was only trouble, no one had any joy from her being alive. The children would be better off when they were rid of her.

But now, as she lay in the hospital's nice bed, she was worrying about how things would go for them. She regretted everything she had done and not done. Now that she could not do anything more.

Emelie wanted to raise objections but Bärta silenced her: she knew. And now she wanted to talk about the children.

Gunnar, he was getting on all right. Emelie had helped him, set him right, and finally he had also found out his father. It wasn't for Gunnar's sake that she had looked up August; Emelie knew that well. But it felt right in any case, now, afterward. And maybe Gunnar would gain some happiness from it.

Erik would probably also manage well, and anyhow he wanted to take care of himself. It wasn't worth trying to influence him. Not Tyra either, for that matter. But if Emelie wanted to help the youngest sometimes. And Beda, of course. It was at Emelie's that those two felt at home.

Emelie tried to calm her. Of course she would do what she could.

And Bärta grew a little calmer. With Emelie's help things would probably work, the boys would manage. Beda too. And maybe the restless Tyra could find a good boy to take care of her.

Somewhere a window either closed or opened, catching a reflection of the evening sun. A pale and brief flicker of light glimmered in the gray face on the pillow.

AFTER BÄRTA DIED

The streetcar rumbled along between the low houses and sheds on Nytorgsgatan, braking before it cut, with a piercing noise, through the curve toward Åsögatan.

Dirty gray awnings drooped over the open hatches; no wind rocked the used clothes that had been hung out for sale. After the streetcar disappeared, the street was almost empty. The customers would not come in any great numbers until nearer to evening. The May sun shone as warm as summer on this afternoon, and some of the sellers had sat themselves in folding chairs along the sidewalk.

Footsteps were heard; a small group of people was coming from Åsögatan, walking down the hill toward Nytorget. They did not stop to look at the wares, only passed by silently. A woman and some young people, noticeably solemn in the smiling spring weather.

Bärta had died, in the hospital for the delirious and the mentally ill. It had happened at night, so quickly that none of her relatives had time to go there. Her heart had not had the strength for the great anguish she had felt, the sights she had seen. The doctor had said that the hallucinations that the patients had these days were more terrible than before. It got that way when alcohol was being rationed and people drank denatured alcohol, disinfectant and hair tonic.

Now the children were going to see their mother for the last time. They had asked Emelie to go along, as if they really could not handle going alone. She had gone in to see factory director Melinder and asked for herself and Beda to have time off, promising they would make up the time. The factory director had said the time was not so important; he was always so kind.

While Emelie walked between Bärta's children, she had to think back, remember how it had been. Something was over now, not just another person's life, but also a period in her own.

She looked out over Nytorget. She had to stop a moment, thought she could discern something of life's otherwise secretly hidden pattern. Over there in the house on the other side of the square was where she had met Bärta for the first time. And behind the woodpiles, toward the school, they had found Bärta after the potato riots. Like a ring that had come full circle.

Bärta had been cast into Emelie's life by coincidence. That was after Grandmother had died and Mama thought they had to take in boarders to make the rent. That was more than thirty years ago. Emelie could still remember what her mother had said: the girl seems nice, there probably won't be any problems with her.

There had certainly been problems with Bärta.

As a matter of fact Emelie had not had so much in common with Bärta. It was Gertrud and Bärta who had been close. But Gertrud had gotten married and moved away. Emelie remained. And it was to Emelie that Bärta confided her secret, that Gunnar was August's son. Perhaps it was this knowledge that had bound her to Bärta. They had moved in together, lived first on Fjällgatan for several years, then on Åsögatan. The proximity had made Emelie connected to her. Now Bärta's children had come to her, asked her to go with them.

But Tyra wasn't there. Hadn't Tyra always avoided anything that was unpleasant or difficult—avoided and chosen something worse?

Bärta had been carried down to a cellar room. They had to wait a couple of minutes out in the hospital courtyard while a guard lit some candles down there. Then they were allowed to come down, enter the cool and dark room with its smell of earth and dampness. The open casket stood on a low bench; the flames of the candles lent their flickering light over the white shroud and the pale face.

Bärta—and yet not Bärta. Death had transformed the familiar to a stranger, a wax mask without life. A silent, unknown person in an unknown land, so close and yet so endlessly far away. Silently they stood and saw her lying there, carefully they placed some flowers between her folded hands. Then they went out to life again.

Emelie felt how they flocked around her. They had no one else now, and their unity was not so strong; it was only Erik and Bengt who were close. Gunnar had left their home early, Beda demanded so much time and interest if one was to get close to her. And Emelie remembered how it was when Mama had died, how safe it had felt that Matilda was there then. Maybe she could give some of what she herself had received then, if they wanted to accept it.

"We have things to talk about," she said. "If you like, we can go home and talk a while. And then I will make a little food for us."

Erik was not in such a hurry as usual that evening. It was as if none of them wanted to go home to their room. They sat around the table and Emelie talked about her last conversation with Bärta. Beda could move in with Emelie when she wanted, if they thought that was a good idea. And what did they think Tyra wanted to do? Could she and the two boys continue to share the room they had, help each other out with the rent?

Tyra did not pay so many öre, said Erik. But if she kept quiet she could still live there. Though if she lived there she had to try to stay somewhat tidy and behave properly.

Emelie had not thought much about it earlier, now she thought she noticed something of the pedant in Erik. He sometimes appeared careless in his fervor and even in his clothing—but one never saw him in socks with holes like Bengt wore. No matter how he behaved his shoes were always brushed, his shirt clean, his pants pressed. Erik could seem hard sometimes; he was probably hard on himself as well.

"You will have to try to get along. Try to overlook things a little with Tyra."

He shook his head.

"Nothing good will come of it, I have seen enough of these things. There is no point in trying to help someone who cannot take care of herself. Better to cut it off quickly."

He grew quiet. The memory of seeing his mother just now checked him a little. But Emelie understood that the memories of Bärta would not hinder him. On the contrary, they would drive him on. Tyra would have to pay for Bärta's shortcomings as well. He had not gotten the better of his mother, but he could force his sister into an either-or.

Emelie felt she would not be able to deter him. Maybe it wasn't even right to try. How much can one require of a brother, a son, a person at all? The boys had had it tough during the years that had passed, in fact it was surprising that they had done as well as they had. That the boys could take care of themselves and become good people was tremendous. That they were to take care of Tyra, perhaps even against her will, was something one could not count on.

"Maybe I will go home with you for a little while tonight," said Emelie. "Then Beda and I can carry her things here afterward. If you want help with anything just tell me."

"We can manage," answered Erik. And Emelie felt like it was an order, maybe a warning: he didn't intend to accept any checking up. He wanted to be his own person.

They walked in the dusk, the few blocks to Bärta's room. Gunnar and Maj stayed at home. It was only Beda and the two younger boys who walked together with Emelie.

She had probably expected a certain amount of disorder. She knew how it usually looked wherever Bärta lived, how it had been in the shed over at Hagen and in the room on Fjällgatan, how often they had argued about the mess in the kitchen at home on Åsögatan.

Now it had been some time since Bärta had lived here. While she had been in the hospital the room had changed. Of course it was simple, poorly furnished, almost completely lacking furniture. But it was clean and neat, the window was open and it felt aired out and fresh.

In front of the window Erik had placed a table that he had bought at an auction. It was there he took care of his business and there he kept the club's minutes and paper. In a few boxes were his repository of books and papers and the books he had bought for himself. On the wall hung portraits of the Amalthea men; they were newspaper clippings and framed in cardboard from shoeboxes. Bengt, who was only an apprentice and did not earn very much—and in addition seldom got to keep what he earned—only had a mattress on the floor.

One could be touched by Erik's attempt at creating a home. But Emelie could not help noticing either, that everything he had gotten was personal, private. It was Erik's table, his shelf, his bed. Bengt had only the mattress on the floor. And Beda and Tyra?

A boundary ran across that room. The innermost and darkest part, farthest from the window and behind the iron stove, had another character. A tattered cloth hung on a string between two nails in the ceiling molding. In front of the cloth lay a bed of old quilts and sacks on the floor. It was Beda's simple, yet still tidily kept, sleeping place. On the other side of the cloth was only a formless and sloppy pile. Beside it stood some cartons and bags where Tyra apparently kept her clothes and food leftovers. A dress and some underclothes were hanging from a nail. On one box stood a candlestick with a half-burned candle.

Everything seemed so helplessly clumsy and wretched.

"Does she usually sleep here?" Emelie asked.

"Sometimes," Erik answered indifferently. "She goes around with some gang member, sometimes she sleeps elsewhere. I don't know if she has a job anymore. It doesn't seem like it."

Emelie did not ask any more, only helped Beda gather up her belongings.

When Emelie was leaving Erik stuck out a dirty yellow piece of paper. "Here," he said. "Take it!"

Emelie looked at it. A coffee ration card with a coupon that entitled the bearer to buy one hectogram of coffee.

"I can't accept this," she said. "You must need it yourselves."

"No, take it," he said. "In the worst case I can buy a new one from the thieves in the Old Town."

Then she thanked him and accepted it. She understood and was moved. He was not closing the door completely, but leaving it open a crack. "We can manage," he had said. But the coffee ration card was a sign that he wanted to maintain some of their connection.

She was free of a responsibility. But for one who is used to burdens it can feel heavy to lose one.

JUNE FIFTH

Maj was late. She looked worriedly at watchmaker Gjörcke's clock outside number twenty-two and began to run down Götgatan toward town.

It was vexing that she was arriving late; Erik did not like to wait. But she had a good excuse and good news to tell him. It was done now; she had talked with the headmistress. She would end school at the end of this term. Her mother and Emelie had given in finally. Only a few more days—then she would be free.

A lot of people were out, mostly workers who had left work.

A Left Socialist creation that was called the Welfare Committee had recommended a general strike. Vennerström and Branting were to receive the answer to their questions raised in parliament regarding complete voting rights for citizens. They had demanded that the old graduated voting scale finally be abolished. People were to gather in large numbers on the open square outside the House of Parliament to emphasize their demand. The high-up gentlemen would hear their rumbling all the way inside.

Erik had warned Maj against crossing Norrbro or Råttfällen, the wooden "Mousetrap" bridge. The police would surely close it off there. She should try Vasabron or maybe Järnvägsbron, the railroad bridge, he had said.

She tried with Vasabron; it was successful. She could see the crowds of people around Strömgatan and Norrbro and wondered if she had any chance of finding Erik. He was going to wait for her on the corner of Fredsgatan and Drottninggatan. She made her way, following the workers from Boliner's who came marching from Kungsholmen. The congestion grew even tighter. From every direction people were coming in droves and were blocked by the police barricades around Norrbro.

No Erik to be seen. Apparently he had not been able to wait any longer, and had gone on toward the House of Parliament.

She was jostled about, pulled along with the crowds who were now trying to get down toward Strömgatan. Over at Norrbro several lines of military men were on the alert behind the chain of police, their bayonets shining. Up on Gustaf Adolf's Square the police barricade had just opened and a streetcar let through. The driver clanged the bell ceaselessly, and decimeter by decimeter the car squeezed through the sea of people.

Maj tried to fight her way through to Norrbro. She reached Strömgatans's railing along the water and felt how she was forced against the stone wall there. It was dangerous to stand here; more and more people kept on coming.

She made her way successfully to a lamppost, that and the wall formed a shield for her. Here she could stand more safely, search for Erik, watch what happened.

The streetcars on the ring line stood in a line along Strömgatan. The police, with sabers drawn, tried to open a channel for them through the sea of people. Mounted police came to their aid.

"Drive on!" the police shouted.

When a woman was rammed by a streetcar and fell over, a tumult ensued. A giant sheet metal worker climbed on board and pulled down the trolley pole despite lashes from the policemen's whips. Once the trolley pole had been pulled down, the streetcar began to roll backward down the hill toward Riksbron, and collided with the car behind that was standing closest. The tinkling of glass from the crushed lanterns was heard, strangely brittle but still piercing.

"Build barricades!" people shouted. The police chains along Strömmen had been broken; some boys had gotten rope from a tool shed and thrown out snares for the police horses.

The police had to retire for a moment. Their chain at Norrbro had burst, but behind it stood the military with bayonets. Now loud cries could be heard that machine guns had been seen up on the roof of the palace. They were aimed at the demonstrators.

In a wild fury the demonstrators tried to overturn the streetcars. But the police got reinforcements and rode at great speed, with whips whistling, into the sea of people.

All of a sudden, in the midst of the tumult, like a sigh through the crowd, "Branting is coming!"

They were coming from the House of Parliament, a small group of members of parliament. They ended up right in the midst of the mounted police. Some had to flee the horses. Hansson, the editor from "The Social Democrat," managed to throw himself out of the way and climb up onto the pedestal of Gustaf Adolf's statue and cling fast there.

But Branting walked on, almost as if in his sleep, between the riding and wildly lashing police, followed only by the bearded Oscar Olsson. He was about to be run over—at the last moment the horse turned aside.

"Calm!" he shouted. "To the People's Hall! To the People's Hall!"

"To the People's Hall!" screamed the masses. The police barricades were burst once more, but now by people who wished to get out and away. Drottninggatan, Malmskillnadsgatan and Regeringsgatan were filled with enormous streams that flowed northward. The police, on horses scared out of their wits, drove the masses ahead of them.

Down at the People's Hall, all of Barnhusgatan was filled as well as the large schoolyard outside of Norra Latin School.

And then Branting was standing on the balcony over the entrance to the People's Hall. The cries were subdued, people applauded. As loudly as he could he shouted out across the sea of people: now they were to go home in a calm and orderly fashion and later give their answer in the autumn election.

That instruction was not well received. It was now that people wanted to negotiate and respond, not in a few months. The otherwise well-respected leader of the people was met by a violent symphony of whistles. Protests stormed in his direction.

"Long live the revolution!"

"General Strike!"

"Down with the police!"

In the schoolyard Major Lindhagen was lifted onto strong shoulders. He tried to give a speech but could hardly make himself heard. Now everyone was shouting at once.

They were calling for Texas to appear. And in one way or another he was able, despite Branting's forbidding it, to get out onto the balcony. He shouted that they should assemble in the People's Hall to discuss the situation.

In a few minutes all the halls, stairways and corridors were filled. Everywhere speakers were in action, out in the corridor Oljelund shouted from a window and Arthur Engberg from one of the inside balconies.

Maj had ended up in Auditorium B where she heard Ragnar Casparsson and others speak. While the meeting was underway, some of those who had been forced to seek medical help for their saber wounds arrived. They were greeted like heroes, carried in to tumultuous ovations.

Suddenly Maj had to jump up. There was Erik coming in! Carried on his comrades' shoulders, with a large blood-stained bandage on his head. All the fear she had felt during the riots suddenly swept over her.

Blinded by tears, she fought her way through the hall, didn't know how she conducted herself, but managed to get to him. She threw herself around Erik's neck and cried hysterically. He held her, smiling at her alarm.

CALM AFTER THE STORM

Far away on peaceful Östermalm. People noticed nothing of the disturbances down in the center of the city.

Emelie had dreaded the rallies and the traffic jams, so she had taken the ferry from Slussen to Grevbron. She had been a little nervous about getting there on time. Because of the coal shortage a lot of the ferry service had been restricted. So naturally she arrived way too early instead, and wandered through the streets for half an hour before it was time to go up.

August had moved a few years earlier, to a larger apartment in a newly constructed building on Karlavägen. Emelie had never been there before. Now he had asked if she wanted to come visit them. She had an assignment to report on, so maybe that was why.

The building had an elevator. Emelie didn't dare try such newfangled things. Imagine if that apparatus got stuck between floors— what a commotion she would cause.

So she walked up the stairs, stood a moment and looked at the sign on the door. She opened her purse and made sure the money, through some trick, had not disappeared on the way there. Of the money she had received to give Bärta, thirty-five kronor remained.

The bills lay where she had put them, had not become fewer when she counted them.

She placed her finger on the bell and rang a short ring. Maybe she had rung too short so that no one heard it. Best to wait anyway. If she rang once more maybe it would sound like she was impatient.

The door was opened by someone unknown to her. For an instant Emelie wanted to curtsey to the well-dressed maid, but she stopped herself, only greeted her and asked for building contractor Bodin. Apparently she was expected; she was asked to come in and was helped off with her coat. She was unaccustomed to this, was used to always taking care of this herself. She would have liked to hang up her coat herself and see where it went, but the maid disappeared with it behind a curtain.

"If you please," said the maid and opened a door. Emelie entered, stopping just inside the threshold. And now August came in, begged her pardon for having to wait, he had just received a telephone call and heard that things were calm in the city once more. Emelie must know that there had been complete Mayhem?

He had thought they would sit a little while in peace and quiet first, discuss business. And then they could have some coffee, and Ida and the children could join them. They were out shopping; they had to get the youngest good clothes for graduation.

"Maybe we can sit in the library," he said and showed her the way.

Reverently she stepped inside, saw the rows of shining leather-bound book spines on tall dark shelves. So many books he had. But August had read a lot already as a boy.

Had August read all the books? She had to ask.

Well... not exactly. He did not have time to read as much anymore, mostly just those that had to do with his profession. But Ida and the children certainly read more. The boys especially needed access to books for their studies.

The chair he offered her was low and soft, she felt like she disappeared in it, had a great deal of trouble working her way out and sitting on the outer edge of it.

Indeed... that was tragic about Bärta, he began. But she had seemed so derelict and miserable. A person living like that would never grow old.

Now he wanted to thank Emelie for all the help he had received from her. He did not know how things would have turned out otherwise. It was probably no exaggeration to say that Emelie had saved him.

Well, they had talked about all that before. Did Emelie have any new concerns now, had she in any way been obligated to help Bärta's children?

She told him how things stood, that Bärta's children were now so big that they took care of themselves. The only one who needed a little help was the youngest girl who was a little backward. But there was nothing to worry about; the girl was working, was kind and not any problem.

So August should receive back… She opened her purse, took out the money. It was what was left over, what had been left at Bärta's death.

No, he did not want anything back. That little amount Emelie had to keep for all her trouble.

Despite her protests she had to put the bills back again, there was no discussion he said. And now he had to talk to her a little about Gunnar. The boy was not married yet?

No not yet. These were uncertain times.

That was true, the boy was sensible. One should wait a while. Not only to get married. August had thought of giving Gunnar a good-sized sum of money that he could use to start his own business. A small carpentry business, for example. More and more small houses and large ones were springing up all over town. A skilled woodworking company could make a good income there. But he should wait a little, that was true. August, who was familiar with the trade, would try to find the right moment.

He looked at his sister unobserved, wondered if she guessed that this wasn't just about helping Gunnar. Everything would be simpler and easier if the boy got something else to do and didn't work on his firm's construction sites. No matter how things stand, one cannot treat one's son exactly as one treats other employees. Sooner or later someone would suspect something. And in tough times one must become tough oneself, be forced to treat people in a way one would not want to treat one's son.

His sister sat there, thin and small, on the edge of the large chair. Of course she was afraid to lean back and make herself comfortable. There were features in her that reminded him of his father, slender and pliant at the same time, eyes somewhat sunken in their sockets, the protruding forehead. But there was certainly a lot of his mother in Emelie too, the dark hair, the indefatigability.

Sometimes he longed for the past. For the poor home, the simple circumstances. The time of his childhood, when he still had no responsibility, when there was someone who could comfort and defend him. He could not imagine a better or more understanding wife than Ida, but not even she could place herself inside all the cares he had, not least during these times of crisis.

The coffee table was set in the living room. Ida and the children had come home and were waiting for them.

It had been a long time since Emelie had seen August's wife and children. Ida was just the same, she thought, just as young and beautiful though she must be approaching fifty. And the children… Emelie had known when they were born and how old they had become, but still it was something of a shock. Even though the eldest was not there. Karl Henrik was of age and was doing his military service.

The girls were ladies. If Emelie had met them somewhere else she would have curtsied for them. Charlotta had turned twenty and Anna would soon be nineteen. Both had finished school but neither of them was engaged yet. Charlotta helped out at the office. And then the two children who were still in school: Fredrik who would turn seventeen in the fall, and the girl who had the same name as Jenny's youngest daughter, Elisabet. She was thirteen and tall for her age.

They were polite and nice to their poor aunt. Probably a little curious too, she noticed.

"Papa has spoken so much of Auntie," Charlotta said. "Of when you were both little and Auntie wrote a letter about a dangerous bear that was at a factory on Söder."

Of course, the bear. That was such an immensely long time ago. By the way, Emelie had run into one of August's old classmates, she hadn't mentioned it yet. Valle, the boy from schoolmaster Hierta's orphanage out at Lugnet, the one who was so clever that he got to go to high school. He had not recognized Emelie but she recognized him. He was an engineer now and had visited Melinder's factory a few times.

Valle, of course he remembered Valle. How they had been chased by the "rats" in elementary school and beaten up by the "sweeps" in Maria School. He told them about it good-humoredly. Now the troubles from the old days were good for hiding the troubles and worries of today.

Emelie was almost surprised at herself: here she was sitting and talking to August's fine family, almost felt like she belonged. And everybody was so nice and friendly to her. When she left, Ida absolutely wanted her to take a large piece of meat and a bag of coffee with her. August had gotten these through his connections; he had surely paid a lot of money for them. And now he was giving them away to her. She was touched, did not know how to thank them.

Shouldn't they try to get hold of a taxicab? Or at least a horse cab; there was beginning to be such a dearth of cars now that there was no longer any gasoline.

Of course not, she would try to catch the steam launch down at Grevbron. August insisted on accompanying her there. He felt like taking an evening stroll and would help her carry her things.

The launch arrived. She sat down and looked out over the water and the shorelines. It had gotten late but it was still so light out, the way it only could be in the beginning of June.

She felt happy and grateful. Not mainly because of her gifts, but because they had been so kind to her.

When she arrived at Slussen a completely different atmosphere from the one she had left met her. Here there was trouble and unrest, anger and hate.

Maj had not come home yet. Where was that girl? Jenny, who was off work and at home, did not know anything, had not heard from her daughter. But Jenny was not worried. Maj would surely be coming along, she was young and wanted to amuse herself. They had been young once themselves…

Now Emelie had to tell her about her visit. What had August said? And what was it like in their new apartment? Did they have a really fancy place now?

"Do you want to help me home?" Erik asked. "I feel a little dizzy. That was an awfully nasty blow I got."

Of course Maj wanted to help him. They took a streetcar to Slussen. Many unknown people began to talk to them, expressed their sympathy and poured out their feelings of outrage over the "Cossacks." Erik was something of a hero. Maj admired him, his way of smiling and pretending not to be in pain. His wound must have been causing him agony.

As she sat there beside him and heard him talk to people and tell about how he had been attacked, it occurred to her: I love him, for the first time I know for sure that I love him. It did not feel like this before, despite the embraces, the kisses. Now it is different, something completely different.

They walked across the bridge at Slussen and watched the dark, glittering water in the locks canal rise bubbling after the bridge had just opened. Around Karl Johan's statue the trees stood dense, intensely light green. A streetcar came up from Brunnsbacken, rolling in the curve around the grove.

This evening they splurged and took the elevator up to Söder. Erik would certainly have gotten tired from walking the whole way uphill.

"Come in for a little while," he said when they arrived. "We can have a cup of coffee. I need one. I have been bought some from the thieves. I can't sit and work at night without coffee."

Any other evening she would have hesitated, but not now. She knew that Bengt was out. How things were with Tyra she had not heard, didn't care either. Now the only thing that mattered was helping Erik.

He unlocked the door, stepped ahead of her into the room and turned on the electric light. She helped him off with his jacket. He had a hard time moving his arms, which were battered blue from the sabers.

He took her hand and looked at it.

"You have received some blows too," he said.

"Lie down now," she said as if deflect him. "I'll make some coffee."

He sat down on the bed, watched while she lit the flame on the primus stove and poured water into the pan.

"Here is the coffee," he said and opened his locked desk drawer. "I have to hide what I have because of Tyra."

"There are some cups in the box over there," he continued. "But it is locked too. I have the key to the padlock here."

She placed the cups on a chair, sat beside him on the bed. She had not drunk such good, strong coffee in months. Erik smacked his lips contentedly. He tried to put his arm around her, but it hurt all over in his pounded body.

"Lie down now," she said and pushed him gently away from her. "I will wash out the cups before I go."

He looked so pale where he lay with the large bandage around his head.

"Can't I help you? You need to go to bed properly."

"If you could help me off with my boots."

She kneeled beside his bed.

"I think I will keep my pants on," he laughed.

Steps were heard on the stairs and the door opened. It was Tyra coming in. She didn't say hello, pretended as if she hadn't even seen them. She only closed the door and went in behind the curtain. A light went on from inside it.

"I'm going to go now," Maj whispered. "Can you manage tomorrow? With your boots and jacket?"

"I will probably have to stay home, go and have my head rebandaged too. Can you come by at all?"

She bent down and kissed him before she left. Waved to him a little from the doorway. Out in the vestibule she heard how he started to shout in there. He wanted Tyra to turn out the light. Maj hurried away, did not want to hear anything.

She didn't know if she wanted to rejoice or cry, was just keenly aware that everything had changed. That she was a whole new person from the one who had gone to school this morning.

WARTIME SUMMER

The big brown wall clock showed ten of six. The office boss had left, but no one dared count on him not returning and checking to see if anyone had sneaked out before it was time. So all the office workers sat there: the bookkeepers at their high desks with books open, the girl who was the typist at her lower desk with the last sheet of paper still in her typewriter. But work had come to a stop.

Maj had brought out her manicure case. She was filing and polishing her nails, one at a time, carefully. In reality perhaps mostly to make the time pass.

After something over a month of office work she had begun to suspect that the life of adults was not as exciting as she had believed. But work brought one advantage in any case; they could not treat her like a schoolgirl at home anymore.

Before the war there had not been so many women office workers. But during the war years, with the long-standing military draft, women had been needed at the workplace and they applied for office jobs in particular. The work could well suit a woman; it must be hard to support a wife and children on an office salary. It was lucky Maj did not have to support herself. She would have barely been able to live alone on her wages.

Polished nails were a symbol of her new life. Office girls had to be well groomed. They should even be a little stylish, claimed Agnes who sat at the desk opposite her. The gentlemen at the office found it gratifying.

Finally the clock struck. Maj slid down from her chair. Her white dress got pulled up and showed a little more of her leg than was considered proper. But she inspected her shiny tan silk stockings proudly, felt pleasure at the sight of them. It was nice that skirts had gotten shorter in recent years; they were almost up to the calves now. She stood in front of the mirror, wetted her fingers and twirled a lock of hair that was supposed to lie flat across her cheek.

Erik was waiting for her. He had not promised to come, but when she saw the beautiful weather holding up she had thought: he's going to come.

He lifted his light-colored straw hat. Erik had changed a great deal during the past year. Before he had been a typical fellow from Söder. Now he was becoming more and more a young sophisticate. What had changed the least was his speech.

An acquaintance of Erik's had started a soap boiling business where they made substitute soap. Dog fat and rat filth were good for soap, Erik joked. And rancid lard was a fine thing if you did not have to be there to boil it and smell it. Erik avoided this; he only did the selling.

A little irritated, he twisted his neck. He had bought a new white collar and it was chafing him. Then he scrutinized Maj's dress with satisfaction; he liked to go out with a sharply dressed gal. It was just a pity that she had inherited her mother's large mouth.

After the spring and early summer's crises and flare-ups, things had grown somewhat calmer. It was as if people were catching their breath before the fall elections and new conflicts. The food situation had improved since the government had gotten on better terms with the English. And in any case, everything seemed easier once it grew light and warm outside.

The city relaxed to its heart's content in the evening sun. Erik took Maj under his arm and she walked proudly by his side along Kungsträdgården's fashionable promenade. When they reached Nybroplan a balloon seller was standing outside the Royal Dramatic Theatre. The colorful gaudy cluster stood out against the dazzlingly white walls of the building, and from one of the wooden cargo boats the sounds of an accordion were heard. Erik hummed along with it; the melody was one of the ones that everyone knew just now. It was the refrain about

Mister Rubinstein's luxury gramophone

That he bought on the installment plan...

He had closed a good deal, sold a large consignment today. These days he had left off his small dealings with razor blades and other junk. He might still be of service selling books and newspapers, but that was really not because of the profit, but out of pure idealism.

Otherwise he was dubious of that notion of idealism. It was certainly not by accident that Marx said the liberation of the proletariat would be by its own production. The slave who burst his chains did this not out of idealism, but because his shackles tormented him. He felt compelled to do so. It was not idealism but compulsion that forced people to become revolutionaries.

Erik could not help but doubt some of the leaders the workers had come up with. Such as Branting... who had taken a step down from the upper class to help and to lead. There was something odd about that, something sick. For centuries the upper class had sucked everything out of the poor and now someone was suffering a guilty conscience, wanted to try and correct the disparities. A sick conscience... wasn't that what he had said, that there was something sick.

But think of all that Branting had risked, objected Maj. Career and reputation. He had had everything to lose. Those who came from the working class had nothing to lose. On the other hand they could gain a lot through political movements; they could become members of parliament, step into society.

That was exactly what he meant; they had excuses that were valid. It was so right and natural for them, that even if they worked out of pure self-interest, they would pull their class along with them. Their own future would become that of their class. But it was clear that they took certain risks. They could lose a whole lot as well, get fired from good jobs, be persecuted by employers and authorities. Many had failed and disappeared, perhaps poorer and unhappier than when they came to the movement. But some would succeed and be carried up to society's higher echelons.

You had to know the rules of the game. Be aware of the risks and opportunities. Many went along as if intoxicated and then after the intoxication the only thing left was the hangover. He had his eyes open and looked soberly both at the movement and himself.

There were those within the movement who criticized his business dealings and said he was dealing in speculation in times of crisis and wartime profiteering. But somebody had to sell soap and since there was money to be earned he sold it. And course those who criticized would gladly accept a bar of soap if they got it for free. Then they would wash their hands like that guy in the Bible...

"Pilate," said Maj.

Right. Washed and shouted that they were so clean and pure, idealists who would never want to earn a farthing under circumstances such as these. But that was just empty talk. Sure they wanted to—but they couldn't.

No, they should be thankful and glad that at least one of their own was plugged in and took a little part of the great bounty.

Maj had understood that Erik's business had given rise to a number of stabs and digs on the part of his comrades. Erik knew all about buying and selling, it was his life. As long as he had practiced his talent in service of the movement, no one had any objections. Now when he was running his own business he had to defend himself. That was why he did not seem really happy despite his successes. And despite the beautiful evening which he would have just liked to enjoy.

He invited her to dinner at a little outdoor café. The food was expensive, meager and bad but they ate with good appetites. They sat and watched the dusk fall over Djurgården, as if it were sinking down through the treetops. Streetlights and rows of lamps around the café were lit; the gates to the amusement park, Gröna Lund, were opened. Soon the first couple would slide down from the high tower of the toboggan ride, or stumble out from the large rotating fun wheel. This year the amusement park had gotten several new attractions; many of the old simple sideshows had disappeared. A new dance rotunda had been built and a restaurant with large verandas. And then there was the "enchanted house" that was also called "Babylon."

They had been to Gröna Lund a few evenings. But now Erik wanted them to see what it was like at the rotunda, Dance-Out. People had been talking so much about it.

She hesitated. Of course it might be fun, but the place still a somewhat dubious reputation.

"Good music," Erik said. He wanted to dance.

And naturally he got his way. It wasn't long before they caught a glimpse through the trees, of the white pavilion and the long, multi-paned loggia on Alkärret, right beside the new art gallery.

Most of the tables in the loggia were already taken, but they finally were able to find a table in a corner, and they ordered coffee. It was made up mainly of the essence of boiled dried dandelions.

"Easy virtue," whispered Erik about the women who were sitting there in small groups of two, three and four at the various tables. They wore large hats and enormous boas. When the boas were drawn aside one could almost wonder for a moment if some of the ladies were not naked to the waist, so deep were their décolletés. Some of them smoked cigarettes. They appeared keenly aware of the gentlemen around, and observed them appraisingly.

The men looked back, fastening their gazes on shiny silken calves and swaying breasts.

Profiteers and filles de joie. But also a whole lot of office workers and shop assistants, some Karlsberg cadets and a few settled married couples. The crowd was mixed and the mixture gave everyone cover, it justified and facilitated.

The music played "Mister Rubinstein" and the pavilion was filled with stepping feet. Dance partners came in from the terrace outside and asked the ladies to dance. Others hurried to the ticket window where they could buy tickets, twenty öre for a dance.

Erik invited Maj to dance. They wedged their way in among the dancers, gripped by the melody's rhythmic pull. He held her tight; in the one-step the dancers had to almost cling together, sticking their knees between their partner's legs.

So much had been written about the indecency of the one-step. In some ways Maj could prove the indignation correct: it was an embrace. But now she was dancing with Erik, Erik whom she loved. What might otherwise be viewed as forbidden was allowed here, in the dance. And the music pulled them along, pushed them onward, made them forget what people might think or believe. They only squeezed closer together and hummed with the refrain.

Erik ordered port wine. The looked at each other and toasted one another. A waltz... wouldn't she like to? And they danced again, fluttered past the lamplights, saw out over the crowds of people who had assembled out on the terrace below.

It grew late before they walked back toward the city, but the summer night was not willing to allow any hurry. It was mild out and lovely, inviting for a stroll. They walked along the quay on Strandvägen and breathed in the fresh smell of the wood stacked there. They stopped at Norrström and watched the white foamy water rushing under Norrbro. Above the bridge the arc lamps shone from the wires stretched up high, twinkling when they swayed in the evening breeze.

Maj felt exhilarated, giddily irresponsible. She had to dance a few steps on the street, whirling away in front of him. The next day seemed endlessly far off.

"Will you come home with me a little while?" he asked.

"But Tyra..."

He had thrown her out. She had begun to keep company with some guy that he did not want to see. Besides, he needed the space and she had not been paying. And Bengt was working outside of town now.

No, it was too late. She didn't dare.

They had arrived at her door. He went in with her, it had become a habit. They stood in the dark and kissed. But then they heard someone coming on the stairs and Maj ran up.

She thought she could hear the music when she went to bed, felt how she was swinging round and round, Erik was pressing against her.

She heard his voice, somewhat dry and a little angry: dog fat and rat filth, not idealism but compulsion, I threw her out. His face glimmered into focus in the darkness of the entryway, his knee pushed in between her legs, his hand went down into the neckline of her dress. And his voice again, he started to laugh, sang:

But Mister Rubinstein's luxury gramophone
That he bought on the installment plan...

The music beat rhythmically—or was it just her heart or the port wine? She didn't know, fell asleep.

TROUBLES AND A KIT-BAG

The winter they were waiting for would be difficult; people could sense it. The city's poor might comfort themselves with the knowledge that the election had yielded a new government which in all likelihood should listen more willingly to their complaints than the right-wing ministers who had been brought down did. Now the socialists and liberals together were in charge. Edén had become prime minister and Branting got the department of finance.

But even if those governing were to listen, the resources were still lacking to remedy the disparities. Many factories closed for want of raw materials. Transportation was restricted even more; the few trains and streetcars that ran were always overflowing with travelers. The most difficult was still probably lighting. Kerosene was unobtainable, gas became ever weaker, carbide ran out. The crown princess began a collection for candles so that the poorest in the city would not have to sit in the dark in their homes.

But outside the Phoenix Palace on Drottninggatan flocked expectant crowds dressed for a party. Inside it soon filled up at every table, lights sparkled, music played—and the Stockholmers' new favorite, Ernst Rolf, appeared on stage and sang: Pack Up Your Troubles in Your Old Kit-Bag!

Emelie had stayed on at the factory preparing for the next day. Previously this time of year would have been the busy season. But this year no general overtime work was required. Factory director Melinder was careful of the company's good reputation, and refrained from manufacturing inferior replacements with the raw materials that were to be had. So there was not much to do, and the personnel had been reduced. Now a reasonably large order had come in for goods that could still be delivered, and it was important to plan so that the few packers there could finish it up.

As was customary, she passed by Adolf Fredriks Kyrkogata over by Drottninggatan. Horses hooves clattered, wagons went past, rolling up toward the entrance of the Phoenix Palace. Now all the cars had disappeared.

She saw the glittering lights, the abundance, the gaiety. Imagine if it were Jenny all the people were coming to see... All of a sudden someone who had earlier been unknown could become everyone's idol. Jenny had been acquainted with Ernst Rudolf since he had performed in the Svea Hall a few years ago. He had sung some of those typical old farmer songs and was known as "the humorous man from Dalarna." Ragnar Johansson had been his name back then. Now he was dressed up in tails and top hat and had become Ernst Rolf. And everyone was fighting to see him.

Emelie sudden had a reason to steal away. There, just a few meters away from her stood August's daughters. Two elegant young ladies accompanied by two gentlemen. They were apparently going to go in and see the cabaret. It was impossible to believe that she had sat down together with them, that they had called her "aunt." Now it was as if there was no connection between them and her.

She heard the girls' laughter, like small sparks of flame. She wondered a for moment if it was her they were laughing at—but no, they had not seen her, not even looked in her direction. They laughed at something that only existed in their world where she did not belong.

And yet they were Gunnar's two half-sisters.

Another evening, about a week ago, she had passed by another half-sister of Gunnar's.

Emelie had tried to hurry over, say hello. But Tyra had slipped away and disappeared. It was possible that she had seen Emelie but pretended not to. Maybe she had been ashamed.

The beautiful untroubled girls who laughed and pushed forward to get inside and listen to Ernst Rolf. And the fallen figure who had sneaked past in the lanes' darkness. Gunnar's half-siblings.

The shack at the end of Värmdögatan was barely more than an outhouse; broken panes had been mended with paper and cloth rags.

A few remains of a chair burned in the rusty brown iron stove. A woman sat huddled on the floor and tried to stuff a piece of wood inside that was a little too long to fit. She began to swear, lifted up the lid on the stove with a rake, slipped the piece of wood in from the top. A few sparks flew out, glowing in the dark room.

The door opened and a tall and thin man slipped in. He looked around suspiciously, as if he feared enemies.

The woman stood up. The light from the open stove lid flickered on her gaunt body in the tightly fitting and stained coat, showing off the round bulge, which stuck out and created a macabre contrast to her skinniness.

"You look awful," he declared. "Do you have anything to line my belly with?"

She threw the bag with the leftovers she had gone around begging for in the building at him. He rooted around in it, fished something out, made a face, looked again, and finally found something he considered edible.

"Didn't they take you?" she asked.

David often feigned illness, was expert at collapsing and getting spasms. This had helped him to get good food and rest many times. People gathered around, someone called for an ambulance and he would get to lie in the hospital for many days before they released him without being able to determine what ailed him. He usually "admitted himself" to the hospital when he did not get enough food or sleep. But finally a policeman who patrolled the area around the locks at Slussen and Kolingsborg grew suspicious; the attacks occurred so often. And in collaboration with the doctor at admissions in Söder hospital, he had arranged so that electric wires would be attached to David and he would receive shock treatment. Now David had dared not have an attack for several weeks.

"I fell on the ground again today. That cop has come back."

She began to laugh, a quick laugh without mirth.

"You can go ahead and cackle," he said sullenly.

"Of course," she said. "I have so much to cackle at."

She sank down on the pile of rags, lay and stared into the fire. She wondered how long it would take before the little one arrived, what she would do when it was time. And afterward. One could not live like this with a kid—she would probably be arrested for infanticide.

She had taken care of herself for a long time anyway. Twenty-two years now, could have had that kid six or seven years ago if she had slipped up. She had hung out with the gangs, gone from boy to boy for a long time now. But for the past few years it was mainly David she had been together with. They had begun to be an item, as people said. In the beginning of their acquaintance he had still been a little snobby, spouted a lot of twaddle about the philistines, sat with his accordion and played the Kungsholm gang's parade march. He had been around when the song was new and popular. He was considerably older than she was, almost forty. She had met him one night when he had nowhere to sleep, had begun to talk to him. He had been a little full of himself, how he had managed to swindle a country bumpkin for a whole fifty kronor bill. But still he had no money for a bed.

Since then they had been together.

David had been a rag nailer, an upholsterer, for a while, probably a long time ago now. But that had dried up he said, it didn't pay. You do better pulling farmers' hair. He had come across some defective watches that ticked unevenly and lost time. He sold them and made a few bucks here and there.

Ever since Erik had driven her out of the room she had only had David to go to. He knew an old shoemaker who was such a drunkard and so dithering that he could not keep people out of his place. It was the shoemaker who rented the hovel they stayed in.

David feigned sickness. But he was also sick, something probably with his stomach. An ulcer, maybe. He needed to get some real food and a bed sometimes. That was why he came up with the attacks idea. But now when he really needed it, it didn't work anymore.

"At least we have a bed," he said soothingly. "And one fine day some other slob will share his money with us too."

"But what will I do when the kid comes?"

"Everything will work out," he said. "As long as I can get enough together for a jacket. You can't be too shabbily dressed when you go out to dupe the bumpkins.

She did not answer, just turned her face to the wall.

"Hey..." he pleaded. "Hey... damn it. You're not going to cry are you?"

He sat down on the pile of clothing next to her, stroked her clumsily. She guessed what was going to happen next. If he got close to her he wouldn't stop until he had her. And she wanted him to come to her, didn't have to be afraid now, what could happen had already happened. There was nothing else, nothing more they could give each other.

She lay there with her face turned to the wall, gave in, received him. And still lay that way when he sat up and began to dig around in the food bag again.

In a little while some of the others showed up. They were in a good mood, bragging about the people they had beaten up and about how much they had managed to panhandle. One of them had gotten hold of a bottle of booze from a bootlegger. The bottle went from mouth to mouth.

Tyra sat up, got a smoke, went to the countertop sink and dabbed her face with water. They sat down around the table, poking at each other jokingly, teasing her because she was knocked up and wondering if she wasn't going to pop soon. And she snapped back at them, invited a street seller who wanted to grab her boobs to go to hell, pulled out the bag of leftovers and tipped it out onto the table.

However things were, and whatever all the sensible people said, this was her world. Here was where she felt welcome and could be happy. They asked so little of her, they were friends.

But a child would not be able to live here. And David was sick. Tyra had a feeling that she would be forced to try and take the difficult route back, get a job, live under the tyranny of everyday toil. As long as she had the strength, as long as she had not gone too far outside the bounds of society. She had to have the strength not only for herself, but for David and the child as well. It did seem pretty hopeless.

"Toss the matches and a cigarette over here," she said.

She sat with her hands clasped around her shapeless belly, blew out smoke, pondered. There was in fact no one other than Emelie for her to go to. She didn't want to go there—but she had to.

BESIDE THE
GARBAGE DUMP

Up on the bare hillocks above Söder's garbage dump and surrounding Söder's poorhouse, which was now called Rosenlund's Old People's Home, lay the newly built tenement housing for the poor, brownish yellow two-story tenement houses. From a distance the groups of freshly timbered and freshly painted wooden buildings give the impression of an idyll. Anyone coming closer would find a tattered and impoverished everyday reality of crisis times.

The heights where the largest group of tenement houses stood used to be called Rackarbergen, Rogue Hill, but now it had been renamed Årstalunden, or Årsta Grove. But the rocky hillside still shone gray and cold between the buildings.

One of the longest tenement houses was on the hillock between the garbage disposal plant and the public cleansing division building. In the dump beside it the wagons rattled against the rails, the garbage thudded down on the sheet metal bottom and the winches clattered. On warm days the smell from the garbage rose up and enveloped the children who played above the precipice.

The formerly homeless were moved to these tenement houses for the poor on the outskirts of town. Some of those who could only temporarily be subdued would soon move on. Others might stay longer but continue supporting themselves. But many belonged to those doomed to ruin. Police, inspectors for poor relief, child welfare workers and temperance officers were frequent visitors in the tenements, lifting their hats to each other in the entryways as their boots thumped on the wooden stairs.

The few and feeble streetlamps were not enough to keep much of the autumn darkness at bay. Children still played on the edge of the steep slope, hid among the bushes and shouted taunts at passersby.

Tyra and David stopped at the foot of the slope; there were a couple of wooden steps there. Tyra sank down, panting after the walk.

David stood and hung over the railing, whistling to himself.

They had failed. Actually Tyra had not had such great hopes. But she had still felt like she must ask Emelie. There was really nobody else.

And then she had not even dared to go in. Because of Erik. Erik had stood in the doorway. And as soon as he caught sight of David he began to curse him out as a scab again.

At that point they left. Fled, actually.

How did Erik find out about everything? Already the first time he had seen David he knew about the secret. It was because of David that she had been driven out of the room that her brothers rented.

It was as if David guessed her thoughts. Suddenly he stopped whistling where he was standing behind her in the darkness. He said, "I know why he doesn't like me, your brother. Maybe it's like he says..."

"You can tell me," she said, though in fact she was not curious.

He stayed standing at the wooden railing behind her and she barely recognized his voice, it was so low. He didn't have his usual self-assurance.

He was marked. Never thought he would get honest work again. That's the way it was. And it was the general strike's fault. Just before it broke out he had managed to get a good job. At that time he had been married, had two kids. When the strike broke out the factory owner asked him to stay on the job and he had been dumb enough to go along with it. The wife had been so afraid that he would have to go begging again and he had thought it can't be that bad to go on working. But then the factory had closed and when he looked for a new job there was nobody who dared hire him. There was trouble everywhere he went. He had been barred from the union; organized workers were not allowed to work with him. He had tried his hand at working as an upholsterer for a while, but they had even succeeded in getting him fired from that little workshop.

He had really believed that it would pass after a time. But still, eight years after the strike, it was just as bad. It had even happened that strangers came up to him and slugged him in the jaw. And old buddies pretended not to know him. Besides that it was also his unusual appearance that made things extra tricky for him—others could hide themselves in the crowd and be forgotten. Him they remembered.

His old lady and the kids had left. Everything had gone to hell. That's the way it was.

He hummed in the darkness:

The word for girls who sin against our Father
And cross the line at the seventh commandment...

He was quiet for a moment, then burst out:

In Kungsholm's Church it is so fine up in the morning
But across the street it is so fine the other times!

"Shut your trap!" she said, more irritated than indignant. He was like a kid who liked to shout dirty words. And his story was also that of a frightened child, a half-truth to arouse sympathy and escape a spanking. Actually pretty typical: the only time David had worked was just when there was a strike.

"Do you think they'll give us a bed?" she wondered.

"Sure," he answered confidently. "Dad has been put away for vagrancy for a bit, but he's home again. We can probably stay till you've had the kid at least. After that we will have to see."

"Then we had better get going," she said and got up clumsily.

His mother was in the hospital they found out. His father had not had time to find any work yet, had just been released from the institution for alcoholics. One of David's sisters was still living there with her child, a five-year-old daughter. The sister looked at Tyra and her belly with hostility. She asked as if Tyra was not present, "Is that going to live here too?"

"This is Tyra," said David. "We are going to get married."

"Are you really divorced from the previous one yet?" asked his sister.

"Keep your nose out of it. You didn't even see who the father of your kid was. He just happened to pass by as you lay with your ass in the air scrubbing the steps of the customs house, right?"

Red with rage she left the kitchen.

"Forget her," said David. "She thinks she's something because she had a kid with a married customs policeman. Actually she's a good sort. You two will probably get along."

They were allowed to sleep in the kitchen. David got a mattress, which they shared. The old man lay on the kitchen sofa. He didn't bother them, lived in his world, drank and slept.

It wasn't long before Tyra was used to her new life, grew inured to the gray everyday of the tenements. The sister, Dora, was not hard to live together with, once one had gotten to know her. The mother came back from the hospital, whined about her cramps and the lack of money, but took it as something completely natural that the family had increased while she was away. Money from poor relief and Dora's earnings from scrubbing gave them the most essential things. David was responsible for himself and Tyra. Sometimes he took his accordion and went into courtyards and played and sang. Other days he hung out in the cafés in the Old Town and sold stolen ration cards. And if the opportunity presented itself he would pinch one thing or another that came his way.

It worked; they lived. And Tyra got used to the clattering of the garbage trucks below them, to the smell, to all the sounds of the people in the thin-walled wooden house, the hordes of kids yelling on the slope outside, the countless cats, the bed bugs. She quarreled with the women and glared at the men when they joked about her large belly. Anyone who said anything about a scab got a piece of her mind. They knew very well that David hadn't understood what he had gotten into.

Besides—David and work, what did they think he really accomplished? He couldn't make anybody who purchased his labor happy.

They had never seen it that way before, never thought of it like that. David as a strikebreaker must have been more of a good joke than the doer of an uncomradely deed. They had to laugh at the thought—David work! And in the laughter there was a fair amount of forgiveness.

In January the child was born; it was a boy and they called him Allan. One week later the police arrived and took David away. Someone had tried to mark him, surely someone who wanted to make life miserable for the scab. Or plain bad luck. It could hardly be because of incompetence, that boy was so smart, said his father.

Even though Tyra was still weak after the birth, she asked Dora if she could go with her to scrub. David's mother took care of the baby for a few hours and Tyra could at least earn a few kronor. She continued to work when David came home after a few days, thought it was best to. He had managed to wriggle out of it this time; they had not had enough solid evidence. Luckily it wasn't David but his friend who had the bundle of stolen ration cards in his pocket when the cops descended on the café. But now David had to lie low awhile, he felt like he was being watched. He went home and lazed about. There was snow in the hollows of the hills but the sun shone and warmed it up.

Tyra felt at home. She even wondered if it was here she had moved for the rest of her life. The other siblings had gone to Emelie, found steady jobs, become some kind of proletarian petty bourgeoisie. But she had not wanted to bind herself, couldn't deal with that kind of orderliness that existed in Emelie's proximity. Whole and clean... poor but honest. All those attempts to make misery honorable, to wear away at your life by darning and mending and scrubbing ever more worn out clothes. No, that was not for her. If she couldn't afford to buy new she would rather go in rags.

In the world of the tenement houses she could assert herself, feel appreciated. She had some of the strength and willpower that many lacked in the family, was often the one who decided things. They asked her advice, they came to her for help. And the women in the surrounding apartments did as well. She had arrived as the scab's girl, someone to pick at, put down. But she elbowed her way forward, was ready to fight for her rights, for her kid and for her man.

The family who had become hers lived close to the garbage dump. David had a brother who had been in prison for several years. His children were in the children's home; his wife was in a home for fallen women. David's father was institutionalized frequently, his mother went from hospital to hospital, David himself could be arrested any day.

Still she was proud of them, they weren't just anybody.

Together with Dora she went and scrubbed buildings, all the steps covered with slush from the winter, the big offices. And the days grew longer and lighter, and when she got home David was sitting on the stairs with his accordion, Allan lay in a margarine crate beside him and all the kids from the tenement house were bellowing the Kungsholm's league's parade march.

THE SONS

August sat alone in his office waiting for Gunnar. When he waited for someone or something it was as if his ability to work was paralyzed. He could not bring himself to start work that would soon be interrupted. As a result he would just sit and think—and that could certainly be needed as well.

It was not easy being a building contractor during these years of war and crisis. Fewer and fewer new buildings were being constructed. Materials were insufficient and the lion's share of the little there was went to so-called public benefit projects. And then housing rents were not allowed to go up in conjunction with other rising prices. It was forbidden by the new rent control law.

Every law has its loopholes—the rent control law made exceptions for properties that were built after the law was passed. If one could not build from scratch then one could always add on. During recent years the business had been struck by fever, "spectacular wartime conditions." Practically anything could be sold. New industries were started and the demand for locations grew. Many residences were expanded into offices and brought in increased rents. There were plenty of people who were willing to pay.

Even if there were opportunities to make money in his line of work, it was not as much fun to work in as before was August Bodin's opinion. Making business deals now was not a case of meticulous planning, it was rather more a game of chance. Instead of creating something new and doing something useful, you had to do double-dealings and build on and contrive legal but not always pleasant methods to get the most possible out of it. And the one who wanted to live honestly had to refuse money that was proffered every day.

He did not like it, neither one way nor the other. But he was forced to do it. He had to keep the firm going and support his family and still maintain his respectability as much as possible.

Quite often he had reason to think back to an earlier period of difficulty in the company's history. Twenty-five years ago, in 1893, the firm
had been on the way to sliding out of his adoptive father's hands. But
that year had been August's own big year; he had managed to help his
father save the company and he had met Ida once again. Since then he
had held the leadership, taken himself through the difficulties of the
crisis years and strikes. Sometimes it felt as if one crisis gave way to
another, as if he just trampled through one problem to get to the next.

He wondered for one icy moment: Am I on the way to becoming
as burned out as Father was then?

No, it wasn't that bad yet. He could allow himself that consolation.
Father had been helpless, without the will or the ability to act, a
wreck. As for himself, he ran just as nimbly and assiduously today as
before, like a squirrel in a wheel.

He would need help, everything would be more meaningful if he
had someone to guide, if he felt someone step in and unburden him.
Just as Father had once needed him, he needed his own son.

But Karl Henrik was no great help. He ought to have been able to
do it. He had turned twenty-two.

Maybe Karl Henrik had been too protected, maybe in general they
had demanded too little of their children. Many times August had had
reason to compare his own childhood with that of his children. They
could not have the same respect for small sums, the same feeling for
the necessity of economizing. They demanded so much, imagined
that they could afford anything. And Karl Henrik believed of course
that work was some kind of waste of time, that everything would take
care of itself and money stream in without any effort at all.

All too often August had grown irritated at his son's manner of
behavior at the office. The boy used his working time and the space
for his private interests. There were continual telephone calls and
meetings with those Finland activists. August had known several of
the boys for a long time; they were Karl Henrik's old schoolmates, fine
and decent youths. And in any case—their cause, the coalition for

. Finland, was widely respected and should be supported.

What was happening in Finland now was upsetting. Since the end of January a real civil war had been going on there. They had proclaimed revolution against the legal government, which had been forced to flee Helsinki for Vasa. The Red Guard was ravaging and plundering. According to what people said, they went out like hooligans, nailed priests to tables by their tongues, raped and burned.

But in the workers' press equally terrible accusations were made against the White Guard, the "butchers," and their German divisions.

August had naturally not believed what stood in the socialist newspapers; educated people could not behave like that. But lately he had been gripped by doubt. Karl Henrik received letters from friends who had joined the Swedish Brigade and read them aloud at home. And those letters could make one think twice.

One of the boys described with obvious delight piles of frozen corpses; he rejoiced at the sight of so many hooligans rendered harmless. Another boy wrote that they hoped the Swedish Left Socialists, Lindhagen and Vennerström, would still be in Helsinki when the Whites reached it. Those were the two they wanted to hang from the nearest lamppost. The same writer also told a story about a misunderstanding regarding the point of something: a Swedish officer had given some Finnish soldiers orders to evacuate a hospital for wounded Reds. After a while the soldiers had come back and asked what they should do with the empty beds. The orders had been interpreted in such a way that all the wounded had been executed.

The story should not be spread so that it reached the wrong ears, explained the correspondent. One did not know what results Branting's "false reports" in the Swedish parliament could have. And one had to be careful not to feed the malicious propaganda of the opposition.

With wonder and some consternation August noticed how enthusiastically Karl Henrik got involved in such letters.

Karl Henrik had wanted to go out with the brigade, follow his friends. August had implored him to desist. Karl Henrik was the one who would one day take over the firm; the whole family's welfare might depend on him. If August passed away there was nobody else who could take over; Fredrik was way too young.

Unwillingly Karl Henrik had agreed to stay at home. Was he taking his revenge now in some way by being so totally uninterested in his work?

Despite everything, August had to take joy in the fact that his son was still at home, safe and secure. In both body and soul. For no matter how great their concerns at home might be, the boys would certainly be brutalized by war.

As he sat here alone in his room and pondered, he reached a conclusion that he barely dared to admit to himself: that there maybe was not such a great difference between the Reds and the Whites, that cruelty can never be defended, that surely there were good and bad people on both sides.

If what was happening in Finland spread here… How would things turn out then? He could guess. The workers, the poor, on one side. The middle class and the upper class on the other. Those who hesitated would be forced into the different camps, scared into solidarity. Of his three sons one would go with the Reds, two with the Whites. He himself would be white, Emelie probably red.

Antagonisms were not as severe here, hatred not as great. Finland was poorer and lay closer to the Russian core of unrest. But he remembered what it had been like the previous spring, the continuous demonstrations, the threats. There were people who were afraid the Socialists would start a revolution on the first of May this year, follow the Finnish example.

He had to smile to himself: here he sat and hoped for and believed in Branting, almost depending on the Socialist leaders not to let something like that happen here.

He waited for Karlsson, for Gunnar. The red son, an enemy if there was revolution here too. Or maybe Gunnar was not so red?

There was doubtless nothing wrong with Gunnar. If it was wrong that the boy would land on the other side, then it was not his fault but his father's, who had left him to grow up on the other side of the wall.

They sat at the office a long time, discussing plans that August had proposed.

Bodin's had taken over a building from an estate. In the basement a good location was available. If would suit a smaller carpentry shop perfectly. Now when so many spaces were being expanded for offices, a carpentry firm that specialized in decoration and furnishings could get plenty of work. At least to begin with, Bodin's could leave a lot of orders with such a company: they had a construction job underway and wanted to avoid hiring new people for small jobs the way conditions were now.

It might be worth a try. It didn't involve any great risks. If it failed Gunnar could return to his old position as boss.

August felt like he almost had to talk him into it. But he wanted to reach a resolution. It went against his grain to have both Karl Henrik and Gunnar in the firm, not least when he sensed that Karl Henrik's activity was discussed and was criticized among his employees.

Gunnar listened, considered, pulled out a notebook and calculated, tried to figure out what it would cost with renting and hiring and everything that was involved. August declared himself willing to put in a certain amount to start with and loan him more if it was necessary. Gunnar's cautious interest and thoroughness got him engaged; he always liked discussing business, weighing costs against earnings. He found that Gunnar came back with pretty intelligent points of view, he tested his son, noticed that he couldn't be fooled: he had his eyes and wits about him.

The strained feeling he had just felt had disappeared. Here he was sitting with a son who was completely engaged in his work and his future, who wanted to take advantage of his elder's knowledge and experience. If he had been able to talk like this with Karl Henrik...

Let's go and look at the location and then get a bite to eat together, he finished up.

He didn't want to part from Gunnar, not so quickly.

The Whites continued to win. Tammerfors fell into their hands in the beginning of April, but many of the Swedish Brigade fell in the bloody fighting. One week later the German troops took Helsinki. At the end of April, Viborg fell and the red leaders fled to Russia. The last of the Red Guard capitulated at Lahtis. In the middle of May Mannerheim marched into Helsinki and the war was officially over.

Karl Henrik walked around as if in ecstasy. In the middle of the day he ran out of the office to participate in receptions and conferences. When Goole Trade landed at Skeppsbron with the returning brigadiers, Karl Henrik was naturally up in front, following them in their march through the city up to Stadion where they were paid tribute. Large crowds of people lined the streets, cheering and waving. But there was a commotion at Birger Jarlsgatan when Nerman, the editor from "Politiken" shouted "Murderer!" He was immediately seized by the police; a few other demonstrators managed to get away via the back streets.

Afterward reports arrived of the Whites' terrible reprisals and of the enormous mortality in the Finnish prison camps. Even some of the Swedish brigadiers described with horror what had happened: *The war is over; the hunt for people has begun.*

Karl Henrik calmed down a little. The group he belonged to had done their job, their mission was accomplished. The spring's hectic activities had left a mark on him. He had a hard time settling down to everyday living, seemed to feel that anything that had to do with the firm was trivial and uninteresting.

As usual, during the summer months the family lived out on the island of Stora Essingen. The city had crept closer, it was easier to get out there and back now that a floating bridge had been put down between Stora Essingen and the neighboring island, Lilla Essingen. To be sure, it was just a footbridge whose middle section was made of a rope ferry, but it was still a large improvement.

One late summer evening when August went home alone to the apartment, he caught sight of a little poetry pamphlet in Karl Henrik's room. The author was a Finland-Swede, Bertel Gripenberg.

A bit ashamed, as if he were poking around in someone else's secrets, he leafed through the pamphlet, reading a few lines here and there.

Drums and trumpets, armored battalions and proud dragoons. Snarling wolves' teeth, roaring mouths of fire, bloody chasms. But August was frightened, felt the hatred and the contempt that gushed forth:

And Finland's brutalized Reds
Who dream of pillage and prey,
Shall be rooted out, driven away
Freeing our earth of them alway.

This poem was one of the ones that had been written since the fighting was over, during peacetime. Distressed, August read of hordes of barbarians who were not worthy of the name of man, and read of the chasm between people and animals.

Like a lightning bolt, like the punishing sword of the Lord, the Whites would go forth and sweep out the piles of the bandits' criminal offenses for damnation:

We are the sons of the gods
Of the white pantheon of Aesir's line...

August threw the book aside, fled the room. He thought he could hear the song that had been sung in there so many times: Sons of a people that bled...

Sons. Red hooligans, white slaughterers. Heroes of the proletariat, liberators of the fatherland, shot down as traitors or thanked as liberators. And all the silent and small that were just forced to go along.

He should bring his sons together, had done wrong in keeping them apart. He himself had gone along with drawing the boundary that should not be there.

Although—on the other hand...

THE BELLS
ARE RINGING

It was raining; gray fog enveloped the city. People who were hurrying through the rain looked poorer and more tired than before. The scarcity of food and clothes had set its stamp on many. And then the fear of the raging epidemic that only grew in strength and size.

News flyers with headlines hung like white rags outside the newsstands and bookstalls, reporting of a giant accident: more than forty people had been killed in Geta when the railroad embankment, which had been dug out by the rain, collapsed and the train from Malmö crashed into the ravine.

The war was still going on, there was still no end in sight. The Germans had forced their conditions of an armistice on the Russian Bolsheviks, but their massive offensive in the west had met with failure. Now they were expecting the fifth winter of the war.

Despite everything Gunnar felt quite happy as he walked home in the autumn foul weather. He certainly was tired. But he liked to work, not least of all when he had his own firm. He hadn't made any brilliant deals, but he supported himself and his two employees.

He could have tried to squeeze onto a streetcar, but thought it felt good to get out a little after the day's indoor work. It was this walk home that he liked. Then he could think about what he had to do and sometimes also let his thoughts wander over things other than work. Now he was walking along and thinking about his father, the building contractor.

There were building contractors who were much closer to their employees. They walked around in their midst, swore and swaggered, drawing attention to some kind of equality at the same time, in a kind of boorish way, talking about who made the decisions. August Bodin always kept a certain distance. Now Gunnar wondered if it was more out of shyness and fear. His father had a hard time making contact, just like Gunnar himself. It took time for them to loosen up; they were afraid of appearing dumb and intrusive.

These days the previously so alien man came and sat down at his carpentry shop, talked to him as an equal, showed so clearly that he liked to be there. It was no small thanks to Hjördis that things had gotten that way. She joked shamelessly with August, had no respect for him at all. The atmosphere had become such that it was suddenly easy for Gunnar to use the familiar form of address with him, something which had previously been so difficult.

This boded well for the future. Through Bodin's he would always be able to get a certain amount of work and help with creditors, good advice also when it was needed.

The time when Gunnar first heard who his real father was, he had felt some kind of hatred. A man who had abandoned his mother, left him to be half beaten to death by a stepfather. They would have starved to death if Emelie had not been there. Now he knew better how it had been. Then—and as it had turned out now—the past could be forgiven.

As if freed from the difficult past he would get to begin a new life. Once he found a decent apartment, or maybe a lot where he could build a cottage, he and Hjördis would get married. At first he had thought to wait until there was peace—but it felt impossible to wait for that.

A car rolled past splashing water up on the sidewalk. Cars did not come by very often now; when he looked up he saw that it was a fire department ambulance. It was probably someone who had gotten the Spanish flu and was on the way to Maria Hospital.

The epidemic showed no sign of abating. The deaths were many. During the summer there had been the first wave of sickness, but then in a mild form. Now that it had returned with the bad fall weather, it was of a much more serious nature, often accompanied by great difficulty in breathing and violent nosebleeds.

But Gunnar felt young and strong, as if the sickness did not really concern him.

When he got home he found that they had an unexpected visitor. Tyra had come; she was sitting in the kitchen and drinking dandelion coffee together with Emelie and Jenny.

His sister looked unkempt, her hair was hanging in wisps out from under a wet ladies' hat that she didn't take off. She had a baby that was a few months old, a boy, she said. Now her husband had been taken to the hospital. The Spanish flu, of course. His parents, the ones they were living with, were also sick. No one besides Tyra could earn any money; she had been scrubbing stairs and worked as hard as she could. Now she was beginning to feel a little distressed herself. Could they help her with a little money or some food?

Gunnar took out his wallet and contributed his share. And Tyra assured them that she would not have come if she had been able to manage any other way.

She had changed, but not just for the worse—there was a clear wish to take responsibility for that child.

Maybe the sickness came with Tyra. Maybe it would have come anyway, almost all the people were sick.

Jenny got a fever, a sore throat and diarrhea. A few days later it was Maj's turn.

At Emelie's job they were talking about a cure that would absolutely do the trick if one got sick with the Spanish flu. The sick person was to be rolled in wet sheets and wrapped in as many blankets and comforters as one could get hold of. They tried this method and both Jenny and Maj got well after a week. They couldn't say whether it was because of the cure or not.

The epidemic reached even greater proportions. Doctors were placed at police stations to be ready to dash out round to clock. The lack of cars was cause for concern. There were only three transport vehicles for the sick and some open cars for the doctors. The doctors wanted covered cars in the bad fall weather, but there weren't any. The tires available in these crisis times did not hold under the heavier cars with roofs—and these cars used more fuel. But doctors on call with identification could ride the streetcars, even if this caused the number of passengers to go over the limit.

The newspapers filled several pages with obituaries every day. At the pharmacies the supplies of aspirin ran out. Many people complained about the continual funeral bells ringing in the churches. It was extra hard for the sick with the eternal reminder of their mortality.

The Bodins were struck too.

First Ida got sick—but it seemed only like an ordinary cold and already after a few days she was well again. Karl Henrik and two of the girls were taken to their beds. In their cases there was no question that it was the Spanish flu, though not in any particularly virulent form.

But the youngest son, Fredrik, had cramps and difficulty breathing, and it was clear that he had to go to the hospital. Several of the hospitals were full. At Sabbatsberg over the last twenty-four hours they had taken in fifty patients, but they would try to find space for him anyway.

They waited for the ambulance a long time. Fredrik had developed a strange dry cough and complained about difficulty breathing. His throat was bluish red and looked like it was varnished. He was placed in the main ward with the others, and August and Ida who had gone along in the ambulance were told to go home; they would call from the hospital if there was any change.

But no one called. They did not feel calm enough to go to bed, so they sat by the telephone in the library the whole night. The maid came with the morning coffee, genuine and strong coffee that August had paid twenty-five kronor a kilo for.

Now being able to pay did not help anything. Now he was left out like all the others. Helpless.

In the afternoon they called from the hospital. He and Ida rushed there. Fredrik was still alive, but it was a feeble and almost imperceptible life. The boy's head had taken on a blue-gray color, he did not have the strength to look up or speak to them.

They sat by his bed, waiting for the miracle they no longer dared believe in. Ida cried and he himself also felt the tears that he had to check. He felt his dry and red eyes smart and burn.

Nothing could be done, nothing. And he had wanted to give his life for the boy.

While they were there Fredrik died.

August's youngest son was only one of the more than twenty-seven thousand lives that the epidemic took. There had been no such deadly plague in the land since they had begun to collect statistics of causes of death.

But for August it still felt like he had reached a precipice. In a few weeks Fredrik would have turned eighteen. In the spring he would have graduated. A short time ago he had still been a child.

August had had his plans for Fredrik. He had thought that perhaps his younger son had greater qualifications for taking care of the firm than Karl Henrik. The two brothers would at least be able to complement each other, help each other.

Now Fredrik was no longer alive.

Yet gradually August had to get used to the fact that life went on. Even if the plague had killed many, there were even more survivors, and they had to be protected from new dangers. That was true of the world in general, that was true of his family.

Now he was completely dependent on Karl Henrik being able to change and become involved. And if not—what would he do then?

But he still had one more son—and that son knew the business. Gunnar was perhaps not the right man to run a large company, did not have the education and the confidence that were necessary. Moreover it would be unreasonable for him to imagine that Gunnar would run a company that would give his unknown half-siblings their secure future. That would not be pleasurable for either party.

In reality, the two sons ought to be able to complement each other, each take care of his part of the company. It was not time to make any changes now, but one day in the future he could imagine doing it.

He wanted to make a try at bringing them together and arranged for a meeting at a restaurant. He suggested that the contacts between Bodin's and Gunnar's carpentry shop would be managed by them in the future. He began with working out the details involving renovating a store. But he soon found that it was only himself and Gunnar who were interested. Karl Henrik sat and flirted with some girls at a neighboring table.

"Do you follow what I'm saying?" he asked.

"Sure. That should work," answered Karl Henrik. "Karlsson should be able to take care of things… Gunnar, I mean, best himself."

The time of the meeting was maybe not so well chosen. Karl Henrik was irritable and in a bad mood because of events in Germany. It was clear that the German defense was in the process of being broken down. There were new socialists in the German government. In Kiel the sailors had held an insurrection and helped build a workers-soldiers council. Uprisings in Lübeck and other cities were reported. A revolution was expected at any time.

The Germans had helped Finland's Whites. Karl Henrik was, like most of his friends, "German minded." When he and his father had gone to the restaurant meeting that evening he had asked if "that Gunnar" wasn't rather red.

"Besides, maybe there will be a revolution here as well and then we will have other things to do than to renovate stores," said Karl Henrik now and laughed.

"Dumb remark," August said curtly.

But he did not feel completely sure. If the revolution had now reached Germany, what if the fire spread.

When they left the restaurant August felt like he was leaving a fiasco.

The German Kaiser fled to Holland; on the ninth of November Karl Liebknecht raised the red banner over the castle in Berlin. Two days later the fighting stopped.

Now the church bells were ringing all over the world, ringing in peace.

The same day something happened in Sweden: the socialist left threatened a general strike, demanded a republic and an eight-hour workday, the expropriation of companies and goods, and the building of workers-, soldiers- and farmers- councils all over Sweden. People could not brush aside the threat as one from a meaningless minority—similar demands were also made by many Social Democrats. Social Democrats as well as Liberals demanded comprehensive constitutional changes. First and foremost they wished to institute universal suffrage, including for women.

But on the right-wing fringes, people were talking instead of a return to the old class-based elections for society and lamented that Sweden had no Mannerheim. He would have only needed a wooden sword to intimidate the democratic revolution that now threatened.

Funeral bells are ringing across the capitalist world, shouted the left's spokesman, Fredrik Ström.

Would the bells of peace turn out to be the bells of death? Bolts were set in the doors of the upper-class houses on Strandvägen, revolvers were bought, money taken out of the banks. And the whole time people listened worriedly for the revolutionaries' first shots.

The labor union held meetings in the People's Hall. Gunnar got there in plenty of time; they were expecting a lot of people. He sat on one of the benches farthest away in Auditorium A.

The rumor made its way through the rows of benches; they were expecting the executive committee to recommend revolution with a demand for the immediate formation of a republic. Branting had arrived. The leaders apparently were still holding a conference; they should have opened the meeting by now. But the enormous attendance meant that several halls had to be opened; the speakers would have to circulate.

Finally Branting stood on the speaker's platform, the decisive moment was upon them.

If he proclaimed revolution now they would follow him. If he demanded a new general strike they would accept. Now anything could happen.

The man on the speaker's platform looked down over the hall with tired eyes. Then he began to speak and his weariness disappeared. Some of the future's Utopia was visible; he showed them the way that he thought would lead them there.

We will lay the foundations for a democratic ordering of society with room for socialist development—but not a war between social classes.

That was the essence, the answer. The revolution would not happen, at least not in the form of a bloody uprising. The questions about a unicameral system and a republic would be decided by a parliament elected according to democratic principles or by a general election. Voting rights graded on a scale of wealth would be abolished and be replaced by equal municipal voting rights. Political voting rights will be expanded through the abolishment of voting restrictions and the introduction of women's suffrage. The eight-hour workday would be instituted. Conscripted military training would be cancelled for the time being and a commission set up to work on suggestions for the development of a new military.

Such were the broad outlines and demands that were laid down in the manifesto that was adopted. Some of the points would certainly be compromised on in the coming negotiations between parties. But there would be no question of any Major concessions, the line would hold.

During the following weeks August came down to the carpentry shop often to talk with Gunnar. He wanted to know what his son thought and believed, how he and his political friends comprehended what had happened, now after the big constitutional debate in parliament.

Of course there had been many who wanted to go farther, demand more than Branting had done. Even among the Liberals there were those who thought that they had given in too much when they set the voting age as high as twenty-three years of age. But at the same time greater gains had been made. It was really a question of a breakthrough for democracy. And the remarkable thing was that it could happen with so much unanimity. It's true Hjalmar Hammarskjöld had said that the decision meant that power would lie in the hands of those who were least competent to handle it. But the first chamber of parliament had still accepted the constitutional revision without a vote and the twelve in the second chamber who had voted against it were the Left Socialists who demanded even more comprehensive reforms.

As Gunnar saw it, Branting had once more been capable of the most difficult task, to set the future ahead of the present. Through not demanding too much he had been able to carry everyone along with him. Now democratization had been decided by the all the people. By this means the new society got a solid foundation. The minorities who placed themselves outside it were so small that they could not ruin the work. Increased voting rights would soon lead to a more radical parliament and then one thing and another that were still just in writing could be worked out.

August nodded. That could likely be so.

If one could start to work in earnest now, build things up after all the years of things only being torn down.

For the first time after Fredrik's death he was able to think of the future again.

IV

A TONE
OF DESPERATION

Ration cards disappeared; things that had long been missed could once again be bought. Hoarders got rid of rancid supplies; stores sold dandelion coffee and reed tobacco at reduced prices. The fuel commission found it had eight million cubic meters of wood left that was standing and rotting in piles. A lot of mismanagement was discovered, but no one really had the energy to condemn any longer. War profiteers and loan sharks disappeared, many just as poor as when then had been cast into the whirl. Only a few managed to push their way up to the thin outer layer of society's traditional and stabilized wealthy members.

Cars began to roll through the streets once more, soon in the same profusion as during the first years of the war when there had been a few thousand cars in the city. Flight had been developed during the war, now a German Captain Göring gave daily ascents over Stockholm with passengers. A regular airline between Malmö and London was inaugurated. The airship Bodensee, a one hundred twenty meter long cigar-shaped zeppelin, came on a visit.

In parliament the eight-hour workday was adopted after long discussions. As a follow-up of the earlier constitutional revision, the first women members of parliament were elected.

Much could be viewed as full of promise. But the gifts of peace were still not as great as one had hoped. Instead of prosperity and progress people soon got long and difficult years of crisis with recession, unemployment and new privation.

Much of their faith had been dashed to the ground by the war; now peace arrived with new disappointments. The many disappointed hopes gave the years after the war a tone of desperation.

One could imagine that tone in much that was new. It was in jazz melodies, in the spasmodic shaking of the shimmy, in the increasingly hectic life of pleasure seeking. It could be sensed in the violent burst of home distilling.

Maybe it was also there hidden in the starkly audacious accompaniments to woman's liberation. Women graduated from secondary school, became parliamentarians and marriage mediators. Their skirts got shorter, layers of thick petticoats disappeared and silky tricot and charmeuse were the rage. On the beaches communal bathing was practiced, and the earlier bathing suits with lots of fabric were replaced by tightly fitting wool sheaths. A lady who tried to walk through the city dressed in coveralls was seized by the police, however. That fashion was seen as too offensive.

Liberation and promiscuity were met with a new puritanism, abuse of alcohol with demands for prohibition. The "Pentecostal epidemic" spread across the country and among those who joined the ecstatic movement was the author Sven Lidman. In Italy a new political extremist group rose up, fascism, which called for a vigorous effort to counter superficiality.

When the big crisis arrived, the workers found support in their solidarity and in their unions. They had won the ability to negotiate and could meet toughness with toughness through threats of common action.

Office workers had it harder. The office worker who wanted to attain any benefit had to speak up alone and there was always someone who was ready to take every position on lower terms.

The office workers' union that existed was more of a social club than a labor union and had relatively few members. An unemployed office worker could not count on any support and instead would be referred to distress relief work. This was often of such a nature that anyone not used to physical work could hardly manage it.

It was especially difficult for those supporting families. Hunched over men with shiny pants seats and worn elbows glanced worriedly at the young girls who could get by on considerably lower salaries. When one position opened up hundreds of applicants would flock to it.

The office workers were held in contempt because they did not have any effective organization, but people were ingratiating to them as well: they held positions of trust and were to be treated as individuals, not as a collective group. During worker conflicts it was taken as a given that they would stand on the side of the companies and be strikebreakers if it were necessary. They stood close to management. And this proximity to those higher up gave them many love-hate relationships, consisting of both self-contempt and overestimating their own value.

The office worker corps had grown immensely during the war years; the women especially had become more numerous. The many young girls on their way to and from their workplaces, or catching some sun during morning breaks, provided a new feature on the street scene.

The flocks of them that came whirling out of the doorways on Regeringsgatan and spread across the sidewalks around there could be compared to a cluster of light-colored butterflies in the sunshine. But under the light and glitter there was a feeling of desperation as well. The office management had just announced that all office workers' salaries were to be cut by forty percent.

UNCERTAIN FUTURE

The traffic rumbled along across Norrbro and Gustav Adolf's Square. Private cars had their convertible tops down and the sun sparkled on the radiators' metal hoods. The streams of traffic from the bridge and from the many streets around the square ran up against each other. Cars squeezed in between horse-drawn carriages and pushcarts. Horns blared impatiently.

Two girls stood outside the enormous bank building, leaning against the rough stone wall. Today they were not enjoying the sunshine as usual; they only felt bewildered and upset. Of course prices had gone down over the past few years. But still they could barely have lived on their salaries if they hadn't lived at home. And now they suddenly were going to receive little more than half of that.

They should protest, quit, show that they would not just take anything. But it wouldn't work. They could only accept and be thankful that they at least had a job. There were several hundred thousand without jobs in the country. It wasn't as if one got any public assistance either if one became unemployed. Only those who had responsibilities to support others got that. The unemployment commission had wanted to cut back on welfare for all women—but then the government had said no after all.

One of the men at the office who was married and had a large family had made an attempt to gather his workmates and get them to demand negotiations. The boss had heard what was going on and called in the culprit. He did not want to hear about any such carryings on, he did not negotiate with office workers, he had had it up to here with what the workers dreamed up.

"The only thing we can do is become more thrifty," said Maj.

"Or find a rich guy," said Agnes. "Haven't you heard from him, by the way?"

"I don't know anyone who's rich," Maj objected. "But he did call."

She had to tell even though she didn't really feel like it. Agnes was her friend, after all.

He wondered if we couldn't meet. Though he didn't ask me to forgive him.

Maj had not dared tell Agnes about the real reason for her break-up with Erik, only said that he had lied to her. For a long time she had gone around afraid, now she didn't think she had to be any longer. But the consequence was that she kept quiet. No one was to know anything. Even Agnes.

"I promised to meet him," she said. "But it's bad luck that it is just today. This thing with our pay has put me in a bad mood."

"Right now you might need some fun," Agnes said consolingly.

Maj wasn't so sure that it was going to be fun. She did not want it to be like before, at least not before Erik promised to mend his ways. And the worst thing was that she did not really dare believe in his promises.

They were on Regeringsgatan now. It was cast in shadow and they shivered. Spring had not come as far as one might believe out there in the sunshine.

Erik stood and waited for her. He had grown almost more elegant since their last meeting a few months ago. A new hat and new spring jacket, low shoes and a walking stick.

He smiled his slightly crooked smile, that expression that she could never quite get used to. One could think that it was friendly or sneering; it depended on what kind of a mood one was in oneself.

"Just as pretty," he said and took her arm. She shrugged him carefully but firmly off, he wasn't going to get any ideas. And besides, it was unnecessary to walk around arm in arm like that. Some of her workmates might see her and think they were engaged.

"And just as sulky?" he asked. "Can't you forget that little incident?"

"Little incident! What if somebody from the office had happened to read it and guessed that it was me!"

"Nobody would have been able to prove anything. Besides it was a good story. A representative from the Office and Commerce

Association got in touch and wondered if they shouldn't try to organize the personnel in your office. But when he heard what kind of
office it was he left it at that. He dealt mostly with department store
office workers, he said. The office workers' association should take
care of all the others."

"Did you say which firm he got in touch with?"

He waited a moment with his answer: "Of course not." She guessed
that he was lying.

She would never dare tell him anything again about her firm. She
would not have told him this either if she had not been so indignant.
With out any further ado they had fired one of the oldest workers in
the company, a bookkeeper who had vacillated about filling some
entries in a way that he considered wrong, even outright illegal. Erik
had gone directly to "The People's Daily" with the story. The office
had not been named, but there was certainly information that
pointed in the right direction.

"That you could have done that, even though you promised..."

"C'mon, no one could know which firm it was. And there is
probably the same amount of crooked dealings everywhere. Nobody
guessed anything, right?"

"But you broke your promise."

"Now we are going to stop. I did not break any promise."

She was silent.

"I thought we would eat at Pelikan," he said. "We can maybe stop
by my place first, I'm expecting a letter."

At one time she had taken it for granted that they would be together all their lives.

Now nothing was taken for granted anymore. They quarreled quite
often. He was so busy with other things; during long periods he hardly had time to meet her except for brief moments. It was his business
dealings and work in the party. The latest had been a large collection
of clothing for Russian children that he had been so involved in.

That's the way it was with Erik. Intensive periods when they were together constantly, when everything else was pushed aside. When he was exuberant, madly happy and in love. And then weeks of chilliness and indifference, when everything else was so much more important, when he was so pressed for time and had so little friendliness and warmth.

The woman who was together with Erik would have to obliterate herself, content herself with just being there and being available when it was convenient. Could she and did she want to do that? Right now it did not feel like she did.

"Things have been so busy," he said. The party had been behind the unemployment demonstrations, gathered deputies from around the country, organized meetings and official visits. He had participated in and organized everything.

And then there were all the complications. A few years ago the party had split and the group he belonged to called itself the Communist Party and had adopted twenty-one theses. Höglund, Ström and Kilbom formed the leadership. Vennerström, Lindhagen and Fabian Månsson had left them and rebuilt the Left Social Democratic Party. But there was no peace within the party now either. They just fought and talked behind each other's backs to the men in Moscow. He himself was with Kilbom; it was clear that world revolution had to be centrally directed.

He was talking on as usual, she thought, everything was just evasion.

He was renting a room alone now, had been successful in finding a small apartment. Bengt had the old room together with a friend. It was too poky and unpleasant. He had rented a room with a kitchen on Mosebacke. They took the Katarina elevator up to it.

The building was not new but was clean and well kept. He asked her to come in, the letter he was waiting for lay in the mailbox. It was an order for some merchandise. He had gotten a telephone and called in the order immediately.

She looked around and as before felt surprised over how orderly he was; everything was so perfect. No clothing hanging out, the pens laid out in order on the desk. Instead of the Almathea men there were now some colorful pictures on the walls. On the bed he had a multi-colored bedspread.

Maj glanced at it out of the corner of her eye: how many had he had up here while they were apart?

Now he slammed down the receiver.

"Such a damned good-for-nothing! Sits and picks at her nails all day and then starts whining when she has to work overtime."

"She works for my friend," he explained. "If she worked for me she would get a foot on her backside the first day. Come on, let's go eat. I've booked a table."

The laurel trees had been placed outside for the summer. They stood there in their green wooden barrels and framed the entrance to Pelikan. On the ceiling of the rotunda that extended over the railroad track, the pelican mother fed her young eternally. A streetcar rolled with squealing brakes down Brunnsbacken, then it swung onto the steep curve toward Östra Slussgatan and past Kölingsborg, whose black roof up stuck up out of the old iron pit.

He had ordered a table inside the rotunda, next to the window. The Stomatol sign up on the elevator had already been lit; red toothpaste was squeezed continually out onto a brush. One was captivated by the display, though this close one could see clearly that it was just red and white light bulbs that turned on and off.

Heinrich Neve's orchestra played. Maj usually was in a good mood as soon as she caught sight of the jolly conductor with the monocle clamped in his eye socket. But today it felt like the music was part of a plan, an attempt on Erik's part to make her compliant.

It was as if he became another person as soon as they stepped into the restaurant. The irritation and press disappeared; he relaxed from his daily life. He spoke no more of his business dealings, nothing about the party either. Instead he asked if they shouldn't take some shimmy lessons, it looked like so much fun. And had she heard about the latest in America, the radiophone? It was sort of like the telephone, you could hear music or the news in an earpiece. But maybe it was just a new American fad, something that was popular for a while and then disappeared.

He talked on, and gradually she grew into a better mood. You had to accept each person as he or she was; there was nothing wrong with Erik. He was like a child sometimes, flaring up, angry when he did not get his own way. He had gotten used to bossing people around. Of course he was capable. And nice and fun, worth liking.

Now he asked her forgiveness as well, both for his recent bad humor and for that affair with the newspaper. It got like that, he had been so rushed that he had not had time to think things through and behave the way he should have. Now he would improve, actually take a week off, maybe around Midsummer. How about traveling together somewhere?

That would never happen, she thought, but it could be fun to talk about it, pretend. She went along with him. Where could they go?

He had some suggestions, one crazier than the other, and coaxed her into laughing where they sat huddled over their liqueur glasses. She pulled the curtains aside and looked out, now dusk had arrived. The headlights of the cars shone yellow as they swept past, the lit up signs on the elevator blinked on and off. He held her hand in his, played with it.

He had an old map of the archipelago at home. Couldn't they go back and look at it, find a really nice place to travel to?

But it was getting so late.

Not that late yet. Just for a little while.

Then it had to be a very little while.

He had a bottle of vermouth, which he opened. The map was spread out on the bed. A wreath of colorful advertisements surrounded the blue delineated water with the many white islands. *Stora Möja, Vindö, Harö*—she tried to imagine how it might look out there. In one corner was a listing of seaside resorts.

Dalarö. Havsbad. Well-known spa and recreation resorts. Beautiful natural setting, healthy climate. Mud, pine needle and effervescent baths.

No, mud was not for him. And pine needles—they were prickly.

Then how about Södertälje? *New bathhouse and social center.*
Specialty soap massage bath. Sea bathing. Sun and open air bathing.

That sounded better: sea, sun and bathing. And probably he could
give her a soap massage, if that was what she desired.

Her gaze followed the printed column. At the bottom was an adver-
tisement with pictures of the steel-bottom bed, Elastic, and a baby carriage, everything from Levin Svenson on Stora Nygatan.

She got up off the bed. Should probably go now.

But she had barely tasted the good drink yet. Here was the glass
standing and waiting for her.

She took a little sip. The smartest thing would be to go now. She
knew what he wanted.

"Come here," he said. "It's been so long."

He pulled her down on his lap and she felt that she was giving in;
her protests would have to yield. Actually what she wanted most of all
was maybe to cry after the day's worry and disappointment, cry and
be comforted. His hands were caressing her, as if they really were trying to comfort her. And she felt how tired she was now.

He pushed the map aside, which fell to the floor. Lay her down on
the bed.

"Turn out the light," she said.

He was kind and walked with her to the outside door afterward.
When she got up to her apartment the others were sleeping. Gunnar
had gotten married and moved away from home so Maj slept in the
kitchen now, together with Beda. And Beda was snoring as usual.

Maj crawled down into her bed, which they had been considerate
enough to make up for her. Now she just wanted to sleep, felt tired
and bone-weary, a little sick too.

But she couldn't fall asleep.

Forty percent reduction, she had not had the opportunity to tell
them about it yet. But it no longer seemed as important, now Erik was
the problem. Again. As long as it lasts this time, as Emelie had said
when they made up last time.

No, together with Erik was nothing constant, that much she had learned. Back and forth now, though it had only been a little while since she had left his bed, she was unsure of him. You know I was joking, you're not dumb after all, he might say.

She rolled over. No matter how she lay she couldn't get comfortable tonight. Outside the window it had already begun to grow light. Beda was still snoring.

This bed was uncomfortable. If she hadn't had her wages lowered she would have bought a new one. Maybe one of those Elastic ones. But then they had better not come offering her a baby carriage instead.

VICTIMS OF
THE CRISIS

The big crisis after the war grew more widespread. It was as if a storm flood of water streamed forth and overturned everything that did not have the strength to stand against it. Old respected, though perhaps moldering, companies disappeared in the maelstrom; new groups of people were hurled into unemployment.

If one were to get by now, one had to be clever and have both luck and capital. The banks wrote off enormous losses; the department store, Nordiskakompaniet closed its luxury departments. One had to adjust to the changing economic circumstances of the depression. Salaries and dividends were cut.

Now it was time to return to the land, abandon the city, according to many. Industry had shrunk production by close to a third. The government tried to meet the crisis by maintaining the value of the krona. Then prices sank by fifty percent despite the fact that a shortage of goods still prevailed. The value of merchandise in stock was reduced enormously. But anyone who wanted to survive had to continue to sell—and buy, even if business ran a loss.

The little cosmetics factory on Stora Badstugatan, which had become Sveavägen, gave an undeniable impression of decay. It was true that the building with the large archway facing the street had once been a small and low-built but beautiful and well-kept edifice. Now the plaster was falling off, the roofing sheets were rusty, the archway had been banged into by delivery trucks. People wondered if it wasn't soon time to tear down the old crumbling places that were still standing on Sveavägen. They belonged to the parts of a "Stockholm that should go."

That the buildings had become run-down was not primarily a

result of economic difficulties. It was because they were condemned to death. The traffic grew more bustling, people expected to widen the street soon even more. Small factories of all types had to move to outlying areas, make way for a growing city center. The buildings in and of themselves were not worth anything, nothing to put money into. On the other hand, the value of the lots was going up.

The years of war and the years of crisis had shaken the Melinder firm, brought huge losses. Now Konrad Melinder might regret that he had not given in and done as many others had: manufactured and sold any old thing. Virtue had not paid off. He had tried to keep up quality and only produced goods that the company could stand behind. But after the war, people had acted as if they were crazy, absolutely refusing to buy anything they suspected was made during the war. If it was good or bad it made no difference.

He had been forced to sell off cheaply top quality merchandise and buy new materials and manufacture new products—that were now being sold at half price. One great loss had been followed by another. He had tried to cut back and save, let people go and lowered wages. Nothing helped; no measures had been radical enough.

What he had left of great value was his land. The company was only a burden. Maybe he could get a loan, but that would only mean that the lot would also be put at risk. In that case it was better to close down, stop in time.

It was difficult, felt like wasting an inheritance. It was like proof that he had misspent his legacy, what he had once received. What would his old uncle have thought and believed if he had been alive? The old man had always been against any plan to enlarge the company. His cautious uncle might have made it through the crisis. He who does not climb so high does not fall so deep, he used to say. But Konrad Melinder had wanted to climb, been proud of expanding the little company. He remembered how afraid the old man had been that time in 1897 when Konrad had rented a pavilion at the exhibition. That pavilion had been the starting signal for the upswing the company had gotten. Or had it just increased the height of the fall?

He had to come to a decision; each day that went only yielded new losses. He could still make a decent settlement. In a month or two it would probably be too late.

But it was hard to part with the factory, with all his plans and dreams. Maybe from the people who had believed in him and been dependent on him too. There were not so many old-timers left anymore. Everyone who had been there in his uncle's day was dead. Wait, one was left: Emelie. The old man had told him that she had begun to work there when she was twelve years old, the same year that he had started the factory. That would have made him 82 then. And that meant that Emelie was 52 now.

Not so easy to find something new at that age. He did have a certain responsibility toward her, had to think if he could come up with something new. And then the senior accountant who had not been there as long but still long enough. Maybe the coachman too, who was called a chauffeur now. But he could probably find him a job with an acquaintance. The rest of them he could do nothing for, if he could even do something to help these three. As for the machines and whatever was left of the stock, he had already made certain preparations. Most of it was impossible to sell and not much worth saving. For many years he had been looking for a suitable site to move to and avoided any great purchases. Now the years of crisis had eaten up the money he had set aside while the machines and other inventory had been completely worn out.

He walked through the rooms, through the office where only the senior accountant and a woman office worker were left, across the cobblestone courtyard, over to the old stable where he used to keep the horses. Now it had become a garage and a junk shed. He passed the soap boiling room where the giant boiler now stood, empty and cold, and the soap cutting machines; only one of them was running. At ink and perfume bottling a couple of girls stood scrubbing the counter. One of them was the mildly retarded girl that Emelie had some connection with. What would happen to that poor thing now? Maybe he could ask one of his friends to do a good deed and take on the girl. She didn't bother anyone and the little wage she would receive was negligible.

Inside the packaging department they were standing and wrapping soaps, Emelie and the two others who were left. He wondered if they knew that the firm lost one öre for every bar of soap they sold. It was just as well to get the thing done right away, it had to happen anyway. He asked Emelie to come see him a moment when she had time.

She came right away. He saw how she grew pale, almost collapsed when she heard the difficult news. He promised to remember her if he came across anything new. He could not do more than that. Oh yes, she would get two weeks' pay and a good recommendation, if she wanted to look for something else.

She said nothing, only thanked him for his promise and for the money. And especially for his trying to arrange something for Beda.

It was worse with the senior accountant.

The accountant himself had understood that they could not go on for long, but still he collapsed and had to be calmed down with a glass of cognac. And naturally it was a hard blow for him. He was over fifty but he had young children and a wife who was sickly.

This was part of being an employer, damn it, in these times. Since the cognac was out anyway, he poured himself a large glass. If someone came along now and saw him—who cared, everything had gone to the devil. His own work, the expanded company, it all went to hell. But his old uncle still haunted him—and helped him. How in heaven's name had the old man managed to buy land just on this street that they were saying would become a Major artery of tomorrow?

When Konrad Melinder had come here the first time, the street had in many ways still been a country road, a road for all the rattling horse-drawn wagons on their way to the farmers' market at Hötorget. There had been breweries here, tanneries, tobacco factories. Inside the courtyards hundreds of horses had stood stamping their feet. The churchyard had stretched almost all the way across the street, only leaving room for a little narrow channel for traffic. Now cars and streetcars rolled along over old graves. Where Kungsgatan now ran,

Stora Badstugatan had crawled up the ridge on a steep slope toward Oxtorgsgatan. There was talk that Sveavägen would run all the way to Gustav Adolf's Square and become the city's new prime thoroughfare.

Konrad Melinder sat sunken in his chair and noticed how the rather large amount of cognac began to do its work. In the shadow of the old man who had died so long ago. The old man, who had only been a little bookkeeper before he began his own firm, had been successful. He himself had failed in everything and now he sat here and drank during working hours.

Emelie tried to keep calm as long as the workday lasted. But when she walked home through the city and thought how soon she would not have any job to go to, she felt the despair and her eyes grew misty. When she got home she hid herself in the room's darkness and cried. Naturally she had to tell Jenny what had happened and Jenny tried to console her. Now it could be her turn to help Emelie a while.

The fact that Beda would get a new job was a consolation, even if it did not mean so many kronor. And Maj had her job. Of course there were those who had it worse. Still, it was so difficult. Emelie was used to being the one who could always manage and help out.

She still had a few weeks left to work, take part in the liquidation. One after another of her workmates came and said good-bye and disappeared. The merchandise was sold off and driven away; machines were dismantled and carried out. Finally the rooms stood empty and cold. As if someone had died, as if everything that once was had to be rubbed out.

Factory director Melinder came down and looked when everything was ready. Emelie asked if she should scrub the rooms and wash the windows, but he answered that it was unnecessary, no one was going to move in. He was already in the process of negotiating a sale. Everything was to be torn down.

She folded up her work apron and placed it in her bag. She received her money from the senior accountant who was still sitting in the office. The factory director checked that he had her correct address, promising once more to get in touch if he had anything to offer her.

In one month she would have worked here for forty years. She had begun the day after school ended. In all those years she had not been sick more than four days total. Then of course there had been the strike. But otherwise she had come here every weekday. The now so empty space had been the place where she had spent the largest part of her life. The table, the shelves and boxes, she could close her eyes and find everything. Everything that was gone now, that was only there when she closed her eyes.

The strike and the war could be overcome. But the crisis had crushed everything.

She didn't really know where to go when she came out on the street. It was not evening yet. Now she no longer had anywhere to go, no job, no security. It was as if home was no longer hers in the same way as before, now when she didn't know how she would cover her share of the expenses.

She had become a burden for them. Now they would get by better without her.

Jenny had her daughters. Gunnar was married and supported himself well. In fact it was only Beda who might need her now. If nothing else, she had to manage for Beda's sake.

Otherwise maybe it would be best if she died. As long as the crisis went on it would be difficult to find any new work. And she was beginning to be too old. Who wanted to hire someone over fifty?

If she died now she would do it honorably. Once, many years ago, she had begun to put aside a little money at a time, collecting it in an envelope: Money for my burial. No one would have to help her, she had thought, she would take care of herself. She had been twenty-eight then, had begun to save at the same time that Olof had moved away from home.

Some of this bitterness she had felt then, maybe it was bitterness that led her to begin saving. She had felt so abandoned and alone when her brother had moved in with his artist friends. Maybe she felt like she had sacrificed her own happiness to take care of him. And then he left.

Then she had thought, no one will have to give me anything. No one will have to take responsibility for anything I've done, no one will pay for me.

That time it was Gunnar who had held her back. The thought that the boy needed her. Now Gunnar was grown and married. But Beda would never really be grown up, would never be able to take care of herself.

In any case, the burial money was still there. And she guessed already that she would be obliged to borrow from it. To pay for her part of everything, to avoid being dependent. But then she would have to live until she found work again and had time to pay everything back. Otherwise she could not die in honor, as she had imagined. The person who was alone had to be prepared. And when it came to herself and what she might need and cost, she was always alone. She could give but had never learned to receive.

OUTSIDE

The summer sun shone across the open area around the locks. The water glistened and a large white Finland's boat was in the process of backing out from the quay at Skeppsbron. The traffic over the lock bridges was directed from the new star-crowned signal tower between Fiskarhamnen and the square. For a few months now the north and south streetcar lines had been connected and the bridges rebuilt to be able to sustain the traffic.

Recently the western bridge's halves had been raised in height; a small cargo boat should be able to pass through. While the puffing and chugging boat took itself into the bay at Riddarfjärden to wait for the railroad bridge to open as well, the lines of streetcars, cars and horse-drawn wagons grew. Finally the boom gates lifted. They were newly painted and shone like wet candy canes. Clusters of pedestrians bent over and rushed out onto the bridge as soon as the gates began to lift.

Emelie hurried after since she had waited obediently for the boom to be completely up. For once she intended to take the streetcar. She saw the car waiting at the end station in the loop around the king's statue. The car she was going to take did not go across Slussen. Line eight, as it was now called, went from Slussen to Enskede.

She had been on her usual visit to the employment office and received the usual reply: they had nothing for her, not yet. Now she had left them the message that she would not be back for a few days, she was going to help a relative.

In a bag she carried with her what she would need for a few days. And a cloth that she had embroidered and was going to give away.

The conductor and the driver were still standing out on the platform talking when she stepped aboard. After a moment the car rolled out of the loop and up toward Katarinavägen—which she had walked along almost every day since it was finished. Now she was being transported up it, very smartly and with a light breeze. The car came to Folkungagatan and stopped only a few blocks from her home. But she stayed seated, rolling along Folkungagatan away toward Götgatan and along Götgatan down toward the tollgate. Here the street had been broadened, rocks blasted away and hill tops planed off—though there was still a lot of the outskirts left: tumbledown shacks, caving-in tenement houses, huge hollows with edges overgrown with weeds.

Down at the tollgate she had to really look around, so much had happened here. For the past few years they had been busy blasting for the Hammarby Canal that would connect the Baltic Sea with Lake Mälar. Farther on, at Danvikstull, a new bascule bridge had been built. It was to be inaugurated in a month. But here at Skanstull the streetcars rolled out on a rickety provisory wooden bridge that crossed the canal in progress.

She stood up halfway, looking out through the window. A remarkable sight—all of Hammarby Lake lay there dry, turned into a giant mud gray grave. When the water was let back in, the lake's surface would lie eight meters lower than before, the former inland lake transformed into a saltwater inlet.

That lake that had been the lake of her childhood! They had rowed and swam there, once they had landed on Mormor's Island and on one of those floating islands. Where were they now? And when Papa was alive they had gone sledding with him all the way down Bondegatan and out onto the ice. And in a hole in the ice out there Mama had drowned.

How everything could change. These days they could let entire lakes just disappear. They were working away out there on the lake floor, building strong stone piers.

Then no more was visible of what had once been a lake. The car rolled out onto solid ground, traveled around the greenery surrounding Fredriksdal, down the old gallows hill and cholera graveyard, up the ascent toward Johanneshov. It stopped beside a large old slaughterhouse that had been finished some years before the war, and then continued on between the houses on Södertornsvägen. When it arrived at Sockenvägen it turned eastward, between the churchyards.

Emelie was going to take it to the last stop near Tyresövägen.

It had been a little over a year since she had been out here last. Gunnar had not had the house ready yet; he and Hjördis were living as if on a construction site. But even then one could already see that it was going to be a big and fine house, and Gunnar had shown her the plans too. August had helped him with the loan.

Just think that that anxious little Gunnar had become a big man with a wife and child and his own house... That poor little thing that she had to take in once upon a time, who had slept in her bed in the beginning, lying there like a worried little mite. And how tightly he had clung to her hand when he had gone with her to the big exhibition the first time.

Now Hjördis had come home from the maternity hospital. And Emelie had promised to help them a few days, while Hjördis recuperated. Emelie had plenty of time of course now. Placed outside of everyday life and work. Shoved aside, on the fringe. But she still could be of some use.

She had assured Gunnar that she would find her way herself. Though now when she was standing there beside the streetcar she felt a little at a loss somehow. The last time it had been winter, with snow. Everything was different in the summertime. And that time Gunnar had met her.

Slender, newly planted trees were coming into leaf behind the fences, newly built houses gleamed. Yes, now she remembered... they had continued a bit in the same direction as the streetcar and then turned off.

She walked the way she remembered—and came to the right place. Tistelvägen. She did not like the name: to name a road after a weed, thistles! Roads should have beautiful names, Rosvägen, Päronträdsvägen: roses and pear trees. She was sure that Gunnar would not let any thistles grow in his yard.

Was it really here? Could it be possible?

The house looked so big, many windows on the ground floor and one in the gable on the upper story. A glass veranda as well. Yes, this was it—there was Hjördis standing in the window, waving.

Carefully, Emelie made her away across the planks that had been laid over the newly dug ditch. A big pile of mud and sand reached almost to the steps. Most of the new neighborhood was not done yet and it would take some time before it was really ready.

Hjördis did not have the strength for much yet, and Emelie made sure that she did not overexert herself, really preferred her to stay in bed. Otherwise there was no point in Emelie coming out.

She washed the dishes after coffee, took the milk can and bag and went shopping. Out here it was quite a long way to the store and she looked around with interest as she walked. A newly built neighborhood where scaffolding and large holes dominated the picture. Naturally there was fresh air and it was healthy to live like this out in the country, though she herself would probably rather live in the city.

Gunnar came home from work and they ate together. They sat in the living room, on the sofa they had received as a wedding gift from August.

Time after time Emelie came back to how much space they had. She compared it with the cramped quarters at home where they weren't nearly as many as they were before, but still they were five living in one room and a kitchen. Here there was only Gunnar and Hjördis and the little one in three rooms and a kitchen, a hallway and a glass veranda. No matter how things were with crises and problems, one had to say that the world was going forward. Something like this Papa and Mama would not have been able to even dream of. Yet most of those who built out here were completely ordinary people, craftsmen and workers.

Emelie went with Gunnar out onto the property for a little bit. He wanted to show her what he intended to do. They were going to have some fruit trees and a few berry bushes, gooseberries of course. Emelie must remember the gooseberry bushes they had in the garden at Fjällgatan? Here they would have a grass lawn, maybe he would have room for a lilac bower as well. And some garden beds next to the house, flowers in front and vegetables to one side.

They walked on planks over the piles of mud, thought they could see some green peeking through. In a few years Gunnar and his family would be living in the middle of a garden. Of course the commute was long and expensive, but they gained a whole lot too. And for a carpenter it felt right to have his own house. He could do so much himself.

Emelie stayed in one room on the upper floor; the other room was the family's bedroom. She sat by the window and looked out in the twilight for a while. In the mud yard below Gunnar was digging, persistently and perseveringly. He should go to bed now, sleep so that he would be able to do his job. But he was working double, first at his company and then at home.

She almost felt something like envy; she would also have wanted to work like that, be young and strong, see the result of her labors. She had been working of course since she was a child—but had there been any results? No house and no garden, nothing as tangible. But maybe still... Maybe her work had had some meaning. She thought about what Gunnar had said about the gooseberry bushes.

Though she would have preferred to have a measure to measure it all by.

He rested a while, looked up and caught sight of her, waved. She waved back.

She felt in almost a solemn mood, and at the same time unusually alone. She had never slept alone in a room before. Here she had this whole fine room to herself. There was also an electric light. And everything was so new, so clean and light.

But the loneliness worried her a little. Here she sat and time passed. She wasn't getting any work. It was strange to sit still here far outside of town, on the side. How were they doing at home now? Only Jenny and Beda were home right now, Elisabet was at summer camp. Maj and Erik should not have taken a trip like that, just them. But if Jenny didn't want to stop Maj so... Jenny was a little free with herself. Just now she was involved in and playing a part in a film where the girls appeared only in bathing suites. Not Jenny of course, she wasn't exactly the right age anymore. Otherwise she probably wouldn't have had any objections to doing it.

No, now she should not waste Gunnar's light anymore. Now she had to go to sleep. She absolutely had to wake up before five-thirty so she would have time to give Gunnar a little breakfast before he went to work.

Emelie cleaned and shopped, made meals and washed the dishes. Still she felt mostly like she was hanging around. Such a time of idleness should not last too long, otherwise she would be completely unfit for work in the future. Hjördis began to resume her activities more and more, but still wanted Emelie to stay—as a real guest for a few days.

Emelie wanted to iron the washing before she left. Then she thought it would feel rather good to come home to her own place— and she had to go and remind them of her existence at the employment office.

But once home she regretted it. She could easily have stayed and helped Hjördis a few more days. At home everything was in order and the employment office still did not have anything.

Was she condemned to going on like this, on the outside?

Maj returned. They had been all the way out to Sandhamn and had good luck with the weather. Much more Maj did not tell. She did not seem happy. Emelie guessed that she and Erik were not getting along again.

Jenny talked even more about her experiences. She had also been out of town for a few days, for the filming in Dalarö. The director, Petschler, and his bathing beauties had been too crazy. One of the girls had slipped on the muddy beach and sat down, thump, on a stone. The girl had howled so that they had to redo all her make-up again— but of course all the others had thought it was funny.

Beda sat there silently, as usual. Emelie sensed that the girl was having a hard time. She had changed jobs and there was no one at the new place who could help her. Before Emelie had been able to look in on her of course.

Everything was as usual. It was only she herself who was on the outside, who all of a sudden had become almost superfluous.

WHILE
TIME PASSES

Prohibition was the general topic of conversation. Big posters reminded people to vote. For the sake of their children. One should vote yes—and stop the flood of alcohol. One should vote no—and stop the flood of smuggling.

VOTE YES! Otherwise maybe your daughter will meet an unhappy future through alcohol.

With a quick, almost angry movement, Maj crumpled up the newspaper.

It was not the alcohol's fault exactly. In her case. Even if they had drunk a little in the evenings.

Now she was sure of it. She was pregnant. And it had come down to that week when she was out in Sandhamn with Erik. She remembered the light-colored curtains that lay like a thin veil in front of the view of the sea, the double bed that took up such a dominant place in the room.

"What's up with you?" Agnes asked.

It felt good to tell someone.

Naturally Agnes promised to keep quiet. But if not before she would certainly tell the others after Maj quit. It couldn't make any difference then. It was now it would feel uncomfortable with all the glances her way.

"My God," said Agnes. "Aren't you going to get married?"

Maj shook her head.

In spite of everything, she felt strangely indifferent to what had happened. She wasn't afraid of talk, not afraid in general. Opposition gave her courage, shame and disgrace gave her strength—that was how she reacted. The person who wanted to could spit and she would spit back, sure of her target. And her manner was perhaps a little bit dissembling, an act: that was how one appeared on the stage. She wasn't the daughter of an actress for nothing.

Suddenly she had to burst out laughing. Agnes looked at her quizzically, almost worriedly.

"I just thought of Mama," said Maj.

Any further explanation wasn't forthcoming.

Jenny had a new engagement. Emil Norlander's big success "Anderssonskan's Kalle" was going to be made into a film and Jenny was going to be one of the quarrelsome and chattering old ladies in number twenty-three. Several of the outdoor scenes were filmed conveniently close by, around the small cottages that were still standing on the old well-known Fjällgatan.

Jenny had Elisabet with her. The girl had come back from camp and got to be part of the herd of kids that were under the command of the energetic Kalle. They soaped the steps so the surprised guests went down on all fours, they placed gunpowder in the stoves and put leeches on the old ladies.

But Elisabet never let herself be drawn into the games. She was always hanging behind, staying a bit apart and didn't mix with the other kids. The girl was oddly withdrawn, as if she felt a little superior. This had no effect on the filming. It actually added a humorous detail to the picture.

Jenny played Pettersonskan, one of the women who was plagued the most. Didn't Jenny always end up with the toughest assignments? As if she was made to have doors slam in her face or fall on her backside so she turned black and blue. Others might be careful and avoid hurting themselves, they could also complain about the difficulty and ask to be excused. She went along with everything, could become completely uninhibited. She didn't understand it herself. But it turned out that way. She thought that what had to be done should be done with conviction, one should not hold back. If the result was funny let it cost what it may.

They had built up a backyard in the provisional studio on the roof of the indoor farmers' market at Hötorget. All afternoon Jenny had chased Kalle around with a wooden rug beater until he, according to the manuscript, trips her so she falls forward and puts her head through a door panel.

The door panel was made of rather thin cardboard and was constructed in such a way that it would split in the right place. But it required several takes before the director was satisfied with the scene.

The afternoon provided even more difficult trials. Then that confounded Kalle would be avenged, oh dear. While she stood on a high step stool by a fence to hang up a wash line, Kalle took hold of her skirt and nailed it to the fence.

Despite all the safety precautions, she thought at one time that Kalle would succeed in his attempts at killing her. When the step stool fell and she was hanging there like a spectacle, screaming with her skirts up and legs kicking, she barely knew herself if she was playacting or being serious.

At last they let her down. And the director said she had been brilliant. The scene did not have to be reshot.

Probably the only audience member who did not laugh was Elisabet. She had not been afraid, was more offended, didn't like them laughing at her mother. Maybe she didn't like her mother either, when she saw her like that.

As they walked home Jenny tried to explain it to her: they made the film so that the people who saw it would have fun. It wasn't a bad aspiration to make people laugh. But Elisabet did not seem convinced.

Jenny had lain down on top of the bed in the room, stretched out and began to feel pleasantly full and sleepy, with tired and buffeted limbs as if numbed for comfort. Maj came in, sat on the edge of the bed. And told her.

It was a shock, a blow. Maj, who she had hoped would have an easier and happier life, Maj who was almost a child herself.

And they were no longer together, she and Erik. But maybe that was just as well. It didn't seem like they could stay stable.

Jenny sat up, grimacing with pain. She did not really know what to say. There was no point in coming with recriminations. If she knew Maj, the girl was more than angry enough with herself.

"We can probably manage if we help each other," she said. "It's just as well to let Emelie know right away."

Naturally Emelie was shaken up. But she didn't say much; maybe she had been involved in this all too many times. At times she had wondered if Jenny had not let Maj live too freely. Now her apprehensions could appear justified, so there was not much more to say. And now when she did not have any work it felt like she had no right to express herself. It was Jenny who had the greatest income, who contributed most to the household. Everything should be the way Jenny wanted it. Clearly they had room for Maj's child.

It was a little more difficult for Jenny to playact the next day. She was still in pain, was sore everywhere. And time after time she had to think of Maj. The whole time she thought that Elisabet looked reproachful. It was probably wrong of her to bring the girl along. It was easier to act if no one in the family was there. And hadn't she done things wrong when it came to Maj, had too little time for her, given her too much freedom—that was what Emelie had said so many times.

Now they were calling, she had to go in and get black make-up on. They were going to film the scene with the old ladies after the stove explodes. If only she could wait a few days before she had to go down the soaped steps on her rear end...

The filming was over; Jenny was at home for a few weeks. Maj was still working; no one could see any signs yet. Prohibition was voted on. It was a slim victory for the opponents of prohibition. Elisabet began school after summer vacation. Gunnar's little daughter got sick and Emelie went out and helped them for a few days again.

And the whole time Emelie was obliged to dip into her burial money. She tried to save and scrape as much as possible, but she insisted on paying her portion of the expenses. Gunnar gave her some money, which she unwillingly accepted and put down as a loan.

During a few weeks that fall she got a temporary job in a grocery store. Emelie had a difficult time standing and talking to people about nothing, but customers were used to a chat. She rang up their purchases quickly and efficiently, then she did not have much to say to them. And it was impossible to get a real overview of the complicated system with credits. Only the owner herself could figure it out. Some got to "sign for credit" who should not have been allowed to and vice versa. There were complaints and arguments and Emelie herself did not know how she would avoid repeating it.

Very often she thought of Melinder, wondered if she would hear from him anytime. Her hope had cooled. Now she barely remembered his words like a promise anymore, more like an uncertain dream.

Still she waited. Those who are able to wait have something to gain. The world is getting better, she thought obstinately. The proof was Gunnar, the house he had built, the home he had created for himself. He had been successful in carrying out something that would have been completely impossible for her parents. No matter how bad the times were, things had come so far that a worker could build his own house. The thoughts of Gunnar buoyed her up.

The pay she received for the hours in the store was not enough to fill any holes back up with. It came to an insufficient contribution to her most necessary expenses. But still the work was meaningful. She did not have to feel as set aside any longer.

One evening Tyra arrived. It had been several years since she had last been heard from. She had borrowed money a few times, said that she would pay it back, but they never heard from her.

Now she had a touch of importance, had bought a new coat and hat—but was dolled up more shabby than elegant, as Maj said afterward. She had her oldest son with her, Allan, who was four years old and was dressed in a sailor suit. She had two more at home, she told them. Both boys too. They were still living in the tenement. David had been doing good business lately, so now she was going to pay back what she had borrowed, if they only could help her by telling her how much it was.

She was able to get a clear reply. Emelie fetched her little notebook, where everything was recorded. There were the sums of what August at one time had supplied. There was the money that Gunnar had given her, the household money from Jenny and Maj and Beda.

All told, Tyra had been lent forty-five kronor by Emelie, Jenny and Gunnar.

Here were fifty even. She wasn't the sort to be stingy. Then she asked Emelie to be kind and divide it.

No, no. She shouldn't pay back more than she had borrowed. Emelie went for one of the last five-kronor bills in her burial envelope.

It was a little too crowded at home for her to invite them over, Tyra said. But if things went well for David in the future as well, then they would move to a bigger place.

Allan stood at the kitchen window and lit matches. He had a box of them in his back pocket. Emelie watched him anxiously but Tyra seemed not to pay attention to what he was doing.

"Does he get to play with matches?" asked Emelie.

"I can't constantly be nagging him," said Tyra. But then he lit couple of matches at the same time and came dangerously close to the curtain.

"Stop it or else you'll get a smack!" she screamed.

He stuck his tongue out at her but put away the box.

They did not stay very long. Tyra had several errands to run.

Just a few weeks later they heard that David was being held by the police.

SNOWFALL

The wind drove the drifted snow into whirling clouds. People couldn't see farther than a few meters, streetcars and automobiles glided out of the white mist like dark phantoms.

A few snow shovelers tried to keep the sidewalk by Norrbro cleared. But the wind blew away their piles to new places and whipped the prickling snow in their faces. A couple of them had a hard time keeping up. They stumbled forward and did not get very much snow in their shovels. Maybe they were unemployed office workers or shop assistants, unused to physical labor. One had a dark overcoat and indoor shoes. Time after time his hat was about to fly off and he pushed it down over his forehead.

Emelie recognized him already from behind, had time to rush over to the other side of the street. "Hello!" The senior accountant—things had gone so far that he was forced to go out in the snow removal force. How would he have the strength? He who used to call for the warehouse workers if even a desk needed moving. Now she had to admire him. He had not given up in any case; he stood there with a shovel and fought for his family's existence.

He had not given up; she could not do it either.

The fall was difficult, even though perhaps it had begun well. The film about *Anderssonskan's Kalle* had become unbelievably popular. Everybody had to see it. Without doubt, Jenny had some small success as well; some of the newspapers had named her by name. She could have expected to get many new offers. But it had not turned out that way. Jenny had gone without work for most of the fall and winter. And now Maj had to stop working too.

Everything hung on Emelie; she had to manage the daily needs. She was helping out in the grocery store a few hours a day again, but it was poorly paid.

To support them she had been forced to do something she had seldom done earlier: borrowed money. She had been forced to look up even acquaintances from her younger years.

Now she was coming back from August's.

The humiliations had been many and felt difficult. Sometimes she had walked around the block many times before she could get herself to impose. Most of them had of course been kind and friendly. But some wanted to know what she needed money for and came back with good advice. In these times of crisis one had to adjust the mouths according to the foodsack, not take on more responsibility than one was able. Jenny and her daughters would have to try to take care of themselves. And wouldn't it be better to put someone like Beda in an institution?

To such talk she answered as little as possible. It was not advice she was asking for. Someday there would be better times again. Those who had so much good advice to give would get their money back first of all.

She recorded the loans carefully. No one would be forgotten, everyone would get it back. Once she got work again.

Beneath the worry and troubles there was something that resembled satisfaction: it was she herself who had to manage.

When it really mattered there was no one else.

But she doubted her ability as well. And soon wouldn't she have borrowed from everybody there was to borrow from? And how would she ever be able to pay everything back?

People said that the worst of the crisis was over now, that it was beginning to brighten. But while they waited for the reversal, time passed. Maybe she would grow too old to find anything new, maybe the senior accountant would perish over his shovel.

A while back she had paid a visit to Tyra. She had to hear how things stood. Could they keep the money Tyra had paid back to them or was it stolen?

Of course they could keep the money, Tyra had answered. She had earned it honorably. That David, easily fooled as he was, had gone along with a break-in—that was something completely different. People who didn't buy proper locks could blame themselves, by the way.

Tyra had had money. And Emelie had been able to borrow five kronor.

Now, when she had gotten some from August, she was on the way to Tyra's to pay her back. She walked up the hill on Götgatsbacken on Söder. Nevertheless she regretted that she had not taken another street, here it was risky to walk. Car after car came rushing down the steep and slippery hill, sliding as they frantically blew their horns. The cars flew like sleds and she tried to make sure she always had some doorway handy to jump into and save herself.

When she had reached the top the worst danger was over. She walked past the old poorhouse and smaller houses alongside Södra Bantorget. Outside the Horse Owners' feed shop in a shed of corrugated metal, stood a horse in front of a cart. It continually shook the snow off and puffed out small white clouds of smoke.

Now there wasn't far to go.

The hill up to the tenement houses was sanded but the children had put in an enormous amount of energy to sweep away the sand and turn the walking path into a slide. She was close to falling a number of times before she got up there. She heard the children being noisy in the stairway. Some of them came out and looked at her curiously, following on her heels as she went up.

David's old father opened the door, let her in unwillingly. He went before her into the room and shouted for Tyra—and Tyra came quickly, as if in defense. When she saw it was Emelie she started to laugh.

"The old man thought you were someone from the home."

Allan had had to go to a home for children with weak lungs. Now they went around afraid someone would come and take Stig as well. There were people from every possible institution running about in this building.

Were the children really sick?

No, not so bad. There was something wrong with most of the kids in the tenements. In Allan's case the authorities probably mostly wanted to put him in a children's home. He had been close to setting fire to the row of outhouses; he was impossible with his matches. But then it had appeared that there was phlegm in his lungs and so they put him in a home for the sick instead. So he had a little luck with his bad luck maybe.

Tyra seemed tired. Three children in four years—wasn't she expecting one now again? What would happen to all these children?

It was still snowing and blowing when Emelie came out. As she walked she left footprints in the snow, but they were soon swept away, disappeared.

It was as if misfortune spanned the generations: Bärta and Johan, Tyra and David, now Allan. They could seem strong and hard sometimes—but it was weakness that condemned them. The person who was poor had to be very strong, have the ability to toil long hours, refuse to give up. It was perseverance that was most important. She had learned that.

Jenny sat and made paper flowers. She had found a few forgotten rolls of crepe paper. Now she had cut garlands and hung a couple of them crossing each other from the room's ceiling.

So that it would look a little more cheerful.

She had not heard from anyone today either.

Emelie thought that Jenny certainly could have undertaken something more useful, darned stockings for example. But she said nothing.

Maj was resting. She was a little difficult to deal with now, irritable and worried. And that wasn't so strange considering the mess she had gotten herself into.

Emelie changed her clothes and went down to the store. She thought she was beginning get a little more order in the system with giving credit, there seldom were arguments anymore. And order in the whole store too. She took one bit at a time when she had the chance.

She cleaned, organized. The owner grumbled sometimes. She was used to having granulated sugar in four different places and butter in one corner and margarine in another. But she got used to the new orderliness too. One could see what there was in the stockroom and not as much was wasted anymore.

But she did not thank Emelie and if there was something she could not find, she complained sometimes that Emelie had arranged it that way.

Thumbs came and shopped. He bought more than he usually did and had big news to tell: Mikael had come back. The boy had been at sea for many years now and had seldom written home. Now he intended to take it a little easier, he was going to turn fifty in a few years. He had saved a little money too, and if times got better now, he should be able to get a job. Maybe at the harbor.

Thumbs had livened up, he was really beaming. He was almost the way she remembered him from the old days.

And now Mikael came into the store too. And he was large and broad, deeply tanned in the face.

Customers came in and she did not have the chance to talk more, only had time to ask if they could come and drink a cup of coffee that evening.

On the way to the potato crate she passed the door to the street, watched them as they left. Mikael supported his father who had become little and bent. It was so nice to see that she could hardly take her eyes off of them.

Meeting Mikael suddenly made everything feel easier and brighter. It was as if he had stepped forth from the whirling snow, without a trace behind him. Wasn't he a promise?

When she got back home she thought Jenny's paper garlands made it festive, like light-filled summer laughter in the winter darkness. Emelie had gotten to take with her from the store a whole bag of left-over coffeebread for free.

They arrived as they had promised. And for everybody in the little apartment it felt like they had been touched by a fresh breeze. Here they had sat, each one in her corner, reeking a little with smoke, dusty and gray. And then Mikael arrived, wandering in, full of stories and rich with experiences, safe and secure.

He had presents with him too.

"It just happens that one buys this and that," he said. "Without knowing who one will really give it to. Just because one sees something interesting and something that doesn't exist here at home."

Emelie could have answered one thing or another to that. But she kept quiet and admitted to herself that naturally it was different for Mikael, who had been away for so long and seen so much. And who in fact only had himself to think of.

Jenny got a Japanese fan and it suited her exactly. She crept into a corner of the sofa and fanned herself with it, really flirted with it, thought Emelie. Maj got a bracelet that he had bought in an oriental bazaar. With gestures and faces, Mikael told how he shopped there and how hard one could bargain. Beda and Elisabeth each received a necklace of red coral. Beda could not get out a word of thanks, but sat there the whole evening with the necklace in her hand, carefully fingering it, seemingly not believing it was really hers.

Then he reached over with a larger package for Emelie. It was silk cloth, made in China. She could sew a dress out of it.

Could she really accept it? It was much too fine and expensive. Wasn't there someone else he ought to give it to?

Emelie felt how she blushed, became embarrassed and annoyed with herself.

They laughed at her, teasing.

"But why give it to me?"

"The one it was meant for has already gotten married," he laughed. "That's the way it goes when you are away for a long time."

"And thanks for looking in on the old man from time to time," he added in a low voice. "You probably don't know how much it meant to him."

Of course the words gladdened her. But maybe she felt a little ashamed. She had not had time to visit Thumbs as often as she would have liked.

Thumbs talked to Maj. If it was a boy, the child that Maj was carrying, in that case he thought she should call him Henning. Since it sounded like Maj didn't intend to marry Erik, the boy would in any case be named Henning Nilsson. It would be almost like getting the old Henning back again, in a new gestalt. And you see Henning, such a man as Henning…

"Maybe it wasn't really like that," said Emelie to Mikael. Thumbs had transformed her father, let his memory create another and prouder Henning than the one who had once lived.

Yes, it had gotten like that. And just as neatly his old man had turned his older brother Rudolf into a hero too, even though they had had a hard time of getting along when Rudolf was still at home. But there were so many who blackened people, so there was no good in complaining if someone painted them in a rosier light.

Rudolf had been able to get into the streetcar company in New York, Thumbs had told them. He was not a driver, he was what they called a collector, took the fares. Mikael had been in New York too but he had not seen Rudolf and Gertrud. And he would no longer recognize their children, even if he tripped over them. The oldest was married of course and had children, he had heard. Emelie confirmed this. Gertrud wrote once in a while.

It felt empty when Thumbs and Mikael had left. For a while they had been able to forget all the usual troubling things, and now they were back in reality again.

After Emelie made the beds she stood a moment at the window. The snow was still whirling about, glinting in the light from the street lamps. She could more sense than see how people were slipping past under the lights, disappearing into the whiteness. She thought about Gertrud and her children, wondered if she would ever get to see them again. No, it was unbelievable. Sailors traveled long distances, ordinary people stayed where they were. Those who were gone were gone.

She looked at the cloth one last time before she went to bed, stroking the sparkling, shiny surface. While she considered what it could be used for she could maybe keep it at the pawnshop. It was absolutely necessary to get more money together.

BOUND AND RELEASED

Two young girls came down the hill on Värmdögatan, each one swinging her enameled milk can to the growing line outside the soup
kitchen. Suddenly they stopped: a wonderful smell of caramel wafted
out from the open windows in one of the low stone houses on the
eastern side of the street. They were airing out the caramel factory.

Imagine getting to work inside there, so close to the candies, with
that smell... The girls stood on their toes to get as close as possible.
But their vision of paradise was suddenly torn in two. Someone
screamed desperately from inside the factory and someone else tried to
quiet her down.

The spell was broken. Frightened, the girls ran away, not stopping
until they reached the line.

The one who had screamed so terribly had probably gotten boiling
candy syrup on her. And the girls themselves decided they would
rather be actresses anyway.

Alfa Candy and Caramel Factory had a dozen employees who
worked in the crowded and dark rooms in the old stone house. Most
of them were young; the work was poorly paid.

Beda had been at the candy factory for one year now. She had come
here directly from Melinder's. Factory director Melinder had been so
kind and recommended her to Alfa's owner. In the beginning she had
had a pretty tough time. There was no Emelie here who could help her
and speak for her to their workmates, no one who she knew. She had
gone around alone. Those who tried to talk to her had grown tired of
it since they never got any answer.

In ink bottling everyone had been women. She had had very little
to do with the male workers. Here it was different. And she was afraid
of the men. Memories from school were still there, boys who had
pulled her pigtails, stuck her with ink pens.

She was no longer as afraid as she had been back then. Something of the fears and feelings of being left out from her childhood years had begun to fade. The years with Emelie had given her a certain security. No one wished her harm; some even had the patience and enough interest to wait for her words. There were people who cared about her and believed in her. She had begun to guess this and it made her anxiously eager sometimes because she wanted to respond to their trust and show her gratefulness. But mostly she was calmer, might think that she felt something good and warm growing inside her, a new confidence, a previously unknown happiness.

Jenny had once taught her to knit. Emelie had taught her to sew. Now she liked to sit at home and work during the evenings. She had made sweaters and mittens that they praised her for and used. She had hemmed tablecloths and embroidered cloths. She knew how to do something, was useful. If she could only overcome her fear of speaking. She had the words as if ready in her mouth, prepared. But when she went to say something it didn't work. She grew excited and desperate, it was so important for her that she became dumb.

But when she sat alone and no one was listening to her, then she talked. During breaks at work she would go out to the yard and sit alone and talk in a low voice to a friend that wasn't there.

Still, one day she would dare speak for real to those at home, say more than a few individual, fumbling words. Preferably one evening when they all had a lot of time and she didn't have to feel like she was holding them up. But it was so seldom that she had enough time so they had gotten used to her only saying a few words. They understood what she meant and filled in the rest themselves. Emelie had so much to think about, was the one who had to think for them all. And Jenny was so eager and lively and had all her plans and ideas. Maj had to take care of the little newborn.

But one day they would maybe have time anyway, and then she would talk for real to them, thank Emelie properly.

That she would ever dare say anything at the factory was something she was more unsure of. A yes or a no—it was never more than that.

And more wasn't necessary either. She received her order slips and
packed according to them and there was not much to say about that.

Beda had a hard time protecting herself against some of the
younger men, there were two especially that were bothersome. Of
course it was crowded everywhere in the old rooms, but not so crowded that they should continually bump into her and take hold of her to
get by. If she stood bent over to reach a tray of candies, they would
come over and give her a spank and holler about her pulling in her
rump. If she stood on a step stool they would pinch her legs and if she
were sitting on the packing table they would come and grab her
breasts. And when she forced out her angry no, then they would laugh
and imitate her. Despite everything it was as if they had a little more
respect for her afterward; they noticed that she would not give in. And
now she noticed that she was not really as afraid of them anymore, not
since she had happened to push one away so that he had fallen over.
He kept away from her then, did not want to be laughed at by his
workmates another time.

Beda had begun to get used to it, feel in place at the factory. It had
taken almost a year, but now she felt like she had become established
in her work and was approved of by her colleagues. Even if she was on
her own for the most part—but she had always been like that, everywhere.

Even in that respect there was a change underway. A few days ago
she had made a friend. Maybe that word was too big, friend. But a
new girl had begun there and she had been put beside Beda. The boss
gave the order that Beda should show the new girl what to do and
teach her how to pack candies and caramels.

The new girl was not more than sixteen years old, a fair-haired and
pretty girl who was also a little shy and afraid in the new environment.
She had not had a job before, had only been at home taking care of
her siblings since she finished school. Beda helped her, mostly using
gestures and showing her how she herself did it. No, she said and
shook her head. So, she explained. Yes, she nodded when the girl

understood and succeeded.

The girl's name was Karin, nicknamed Kajsa. She followed Beda out to the yard during breaks. They climbed up a bit on the hill above the backyard where the sun reached. They found a place in a crevice, enjoying the warmth.

One day when Beda sat with her eyes closed to the sun, she heard that Kajsa was saying something to her. The girl was asking if Beda had heard that they were going to work late.

She didn't know how it really happened, but suddenly she answered. Not with just a yes, but with five or six words. Of course she spat them out, thought herself that they sounded a little strange. But she had still spoken, managed to answer. Maybe she had dozed off and thought she was alone and was talking to that listener that wasn't really there.

Beda was so surprised and shaken up that the rest of the day she could only nod, yes, or shake her head, no. And it felt almost like a relief when the day was over. Then she could go home and think through what had happened. She had answered and it had sounded almost real. Kajsa had understood her. If Kajsa said anything during break the next day she would try to answer again. Quickly, just like that without thinking, as she had done today.

Kajsa was pretty, attracted the boys in a completely different way from Beda. The two bothersome ones would not leave the girl alone. Beda tried to push the table so Kajsa would have a protected corner, putting herself in front of it, ready to block them. But the boss apparently thought that it was impractical for Kajsa to squeeze her way past Beda every time she had to get new boxes. When he passed by he pushed the table back. Beda wanted to say something but the boss did not notice or else did not take the time to listen. Now she did not dare move the table again. The uneven battle continued. Beda was shoved and she grunted but she could not watch out for the boys every minute. Kajsa complained that she was pinched black and blue and wondered what her mother would say if she saw it. They pulled a button off of Kajsa's blouse too. Beda helped her sew it back on at break.

One of those boys had something wild and dangerous about him, Beda thought. She had been able to scare the other, but not this one. Sometimes she almost had to pull him off of Kajsa, like when that button had been pulled off. Then he had pulled Kajsa's blouse aside and bitten her in the shoulder, so hard that the marks were there for several days. When Beda pulled him away he tried to hit her, wildly and ruthlessly. If she had been able to talk like other people she would have gone to the boss and complained. Since Kajsa did not dare. She only cried.

Beda wondered how it would all end. Mostly she was frightened by the thought that Kajsa would not have the strength anymore and would leave her job. Then Beda would feel more alone than ever before. But if that was the only way out, then Kajsa would have to quit. So far she had not mentioned anything like that but she could not take it forever, that much Beda understood.

Beda went to get more order slips. The boys were not visible; they had to be useful sometimes too.

She had to wait a while in the office. The clerk was busy on the telephone. While she was still standing there, break time came. Through the window onto the yard she saw how some of the employees were coming out of the doorway and climbing up onto the hill with their foodsacks. Kajsa was not to be seen. Beda felt a shiver of worry, but just then the clerk laid down the telephone receiver.

She hurried back. The cubbyhole-like room where they stood and packed was empty; the door to the candy boiling room was ajar. She put the order slips down in the basket and thought that Kajsa must have had time to go out to the yard after all. Just when she was about to leave the packing room she heard the scream.

She flung open the door to the candy boiling room. It was shadowy in there, low ceilinged with frosted windows. The large oven and boilers blocked the light. But she heard them. They seemed to be in the corner behind the boiler wall. The scream sounded almost half smothered now.

She rushed over. The boys had thrown Kajsa down over a large packing crate, sprawled backward. Desperate, she tried to defend herself. One of the boys held her down and held a hand over her mouth. The other one was squatting down in front of her.

The boy who was holding her down became aware first that Beda had come in. It was as if he understood all of a sudden what he was involved in. He let go of the girl immediately, shouted a few words of warning to his friend and took off, disappeared. The other, the wild one, seemed to neither hear nor see, had only one goal and one desire now.

Beda threw herself upon him with all her strength, gripped by rage. He went to hit her but lost his balance and fell backward down on the floor. Beda started to kick him without restraint until, crawling, he had to get away.

"Brute," she screamed. "Cowardly brute, tackling a little girl who can't defend herself."

She had arrived in time, in any case. Kajsa had managed to defend herself.

And now Beda wasn't even thinking about talking. One calming and consoling word followed after another. The words were needed, the tongue obeyed—and the words came. She wasn't surprised, hardly noticed it. It was Kajsa now who was important.

The girl was still sniffling when break was over. But eventually she calmed down, tried to work again, smiled bravely and nodded when Beda asked if she was able to continue.

The one boy came and asked her forgiveness, begged Beda not to tell on them, promised never again to bother the girls. The other, the worst, just disappeared from the factory without even asking for wages for the days he was owed.

A memory had arisen for Beda. She saw so clearly in her mind the time she had lain bound in the woodshed on Fjällgatan, how they had stood over her with the leather strap, all the children. How hard Tyra had lashed her.

Of course she had been hit many times, much worse than that. By her father so that she could hardly walk to school sometimes, by her mother, though never with a strap or a cane. By the teacher.

Her childhood had been filled with fear and torment. But that time in the woodshed was still the hardest. Then her peers, her own kind, had ganged up. The world had been entirely without mercy.

Since then better days had come, at Emelie's. But that fear of being punished and berated remained.

It wasn't until now that she could think of that time in the wood-shed without getting upset. It wasn't until now that she could truly forgive them. Now she had gotten over it, she realized. And she had even been able to help another person, set someone free.

Together with Kajsa she left the factory, took the long way around through the park to accompany her friend home. She felt like she did not dare let Kajsa go alone, in case that wild boy was standing some-where, lying in wait. And Kajsa was grateful, embraced Beda warmly before they parted.

Beda surprised them when she suddenly started to talk at the din-ner table. They looked at her, astonished. What had happened? Beda could talk.

She had, to be sure, said some words from time to time, but never so many at one time. She was going to meet a friend, she said. Go out and walk a little while.

They did not ask anything, as if they did not dare, as if this remark-able and happy change could be damaged by questions and curiosity. They just nodded. Of course Beda should go out while she could, she sat inside so much.

She dressed up as best she could. They watched her as she left, smil-ing in bewilderment at the miracle, the release that had come so late.

HENNING THE SECOND

The summer that was now almost over had been unusually eventful. The new city hall had been inaugurated with great festivities, dances in the parks and regattas on the bay at Riddarfjärden. Above the hills on Söder's Mälar strand, rose the new Högalid Church. On Kungsgatan the first skyscraper, the king's tower, was finished. And the city now had bus traffic. Now there was an omnibus that went between Odenplan and Gustav Adolf's Square. Earlier busses had only gone out to the steadily growing suburbs beyond the toll gates.

At the stadium Nurmi and Wide had met in a series of exciting running races and a Russian football team had been guest players in Sweden for the first time since the revolution. Several thousand people had bought radios and now sat with their headphones and tried to tune in to whatever private broadcasters there were.

There was a lot that happened, a lot of new things that had come about. But Maj had not experienced all the new. She had had more than enough with her own life, with the little life she had brought into the world. All the big and marvelous things out there disappeared, overshadowed by the new little person who was close by.

She sat on one of the benches in the park on Folkungagatan, gently rocking the baby carriage. The boy was falling asleep.

The dense and high trees built a green vault that protected them against the burning sun. Where the vault ended the cobblestones shone brightly. A blue streetcar with an open trailer car in tow went past, on its way from Danvikstull over to Götgatan.

Even if she was living on the sidelines and in her own world, she understood that the crisis was on the way to being overcome and that there was reason to see the situation in a better light again. Unemployment was still high, but the economy was looking better, she had read in the paper. The Swedish Match Company was in the process of conquering the world. And there was a lot of construction going on, the city was being renovated and was growing.

She looked at the boy. He was asleep, but making faces; a fly was bothering him. Carefully she waved it away.

Henning. Henning the second, as Mikael had said. Then Thumbs got mad. He got so easily irritated sometimes.

"Regular, decent people don't aren't numbered like kings and knaves," he sputtered. But Mikael wasn't the type to take offense, he just laughed. He wasn't without a reply either.

"I thought dock workers had numbers too," he said. Then Thumbs was silent.

It wasn't only Thumbs and Mikael who had worked in the harbor. The first Henning had done that also. Worked himself to death, Emelie had said, dying before he turned thirty-five.

Maj hoped the name would not be a bad omen. Times were different now, and as bad as they had once been surely could never happen again. Of course she would do what she could to protect her little one, help him along.

A boy needed a father, and Erik needed contact with the child too. If he got to see the child grow up he would feel love and responsibility toward him in a completely different way.

Once upon a time she had thought: never again. She did not want to become an appendage to Erik, she wanted to live her own life. And it was difficult in Erik's proximity. He was so domineering, so taken up with himself and his life. He took on so many tasks, had such a need to always be occupied. Home and private life had to fit in the slots that were left after work and the party had taken their share. The person who was going to live with him would have to do the adapting.

Now she had come to a decision. She wanted to try one more time. Not as the victim of an emotional rush like before. Instead, clearly conscious of the difficulties and determined to still live her own life. For Henning's sake she wanted to try—and also maybe because she still, and despite everything, liked Erik.

He had come with flowers to the maternity hospital as soon as he had heard the child was born. Asked her to come back to him. He would get them a good apartment, try to be rid of his multiple duties in the party. Just now he could not walk away from everything. The party's economic situation was so constrained. He had been obliged to be involved and organize the Russian football team's tour. He had traveled around the country with the players. The tour had earned the party close to thirty thousand kronor, so it was a very good business arrangement. And then there had been the conflicts. Höglund had received his dressing-down from the Russian leaders, but persisted in his private opinions. Erik, who supported Kilbom, had to be present and watch out for the interests of the minority within the party's executive committee. He said that in spite of everything they represented the Majority, those who wanted to be faithful to the international leadership.

She did not believe him when he said his duties would be fewer. Year after year they had only multiplied. The party had swallowed him up. She knew that and that was something she took into consideration. He would get to live his life; she did not intend to stop him. And she would live hers, together with the child. But somewhere in his vicinity.

For this they would not have to get married, it felt safer to be free. And it could not mean anything to the child if his name was Karlsson or Nilsson. She frankly that thought Henning Nilsson sounded better.

Best to be free, she thought. Erik would feel safe if they got married. He would be more careful if he knew that she could leave at any moment. She needed all the weapons she could get.

This did not sound too promising. But she had determined to go to him with eyes open, not ignore the difficulties.

Erik knew she sat in the park during the afternoons when it was fine weather.

He came along, sat down on the bench beside her. A little tired after the day's work. He was still a salesman, now for an import firm.

He told how he had run into Tyra's husband, the scab. David frequented the cafés around Slussen; Erik had seen him in Klotgränd. It seemed like he was involved in smuggling. That was what many people were doing these days. Estonian liquor, mostly. There was a lot of money to be made but David was surely one of the petty dealers.

It annoyed him that someone like that was earning money; it was unjust. He himself wasn't making such large profits anymore. He sacrificed too much time and energy to the party.

Maj had to feel sorry for him. Erik did not have it so easy and he did not spare himself. It wasn't strange that he grew hard sometimes. He wasn't cruel—except for possibly when it came to his sister, Tyra. That she was together with someone like David was too hard for him to swallow.

Henning woke up; Maj picked him up. And Erik played with his son. His slightly whiny tone disappeared; he tried to get the boy to laugh.

And Maj felt that her decision was right, father and son needed each other.

For once Erik had time; he went home with her. Her heard that Emelie's brother, August, was coming to visit and he decided to stay. It might be interesting to see that remarkable building contractor.

Emelie talked about her work. She was little a worried that the owner was thinking of selling the store. If there was a new owner she might be out of a job again. Some people had come by to inquire about it, a couple of gentlemen who had owned several stores previously.

Erik calmed her: capable people were always needed. It could be conceivable that it would be to Emelie's advantage if enterprising people took over the business. But in truth he did not believe so much of what he said. Emelie was probably beginning to be a little old. Clearly they would want someone younger.

When they had almost finished eating, Jenny arrived. She was working on the filming of the sequel to Anderssonskan's Kalle and work had been intensified during the final days in the studio.

Beda and Elisabet disappeared, each going in her separate direction.

Maj had told Erik about the change in Beda, that she talked really well now. Erik did not think he noticed any difference. In fact he was not so interested either, had always thought that Beda was dumb. Even if she could talk now she couldn't have very much to say.

Emelie set out the cups and saucers in the room. They were going to drink coffee when August arrived.

He came a little later than he had said. But he was not alone. Beside him stood an older woman. She leaned heavily on August, panting after her walk up the many steep stairs.

They must really excuse that she imposed this way. But when August told her... well, she knew Henning so well, the old Henning.

Before August had a chance to explain, Emelie realized: this must be August's adoptive mother, Annika Bodin. Emelie remembered Mrs. Bodin as a very stately and commanding woman. But this was a little plump and wrinkled old lady who had now stepped into her kitchen. As a matter of fact she looked rather harmless. Though she had not been so easy to deal with, that much Emelie had gathered from August sometimes.

Emelie curtsied, invited them into the room.

Mrs. Bodin looked around. It had been a long time since she had seen how simple people lived. Probably a lot had happened since she had been young herself and grown up in a hovel among a bunch of boarders and foster children. But August did always say that his sister was such a clever and hard-working person, and then there was that actress living here too.

Henning slept in his carriage.

Maj looked at Mrs. Bodin a little anxiously when she approached. She hoped she would let the boy go on sleeping in peace. For safety's sake—and for Emelie's— she had taken the opportunity to give Erik strict orders in the kitchen. He was not to say anything that might be provocative to the visitors. He promised to keep quiet and obey.

Annika bent over the child. She was probably looking for a recognizable trace, the memory of someone disappeared long ago. She could barely remember how the old Henning had looked; it had been so endlessly long ago, everything. The last time she had seen Henning was during that trip to their summer house. At that time her husband Fredrik was still dealing in herring and Henning was working as a herring packer. They had arranged an outing for the employees and their families, and Henning and Lotten had been there and brought August with them. That was when she saw August for the first time. And hadn't she decided already then, thought: that's the boy I want?

When could that have been? That's right, it was when the company celebrated its twenty-five year jubilee, must have been in 1874. Soon fifty years ago.

Henning. So this is little Henning.

As if some of the old Henning was still living. Children, grandchildren, great grandchildren. After her and Fredrik there was no one, only a loan: August. And she certainly would have liked to thank Henning for that loan. August had meant so much to them.

She looked up, looking for Maj. She opened her bag, looking for the gold ten-krona piece she had placed in an old case.

"Let him have this as a memento from an old acquaintance of the old Henning," she said. "It should really have been printed with the little one's birth year—but these haven't been made for several years they told me at the bank."

Emelie asked if they wouldn't like to have a little coffee, nothing fancy. They of course had not known that Mrs. Bodin was coming. Now if she would be so kind...

Annika Bodin said yes. She was happy she had been able to convince August. She sat all alone quite often. August had a family and the firm to think of, of course. She herself had never had that many friends. It was refreshing to meet new people, especially when they were in some sense old acquaintances.

For a long time she had been afraid of all the old things, afraid of being unmasked. It was forbidden to reveal that she was the daughter of a coalbearer. Now her childhood and parental home were so far away in time that the period of the prosecutable offence had expired.

For she had seen her poverty as an offence, something to be ashamed of.

Naturally she still did not tell anything about her childhood to friends and acquaintances. They had grown up under different circumstances, they would not have understood. But here she could feel like she was among fellow offenders. Maybe they would actually like her better if they knew how her life had been at one time.

She talked about when Henning worked as a brick carrier, how his hands were bloody, he was so unseasoned. That was during the time he had been a boarder with them. And Henning's friend named Thumbs; he had helped her wash her clothes down at the washing dock at Hammarby Lake. He had worked at the dyer's then. So, he was still alive... She grew pensive, was silent a moment. Once she had really liked Thumbs, but he had chosen someone else. Or was it she who had chosen first, chosen Fredrik and his money?

August sat and listened. Thought that his mother really never would be able to prefer Thumbs. If Thumbs entered the conversation any time over the years, she had never been able to resist coming out with some little nasty remark.

Some time August had to be kind and drive out there with her. She had to see if the house she had lived in was still there.

Emelie sat quietly, felt a little unsure as to what to say. Erik, who could dare to speak, had of course promised Maj to say next to nothing. Luckily there was Jenny who was used to moving in all kinds of circles. She asked questions and answered them and did not seem in the slightest way troubled or nervous. August, on the other hand, was unusually silent. He would probably have preferred to come alone.

When Emelie went out into the kitchen to get more coffee, he followed her. He hoped she wasn't mad—but Mother would not be gainsaid. They would leave soon, he would make sure Mother got back safely and then he had some work waiting at home.

Emelie assured him that it was a treat to have Mrs. Bodin come with him. It wasn't clear that August believed her.

As they stood in the kitchen saying good-bye, someone rang the doorbell. Thumbs and Mikael were standing outside the door. They had taken an evening stroll and thought they would drop by for a little while. But maybe it wasn't such a good time, didn't they have company?

Mikael thought they should leave. But Thumbs stepped inside, looking with astonishment at the visitors.

"What the hell…" he said. "It can't be Annika?"

August looked nervously at his mother; she had grown completely pale. For a moment he wondered if she was going to faint. But there was probably no risk of that. Quite the opposite, she could really get angry sometimes.

"One should say hello, in any case," said Thumbs and extended his hand. Annika Bodin took it but dropped it just as fast.

They stayed standing, staring at each, as if waiting to see who would be the first to attack.

August might very well have reason to be mad himself; Thumbs had been so caustic to him once. It was Thumbs who was the reason for the break between August and his siblings back then, when they were young. Thumbs had never been able to accept August's new environment and its demands. He had seen him as a traitor.

Now Thumbs was an old man. Maybe there wasn't much of the revolutionary fervor left.

"You see, we were just passing by," said Mikael.

August and Mikael had never spent very much time together. Mikael was several years younger. Now they shook hands and when August felt his strong grip he remembered that he had heard Mikael had gone to sea.

"Have you settled down on land now?" he asked, a little unsure if he should say this or not.

"Yes," said Mikael. "And you're building houses I've heard."

"Yes, things are beginning to pick up a little on the construction scene."

"Your boy has done well for himself too," said Mikael.

August had to think a moment before he realized it was Gunnar that Mikael meant. August nodded. Yes, Gunnar was getting by all right.

"I did a small job for him," said Mikael. "I'm not a craftsman, but I can always do a little heavy work."

They were just on their way out, August said. It was nice to have met again but now he had to see his mother home.

They left. A threatening collision had been avoided. But Thumbs paced back and forth, gently swearing to himself, chewing over the plain truth he should have told that August but never come out with. They had run away, those fine people, with their tails between their legs.

He went over and opened the kitchen window.

It needs to be aired out. It smells like prostitutes in here.

Jenny asked when he had last seen Annika. Thumbs had a hard time remembering. More than twenty years ago for sure.

And Jenny laughed, a ringing laugh.

"Oh my God," she said. "An eternity ago... and you were just as impossible, just as stubborn. Are you never going to be able to accept each other?"

"The old lady was actually very nice," stated Erik.

"You don't know that snake well enough, my boy," Thumbs snapped. "But if you have any coffee left give me a swallow to down this bad taste with."

The baby woke up and started to cry. Thumbs tried to rock the little one in his buggy, but it didn't help. Henning was hungry. Maj had to pick him up and shooed the men out of the kitchen.

"It was because his name is Henning that she showed up," Thumbs said. "Annika always had a weakness for Henning. That was why she bought August. If she had been able to she would have bought Henning too."

In the late fall Erik found an apartment that was acceptable. It was big enough as both a place to live and an office. Maj and the boy moved there. It was so quiet and empty after they were gone in the little apartment on Åsögatan. Now there were only four left. Beda and Emelie slept in the kitchen now and Jenny and Elisabet in the room.

It was still not apparent how things would turn out with the grocery store. Negotiations were still underway. And Melinder had not been in touch.

Jenny was performing in the Record Theater on Götgatsbacken, Elisabet was together with her schoolmates, Beda had gone with Kajsa to an evening class to learn to make clothes. Emelie felt alone, a little superfluous.

NEW BEGINNING

Folkungagatan, which at one time had been a minor side street along-side the livelier Tjärhovsgatan, had gradually turned into a main street for eastern Södermalm. The streetcars of four different lines had a stop on the corner of Renstjärnasgatan, and beside the park at Stigberget stood the new big busses that took care of the traffic toward Björknäs and Värmdön. Many of the low rows of factories that had edged the streets had been torn down. Small shops and craftsmen's workshops were beginning to be replaced by modern stores.

Still, much of the outskirts of town was the same. Rotting wooden buildings crouched beside newly built apartment buildings, and on Stigberget's slope red fences wound between the gardens' greenery. And only a few blocks from the big thoroughfare were enormous undeveloped lots where gray rock emerged between thistles and bushes.

The grocery store where Emelie worked did not differ very much from the unpretentious small stores one found on the back streets, even if the premises appeared large from the outside. The owner had not been able to keep up with progress, had not been capable of pulling in the streams of people from the street outside. The stores next door had changed. In her store time had stood still, and those who passed by hardly noticed the small windows with their humble attempts at display.

Now she wanted to sell the store, give up.

Emelie realized that the decisive moment was near. And she guessed which people would be the new owners. They didn't rush things either, had negotiated for a long time, paid many visits to the store. Their names were Lundin and Fredriksson and they were business partners. They already owned a couple of grocery stores downtown.

It was the elder of them especially, director Lundin, who was interested in the purchase. He came back time after time. Emelie understood that he probably wanted to evaluate how they were doing for

customers. She felt observed, tried to pretend not to notice the scru-
tinizing glances. She had no great hope of staying; they would
certainly want to hire someone younger and more experienced in the
business. If they even needed an employee at all. They may have some
people to move over from the other shops.

Then it was decided: on the first of October they would take over
the store. Was she interested in staying on, they asked? And did she
have references from previous employers? She could come down to
their shop on Drottninggatan and discuss the matter.

Emelie took a few hours off, went home and changed her clothes
and took out the letter of recommendation she had gotten from
Melinder. She felt it was almost vexing to show it. She had not merit-
ed such a fine recommendation in any case. But Melinder had wanted to do everything he could to help her, must have felt he bore some
responsibility for her after all those years at the factory.

It was raining. In order not to arrive completely wet she took the
streetcar. She got off at Norra Bantorget and walked up Barnhusgatan,
passing the shop and glancing sidelong in the window. It looked large
and elegant inside. She wondered if they intended to make the store
on Folkungagatan as elegant. Since they had asked her to come she
could at least hope to stay on. Maybe they would hire someone as a
shop supervisor as well. It would not be so easy if she got a young, self-
confident gentleman over her.

Both of the directors were there. They asked her to sit down. She
brought out the reference letter and they read it carefully. She felt
herself blush at the thought of the overly favorable words.

"This is a fine recommendation," director Fredriksson said.

Director Lundin asked if she really had been with the same firm for
over forty years.

Yes, she had begun there when she was twelve, right when she
finished school.

Then it must have been a hard blow.

Yes indeed. Indeed it had been difficult.

And now she had been at the grocery store for a little over a year.

Well, the store wasn't exactly well run. But they had had the opportunity to observe her, seen that she liked to keep things in order. Which must not have been easy, given the circumstances.

They would prefer to have someone there who was familiar with the customers and the area. Therefore they were asking her to stay. The salary they named was not big but bigger than she had been receiving. She said yes, of course.

Before she left they asked to keep the letter of reference a few days.

The new owners began by closing the shop. All the goods were taken away, the windows painted over, the inventory carried out and old shelves and boxes broken up. Craftsmen of different types began to renovate the premises.

Emelie got to be in the store on Drottninggatan while the renovation went on. She took it as a training period, tried to master how they worked, tried to see what merchandise they had that was not in the shop on Söder.

Director Lundin had plans that showed how the store on Söder would look when it was rebuilt. He showed them to her, wondering if she had any ideas. She had some. There were details that were not really practical. And she had heard a lot of how they were furnishing stores; Gunnar worked a lot with that. And director Lundin, who had maybe mostly asked as a joke, became interested, asked her to tell him how she would want to have it.

What she had to say had mostly to do with solutions for keeping it clean easily. And then she thought that there should be a glass shield for the cheese counter, so people wouldn't sniff the cheese or touch it.

Almost every day director Lundin came to her with something to talk about. He wanted to know how many customers had credit and how they paid, and if Emelie thought they should keep the credit system. He wondered if there were many people shopping in the store who rode the bus, and if one could reach more of them. Which stores were the biggest competitors in the area?

She gave as exact answers as she could, asking sometimes for time to think it over. She tried to give reasons for her opinions, wanting to show that it was not just a question of guessing. As in the answer about credit: she knew that many people were dependent on credit and which ones could be trusted. But they had to come up with a new system. Up until now the purchases had only been written on slips of paper and sometimes there was a disagreement when people did not remember what they had bought. If they were going to sell on credit they should have books that the customers took with them when they shopped and there one could record the entries. It wasn't enough with just writing up the sums in the store. Or else one could write out slips with carbon paper in between so the customers who wanted to could keep their accounts themselves and check what they bought.

"Miss Nilsson seems to know how she would like to have things," he said. This frightened her a little. Now she must have sounded too self-assured and spoken as if she had any say in the matter. But he had asked.

A few days later he said the exact same words again. But then added, "So it is just as well that we decide at once that you should be the manager."

She had not expected that. Maybe hoped… but said to herself that it was a fruitless hope. She said nothing, felt nervous about the responsibility, had to wonder if she was up to the task.

"You are used to leading workers," he said.

That must have been thanks to Melinder's recommendation.

"I will do my very best," she finally came out with.

The store was finished. One could hardly believe that it was the same space, everything was so transformed. The windows had been enlarged, the store was light and clean, rows of cans stood neatly arranged on the long shelves. In the glass cases were cookies, cakes and candies. Instead of putting the money in a wooden box, they would use a new and sparkling silver cash register. Stools to sit on stood in a row on the outside of the counter. On one of the short walls large woven baskets hung filled with fruit. A new automatic scale had replaced the old one with loose weights. Powerful globe lamps lit up all the corners.

The younger of the directors, Fredriksson, had set up window displays. Offers arrived with bouquets of flowers from the firm's suppliers.

Emelie thought it felt as ceremonious as the time Melinder's pavilion had been inaugurated—at the exhibition in 1897.

Two young shop assistants had been hired, a girl and a boy. Many curious people came and looked the first few days. They came on the streetcar and often only had a few minutes to shop. Some telephoned in their orders so they only had to pick them up when they came. It was easier to call now that the telephone companies Riks and Allmänna had merged.

Emelie had been able to start all over again, once again had important and responsibility-filled duties to carry out. Of course she felt at times that she had grown older, that the work strained her sometimes—not least of all when Christmas shopping began. But she had never been afraid of digging in, liked it when there was a lot to do. And she was happy with the results; the number of customers was growing.

Emelie thought of Melinder quite often. On the opening day, when she remembered the exhibition. And almost every day when she took pleasure in her new job.

It was Melinder she had to thank for that.

What was factory director Melinder doing now? Would he come one day and tell her he had started all over, wanted her to come back? And what would she answer then? It might be hard to choose; she did not know if she really dared and had the energy to start over one more time. And then she was so happy with what she was doing now.

Now it had gotten to the point where she hoped that he would not come; the choice would be much too difficult. If she thought she saw someone who resembled Melinder out on the street she would feel a stab of worry and fear a momentous decision.

Then one day he was standing in the shop.

It was not much he had to offer. Indeed he had started a new company but it was not particularly extensive and he was not manufacturing anything himself. He was a wholesaler for a paper manufacturer and sold mostly bags and wrapping paper to stores. He arranged to have store names printed on labels through a printer who did this at his factory.

Emelie could see that he had been having difficulties, that he still had worries. He was not the jolly factory director from other days standing at the counter. When he learned that Emelie supervised the new shop he said right away that what he could offer her was worse, not worth thinking about now. He had wanted to look her up because he had promised. If she was going without, a bad job would have been better than no job. But he thought that she probably had something, knew what she deserved.

He hoped of course that he would be successful in building his new company, but still there was the risk that he would fail. She was more secure where she was. The senior accountant had come back in any case. Though he had grown old and out of sorts, seemed a little crazy.

So Emelie was relieved of having to choose. There was no choice.

She thanked him for the recommendation; it was surely that which had gotten her the job. It had been much too full of praise.

No, not one word too much, said Melinder with a smile. It was nice if he could have been of some help somehow.

Before he left he asked who was in charge of ordering wrapping paper and bags. He was going to go by the main store and speak with them. But it was difficult for a newcomer to start competing with the old established suppliers. It was easier when he was dealing with completely new companies.

Emelie suffered. She understood that it must feel humiliating for him to stand like this in front of her. And she did not have the option of buying something from him. All the purchases were made centrally.

He disappeared. Maybe she would never see him again. The city was big, their ways so separate. It was the end of the dream of returning to the old.

It might feel like some kind of a betrayal that she had not gone with him, that she so quickly accepted his assurance that she was better off where she was. But she had large debts after the tough years. She dared not risk anything. She had no choice—and still it felt like she had let him down.

DAY BY DAY

Everywhere people could hear the melody that Ernst Rolf had launched in his big fancy revue at the Oscar Theater: *It's Getting Better and Better Day by Day!*

Maj hummed it as she walked around the apartment on Dalagatan. Outside the windows she saw the still bare trees of Vasa Park and the winter-yellow grass lawns. Little Henning crawled across the floor, found a rattle lying on the rug, reached for it, lost his balance and sat down heavily on his bottom.

Better and better? She wasn't so sure about that; sometimes the words of the refrain sounded a little ironic. But of course she had it good in many ways. The apartment that Erik had found was marvelous. She had never lived this well before. And the boy was healthy and good.

There was much that was good. And what was not good she had prepared herself for, counted on. She had never believed that Erik would pull back from the arduous work within the party. She had counted on being left alone very often. And that he would be irritated and anxious, difficult at times.

Men, she well might think, men and politics. She could not fathom their way of operating. One might believe that the little communist party needed every adherent, that they should stick together and try to unite their efforts. But most of the strength and energy was wasted on intrigues amongst themselves. The party had already had time to split one time, and now they were preparing of course for the next split. The gentlemen in Moscow apparently wanted to get rid of Höglund who would not yield to the Comintern's commands. There were more representatives of the executive committee arriving. There would soon be a half dozen of them in town.

Erik was welcome to bring home one of those executive representatives for coffee she had said. It might be interesting to see one of those mysterious old men. But apparently it wasn't allowed.

Others came instead, sometimes sitting in the kitchen at night and discussing with Erik. Especially those from the Communist Youth League. Maj would offer them sandwiches and exchange a few words with them. Preferably with the Youth League's representative, a round and jolly youth with curly light hair. His name was Einar Olsson and a lot of hopes were pinned on him, especially within the party. He was full of suggestions and ideas. He could round up a lot of money, but seldom his own salary. He had been hired on the terms that one hundred members had promised to pay one krona per week as his salary—and this salary the representative himself had to collect from the members.

Everyone who came belonged to the Kilbom faction, like Erik.

One afternoon a week Maj would go see her mother. She would choose a day when she knew that Jenny was not rehearsing or filming.

The streetcar, Number 9, stopped at the corner of Vasa Park. There were plenty of seats in the middle of the day. Maj would sit with the boy on her lap next to a window. She went downtown so seldom that she would take the opportunity to look around as she rode the streetcar.

At Tegelbacken cars and streetcars stood in line and waited while a locomotive was being changed. It rolled out and chugged back in again while they lifted the boom gates. Small cargo boats lay alongside the quay and blocked the view of Riddarholmen on the other side of the water. They were unusually high because the spring floods had been strong this year after the hard winter. At Mälartorget and Kornhamnstorg a lot of the quays lay under water and several cellars in the closest buildings had to be evacuated. Cars plowed through and sprayed cascades of water around them, rows of white steamships in the Lake Mälar harbor could only be reached by temporary wooden bridges that passengers and crew members had to balance their way across.

Her journey continued on up to Södermalmstorg; the car went into the loop past the International Red Aid center and up toward Ragvaldsgatan. In the evenings there were always many youth who gathered here and outside the Biograph Palace. Now there were only a few sailors standing on the corner and housewives with shopping bags looked in the windows of the low row of shops along Hornsgatan.

The buildings crowded closer, the streetcar slowly took the curves on Sankt Paulsgatan, and continued up Götgatsbacken to the top and then down toward Södra bantorget and Folkungagatan. Here Maj felt at home again. Not maybe so that she wanted to move back. The road led onward, away from what had been. And she wanted to try and stay with Erik, for the boy's sake if nothing else. Well, for her own sake too. She and Erik belonged together, despite everything.

Though he certainly behaved strangely for having a family. Usually he completely forgot they existed. Evening after evening he sat at his meetings, Sundays he gave lectures, during the days he was out selling. For him to accompany her and visit her mother or Emelie some evening was unthinkable. Or that they might go out and have fun, see a film or eat out. He never had time. There was always something that was more important, something he had promised to participate in. And Maj did not want to force him. Wanted him to give some of his time and some of his life of his own free will.

She had known how it would be, decided to accept him as he was. Though it was hard to follow through on her decision; time after time she forgot herself. Not so that she fought with him—but she blamed him in her thoughts. When she had gone along a few days and felt bitter, it sometimes felt as if she had taken poison herself. As if she had inflicted wounds on herself that perhaps would not heal.

Jenny was waiting for her, happy and eager as always. She had so much to tell, as she usually did. Maj often had reason to admire and even envy her mother: for being so exuberantly vital, so unspoiled and almost childishly happy. Most children usually thought their mothers were old, maybe remnants from a past world. She had never been able to view her mother this way, rather she felt herself sometimes more adult and experienced, more disillusioned. Though these recent years she had noticed that her mother was aging somewhat, that her laugh lines had grown a little too deep, her vitality something of a mannerism. That eagerness and liveliness seemed more nervousness than it used to, some of the spontaneity had disappeared.

Thumbs was in the hospital, Jenny told her. There was some indication of a small stroke. And Gunnar's daughter had gotten chicken pox. Tyra's oldest son had been taken into the juvenile reformatory, or children's home, or whatever it was, even though he hadn't even turned seven. But he did not have the best heritage. His father had gone to jail several times.

What did Maj think of the new mirror there? Did she recognize it? Well… maybe it wasn't so easy. It had been in the Panoptikon Wax Museum before. Jenny had gone to the auction. If she had had room she would have bought some of the wax figures. The bard Wennerborg had been sold off for one krona and Kaiser Wilhelm I on his deathbed for ten, without the bed. A pity she had not thought of it… Maj had more room, could have had some funny figure in her entrance hall, someone people who visited could think was alive and say hello to.

No thanks; she was just as happy to do without.

But if Maj could get free some evening they could go and see the Saga of Gösta Berling; the first part was showing at the Red Windmill now. Jenny really wanted to see it. One of the girls in that film they made on Dalarö a few years ago played the Countess Dohna. Imagine, that crazy girl who howled so when she fell down and hurt her backside on a stone. Some people advanced, she had to say.

But then others shouldn't be down in the mouth about it. Jenny had gotten a role in a film called *Constable Paulus' Easter Bomb*. The screenwriters called themselves "Three Gentlemen with a Whiskey and Soda" and maybe that said it all. But there was always something one could do with a role, play yet another old bag. Though sometime she would like to play a real person, if for nothing else than to see if she could.

They went out together for a while, walked past the store where Emelie worked and waved to her through the window. She came to the door and said hello. But when Emelie was at work it was not good to disrupt her for very long. Maj knew that well and got her mother to move along with her. Emelie didn't feel she had the time and the right to relax, even for a moment. When Emelie talked about working hours it was as religious people talked about the hours of high mass.

While Maj sat with Jenny and the boy in the park, a funny little question popped up that she did not have the answer to. Did she envy her mother and Emelie? Or did she feel sorry for them? They had gotten a little bit set in their ways, been shaken and damaged by life. Jenny's hectic talk and Emelie's persevering industry, they were both manifestations of the same fear—a fear of not fitting in. They did what they could to fill their place in existence. And she herself just sat there, in the park or at home, letting day after day go by without really participating in the struggle for existence. Of course she had her child and her home, the tasks could certainly be enough. But still sometimes she longed back to her job, missed that feeling of participation, sharing in a greater context.

Why did she always have such a hard time being satisfied? Like everyone else, wouldn't she too get set in her ways—whether it were from dissatisfaction or dispiritedness? Was that the price she would have to pay to get to live with Erik?

The summer that came was trying for Maj, gave her many occasions to wonder.

Antagonisms within the party grew even stronger—things were heading toward a crisis—and the fighting took up all Erik's time and thoughts.

Those who belonged to the Kilbom faction held to unbroken solidarity with the Comintern. The Höglund movement counted on breaking away. And it was Höglund who edited the newspaper, "People's Daily." If the opposition wanted to get their ideas out in the party's newspaper they were forced to advertise. And they would later find in editorials and articles scathing criticism of their "ad campaign." It was a bitter pill for those who had built up the network of subscription canvassers and advertising agents.

One Thursday evening in the middle of August the most active within the opposition gathered to talk over the situation. As a place for the meeting they had chosen the Union of Civilian Salaried Employees in Defense Establishments headquarters on Smålandsgatan. One of the members of their group was a representative in the employees' union. The location had been chosen with a thought to the fact that no one within the Höglund camp would gain knowledge of their meeting.

Nils Flyg, who was always a little undependable when it came to meetings and business, did not come. He had to lead a study circle he gave as an excuse. But otherwise the conspirators were there: Kilbom, Einar Olsson, Jeårg Lundström, Carl Winberg and a few others. The discussion led to a decision: they would act immediately, take over the party and the newspaper.

At nine-thirty in the evening the little group arrived at the newspaper's premises in the old bordello on Luntmakaregatan. Höglund and some of his supporters were still at the editorial office. The conspirators explained that they had come to prevent further division and party polemic in the newspaper. An enormous argument ensued and while it was underway, reinforcements arrived from the Kilbom loyalists' youth league. The entryway, stairway and printing office were filled with people. Guards were put in place. Kilbom went out to the printing office and got the manuscript of Höglund's editorial, explaining that it would not be printed. Hesitant typographers listened to the party leaders' fighting and did not know which one they should obey. The foreman was sent for to resolve the dispute over who would decide, editor-in-chief Höglund or the printing office's managing director Kilbom. The foreman determined it was the director of the printing office that should decide.

On that night of the coup, copies of the paper were printed saying that the newspaper was under new management. It also contained a letter to the party members from the Communist International Chairman, comrade Zinoviev. In the letter all of Höglund's sins were enumerated.

Now there were two Communist Parties. A week or so later Höglund began a new newspaper, "The New Politics." The Höglund supporters had requisitioned the party mailing address on Torsgatan, but Erik came up with the idea of forwarding the mail to a new address. In this way the Kilbom faction received all the letters that were sent to the party for several weeks. It was a great advantage to be the first to answer all the worried letters from members around the country.

And the parliamentary elections awaited. Einar Olsson began a huge campaign, "Forge the Weapons to Fight for the Party." Erik worked feverishly. Now the important thing was to salvage the votes, make sure that as many as possible chose the correct Communist Party. It was quite successful. The Kilbom followers got four parliamentary representatives and the Höglund faction got only one. But many voters had probably grown tired of the bickering and squabbling.

Erik had pushed himself beyond his limits. When the election was over he was worn out, sick from late hours, exertion and worry. Maj was able to convince him to take some time off. They traveled with the boy to a boardinghouse. For a few weeks she had Erik to herself, lived together with him. Those weeks in the fall were the best she had all year.

When they came back to town she went and had her hair bobbed. It was the new style and it suited her, she had always been something of a tomboy. But Emelie was almost shocked when she saw her, could not bring herself to say it was beautiful.

Emelie told them that Thumbs had died. He had been in the hospital. For a while they had hoped he would get better. But then he got pneumonia too and then he couldn't hold on.

The old Henning's friend, a faithful friend to them all. Did such friendship exist anymore? Weren't the times all too hectic?

Mikael had telegraphed Rudolf. In case his brother wanted to send money for a funeral wreath.

Maj remembered Thumbs' laugh, his stories, his animated zeal. She should have listened to him more closely, so that she herself would be able to tell the little Henning about the old one.

Now it was too late. While people were alive it felt like time stretched on, that so many opportunities were left. And then suddenly the days were over and the opportunities gone.

Erik was in full force again, had no extra time for her and the boy. It would not be until he was worn out that they would have the chance to really live together again. She would have to wait, day after day, wait until he no longer had energy for anyone else. It felt harsh to hope it would happen soon, harsh to hope that it would not be for a while.

FAMILY GATHERING ON TISTELVÄGEN

The truth was that Emelie did not like going out into the city in broad daylight, during working hours. It was a waste of time and she had to wonder, time and again, how things were going in the store while she was away, if any problems had arisen that the others could not take care of.

But sometimes she was forced to anyway, and once she was out it was indeed quite exciting and fun. Usually the reason was a meeting in the main store on Drottninggatan.

Today she had first been on Drottninggatan and then on Norrtullsgatan at a display window painter's studio. He was going to do the decorations for their Easter display. And then director Fredriksson wanted her to go to a company on Kungsgatan and look at some display stands.

She walked along Odengatan down toward Sveavägen. The low row of bazaars that used to line the foot of the gravel ridge was gone now. Work was underway for the big city library that would be erected here. But the farm beside the observatory was still there, on the farthest edge of the slope.

The old and narrow Stora Badstugatan had become the new broad Sveavägen and had swallowed up the whole neighborhood. New and large buildings were being built everywhere. She arrived at the corner where Melinder's factory had stood. It was gone now too, and a new building had risen up in its place. It was strange to think that no traces were left of the once solid and successful company where she had worked for so many years. She still had a bar of soap at home in a dresser drawer leftover from the exhibition. Otherwise nothing, only memories, shadows of something disappeared.

She felt like she did not dare stay and remember, was frightened by the amount of memories that welled up. Though she did walk a little more slowly, as if some little memory might still catch up with her.

At Adolf Fredrik's Church the street was still constricted by the churchyard. From a distance it almost appeared that a wall of trees and gravestones closed off passage. But there was still a narrow opening close to Reinhold the baker's large building, which was now owned by a publisher. The streetcar could wind its way through, hard by the edge of the sidewalk.

Now she could see the grave between the trees. It was still shrouded in wreaths and flowers.

Branting's grave.

He had built his government shortly after the elections, his third and biggest government. Early on in the new year he had gotten sick. At the end of February he had died. On the first of March, a Sunday, Emelie stood among the many tens of thousands who lined the streets as the funeral procession slowly rolled onward.

She walked in among the dark tree trunks, stopping carefully a distance from the grave.

It was as if not just a man, but a whole era had disappeared.

She had heard him speak many times. The first time she had not been more than nineteen. That was out at Lill-Jans Park, and that had been about voting rights. And two years later it had been out on the field at Gärdet, the first time anyone had demonstrated on the first of May. Gertrud and Rudolf had been there both times. At Gärdet Olof had also been along. He had been little then and she remembered how tired he had gotten.

A completely different era, people who had disappeared. A fight for goals that long ago had been achieved.

She might feel that the man who lay there in the grave had transformed the era, had had so much power that he had been able to turn dreams into reality. It had felt safe as long as he had lived. How would it be now, was there someone who could continue his work? Everyone seemed so small compared to the one who was dead. There was no father anymore, just many children, perhaps children at a loss.

That's how it might feel. For her. But she was so little informed about all the politics. She didn't know anything, didn't understand anything.

She took out the bunch of cowslips she had bought on the way there, lay them farthest out at the edge of the grave. Then hurried off so as not to be seen by anybody.

The same evening they were to go out to Gunnar's—Emelie, Jenny and Mikael. Hjördis had called the store and invited them out, it was beginning to be so lovely in the garden and it was her birthday. But they didn't have to even think of that. It was just a little excuse one had to find in order to get together.

They went out on the streetcar, across the rickety wooden bridge at Skanstull. A few days ago Hammarby Lake's water had slowly been refilled. The water had been let in through an open hatch in the cofferdam facing the Baltic Sea. Now it was like a thin film of water in the pit beneath them. It would take a month for the new lake's surface to be at the same level as the Baltic's.

Trees and lawns shone a brilliant light green. In some of the gardens people were burning leaves, and gray clouds of smoke billowed up and slowly dissipated into wisps.

Gunnar stood at the gate and welcomed them. He thought they should look at the garden before they went in. He showed Mikael the stones he had laid and the fence that was new. Emelie and Jenny looked at the flower beds where the flowers were beginning to come up. The garden was turning green but the spring evening was cool and Hjördis called to them that it was time to come in.

August was coming, Hjördis told them. He usually remembered her birthday and had called Gunnar's carpentry shop and said he would swing by. He had bought a car, did they know?

He arrived, stopped outside the gate and beeped his horn. Everyone had to go out and look. Proudly he showed them the wonder. It was a Dodge Brothers he had bought at Philipson's on Strandvägen. Shiny new, with glossy black steel sides and a gray cloth roof that extended like a big visor on a cap. It had four doors and metal hatches to open and fold down around the radiator. On the back were a spare wheel and a baggage rack that could be folded out.

August was sportily dressed, with a big scarf around his neck—it was naturally a little drafty to ride in such an open car.

The present he had for Hjördis was another technical wonder. Emelie had heard so much about these radio apparatuses, but never seen one. Since New Year's there were real radio programs. Every day there were broadcasts of music and news and readings.

A little rounded closed box with cords and some holes in which August stuck small plugs. To the cords were connected some headphones to put on your ears. There were two pairs so Hjördis would not have to fight with Gunnar, August said. In the middle of the round box sat a little glass container. In the container was something that looked like a piece of coal, and against the piece of coal your were supposed to place a little spiral wire. It sputtered and crackled in the headphones as they lay on the table when August fussed with that wire. Then he found the right place on the piece of coal and told Hjördis to put on the headphones.

Hjördis listened with bated breath.

"Imagine…" she said. "Someone is playing! Do you want to hear?"

She handed the headphones to Emelie who a little nervously put them on. And now she heard the music, as if by magic.

What people could come up with. When you telephoned there were wires, but here beams, or whatever they were, were going through the air. And here one could sit out in Skarpnäck and listen to what they played in Stockholm's round radio station on Malmskillnadsgatan.

It was incomprehensible.

August instructed Hjördis and Gunnar. They could twist and turn that little piece of coal—the crystal it was called—and buy a new one when it wore out.

Emelie sat silently watching August and Gunnar as they stood side by side, bent over Hjördis. Father and son. And things had gotten so good between them. August seemed so happy when he saw Gunnar and Hjördis. Once he had seen Gunnar as a threat, taken it as unpleasant news that he had this son. Now he probably saw Gunnar as a support. He certainly didn't always have an easy time of it with the son from his marriage, Karl Henrik.

Everything, everyone she knew had disappeared. She had thought that as she was standing by Branting's grave. Gertrud and Rudolf and their children had emigrated, her parents were dead, and Thumbs, Matilda and Olof. She may have deserted Melinder.

But now she saw how much was left, many near and dear ones. August, who she felt like she had gotten back as a brother. And Jenny. And Mikael who she valued more and more. Gunnar and his Hjördis. And Beda and Elisabet and Maj who were not there this evening.

Her existence was not empty. Something was still there, and she got to have some of those she knew and liked around her in this new and incomprehensible world, with all its technical marvels that she could not understand but might derive some pleasure from anyway. The world that her brothers' children's children would grow up in.

Of course it was an interesting time to live in, with all the new things. What would Mama and Papa have said if they had been able to see them now? August with his new car outside, his son with those headphones playing music around his ears. And Gertrud off in America and Olof's widow with bobbed hair, she too. And Emelie herself, a little old and tired but still manager of a high-class store.

She had wanted to preserve the parental home, provide a home for those who otherwise might have been homeless. Now it felt as if she had succeeded. She did not think it was thanks to her; it was thanks to more than one person. It was grace.

REMEMBER
THE
CITY

That spring evening in the beginning of May 1925, was cool and light. The dusk lay like a gray blue mist over the small gardens. The windows of the houses shone like yellow lanterns through the delicate greenery of the trees.

Jenny and Mikael thought the evening was so beautiful, wanted to take a walk back into town. Emelie was going to get a ride with August in his car. He went outside beforehand and started it. When Emelie came out after a while, the car was standing there impatiently shaking with the many small explosions of the motor. August lit the head-lamps that glowed like two giant yellow eyes. Then they glided slow-ly forward between the gardens and houses, came out to the big road and increased their speed. After a moment they drove past Jenny and Mikael. August leaned on the horn and the two walkers jumped aside and apart—they had been walking arm in arm Emelie saw. And she wondered if that might mean something or if it was just Jenny's nor-mal, slightly careless familiarity.

Up on top of the old Rackarbergen the lights in the rows of yellow tenement houses were shining. Across the greenery of the White Hills, Sofia Church stood like an enormous upside down cone.

"Do you remember that windmill that burned down?" he asked.

She nodded. Mama's fortieth birthday. They were living on Nytorget then and August had come home to celebrate. It was long before the church had been built.

"That evening I learned that Bärta was pregnant," he said. "I was terrified at first that it was mine—but then someone said it was that chimneysweep, Johan's child. And people believe what they want to believe. But now I want to thank you for everything you have done for Gunnar. And for me. You should know that I am both happy with and proud of him. You have unquestionably meant a lot to him, made him who he is."

She stayed silent, felt too happy to be able to answer.

"Let's drive past Nytorget," he said.

They drove in slowly, glided past the uneven rows of dilapidated houses. There it still stood, their house. The window in the upper story, facing the square, had been theirs. Though of course that was after August had moved away from home.

The arched entryway opened like a dark tunnel onto the yard. Emelie felt like she could still see old Washer-Johanna on her way to scrub the stone steps, hear the howling of the dogman's mongrels, the gushing of the water hydrant. And the sound of the ironclad wheels of the open sided wagon that carried their dead mother home.

Take care of Olof. That was her last wish.

Emelie felt like she had never been able to fulfill that duty. Olof had not let anyone take care of him. But she had tried as hard as she could, first with Olof and then with Jenny and Maj. But the memory of Olof would always be bound with something that felt like a broken promise.

"Do you remember?" August asked again. Old Malongen, the school where he had gone those first years. Together with that drummer boy from the city guard. And Rudolf. The teacher they had called Olle the drunk and who had been fired later on. Everything seemed so incredibly far off now. But it was he himself who had lived it, it was that close.

He wanted to see the house on Åsöberget again too. The car had a little difficulty getting up the steep ascent of Duvnäsgatan, which had been called Sopgränd before. But they made it. They saw the gate in the fence. August felt the handle carefully, but did not try to enter. He only wanted the feeling of it in his hand.

The house within lay dark. Those inside were probably sleeping already; it was late.

Sleeping, dreaming houses on the back streets. The neighborhoods that had been left behind, remains of a forgotten time. But from the open hillside that was right beside them, the view was of the city of today.

Do you remember?

Do you remember the houses, the events, the people? All that is now gone and doesn't seem to have left any traces behind. All that is forgotten, so forgotten that one has to ask oneself if it was completely meaningless.

Still, every occurrence and every choice did have its meaning, staked out the route to the present, created the foundation and the continuation for the city and life of today.

The route disappears in the mist, behind us and before us. And we stand on the little piece of ground that can be illuminated by the spotlight of our consciousness and that can be made to serve our purposes, as we put down our stakes. There are routes to a time and the foundations of a city that we will not reach and where new generations will stand, wondering at what may appear meaningless patterns that we have left behind.

August took his sister's hand, helped her down the hillside toward the car. The giant yellow eyes slid over their childhood house that lay closed and silent, familiar yet unknown.

MAIN CHARACTERS AND FAMILIES
IN THE STOCKHOLM SERIES

NILSSON
Henning (b. 1845, d. 1879) and *Lotten* (b. 1848, d. 1889)
have the following children:
August (b. 1868, see Bodin), *Emelie* (b. 1870),
Gertrud (b. 1871, see Lindgren)
Olof (b. 1879, d. 1902).
Olof marries *Jenny* Fält (b. 1881); their daughter is *Maj* (b. 1900).
With the singer Julius Törnberg Jenny has a daughter,
Elisabet Törnberg (b. 1910).

LINDGREN
Thumbs (Ture, b. 1845) and *Matilda* (b. 1845) have three sons:
Rudolf (b. 1868), *Knut* (b. 1870) and *Mikael* (b. 1875). Rudolf
marries Gertrud Nilsson. They have two sons and three daughters.
Knut is married and has a family; Mikael goes to sea.

BODIN
Fredrik (b. 1835, d. 1898) and *Annika* (b. 1846) adopt August
Nilsson as their son; he receives the name Bodin.
August marries *Ida* Wide (b. 1868); their children are:
Karl Henrik (b. 1895), *Charlotta,* (b. 1897), *Anna* (b. 1898),
Fredrik (b. 1900) and *Elisabet* (b. 1904).
With Bärta (see Karlsson) August has a son,
for a long time unbeknownst to him,
Gunnar (b. 1889).

KARLSSON
Johan (b. 1870) and *Bärta* (b. 1868) have the following children:
Tyra (b. 1895), *Beda* (b. 1897), *Erik* (b. 1899) and *Bengt* (b.
1900). With August Bodin, Bärta has a son, Gunnar Karlsson
(see Bodin).

In *City of My Dreams* the years 1860–1880 are depicted. *Children
of Their City* covers 1889–1900, and *Remember the City* spans
1900–1925. Two more novels follow in the Stockholm Series.